SHW

ALLEN COUNTY PUBLIC LIBRARY

P9-EDG-904

MAY 2 5 2004

PRAISE FOR CHRISTOPHER HYDE'S ELECTRIFYING THRILLERS

The Second Assassin

"This is different . . . a standout thriller combining real period charm with brutal up-to-the-minute suspense . . . like Caleb Carr meets Frederick Forsyth."
—Lee Child, author of *Echo Burning*

"A twisty, tense, and meticulously researched thriller that raises some very unsettling questions about what might have been."—Peter Abrahams, bestselling author of the *The Tutor* and *The Fan*

"A perfectly realized sense of the times, places, and people in one of the greatest stories of intrigue never told."
—Jack Du Brul, author of *Deep Fire Rising*

"Both Jane and Thomas emerge as the unlikely but compelling heroes of this tale, which Hyde insists is based largely on actual events and persons. Whether or not the reader chooses to accept Hyde's claim, this is still a rousing political thriller that bursts with nonstop action, rapid-fire dialogue, and eminently likable characters."
—*Publishers Weekly*

"It's odd that Christopher Hyde's thrillers haven't received greater attention, for they're truly rollicking reads. Period details are well presented, as are cameo appearances by real-life figures such as rising-star congressman Lyndon Johnson and a very young Frank Sinatra."
—*January Magazine*

continued . . .

A Gathering of Saints

"A baroque, delightfully gruesome serial-killer whodunit set in WWII London. . . . Hyde accomplishes a superb turn with his latest." —*Kirkus Reviews*

"Densely atmospheric. . . . Hyde's scrupulous research and deep knowledge of the political realities surrounding the Blitz make his story utterly convincing. . . . [You] almost smell the fear and death. . . . Readers who relish the raw truth of human, and inhuman, history will find here what they are looking for." —*Publishers Weekly*

"What a read! Hyde's ability to describe people and places is fantastic. . . . Some readers prefer suspense; others like mysteries. This book gives you both, with all the force of an exploding bomb."
 —*The Herald-American* (Syracuse, NY)

"A gripping combination of history, spy story, and mystery . . . unrelentingly readable and vividly realistic. . . . Life outside this captivating book simply ceases."
 —*Ottawa Citizen*

"Brilliantly realized and compulsively readable . . . [with] a jolt of malice and mayhem." —*Maclean's*

Wisdom of the Bones

"Extensive historical research. . . . Hyde manages to capture the essence of a changing world."
 —*Publishers Weekly*

Hard Target

"Exceedingly suspenseful thriller . . . powerful resolution and final stunning surprise."　*—Publishers Weekly*

"Strong in local detail and precise descriptions of objects and places, this tale of arrogance and subversion will engross readers."　*—Library Journal*

Black Dragon

"Smooth, literate, and thoroughly cynical. Well done."
—Kirkus Reviews

"[Hyde's] dark, stately style suits his characters well, and the sheer multitude of pieces he fits into his puzzle inspires awe."　*—Publishers Weekly*

MORE PRAISE FOR THE NOVELS OF CHRISTOPHER HYDE

"A model of plotting so dazzling it makes other page-turners look positively anemic."
—Kirkus Reviews (starred review)

"Mr. Hyde spins a great yarn with a likable hero."
—The Spectator (London)

"Not a dull page, not a false note."　*—Ottawa Citizen*

"The best-written, best-plotted heist novel ever published—bar none."　*—Los Angeles Times*

"Hyde's storytelling is pure genius. This is historical fiction at its finest."
—New York Daily News

**Other Onyx Books
by Christopher Hyde**

Wisdom of the Bones
The Second Assassin

THE HOUSE OF SPECIAL PURPOSE

Christopher Hyde

AN ONYX BOOK

ONYX
Published by New American Library, a division of
Penguin Group (USA) Inc., 375 Hudson Street,
New York, New York 10014, U.S.A.
Penguin Books Ltd, 80 Strand,
London WC2R 0RL, England
Penguin Books Australia Ltd, 250 Camberwell Road,
Camberwell, Victoria 3124, Australia
Penguin Books Canada Ltd, 10 Alcorn Avenue,
Toronto, Ontario, Canada M4V 3B2
Penguin Books (N.Z.) Ltd, Cnr Rosedale and Airborne Roads,
Albany, Auckland 1310, New Zealand

Penguin Books Ltd, Registered Offices:
80 Strand, London WC2R 0RL, England

First published by Onyx, an imprint of New American Library,
a division of Penguin Group (USA) Inc.

First Printing, May 2004
10 9 8 7 6 5 4 3 2 1

Copyright © Christopher Hyde, 2004
All rights reserved

 REGISTERED TRADEMARK—MARCA REGISTRADA

Printed in the United States of America

Without limiting the rights under copyright reserved above, no part of this
publication may be reproduced, stored in or introduced into a retrieval system, or transmitted, in any form, or by any means (electronic, mechanical,
photocopying, recording, or otherwise), without the prior written permission
of both the copyright owner and the above publisher of this book.

PUBLISHER'S NOTE
This is a work of fiction. Names, characters, places, and incidents either are
the product of the author's imagination or are used fictitiously, and any resemblance to actual persons, living or dead, business establishments, events, or
locales is entirely coincidental.

BOOKS ARE AVAILABLE AT QUANTITY DISCOUNTS WHEN USED TO PROMOTE
PRODUCTS OR SERVICES. FOR INFORMATION PLEASE WRITE TO PREMIUM MAR-
KETING DIVISION, PENGUIN GROUP (USA) INC., 375 HUDSON STREET, NEW YORK,
NEW YORK 10014.

If you purchased this book without a cover you should be aware that this
book is stolen property. It was reported as "unsold and destroyed" to the
publisher and neither the author nor the publisher has received any payment
for this "stripped book."

The scanning, uploading and distribution of this book via the Internet or via
any other means without the permission of the publisher is illegal and punish-
able by law. Please purchase only authorized electronic editions, and do not
participate in or encourage electronic piracy of copyrighted materials. Your
support of the author's rights is appreciated.

With Love
For

Mariea,
Noah,
Chelsea
&
Gabriel

You are my heart.

On the threshold of the grave
Breathe power divine into our clay
That We, Thy children, may find strength
In meekness for our foes to pray.

—Last verse of an anonymous poem found in the
tsarina's Bible at the House of Special Purpose

Revolutions are always verbose.

—Leon Trotsky, *History of the Russian Revolution,*
Vol. 2

Prologue

July 17, 1918
Yekaterinburg, Western Siberia

Alexander Mikhailovitch Levitsky slipped quietly toward the gate of the wooden palisade that almost completely hid the house from view, showing his pass to Gorshkov, one of Yurovsky's Cheka guards. Behind Levitsky, parked close to the basement windows at the side entrance of the house, was a canvas-topped truck with its engine running.

Gorshkov examined the pass:

SOVIET OF THE PEOPLE'S COMMISSARS

Petrograd
12 February 1918
No. 567

I request all Organizations, Soviets and Commissars of Railway Stations to give every assistance to the holder of this letter: *Comrade Alexander Mikhailovitch Levitsky.*

State Commissar,

V.I. Lenin

Commissar, All-Russian Extraordinary Commission to Combat Counterrevolution and Sabotage,

Feliks Dzerzhinskiy

The signatures were overstamped with the seal of the Yekaterinburg oblast. The document was capable of taking the slim, fair-haired young man anywhere he wanted to go, but Gorshkov was as methodical as he was stupid and took an inordinate length of time examining the one-page letter. After a few moments it occurred to Levitsky that the reason Gorshkov was taking so long was because he couldn't read.

"As you can see, it's signed by Comrade Lenin as well as your own commander of the All-Russian Extraordinary Commission to Combat Counterrevolution and Sabotage." Levitsky seriously doubted that the guard had ever heard the organization he worked for described by its full official title.

"Yes, I can see that." Gorshkov scowled. "But it doesn't explain what you're doing out on the street at this hour of the morning, or the reason for it." The sound of the running truck engine aside, Gorshkov was almost certainly aware of what had just transpired inside the euphemistically named House of Special Purpose. Levitsky had no doubt the rifle fire and the screaming from the room in the half basement could be heard halfway across town. The large residence on the northern edge of town had originally been owned by the Jew engineer Nicolai Ipatiev and had previously been known by his name, but as the whole city knew by now, for the last two months it had been used to accommodate and imprison the tsar, Nicholas II, and his immediate family.

The guard was still staring balefully at Levitsky, waiting for an answer to his question. Levitsky leaned into the flat Mongol face. "I am returning to Moscow on urgent business. I have a meeting with Comrade Dzerzhinskiy in Lubyanka Square in two days' time. I don't think Iron Feliks would appreciate you detaining me."

"You are taking the *Rossiya*?" Gorshkov asked, using the proper name for what most people outside of Russia called the Trans-Siberian Express.

"Of course I am taking the *Rossiya,* comrade. How else does one get out of this godforsaken place?"

"Comrade Lenin tells us that God is dead."

"Comrade Lenin may very well be correct, and if God is dead, He is almost certainly buried in one of the fly-infested swamps around this place or drowned with chains around His ankles in the river Iten." Levitsky reached out and snatched the priceless pass out of Gorshkov's hand. "Now if you'll let me go on my way."

Gorshkov made a final attempt at exerting authority. "The westbound *Rossiya* does not arrive at the station until almost noon."

"This place has proved to be a little too unhealthy for my tastes, comrade. I prefer to wait at the Yekaterinburg Station rather than here, if you don't mind." Not to mention that he had no intention of taking the westbound express, or of meeting with Iron Feliks, for that matter. Levitsky pocketed the pass, gave Gorshkov a curt little nod and turned on his heel, heading north toward the station, his boots clumping loudly on the wooden sidewalk.

Including Yurovsky, there had been fourteen men in the basement behind him, most of them members of the First Kamishl Rifle Regiment. When Yurovsky was finished with disposing of the bodies, he would turn his attention to the smaller but equally vital details of the plot, which included removing any witnesses to the atrocity with a single shot to the back of the head using the .32 caliber Mauser he carried with him everywhere. Everyone, right down to Leonid the kitchen boy, would be silenced and given their own spot in the swamps to wait out eternity. Even a lummox like Gorshkov would be a liability.

Levitsky was not Bolshevik, Menshevik, Royalist or White. He was an artist, and like all artists he bore no allegiance to any political organization. His only allegiance was to his own survival, and the only way to keep on breathing was to beat a hasty retreat from the hell house he had just left and to cover his tracks while doing so. That was precisely why he had informed Gorshkov that he was going to wait for the *Rossiya* at the railway station.

To allay any suspicions the Chekist might have, he would head in that direction, but at the earliest opportunity he intended to follow a series of side streets, eventually coming out at the railway track well to the east of the station. From there he would follow the track to the

old Jewish cemetery by the freight yards close to Lake
Shartash on the eastern edge of town. At the first sign
of a freight heading in the direction of Omsk he would
jump a boxcar and simply disappear. He was well aware
of the telegraph poles that ran along the same route as
the *Rossiya,* and he had no desire to be trapped by those
whispering wires. With a nation starving to death, divided and still at war with Germany as well as itself,
freight trains had priority over the *Rossiya* and everything else on the tracks, with the exception of those terrifying armored trains he had seen on sidings when he
had come up from Moscow. If his luck held and he
wasn't captured by the Czechs, the Reds, the Whites or
Comrade Lenin himself, Levitsky could be in Vladivostok within a week.

Walking north, he heard the loud sound of a truck
backfiring and felt his heart leap in his chest. Instinctively he reached under his jacket and touched the precious object he'd slipped under his shirt. Still there. The
truck backfired a second time, accompanied by the crash
of gears grinding. Lyukhanov wasn't much of a driver.
He resisted the urge to turn around and look. He kept
on walking, forcing himself not to panic, and eventually
he heard the sound of the truck engine receding. For
the moment, at least, he was safe. He turned down a
side street between a tobacco shop and a fishmonger
with an iced-down display of pike and grayling in the
window, perfect for making *ukha*. He had a vivid memory of the smell of his grandmother's recipe for fish soup
and he sighed. Desperately trying to ignore the hungry
rumbling in his stomach, he increased his stride, and with
that, Alexander Mikhailovitch Levitsky marched into
history.

The military evacuation of Yekaterinburg began two
days later on July 20. On July 21 there were a few minor
clashes between the advancing White Army and a few
Red Army units retreating toward Perm. On the night
of July 24–25 troops from the Siberian White Army
under the command of Colonel Voitsekhovsky occupied
Yekaterinburg, meeting no resistance whatsoever. The
House of Special Purpose, once known as the Ipatiev
House, was empty and bore traces of havoc and hasty

flight. On July 25, the head of the Yekaterinburg garrison, Major General Golitsyn, assigned a military guard to the house in an attempt to stop the looting that had begun there.

On July 29, twelve days after the execution of the entire family of Tsar Nicholas II, Alexander Levitsky arrived in Vladivostok after a relatively uneventful, although hungry, journey. From there he joined a group of refugees and boarded the SS *Ida,* a tramp steamer bound for San Francisco by way of the South China Sea, the Philippines and the Hawaiian Islands.

Chapter 1

Tuesday, November 18, 1941
New York City

Jane Todd walked stiffly down the steps of the Genero-Taglia Funeral Home, the darkly varnished copper urn containing the small bones and ashes of her sister's remains held firmly in both hands. Above her a hard rain battered the faded maroon awning that sheltered the worn granite steps leading down to the sidewalk in front of 49 Second Avenue. The sky over Manhattan's Lower East Side was the color of hammered pewter, and a block and a half away the First Avenue El provided regular peals of racketing thunder. It was a good day for a funeral if such a thing was possible.

Behind Jane came the few guests she'd invited to the brief service. Her scrawny friend Rusty Birdwell from the *Daily News,* who'd called her in Los Angeles with the news of Annie's death at the Blackwell's Island Asylum. Detective Sergeant Daniel Patrick Hennessy, with whom she'd had her share of adventures over the years, and Noel Busch, her high-class friend from the *New Yorker* and *Life* who'd insisted on making all the funeral arrangements.

"I still don't know why you chose this place," Hennessy muttered. "Everyone says it's a stiff locker for the Mob, a place to park bodies until they can get them across the river to the swamps in Jersey."

"It may be owned by the Mob, but they do a good job and it's convenient."

"Convenient?"

"Come on."

As Jane reached the sidewalk and stepped out from under the awning, Noel snapped open his umbrella and had it above her head before a single drop of rain could strike. She was tired and grieving and her blond hair was lank against her neck, but she still looked ten years younger than her age of forty-one. More than one of her friends had commented that there was something about her that would always keep her looking young.

"You got class, Buschy, I'll give you that," Birdwell said in admiration.

Busch's big black Lincoln Zephyr, Birdwell's brand-new Hydra-Matic Olds in bright yellow and Hennessy's dark green unmarked and slightly battered-looking '35 Hudson Terraplane coupe were parked right in front of the funeral home, but instead of guiding Jane to one of the cars, Noel took her by one elbow and turned her to the right.

They all ducked into a narrow alley between the funeral home and a tenement next door. Directly in front of them was an ornate wrought-iron gate fitted with a very heavy-looking old-fashioned lock. In scrolled metal letters above the gates it said:

NEW YORK MARBLE CEMETERY

"You're kidding me," said Birdwell. "There's a cemetery here?"

"Since the 1800s," Busch answered. He took a huge key out of the pocket of his suit jacket and inserted it into the equally large lock. The key turned and he pushed on one of the gates. It opened smoothly without so much as a squeak. In front of them, protected from the rain by an arched stonework roof, was a long alley-way leading down to another set of gates.

"Just a little spooky," said Hennessy as they went through into the alley.

"Last resting place for a lot of famous families," offered Noel as they headed down the alley. "Scribners, Varicks, Beekmans, Van Zandts. Even a sprinkling of Busches."

"Are you sure this is okay, Noel?" Jane spoke quietly, and there was still a slight, haunted crack in her voice.

"I asked my mother," he answered, patting her on the shoulder. "She thought it was a fine idea." He patted his jacket pocket. "She was the one who gave me the key."

"How do we get down into the vaults?"

"Don't worry about that either. Mother's arranged everything."

They reached the end of the alleyway and Noel took out the key again, opening up the second pair of gates. They stepped through into a parklike area a hundred feet wide and two hundred long. Grass had been planted and was neatly tended, as were the scattering of small trees. There were no visible headstones anywhere, but there were marble plaques on the stone walls that surrounded the cemetery. The plaques were set into metal slots so they could be either removed or added to. Each row of marble plaques had a metal number welded to its holder. In front of row 103 a workman had a pulley tripod over a hole in the ground. The top plaque in the holder read EZEKIAL BUSCH 1882. The workman, dressed in overalls and a broad-brimmed hat, had sliced off a square of turf, dug down a few inches and then reached a granite capstone. Threading a rope through the attached U-bolt, he had hauled up a heavy slate trap-door, revealing an iron ladder fixed to one wall of a dark shaft. The workman stood upright as the little group of people appeared, and even in the pouring rain he removed his hat.

"Now what?" Jane asked.

"Each of the vaults has a dozen or so slate shelves fitted into the marble sides."

"Are all the shelves being used?"

"There's one or two empty ones. Marco here will put the urn anywhere you'd like."

"Not on an empty shelf," said Jane. "I don't think Annie would like that. She was used to being around a lot of people, even though I'm not sure she knew exactly where she was."

"I find you a nice place, lady. Don't worry," said Marco. He held out his hands. "She'll be safe. Don't worry," he repeated.

Reluctantly Jane handed over the copper urn. As Marco took the heavy object from her, she was surprised to see a certain reverence in his expression. He ducked under the tripod scaffolding, expertly lowered himself onto the ladder one-handed and disappeared into the darkness.

"I should have been here for her," said Jane.

"You had to live your life, kid," said Birdie. "And Annie didn't know one way or the other." Which was true enough. Her sister had never recognized her or even acknowledged her presence in all the times she'd visited when she'd lived in New York. But the guilt was still there, deep and abiding, hard in her heart, even if it was only the guilt that she'd been born the normal one and not like Annie. Or maybe the guilt came from the relief of knowing she'd never have to visit that terrible place again.

Marco came up the ladder and climbed out into the rain. He gave Jane a soft, gentle smile. "I find her a good spot, lady. She'll rest happy here." He looked up at the dull sky and shrugged. "On a nice day, this place is very beautiful. Marco makes sure of that. I do grass and flowers and trees too."

"Thank you, Marco." Jane glanced at her friend, wondering if she should tip the man, but Noel gave her a barely noticeable shake of his head. She watched for a moment as Marco went about his business, lowering the slate capstone back over the dark burial shaft, then let Noel lead her away, back to the gates and to the street.

"Oak Room at the Plaza in an hour?" Birdwell said as they reached the cars. "Pelay's laying on a bit of a spread. Drinks on the house."

"Make it an hour and a half," said Busch. "Jane and I have an appointment."

"We do?" said Jane.

Busch nodded. "Somebody wants to meet you." He pulled open the passenger-side door of the Lincoln and handed her inside. He went around to the driver's side, furled the umbrella and slid behind the wheel.

"Where are we going?"

"Palm Court at the Roosevelt." Busch switched on

3 1833 04558 5095

the engine, put the big car into drive and pulled away from the curb, heading uptown.

As the Lincoln sped away Jane wondered what her old friend was up to; she glanced at him across the seat. He had a grim, serious look on his handsome, aristocratic face and it wasn't just from the funeral. Something was going on and she didn't have the slightest idea what.

Captain Guy Maynard Liddell, MC, late of His Majesty's Royal Artillery and presently a high-ranking officer in Great Britain's MI5, stood leaning on the parapet of the narrow stone bridge that spanned the Beaulieu River, smoking his pipe, admiring the setting of the sun and waiting for his friend to appear. To his right was Beaulieu High Street with its few shops and the sturdy brick bulk of the Montagu Arms. To Liddell's left, hidden in the trees on the far side of the bridge, were the ruins of Beaulieu Abbey and beyond that the country house belonging to the estate, now used as one of the training schools operated by the Special Operations Executive, or SOE, and the present home of Morris Black, the ex–Scotland Yard detective inspector he had come to see on urgent business.

He tapped out the cooling ash from his pipe and recharged it from the pouch he carried in his jacket. The sound of the pipe on stone sent a skittering flock of oystercatchers jumping into the air, small anxious shadows rising above the silhouetted shapes of the abbey ruins. The Beaulieu River was an ocean estuary, and low tide had left a few small boats stranded on the muddy banks.

Everything looked much as it had the last time he'd seen Black, almost six months ago. According to Black the abbey had once been one of the few places in England that could offer someone full rights of sanctuary within its grounds. The river and its estuary were inclined to more warlike pursuits.

Two miles downstream was Buckler's Hard, one of the locations where Nelson's fleet had been built, including the great admiral's favorite, *Agamemnon*. Beyond the long-abandoned town was the English Channel, and beyond that France and a war that had swallowed Europe whole and was poised to suck in the rest of the world at the first opportunity.

Liddell heard the scraping of a shoe on stone. Morris Black was approaching him, hands stuffed into the pockets of an old shooting jacket that seemed to hang too loosely on the detective's shoulders. The man seemed to have aged ten years since their last meeting. His hairline had receded even farther, and gray showed at the temples now. His dark, intelligent eyes seemed sunken into their orbits, and though always lean, he seemed to have lost a great deal of weight. The word "cancer" leapt into Liddell's mind—the same disease that had taken Black's beloved wife, Fay, from him only two years before.

Black stopped a few feet away and stared at Liddell. "I didn't expect to see you quite as soon as this."

"No. It's been less than six months."

"The last time I saw you, you wanted me to be MI5's cuckoo in the SOE nest."

"That's not why I'm here, Black. It's rather more important than that."

The detective looked surprised. "I see."

"I doubt that you do, actually. I'm not sure myself. At least not entirely."

"That doesn't sound like you, Liddell. You're the type that likes to know more than anyone else. I suppose it's what makes you such a good spy."

"Perhaps. The point is, you're needed."

"I'm needed here." Black smiled. "Or so they tell me."

"This is King and Country, I'm afraid. Quite literally."

"The royal family?"

"Not the present one. The previous."

"Oh, Christ, not that little Nazi fop and his American tart."

"Presumably you are referring to the duke and duchess of Windsor. The answer is no, not that little Nazi fop and his American tart. I meant George the Fifth."

"He's dead," said Black wearily. "The royals bored him to death. There's a rumor that his doctor put him out of his misery before midnight so they could meet the *Times* deadline for the following day."

"Droll, Black, very droll."

"I'm quite serious," the detective answered. He brought a flat tin of Players out of his jacket pocket, removed a cigarette and lit it. "Only one king at a time. If the one you're concerned about is dead, then you're not talking about King and Country. You're talking about history. Once upon a time I was a policeman, Liddell. I've never been a historian."

"Then consider this a matter of historical detection."

"You're being obtuse, Captain. Get to the point."

"I'm afraid the point *is* a little obtuse. Sorry."

"A hint, then."

"All I can say at this point is that it has rather a lot to do with Mr. H. G. Wells."

True to its name, the Palm Court at the Roosevelt was full of palms, all of them planted in enormous Oriental-style pots. The room was round, the circle marked by alabaster Corinthian columns with gilded capitals. The furniture was bamboo, done in blue and gold, a settee and three comfortable chairs for each small round cocktail table, surfaced in black and white marble.

Only one table was occupied when Jane and Noel Busch arrived at the hotel. Two men sat on the settee and a third occupied one of the chairs. Jane recognized him: Percy "Sam" Foxworth, the deputy director of the New York FBI. The two men on the settee were strangers. All three men stood as Jane approached. She smiled politely. One of the men on the settee was short, silver-haired and pudgy with very pale blue eyes. Put him in a cassock and he could have been an Irish parish priest. The other man was in his forties, dark-haired and wearing a very outdated brown suit. The silver-haired man was drinking what was either the largest brandy Alexander in the world or a glass of milk. His companion was drinking beer, and Foxworth wasn't drinking anything. The only thing in front of him was a slim file folder. The silver-haired man gestured to one of the chairs directly opposite the settee. Jane seated herself, beginning to feel a little uneasy. Noel took the other one.

The silver-haired man made the introductions. "My name is William Donovan. Most people call me Bill. I'm a lawyer."

Jane nodded, recognizing him now. He was a war hero and was known for his political ambition. He was also a friend to presidents.

"That's like calling Moses a stonecutter," put in Noel. "Wild Bill has Duponts and Vanderbilts for clients. He's also a major general."

Donovan glared at Noel, then turned to the man beside him. "This is William Stephenson. We call him Little Bill because he's so quiet." Jane examined the man. He looked like an accountant.

The man in the brown suit leaned forward and extended his hand. "Very pleased to meet you, Miss Todd. I've heard a great deal about you." The handshake was firm, and the hard, flat accent identified the man as a Canadian.

Donovan tilted his head in Foxworth's direction. "Sam I believe you already know."

"I've had the pleasure." Jane smiled, though it was hardly that. Two years before, Foxworth had had her in handcuffs stewing in a makeshift jail cell at the New York World's Fair.

Foxworth smiled in return. "Exciting times."

"Exciting enough to almost get me killed, and I didn't even get any pictures for my troubles."

The FBI director flushed. "Well, that's all in the past anyway."

Jane took a deep breath and let it out slowly. "Gentlemen, I've just come from my sister's funeral. I'm not really in the mood for reminiscing."

Donovan got right to the point. "Do you think there's going to be a war, Miss Todd?"

"Certainly." Any idiot knew that. Hitler was crazy as a bedbug.

"Where?"

"Where it already is. Europe. Russia. The Mediterranean. North Africa."

"That's not our war."

"That's the whole point, Mr. Donovan. We'll be neutral right up until the minute someone drops a bomb on the Empire State Building. FDR needs a war all his own if he's going to drag us into this thing without being thrown out of the White House once and for all."

"You think we'll ever be directly at war? On our own?"

"Yes." With FDR at the helm, it was probably inevitable, she thought.

"With who?"

"The Japs."

"Why?"

Jane sighed. "Is this all completely necessary, Mr. Donovan?"

"I believe so."

"All right. I think the Japs don't have any choice. They want to take over China and the Far East and maybe even part of Russia. Hitler's helping them do that and we're trying to stop them. We've frozen their assets in America; we've got an embargo on oil, scrap iron, coal and every other strategic material you can think of. So do the Brits. Japan is an island and they don't have many friends. Even according to Tojo they've only got enough oil for a year and a half. They either strangle economically or come to some kind of diplomatic agreement, which to them is the same thing as surrendering. They'll fight to the death."

"But we're already negotiating with them."

"They're buying time," said Jane, realizing the older man was simply leading her along.

"To what end?"

"To strike."

"You really think they'll strike first?"

"Yes."

"Why?"

"They don't have any choice. They know they can't actually win a long war with the United States. The best they can do is quickly knock us out of the running."

"And how would they do that, Miss Todd?"

"By catching us flat-footed, probably in Hawaii. A sneak attack. Take out the Pacific Fleet and you own the Pacific. A perfect staging base for long-range bombers once they've invaded. A break in a six- or seven-thousand-mile supply line they can't realistically hope to service."

"Anything else?" asked Stephenson dryly.

"I'd say the Aleutians are a pretty good bet. They could hopscotch their way right onto the mainland."

"You've thought about this a great deal," said Stephenson.

"I read the papers." She turned to her friend. "I read Noel Busch in *Newsweek*." She shrugged her shoulders. "It doesn't take some kind of swami."

"There's a lot of people out there who would disagree with you."

"These days there's two kinds of people walking around the streets, Mr. Donovan. People with their hands over their ears and their eyes closed who refuse to even think about the possibility that war might come, and the ones who know it's coming and that it's only a matter of when."

"I'd say that's fairly close to the truth." Stephenson nodded. "Most people seem to be in a fog about the whole thing."

"I'd like you to come and work for us," said Donovan, leaning forward, his eyes locked onto hers.

"Us, as in a law firm?" Jane smiled. "But that's not really what you are, is it? Not with Sam here and your mysterious friend."

"She's a very intelligent woman," said Donovan, glancing at Noel.

"She's also in the room," Jane answered. "And she doesn't like being talked about in the third person if you don't mind."

"Mr. Stephenson is the director of the British Security Co-ordination Office here in New York. General Donovan heads up the Co-ordinator of Information Office in Washington."

"Lot of coordination going on," said Jane. "What you really mean is that you're spies." She turned to Noel. "And I suppose you're one of them?"

"I work for General Donovan on an occasional basis."

"You're a recruiter."

"I suppose you could say that."

"What made you think I'd want to work for these people or vice versa? I'm no spy. You know that, Buschy."

Foxworth flipped open the plain file folder in front of him. "You live in a fourth-floor walkup off Harlem Place in downtown L.A., you're two months behind on your rent, and your last two assignments have been for Hollywood *Pic*, one on William Lundigan doing *The Man Who Talked Too Much* and then a 'where is he now' piece on a cartoon character named Andy Pandy. You've got twenty-three dollars in the bank." Foxworth looked at Jane benevolently. "You've been running away from yourself ever since the World's Fair thing and getting that scar on your cheek. We're offering you a place to come home to."

"Golly, you make me feel warm all over," said Jane. "People like you don't give something for nothing, Foxworth. Last time I had anything to do with you, I had my office blown up, various burns, cuts and broken bones, not to mention all my equipment being destroyed."

"Anything you lost will be replaced," said Donovan expansively. "And then some."

"Why?"

"Because we need you, Miss Todd," Stephenson murmured.

"One more time," said Jane. "Why?"

"COI and BSC are working together," said Donovan, pushing his pudgy face forward. "We share a lot of people and a lot of information. Little Bill here is of the opinion that we've got a traitor in our midst."

"So arrest him."

"It's not quite that easy," Donovan answered. "In the first place, we don't know exactly who he is, and in the second place he's got some documentation, or knows where it is, that could be very damaging to both England and the United States."

"I still don't see what this has to do with me."

"According to both Mr. Busch and Mr. Foxworth, you are an eminently courageous woman capable and willing to take risks. You're also a photographer, and photography has a great deal to do with this particular assignment. In fact, it is fundamental."

"And I'm supposed to do this so I can get a few bucks and my cameras back?"

"Perhaps you should do it for patriotic reasons," said Donovan, a little coldness creeping into his voice.

"No offense, General. There's nothing wrong with patriotism, but getting the first bullet between the eyes is usually its only reward."

"What reward are you looking for?"

"The one every journalist and photographer like me is going to be looking for in six months or a year."

"Which is?" said Foxworth.

"Credentials as a war correspondent. Both sides of the Atlantic and anywhere else you guys are going."

Donovan gave Stephenson a quick glance. He nodded. Donovan turned back to Jane. "Done."

"Then I guess I'm your girl." She smiled, wondering just what in hell she was getting herself into.

Chapter 2

The taxi pulled up in front of No. 13 Hanover Terrace, and Morris Black and Guy Liddell climbed out into the watery early-morning sunlight. On the far side of the long, curving terrace of imposing town houses was Regent's Park. A few shovelers cutting through the thin mist stood motionless and ghostly over the lake, while the ducks left little waggling v's in the gunmetal water like a breeze blown over mercury. A breath of frost on the grass. Too early for little boys and their boats, if any still existed in London, a little too late for civil servants from Primrose Hill taking a shortcut to Baker Street Station.

"I'm still not entirely clear about all of this," said Black at the bottom of the steps. The tall windows on either side of the darkly painted front door were covered by long indigo-colored drapes. The house looked almost as though it was in mourning.

"It's a very delicate political situation," Liddell responded with a worried look.

"Wells is hardly a political figure. He's a writer."

"And a social critic. A powerful one."

"He writes stories about invasions from Mars and people who travel through time," said Black, grimacing. "If that's social criticism, I'm a little green man."

"He also wrote *The Outline of History,* not to mention his friendship with Lord Beaverbrook. To compound the situation he stole away Maxim Gorky's mistress."

"Another writer?" Black shook his head. "This is becoming absurd, Liddell. We're in the middle of a bloody war and you're going on about Russian writers and their paramours."

"Gorky's mistress was a woman named Countess Moura Zakrevskaia Benckendorff. Her real name is Moura Budberg."

"Is stealing away a man's mistress some kind of crime?"

"As well as being Wells's mistress, Moura Budberg is an NKVD agent."

Black looked startled for a moment. "Then arrest her."

"Can't be done." They climbed the steps and Liddell tapped the knocker.

"Why not?" asked Black. He was beginning to sense some sort of hidden agenda coming into play.

"Because other than Moura herself the only person who says she's a spy is Wells, and Gorky before her."

"She admits to being an agent of the secret police?"

"To them, yes. It seems to be her ploy. She throws herself on the mercy of her gentlemen friends and tells them how she was blackmailed into becoming an agent. She supposedly fled to England by escaping through Finland and was introduced to all of Wells's important friends—Beaverbrook included. Wells found out she was a complete fraud. He was doing a series of articles for the *Guardian* about the Latvian crisis a few years ago and ran into her in Riga. Apparently she returns to Russia three or four times a year, or she did before war broke out."

"Does she have any connection with the Soviet embassy here in London?" What primrose path was Liddell taking him down?

"Not to our knowledge."

"Then I don't see your so-called delicate political situation."

"It doesn't stop with Gorky or Wells."

"She's someone else's mistress as well?" This was becoming farce.

"I'm afraid so."

"Who?"

"I can't say at the moment. The man concerned is married, has children, and the word is he's on next year's civil list. He also has a position of some power in the Foreign Office."

"Foreign Office?"

Liddell let out a long, heartfelt sigh. "Supposedly he works for the Political Intelligence Department, but I'm afraid he's also one of us. SIS. Has been since Cummings's day."

"A spy?" Black made a snorting sound. "Speak for yourself, Liddell. This man sounds like a lifetime professional. I'm only in for the duration. One of these years I'm going back to the Yard."

"His career aspirations are irrelevant, Black, as are yours. This has to do with a single event in his life. Twenty-three years ago."

Black did the calculation in his head: 1918. The end of the war. "Presumably a mistake."

"A stupendous one."

"To do with this Budberg woman?"

"No, but there is no doubt that she would use the information to good effect if we ever saw fit to move against her."

"She's blackmailing His Majesty's government?" God, where was Victoria when you really needed her? She'd have had the woman's head, literally.

"She's blackmailing His Majesty if you want to put it that way."

"And Wells's interest in all of this?" Irritated by the delay, Black knocked again, a hard, insistent copper's hammering.

"You can look at it in one of two ways," Liddell said, smiling thinly. "Either he is doing his duty or getting revenge on Miss Budberg and her friend at the F.O."

A servant met their knock, and after Liddell produced his warrant card, the man took it off into the dark recesses of the house, returning a long moment later. He handed back the warrant card and led Liddell and Black down a long oak-floored corridor fitted with a somewhat tattered but obviously expensive runner. They found

Wells in front of a large bay window overlooking the back garden. He was sitting in a comfortable leather armchair with a blanket wrapped around his knees.

To Black he looked like the complete Edwardian gentleman, wearing a three-piece tweed suit, a stiff-collared white shirt and a four-in-hand tie. The feet poking out from the bottom of the blanket appeared to be very small and fitted with extremely expensive shoes. The eyes behind the thick rimless spectacles seemed bright and lively but the rest of the body was not keeping pace. There were liver spots on the man's face and the top of his balding skull, dark sagging circles under his eyes, and the sagging skin of his face seemed that of a much heartier man.

"You're here about Moura," he said, looking away from the view out the window. At the far end of the garden there was a more modern-looking Mews flat and in between several beds of late vegetables.

"Yes," said Liddell.

"Who's this one? Another troll lurking under Westminster Bridge? Quasimodo swinging about among Big Ben's little bells?"

"His name is Morris Black, Mr. Wells. At one time he was a detective inspector for Scotland Yard. Now he works for another branch of government."

"Special Branch?"

"No, sir," Black answered.

"Well, that's good. Should leave the bloody Irish alone."

"Yes, sir."

"About Miss Budberg."

"What about her?" said Wells. "You should be more concerned about that nest of Nazi vipers at Broadcast House."

"Let us choose our concerns," said Black coldly. "It's our job."

"You called *us* about Miss Budberg, sir," Liddell reminded gently. "Through Mr. Beaverbrook."

"I suppose I did, didn't I?"

"Yes, sir."

"Bit of a trollop." Wells let out a small, surprisingly feminine laugh. "Not Beaverbrook, of course. The countess."

"She does sound a bit wicked." Black smiled. He was rapidly coming to the conclusion that Wells was a bit bonkers. Or going senile. There was a faint smell in the room—death tiptoeing in through the shadows.

"Delightfully so on occasion," Wells answered, giving Black a wink. "Gets the sap running even in a buggered-up old tree such as myself. First diabetes, then this damnable liver thing." He pushed out his small lips like he was a pouting child. "Not bloody fair, I tell you."

It rarely is, Black thought, but he said nothing.

Liddell nodded. "No, of course not."

"Why are the two of you standing over me like that?" said Wells suddenly, his voice flaring imperiously. "I'm not the bloody king of Prussia, man! Sit down! Sit down!" Black and Liddell did as they were told, pulling up a pair of old and very creaky rattan armchairs.

"Miss Budberg?" said Liddell.

"Quite."

"You reported to Mr. Beaverbrook that she was an agent of the NKVD, Soviet State Security, and that she had been for some time."

"Quite so. At least from the time of her relationship with Gorky. Poor fool that he was. Another one of Stalin's victims."

Black was vaguely aware of the controversy of the playwright's death seven or eight years before.

"And when was Miss Budberg's relationship with Comrade Gorky?" asked Liddell.

"Back when the NKVD was called Cheka: *Vserossiya Chrezvychaynaya Komissiya po Bor'be s Kontrrevolyutsiyey i Sabotazhem.*" The writer's accent was surprisingly fluent.

"All-Russian Extraordinary Commission to Combat Counterrevolution and Sabotage," Black translated, his accent equally fluent.

"Well done!" said Wells, his eyes twinkling behind the thick lenses of his spectacles. His small feet did a delighted little tattoo on the floor.

"I thought you were a German Jew," said Liddell, surprised at Black's facility with the language.

"Jews come from nowhere and everywhere," said Wells pedantically. "Hence the Wandering Jew."

"Bielozersk, actually. North of Moscow on Lake Bielo. My grandfather took the family to Germany to work in the coalfields, but they moved on before the Great War. My grandfather insisted that I learn the language of my roots."

"Well, good for him!"

"I'd very much like to talk about Miss Budberg if you don't mind," said an exasperated Liddell.

"Is he always this boring?" Wells asked seriously.

Black smiled at Liddell. "Frequently. But I think he should be indulged in this case."

"If you insist."

"When did you discover that she was NKVD?"

"Gorky told me when I visited Petrograd—Leningrad, if you prefer—in 1918. She styled herself as his secretary."

"Why were you there?"

"Gorky asked me to come, of course. He'd written Beaverbrook saying they were terribly short of food. My luggage was full of butter, if you can believe it."

"And Miss Budberg?" Black asked. "She had a suitcase full of scones, I presume." The man really was a lunatic.

"She said Zinoviev wanted her dead," Wells answered. "Why?"

"Because of what she knew through the British Foreign Office representative there. Lockhart. She was having an affair with him as well. On NKVD orders. I tell you, the woman was not far from being a whore."

The name Lockhart stopped Black cold. The man Wells was referring to was obviously Robert Bruce Lockhart, who'd written the book *Memoirs of a British Agent*. It had been made into a popular film of the same name, portraying him as a romantic hero. Lockhart, then, was Liddell's "delicate political situation"—a man in the upper reaches of the Foreign Office who'd once been entangled with a Communist spy.

"What did she know?" asked Black, pressing on even though a look from Liddell suggested that he should leave well enough alone.

"She knew that it was all fudge and flummery," snorted Wells. He reached under his blanket and took out a small leather humidor and an ostrich-covered Dunhill Sport. He took out a stumpy, half-smoked cigar and lit it, blowing happy puffs of aromatic smoke at the bay window.

"Fudge and flummery?"

"All of the king's supposed hand-wringing about poor cousin Nicky and his unfortunate position."

"Nicky?"

"The tsar. Nicholas the second. Dear Nicky asked King George for asylum in England. The king refused, although not in so many words. He let his secretary do all the work for him. And the prime minister. He was relieved when he found out they'd all been massacred, believe me."

"Why do you say that?" asked Liddell.

"Because it's bloody true. In 1918 this country was as close to a revolution as Russia was. The last thing the king needed was a despot like Nicholas lolling about in Kensington Palace or sharing a bit of borscht at Balmoral. That's the real reason Lockhart was there."

"What reason?"

"To botch a rescue attempt so the F.O. and the king could say they'd tried their best. Lockhart was special consul there."

"Where?"

"In St. Petersburg as well as Moscow." Wells nodded.

"Miss Budberg informed you of this?" asked Liddell.

"Indeed. If you read Lockhart's published diaries for that time period, or that wretched penny dreadful he wrote, he barely mentions the death of the tsar. Tosses it off as a mere bagatelle."

"I was always under the impression that he was there to broker some kind of rescue," said Liddell.

"That was supposedly the plan. And all poppycock. There were no rescue attempts of any kind. They were marched down into the basement of that house and executed. Shot, then stabbed with bayonets, then covered with some sort of vitriol to disfigure them and finally tossed down a mineshaft. Good old King George! How he cared for his dear cousin!"

"You only have Miss Budberg's word for this? There's no real evidence?" asked Liddell.

"Well, there's the rub, you see," Wells answered. He twirled the wet stump of the cigar in his mouth. "There are pictures."

"A photographer was present?"

"Rather better than that," said Wells. "According to Moura she was actually in the room when Lenin discussed the possibility of dispatching a cinematographer to Yekaterinburg to document the proceedings. He was quite a film buff, you know. Moura even saw him write out the pass for the man."

"Did she tell you his name?"

"Certainly. Alexander Mikhailovitch Levitsky."

"He shot the film?"

"He did. A ten-minute reel." Wells smiled. "There's always been a smelly one about the possibility that Lockhart was actually on the scene. Watched the murders himself."

"I don't believe it," Liddell scoffed. "Lockhart was imprisoned. We had to trade him for some fellow named Litvinov here in London. If the NKVD had a film like that, they would have made use of it. It would have proved their case against Lockhart and dreadfully embarrassed the crown."

"To what end, sir?" Wells shrugged. "They were different times, young fellow. And I don't think Lenin would like to have seen himself publicly portrayed as a savage executioner. Not at that point in the revolution. It was all a bit dicey then. Anyone's game. It's all moot, of course, since Lenin never received the film."

"Miss Budberg told you this?"

"Yes. According to her it turned out that this man Levitsky was a Trotskyite."

"He gave the film to Trotsky?"

"It would seem that he didn't give it to anyone, not then at least. He was last seen with a group of refugees boarding an American tramp steamer in Vladivostok."

"Heading where?"

"San Francisco."

"Something of a cold trail. Twenty-three years. Not a terribly reliable source either."

"Why would she lie?" asked Wells.

Liddell grimaced. "To foment exactly this sort of intrigue, especially now that the Soviets have suddenly become our allies in the face of the German invasion."

"A hole card," murmured Black.

"I beg your pardon?" said Wells.

"An Americanism from their Wild West," Black explained. "The hidden card in a game of stud poker or blackjack—what we call vingt-et-un. A secret that can win or lose the game."

Liddell nodded. "Give us what we want out of this alliance or we'll reveal your nasty secret."

"Something like that," Black agreed.

Wells gave a puff on his cigar. "You're all being much too complicated. Moura's just being her bitchy self, believe me."

A few minutes later, the two men left the house on Hanover Terrace, crossing over to the park and walking down toward Baker Street. To their left, on the far side of the lake, was the circular court of the Royal Botanical Society. To the right, rising over the rooftops, was the ornate, smoky presence of Marylebone Station.

"He's crackers, you know," said Black.

"A little. Eccentric's more the word. He's a dying old man."

"He's a dying old man who's trying to tell you something, and you can bet that other people already know it," Black responded.

"Such as?" asked Liddell.

"If there's film of the assassination of the tsar's entire family, making it public would be an unmitigated disaster," said Black emphatically. "We have the Americans poised to join the war. What do you think all those America First types will do when they discover that George the Fifth was an accessory to the mass murder of part of his own family? Have you ever seen pictures of them together? They look like brothers."

"I've been instructed to find the film," Liddell said.

"You knew about the film before you talked to Wells?" asked Black. "That was all for my benefit?"

"We knew there was some kind of evidence. We both needed to know what you'd be looking for before we sent you off."

"Sent me off?"

"Yes. You're going to America. There will be a Sunderland awaiting your pleasure at dawn tomorrow in Southampton."

"And if I don't want to take the assignment?" He was a fan of the Yanks, especially their Old West. At least in concept. He was skeptical about the reality. On the other hand it would get him out of Beaulieu and a life of utter ennui.

"You'll be classified as a security risk. You can sit out the rest of the war reading your books about Buffalo Bill Cody and Wild Bill Hitchcock in that Shepherd's Market flat you keep."

"Hickok," said Black. "It's Wild Bill Hickok. And you are a right bastard, Liddell."

"Quite so. A right bastard who's just following orders, old son."

"The motto of the whole war: 'Just following orders.' "

"So what's the answer going to be?"

They came out through Clarence Gate and walked down Upper Baker Street to the Underground entrance. "I'll go," said Black. He disappeared into the Underground station.

Liddell smiled. "Never doubted it for a minute." He took out his pipe, lit it, and continued on down Baker Street.

Anatoli Borisovich Gorsky, alias Boris Gromov and sometimes known as Henry by the covert agents he controlled, sat in the attic radio room of the Soviet embassy on Chesham Place in Belgravia and worked on the message he was about to send to Moscow Center. Gorsky was fundamentally a very unattractive man, short with upswept reddish hair that was already receding even though he was only in his early thirties, small eyes turned owlish by the thick lenses and plain black Bakelite frames of his glasses and a double chin that predicted more of the same as the years rolled by. Gorsky had been a relatively low-level functionary in the NKVD for years before the war, but he had been promoted by attrition during the 1938 purges. What he lacked in real judgment he made up for in dogged perseverance and bullying. Every single agent he controlled in the field loathed him. Nevertheless, he produced results. His use of the Budberg woman had been a stroke of genius, putting the cat among the pigeons, and perhaps blowing a warm breath on embers long thought cold. Information from Vassili Zarubin, his opposite number in Washington, suggested that the Americans were now curious enough to take the bait as well. Gorsky blinked behind his heavy glasses and smiled. He sat up and stretched, taking a moment to carefully extract a Kreml from its package, twisting the end closed before lighting it with a rather nice Ronson he'd picked up at Burlington Arcade. He took a deep inhalation of the harsh tobacco, coughed for a moment and then inhaled again. This time he let the smoke out in slow steady streams through his pursed lips and nostrils. Why shouldn't the British and the Americans help to find Levitsky's long-lost secret? After all, with the Nazis at the gates of Moscow, weren't they all allies now?

Chapter 3

It was barely dawn as the train reached Southampton and, as he had all the way down from London, Black had a compartment to himself. He wasn't particularly happy with the way the assignment had been foisted on him, but he was secretly pleased to be away from the cloistered confines of the SOE training school at Beaulieu Abbey. He knew that his work teaching interrogation methods had real value, but his skills as a detective—his greatest skills—were lying fallow. He was in a backwater and both the war and his life were passing him by.

He was also thrilled to be going to America at last. From childhood he had been fascinated with the place, especially its rough-and-ready, insistently violent history. Above and beyond that there was the possibility of reuniting with Katherine, the only woman other than Fay ever to have touched his heart. Nothing explicit had been said during the Queer Jack investigation the year before, but she was almost certainly working with Donovan's fledgling intelligence-gathering organization in Washington, the same organization Liddell had instructed him to cooperate with through this Stephenson fellow's group, British Security Co-ordination in New York.

Even with the compartment window shut against the chilly air Black could smell the sea as the train slowly clattered into the dock area. It rolled past the huge customs sheds of the piers, the loading cranes and the berthed liners, their once colorful livery now a uniform gray as they were transformed into hospital ships and troop carriers for the war raging in Africa. He shook his head, thinking of that. A skin of ice on the ponds and streams here and the blazing heat of Africa not so very far away.

The train came to a complete halt in front of a modern-looking building with a sign that read IMPERIAL HOUSE. The building had a faintly nautical cast to it, enhanced by its dazzling camouflage paint. This had clearly once been the Imperial Airways terminal for the short-lived transatlantic passenger service.

Grabbing his single suitcase and a bulging folio containing the mass of briefing documents Liddell had given him to read on the long journey, Black shrugged on his overcoat and left the train. Its wheels shrieked as it shunted backward almost immediately, and he was jarred to find that he was the only passenger who had exited the train. He crossed the narrow concrete platform, even more aware of the salty tang of the ocean, and pushed through the glass doors of Imperial House. The building was empty except for one young man in RAF uniform sporting the single wing and crown WAG insignia of a wireless operator–air gunner. He saluted as Black approached and then stepped forward to relieve him of his bags.

"You'd be Detective Superintendent Black?"

Black smiled at the upping in rank Liddell had managed for him. "Yes," he said, "I am." He looked around the deserted room. "No other passengers?"

"I'm Wiggins, sir. Sparks for this trip. Follow me and I'll take you down to Mother Brown. And you're the only passenger I was sent to fetch, sir."

"Mother Brown?"

"It's what we call the crate, sir."

"Ah," said Black, praying it was anything but.

Hefting the luggage, Wiggins used his hip to open the doors at the far end of the room, and they stepped directly out onto the quay. Black paused and stared. The aircraft moored a few dozen yards away was enormous, like some sort of flying whale. She was painted in a suit of brown and gray camouflage, which seemed to be completely useless since she was also fitted with gleaming targetlike RAF roundels on her flanks and wings. The name Mother Brown was neatly painted in white on the blunt, boatlike nose.

The aircraft bristled with weaponry. Even in the dawn gloom he made out the machine guns in the nose turret, another pair in a mid-upper turret, a pair of waist guns poking out an open hatch on the side he could see and presumably their mates on the opposite side, and at least four more machine guns sprouting from a rear Perspex blister.

"Not quite the sitting duck you might think," said Wiggins proudly.

"No," agreed Black. "I can see that."

"Even got the capability of torpedoes and bombs we can run out under the wings," said Wiggins. "Bean the odd submarine or E-boat in the Channel from time to time. Great fun."

"I'm sure."

"Well, come along, sir. Met says the weather's closing in over the Irish Sea, so we've only got an hour or so to get past it."

Black followed Wiggins down the concrete quay and onto a gangplank that slanted up to the open front hatch. Wiggins traversed the gangplank easily, even loaded down with Black's bags, but the detective was a little slower. A lurching drop into the oily depths of Southampton Water was definitely not his idea of great fun.

He made it across and ducked his head as he stepped through the hatchway. Wiggins had vanished into the complex interior of the aircraft, and Black had no idea which way to turn. On his left was a low-ceilinged storage area that appeared to contain an anchor and several bound-up and uninflated dinghies, while to the right was a small compartment with several trunklike lockers welded to the deck, a rack of carbines and a metal-clad stairway. A pair of legs came down the stairs and resolved itself into a man a little older than Wiggins wearing a pilot's cap and a leather flying jacket so old the sheepskin at the collar had turned the color of tobacco and the leather itself was cracked and worn down to the canvas underlining. The expression on the man's face was not particularly friendly.

"Crofton," said the pilot. "You'll be Black, our illustrious passenger." There was a sour edge to the comment.

"Passenger?" asked Black. "There's really no one else?"

"Just you and the crew. You must be some sort of boffin or a politician to rate an entire Sunderland all to yourself."

"I had no idea," Black responded, shaking his head. "I thought I was hitching a ride."

"No, we're using twenty-five hundred gallons of very scarce aviation fuel just for you." He paused. "I hope you're worth the expenditure."

"Somebody in His Majesty's government appears to think so," said Black. "It certainly wasn't my idea."

"I suppose there's some cloak-and-dagger need for speed. A convoy would take weeks, if you got there at all."

"Something like that." Black nodded. "Ours but to do or die and all that."

The pilot gave the detective a speculative look, then shrugged. Crofton's voice softened slightly. "I suppose we all have our jobs to do."

"Yes."

"We'll be using the old Pan American route," said the pilot. "Southampton to Foynes in Ireland, Foynes to Botwood, Newfoundland, Botwood to Shediac in New Brunswick and then a straight run down the coast to New York. The old way was here to the Canaries with an overnight in Bermuda before New York, but there's too much chance of running into a *Gruppe* of 109s heading up the Channel. Nasty buggers they are too. Like great bloody hornets swarming all about you." He paused. "You'd better follow me and get yourself kitted out before we take off." He jerked a thumb back over his shoulder. "Two toilets back in the nose, port and starboard. He pointed upward. "Cockpit and navigation station directly above." He headed for a narrow bulkhead door. "This way to the wardroom."

He led Black through the small galley kitchen on the other side of the bulkhead. There was a small electric cooker and a coffee urn on the starboard side, a table bolted to the deck in the middle of the tiny room and a pair of cots slung one above the other. "Come up here if you're hungry. Food in the pantry, even some bacon if you'd like, but I'd wait until after Foynes. They do quite a nice Full Irish, and we'll be there for an hour or so topping up and checking the Met again."

They went through a second hatch leading after, and Black squeezed down a narrow corridor lined with various cables and lines. They exited into the waist of the aircraft. Black spotted an empty bomb rack and commented on it. "Saves weight and gives us a longer range. We're not carrying any flares either." The pilot pointed to a pair of large containers fitted to sliding rails.

"Where is the fuel?" asked Black as they passed through another hatchway.

"Wings," answered Crofton. "Four big tanks and another pair fitted into the tail section." They stepped out into a large compartment that contained a pair of leather-covered padded benches, some webbing holding back a supply of parachutes and a rack of extra propeller blades and another rack of dinghy paddles. It was the full height of the hull, and Black could see a ladder bolted to the bulkhead leading up to the upper deck.

"Cozy," he said.

"Bloody cold this time of year," said Crofton. "We'll be nudging the toe of Greenland." He found a locker, opened it and withdrew a crumpled flight suit, a sheepskin-lined jacket like his own and a pair of heavy sheepskin-lined boots. "Put these on or you'll freeze."

Black took off his overcoat and began slipping into the heavy clothing. Crofton watched him do up all the requisite snaps and tabs. When Black was finished, Crofton gave him a brief nod, then went up the ladder to the upper deck of Mother Brown. At the top of the ladder he turned and looked back down at Black. "Sit down on one of the benches and use the harness bolted to the wall to strap yourself in. There's a bit of chop, so takeoff might be a little rough."

Black nodded and did as he was told. A few moments

later he heard the gangplank scraping on the quay and then the engines fired, one by one. Within a few minutes they were hurtling down Southampton Water in the dawn light, their passage throwing up spray that completely obscured the portholes along the side of the hull. He felt a brief moment of stomach-lurching vertigo, and then the nose of the ponderous-looking flying boat rose up off the water and they were airborne. Black took a deep breath and let it out slowly, trying to ease his anxiety. Fighting the immediate urge to urinate and trying to ignore the continuous vibration of the hull and the thundering of the four Bristol Pegasus engines, Morris Black flipped open the folio case Wiggins had carried aft and began to read through his briefing notes.

The two-tone blue-and-white United Air Lines DC3 did a short turn over the Washington Monument and the Tidal Basin, slowly descending as it crossed over the Potomac and the huge construction site of the new military headquarters building being built with disturbing proximity to the neat rows of crosses that made up Arlington National Cemetery.

The aircraft dropped with a sudden lurch, and Jane grabbed the arms of her seat, trying not to think of the way her belly was doing flip-flops. None of the other passengers on the plane seemed to be paying the slightest attention and continued reading their complimentary copies of the *Washington Post* or *New York Times*.

Gathering up all her courage, she took a quick peek out the porthole window beside her and saw a confusing, snaking tangle of roadways under construction and then the end of the runway, which seemed to be rising toward her at an alarming rate. She had just lit a cigarette when one of the stewards came by telling her to extinguish it and to help her with her seat belt. Less than a minute later the flight touched down right on time and taxied toward the newly built terminal building of Washington National Airport. By the time the aircraft reached the terminal and the airstairs were being rolled into place, Jane was almost at the head of the line in front of the main door. She had flown a few times before, and each time she did so she liked it less. For her, trains and automobiles were the only natural form of transportation on land and ocean liners for oceans. In a car or train wreck you had a chance of walking away, and if a ship sank there was at least a possibility of getting aboard a lifeboat. If a plane went down, you went down with it, usually in flames, and that was all she wrote—no second chances.

She'd met a pilot at the derby last year who told her a DC3 could fly on one engine and even coast a good long time on no engines at all, but she hadn't been convinced and he hadn't managed to charm his way into her bed. Not many did these days, given the hideously unromantic and recurrent memory she had of emptying all eight shots from a Brazilian Walther automatic into the face and chest of a man who'd been making exquisite love to her only a few minutes before.

The airstair cleats snagged into their appropriate slots, and the steward, a woman this time, unsealed the door and pushed it back. She smiled, showing every perfect, gleaming Ipana-buffed tooth in a completely insincere smile and saying the same thing over and over.

"I hope you had a wonderful flight with us today and thank you for flying United Air Lines." Jane almost expected the girl to stick her paw out for a tip. She brushed past the woman, stepped out into the sunshine and took a deep breath of fresh air. As she went down the airstairs she could see the baggage guys unloading the rear compartment. All she had was an overnight case she'd carried on board—at this point she still wasn't sure she wanted the job she'd been offered. She smiled at that as she stepped off the airstairs and headed across to the bone white terminal building. At this point she wasn't sure she even knew what the job really was.

She stopped on the tarmac and dropped her overnight bag, letting the rest of the passengers swarm around her. She lit a cigarette at last, pulling the smoke down deeply into her lungs. Here she was in Washington, D.C., and for the life of her she didn't know why. Spies and traitors and secret organizations—it was Black Mask comic book stuff or Lamont Cranston and the Shadow. Shaking her head, she followed the last of the passengers from her flight into the terminal.

Once inside she paused, looking for a sign that would tell her where the taxi rank was, but she was surprised to see a nice-looking young man with dark hair wearing a blue suit and carrying a cardboard sign in his hand that read MISS JANE TODD. The man smiled as she approached him.

"I'm Jane Todd."

"Well, that's a relief," he answered, still smiling. "There was a very unpleasant-looking woman with her hose rolled down to her ankles who just went by. For a nightmarish moment I thought she might be you." He lowered the sign, putting it under his arm, and extended a well-manicured hand. "My name is Fleming. Ian Fleming."

"You're a Brit," said Jane.

"Quite so." He took her by the elbow and guided her across the terminal to the main doors. "Born and raised."

"So why are you kidnapping me?" Jane asked.

"Because you're in need of kidnapping," Fleming answered with a laugh. "Too easy to get lost in this city, I'm afraid. If someone doesn't kidnap you and show you the ropes, you're bound to wind up in some terrible den of iniquity."

"Dens of iniquity are some of my favorite places." She smiled pleasantly, cocking her hip.

"Then I shall have to take you to the Casino Royal at Fourteenth and H. Extremely iniquitous."

"You're very charming," said Jane as they stepped out of the terminal and into the sunshine again.

"Thank you."

"It wasn't necessarily a compliment," she said. "In my experience the majority of charming men are also not to be trusted."

"Part of the charm." Fleming laughed. "In my experience women love cads. Thrive on them, as a matter of fact." He raised his hand and a nondescript dirt brown Dodge slid forward from where it had been waiting in a no-stopping zone. Jane took a quick look. It had U.S. Army plates and the man behind the wheel was wearing a khaki uniform, not a cabbie's cap.

"Curiouser and curiouser," said Jane as Fleming

handed her into the backseat. "What Alice said when she drank from the Drink Me bottle."

"Good for you," responded Fleming. "I've come to the conclusion that with only a few exceptions no one in this country reads books."

"Then you've come to the wrong conclusion, Mr. Fleming."

"Commander, actually."

"Commander of what?"

"Naval Intelligence."

"British Naval Intelligence?"

"Indeed."

"Shouldn't you be off fighting a war somewhere?"

"Shouldn't you?" Fleming replied.

"This exchange of bon mots is terrific," said Jane, "but I really would like some straight answers."

"You'll probably get a few if you wait long enough." Fleming reached forward and tapped the driver on the shoulder. "Let's have the grand tour before we go to the hotel, Billy."

"Sure thing, Commander." Billy put the car into gear and they moved away from the curb, easing into the congested traffic in front of the terminal.

The little Irish village of Foynes lay far up the Shannon River, past Kerry Head, Tarbert, Killrush and Glin. By then the river was half its width at the mouth, her small bays protected by steep hills and headlands that kept the wind from turning the surface of the water into a spuming froth that would have made landing any sort of flying boat impossible.

Unlike Southampton there was no mooring quay, and Mother Brown had to make do with a bobbing buoy and chain out into the estuary, a rope attached to it and to the collapsible capstan on the nose of the aircraft. The front hatch was cracked open by the pilot, and both Crofton and Morris Black stepped out of Mother Brown and into a small launch that had motored out from the village. Potts, the navigator, Stroker, the copilot, and the engineer, a man named Podborsky, joined the other two men in the small boat, leaving Wiggins in charge of the aircraft and the refueling. On their descent Black had managed to catch a glimpse of their destination: on one side a small island and on the other the village itself, no more than a fisherman's wharf with some large, industrial oil tanks. A scattering of cottages and shops lined the cobbled length of its single high street.

As the launch puttered toward the shore, several lighters loaded down with oversized metal fuel tanks were already making their way out to Mother Brown. Black thought it was a little old-fashioned, but he said nothing to Crofton. The launch burbled across the smooth water, barely ruffled by a faint, salty breeze. They reached the main dock, stepped out onto a floating pontoon and then climbed up onto the dock itself.

Crofton pointed to a large shedlike building with the handful of documents he carried in his hand. "I have to go in and placate the *Gardai* and the lads at customs; this is supposedly a neutral country, after all. You can go up to the terminal building while the lads check on the Met again. If you're wise, you'll order some takeaway as well for the trip on."

At the end of the wharf Crofton veered off toward the customs shed, and Black followed the others to a solid-looking building that might once have been a country inn. Now it contained a wireless room and operations office on the upper floor and a pub and tearoom below. According to Podborsky, the engineer, this was the very place where Irish coffee had been reasonably sure the concept of adulterating coffee with whiskey, Scotch or Irish, was probably as old as the existence of either beverage.

The crew ordered their breakfasts from Mrs. Walsh herself, then thumped up the stairs to the Met Room. The pub owner led Black to a small table by the fire and took his breakfast order as well as an order for half a dozen takeaway sandwiches for later. Black took off his flying jacket, unzipped the coverall beneath it and sat back in his chair, pondering what he'd read of the file Liddell had given him, all neatly typed on flimsy onionskin paper by the pipe-smoking spy himself.

The official report on the assassination of the tsar and his family, and the commonly accepted myth, had been written in 1924 by one Nicholas Sokolov, a White investigator who published a book in Paris, where he was then living, called *Judicial Enquiry into the Assassination of the Russian Imperial Family*. The fact that the man was utterly anti-Bolshevik left his objectivity somewhat in question, but he did seem to have marshaled all the salient facts together in a single volume.

According to Sokolov, late on the night of July 17, 1918, Yakov Yurovsky, leader of the executioners, entered the Ipatiev House in Yekaterinburg and awakened the tsar and his family, explaining that due to civil unrest in the town they were to be taken to a safer part of the house. At the same time they were to be photographed as proof that they were still alive and in good health. The family took some forty minutes to clothe themselves, and then they went down to the lower reaches of the house. They found themselves in a small, wallpapered room, and there was no sign of a black-hooded photographer. According to Sokolov there was no cinematographer either, although for some reason the tsar and the rest of his family showed no hesitation in lining themselves in rows with the tallest at the rear, just as though they were about to be photographed or filmed. The group included Dr. Eugene Botkin, the imperial family's physician, especially important for the ailing tsarevitch, Alexei; Trupp, the tsar's personal valet; Demidova, Queen Alexandra's maid; Kharitinov, the pudgy cook; and last but not least Jemmy, a spaniel owned by Anastasia, the youngest of the tsar's daughters.

According to Sokolov, at this point the photographer was to be brought in, but instead, led by Yurovsky, a dozen assassins appeared and began to fire, some with rifles, others with an assortment of pistols, and Yurovsky himself emptying the clip of his Colt Automatic as well as his Walther, firing a total of seventeen bullets. Within seconds the entire room was completely filled with smoke, and out of the fog Yurovsky and his men could hear the moans and groans of dying men and women.

Approaching the dying family of the tsar, Yurovsky immediately realized why so few of the shots had been fatal: the brassieres and girdles of all the women had been stuffed with jewelry, and any shots to the body had either been slowed or ricocheted. Reloading both of his weapons, Yurovsky went from one to the other, putting a bullet into their brains while his men stabbed the writhing bodies on the floor with the bayonets of their rifles. It was all over within a few minutes. Yurovsky then had the corpses loaded into a waiting truck, which then disappeared.

From that point, the rumors began to grow. There were several versions purporting to show evidence that King George had tried to make a last-minute rescue attempt, knowing the lives of his "dear" cousins were truly in danger. There were an equal number of rumors that George conspired with another cousin, the kaiser, to have the tsar and his family killed so that England and Prussia could jointly rule Russia and mount a war against the Bolsheviks and anyone else who got in their way. There was even one extraordinary rumor about an American army officer named Fox who managed to spirit the entire family away before a single shot had been fired. In the end, of course, there was no evidence to substantiate any of it. Some said that George V had stalled in his decision to allow his cousin to spend a life in exile in England, waiting until it was too late to save them. Clearly Robert Bruce Lockhart, now a high-ranking official in the Foreign Office, had been in Russia at the time and was known to have traveled to Yekaterinburg on more than one occasion, supposedly to meet with the British consul there, a man named Thomas Preston. No doubt this is where the rumors had begun.

Any information regarding the cinematographer alluded to by Wells's mistress, the mysterious Countess Budberg, was thin on the water. Levitsky existed, that was well enough documented; he had been the cinematographer for a number of films made both prior to and during the war.

A thin skein of circumstantial evidence connected Levitsky and a man named Alexander Beloborodov. In 1918, the latter was head of the Yekaterinburg Soviet and also close friends with both Lenin and Trotsky. Both Lenin and Trotsky had grandiose plans to have a show trial for the tsar, but a series of telegrams from Beloborodov to Lenin suggested that in the event that there was any chance of the tsar being captured by the Germans or the Whites, he was to be shot and proof made available. In lieu of the tsar's head in a jar of alcohol, what could be better than a film of the event?

Liddell had dug as deeply as he dared into both the Public Records Office and the early SIS files from the end of the previous war and had discovered that when the "real" revolution came, Beloborodov was slated to back Trotsky, not Lenin, and it stood to reason that Levitsky was an ally of Trotsky's as well. There were several reasons to assume this. The first was the fact that the film was never delivered to Lenin as ordered. Second, it transpired that several years later, in 1924, Beloborodov helped Trotsky escape from Stalin's clutches. The only evidence that the film really existed was a passing reference to it made by Diego Rivera, the Mexican painter, less than a year before Trotsky was assassinated. According to Rivera, the film had been used by Trotsky as a form of blackmail against Stalin and was well hidden at Trotsky's villa in the Coyoacán district of Mexico City. According to Rivera and also to his wife, Frida Kahlo, purportedly Trotsky's lover for a brief time, the conversation took place between Rivera and one of Trotsky's most trusted bodyguards, the American Joseph Hansen.

Flipping through the last of the documents as they approached Foynes, Black had spotted what he thought might be the true motive for all this interest in dead kings and assassinated tsars. Both in England and America, Nicholas II had left huge amounts of money and stocks on deposit, money that would lie unclaimed in lieu of incontrovertible evidence that there was no one left alive to claim it, to wit, a reel of film showing the imperial family being gunned down like so many desperadoes in *Riders of the Purple Sage*.

The amounts were staggering—more than a hundred million pounds in Barings Bank in London alone, and ten times that in the Morgan Guaranty Trust and various other banks in America. According to Liddell's estimation, the only possible heir to any of the money other than a direct descendant of the tsar was the patriarch of the Russian Orthodox Church, of which Nicholas II had been the putative head—something like saying that the

Archbishop of Canterbury could dip into the C of E till whenever the spirit moved him.

The truth was, with proof like Levitsky's film, the money would be forfeit to the government of whatever country had it on deposit; in the case of England, a country desperately in need of money to fund a war that could easily go on for years. In America, a secret cache of money could be used to help their allies in a thousand different ways. One man's famine was another's feast.

Black took a last bite of sausage and pushed a rather suspect-looking slice of white pudding aside with his fork. He wiped his mouth with the linen napkin he'd been provided with, then lit a Silk Cut and sat back in his chair.

"It's the money," he said quietly to himself. "They're trying to get the money."

"Oh, no, sir," said Mrs. Walsh, the pub keeper, suddenly appearing at his table. She had a paper bag in one hand and a metal thermos jug in the other. "That's all been taken care of." She put the bag on the table and the thermos beside it. "Now there's your sandwiches, and a t'ermos of good hot coffee to be getting along with. Just leave the empty jug in the airboat and the boys will bring it to me on the way back."

She stood back and smiled as though she'd personally witnessed the miracle of the wine and fishes. Black thanked her and managed to slip a pound note under his plate after she was gone. He picked up the bag and the thermos, bought a packet of Kenilworths on his way out of the pub and headed back down to the wharf.

Chief of NKVD operations in the United States, Vassili Zarubin, also known as Vassili Zubilin and sometimes called Squirrel Cheeks by some of his comrades, although not to his face, sat in the passenger seat of the dark green Chevrolet Coupe. Pavlich Kalugin, his driver and adjutant, was careful to always keep several cars between them and the brown army vehicle up ahead. They had been following it ever since their quarry arrived at Washington National Airport earlier in the day.

"So far we have visited Arlington National Cemetery, the Lincoln Memorial, the Tidal Basin, the Washington

Monument, the Library of Congress and Griffith Stadium for three innings of a Yankees versus Senators game in which Mr. DiMaggio hit a home run. Commander Fleming ate two hot dogs while the woman with him ate only one. We have also been to the roof of the Washington Hotel for drinks and the commander was overheard on the telephone making a reservation at Harvey's for dinner. At no time have they gone anywhere near the Apex Building or the old school at Twenty-third and E."

Zarubin leaned forward, pushed in the cigarette lighter on the dashboard and took a crumpled package of Spuds out of his suit jacket pocket. The lighter popped out and he lit one of the menthol cigarettes, then leaned back against the seat, his eyes dully watching for the brown car a few dozen yards ahead. "Do you think, Comrade Kalugin, that our friend Commander Fleming knows that he is being followed?"

"It is possible," said the heavyset driver.

"I think we should let the commander and his new friend have a romantic dinner alone," said Zarubin. "Contact Stowaway as soon as we get back to the embassy. I want to arrange an immediate meeting. Sometime tomorrow afternoon if possible. The usual place and alternates. Perhaps he can throw some light onto the subject of the lady's identity."

"Yes, sir." Kalugin nodded. He turned down a side street and headed north. Within a few seconds the brown car was lost from view.

Chapter 4

Commander Ian Fleming, RNVR and personal assistant to Admiral Sir Charles Godfrey of British Naval Intelligence, was sitting at a small table in the Willard Hotel's opulent Round Robin Bar drinking mint juleps with Jane Todd when Morris Black appeared at the door and looked around. His eyes lit up when he saw Fleming, and a smile twitched across his face briefly. He threaded his way between the tables in the room and crossed over to where Fleming was sitting.

"Fleming! I didn't expect to see you here!" He shook the younger man's hand and then glanced briefly at Jane.

"Morris. This is Jane Todd. Jane, Detective Inspector Morris Black, once of Scotland Yard and now involved in more secret occupations."

Jane smiled up at Black. "Sit down. Have a mint julep. You're in the Old South now."

"I'll sit, but I won't have a mint julep if you don't mind. Someone once made me one and I'm afraid it made me rather sick." He sat down at the table between Jane and Fleming.

"I really do insist, old man." Fleming lifted up a finger and twirled it in the bartender's direction. "I mean, after all, this is the place where the mint julep was invented."

"Odd you should say that." Black smiled. "I just stopped at a place where they insisted Irish coffee was invented." Black's drink arrived a few moments later. He pushed aside the jungle of mint leaves standing in the middle of the glass and used the straw to suck up a minuscule amount of the drink.

"Well?" asked Fleming.

"Not bad," said Black. He took another, longer sip. "I shall become a drunkard by the time this trip is over. Whiskey-laced coffee across the Atlantic, some filthy brew they gave me in Newfoundland called Screech—and well named too—now this."

"Maker's Mark bourbon, mint, sugar and branch water, according to my friend Arnold over there." Fleming waved at the bartender and the bartender waved back.

"Let's get down to business. Ian here tells me I'm going to be a spy." Jane gave Black a long, calculating look. "And by the way, Detective Inspector, Ian's told me a great deal about you. I'm impressed."

"Ian is a great creator of fictions, Miss Todd. I'm afraid he might have misled you." Although he hoped not. Against his better judgment, he found her quite attractive.

"I don't think so," said Jane.

Black took a long sip of his drink, patted his pocket and brought out the crumpled remains of his pack of cigarettes. "Anyone mind?"

Fleming brought out a flat tin of handmade Morlands, Jane took out her Camels, and Fleming plucked the little box of matches from the porcelain holder in the middle of the table and lit everyone's cigarettes.

"Three out of four doctors recommend Camels," said Jane.

"I beg your pardon?" said Black.

Jane waved away the cloud of smoke in front of her face. "Forget it." She shook her head, realizing that Black didn't get the joke. "Maybe we should just get down to whatever it is we're supposed to get down to." She glanced at Fleming and then at Black. "I don't even know who's running this show."

"I suppose for the time being I am." Fleming tapped his ash over the edge of the ashtray with a neat flick of his wrist. "Right at the moment I'm acting as liaison between British Security Co-ordination and the American Co-ordinator of Information Office. BSC and COI."

"All I was told was that Donovan and this Bill Stephenson guy who's in charge of BSC in New York are worried about commies under their respective beds and somehow I'm supposed to find them, I guess along with you two."

"Just Detective Inspector Black. The two of you will be doing the winkling out from under the beds, and it's only a matter of one commie and one bed really."

"There's more to it than that, Ian, and you know it."

"Do tell," said Jane. She saw Black toss a dark little look of inquiry at Fleming, and the naval commander nodded back. She was beginning to realize that there was more than one level to the game she'd been asked to play, and some of the players knew more than others.

"Am I allowed to bring my toys into the sandbox or is it just you boys?" she asked, making no attempt to mask her irritation.

Black turned to her. "I'm not entirely sure I understand your reference, but in my brief experience with the subject I would say that women make much better spies than men." Black paused and took a deep drag of his Kenilworth, swooshing the smoke out through the nostrils of his long thin nose. He was older and not as good-looking as her onetime friend and colleague Thomas Barry, but she could feel a dark, almost angry passion under the soft English accent and the proper manners.

"Do you see much of Thomas Barry, Detective Inspector? He mentioned you once or twice."

Black's expression was hard. "He resigned from the Yard just after the war broke out. Joined one of the Military Intelligence groups. He went on an assignment into France and never came back. Presumably he's dead." Black noticed the tears forming in the corners of the pretty woman's eyes. "I'm sorry if I was a little blunt, but I'm afraid you get used to it after a while, losing friends. Did you know him well?"

"Not as well as I should have," Jane answered quietly. She cleared her throat and stubbed her cigarette out. "You said there was more to all of this than just sweeping the odd commie out with the dust bunnies."

"Donovan told you what you needed to hear at the

time," said Fleming. "Taking it all in at once can be a little much," the naval spy said patronizingly.

"Try me."

"I've been authorized to tell you this," Fleming said. "There apparently is a reel of film in existence which shows the assassination of the entire Romanov family. Right down to Princess Anastasia's cocker spaniel being bludgeoned to death with the butt of a Mosin-Nagant rifle."

"That was more than twenty years ago." Jane shrugged. "Water under the bridge. What's the problem?"

"The problem is, the film has been lost, and now recently recovered by an NKVD agent working either in COI or BSC. The release of the film to the general public could be disastrous."

"Why?" Jane asked. "Everybody knows Lenin or Stalin or one of those types had the tsar killed. It's not like it's fresh egg on their face or anything." She shrugged again. "Except for that loony who keeps on saying she's one of the princesses and managed to escape."

"Anna Anderson," supplied Fleming.

"That's the one. No Fabergé eggs for her, I guess."

"That's exactly the point," said Black. "There are branches of the Romanov family everywhere. I think one of them owns a restaurant in your Los Angeles."

"Romanoff's." Jane nodded. "Two f's, no v. Ugliest wallpaper in the world, orange, green and yellow. Best place to get a shot of Bogart in L.A."

"Fascinating," said Fleming.

"Cary Grant and Darryl Zanuck are Mike Romanoff's partners, and Mike himself eats with his two bulldogs, Socrates and Confucius." Jane batted her eyelashes and took a sip of her drink. "Am I a girl spy now?"

"I was trying to make a point," said Black.

Jane sighed. "Well, I wish to hell you'd get around to it, Detective."

"Money," said Black flatly. "No matter what Stephenson or Donovan has to say about it, I guarantee you the whole thing revolves around money."

"Slowly," said Jane. "The julep has clouded my brain a little."

Black sighed. "I spent three boring hours on the aircraft I came over on reading an enormous file on everything you could ever possibly want to know about the Romanovs. It actually put me to sleep. I would agree that by this point no one really cares very much about who killed them or why. Even the king's oversight in not seeing to it that they were saved is, as you say, water under the bridge. In a word, the subject of their deaths is moot except for one small item."

"Go on."

"There's no actual proof. The fact that there is no proof has given rise to dozens of claims on the Romanov fortune, including two dozen supposed heirs who claim that the tiara of the Grand Duchess Vladimir, which was 'rescued' from St. Petersburg in 1919 and is now owned by the Dowager Queen Mary, the present king's mother, was in fact stolen and belongs to one of twenty-four people who say it actually belongs to them.

"This Anna Anderson creature seems to know a great deal about the tsar's fortune, but that might easily have something to do with a possible intimate liaison she had with Lord Peter Bark, who before he became a trustee of the Bank of England was Nicholas the Second's last finance minister and in charge of all the tsar's personal bank accounts, the gold reserves in the Narodny State Bank, and not one but a total of eleven so-called secret funds. From what I can tell, the tsar had accounts in Barings Bank, Coutts Bank, which is the bank the royal family uses, the Bank of England itself, the Bank of France, the Anglo-Austrian Bank, the Bank of New York, the National Bank of San Francisco, the Morgan Trust . . . the list goes on and on."

"What's the total?" asked Jane.

Black lifted his shoulders. "Impossible to assess. Three or four hundred million pounds all told. Perhaps a great deal more."

Jane turned to Fleming. "What's the pound worth these days?"

"About four dollars."

"Christ on a crutch! That's a billion and a half dollars."

"More," said Black. "A lot of it was in gold and gold certificates. The price of precious metals has gone up considerably since 1918."

"And no one with proof to claim it."

"The real key is, the claims might be factual, or at least that's the banks' stance. Ergo, until a claim is proven beyond a doubt the money and the gold and the jewels and the stocks and bonds and everything else stay right where they are."

"My God, now I see." Jane lit another Camel. "The film is proof that all the claims are false. No one survived. All the claimants are bogus."

"Exactly, at which point the deposits, here, in England, and everywhere else you'd like to look, are forfeit to the governments of the countries where the money is deposited."

Fleming lit one of his Morlands. "England has been liquidating its assets and selling off its gold for the better part of three years now. We're almost bankrupt. Even if America comes into the war, we'll be hideously debt-ridden until the end of this century and perhaps beyond. A billion dollars or so would go a long way toward relieving some of the strain."

"Find the film, save the world," Jane said. "I'm game. What's the first step?"

"School," Fleming answered. "For both of you. Tomorrow will be your first day."

In 1906 a Mr. Frank O. Lowden of Illinois was elected to Congress. His wife was the daughter of George M. Pullman, the inventor of the Pullman sleeping car. Needless to say, Mrs. Lowden had an almost bottomless well of money to draw on and for some reason assumed that she and her husband would be staying in Washington forever.

They purchased an empty lot at 1125 Sixteenth Street, and Mrs. Frank O. Lowden proceeded to order up a gigantic eighteenth-century-style Italian-French monstrosity of cupid and swag, richly encrusted with gilt accents, marble staircases and mahogany paneling on the walls.

Sadly, within two years "poor health" forced Lowden

out of Congress—poor health being the pseudonym of a young congressional page named Kevin Starr with whom Congressman Lowden had a brief dalliance up in the congressional attic. Thus the mansion on Sixteenth Street between L and M was put up for sale and the Lowdens moved back to Illinois. Lowden seemed to recover quickly from his poor health, becoming governor of the state for a number of years as well as running an unsuccessful campaign for president. Mrs. Lowden seemed very much interested in coming back to Washington in any capacity, including as first lady.

In 1913, the tsar Nicholas II purchased the pseudo-Italianate conglomeration of towers and turrets for use as an embassy but never had time to implement his plan. The newly created Soviet Union took over the building in 1917, shortly before the tsar and his family were assassinated, but since the United States refused to recognize the USSR, the building languished, empty except for a single caretaker until 1933. When the Soviets decided to move in, they wanted the entire interior redone in a hard-edged Stalinist version of art deco, but they couldn't find an architect willing to do it. In the end they gave in and used the embassy as it was.

Vassili Zarubin, who secretly enjoyed the irony of the building's utterly bourgeois aspect and decadent history, sat in a straight-backed wooden office chair on the southwest corner of the roof of the embassy, his powerful and expensive British "Heath" Binoculars raised to his eyes. If the Sheraton Hotel on K Street had been located only a few yards farther to the west rather than locating its parking lot there, Zarubin's surveillance would have been ruined, but as it was the NKVD *Rezident* had a clear view all the way to the seven-and-a-half-story roof of the triangular Apex Building at Pennsylvania Avenue and Sixth Street, some ten blocks to the south and east.

Zarubin's signaling system was as simple and basic as he could make it. An empty package of Lucky Strike cigarettes left underneath the mailbox at the single Constitution Avenue entrance to the building would tell Stowaway that a meeting was required immediately.

In turn, as soon as he could manage it, Stowaway,

supposedly an avid gardener, would climb to the above-the-attic roof of the building and place a pot of red geraniums at one of the three corners of the roof. Each position represented one of their meeting places. To add to the number of possible rendezvous, sometimes a second pot of geraniums would be added to one or more of the corners. In this case Zarubin spotted two pots of geraniums on the southwest corner of the building. Stowaway had chosen the Pierce Mill site in Rock Creek Park. The time for their meetings was always the same: four in the afternoon.

Riding the elevator down from his fifth-floor office in the Apex Building, Maurice Halperin pushed his bifocals up onto his nose and lifted his wrist, reading the time off the Tiffany-Longines wristwatch his father had given him when he received his Ph.D. and became Dr. Maurice Halperin, professor of Latin American Studies at the University of Oklahoma. It was three thirty, plenty of time to get to his meeting.

Maurice Halperin had been a member of the Communist Party of the United States of America—CPUSA—since the early twenties, and long before gaining his doctorate he was well known for his support of extreme left political causes, although on direct orders from his CPUSA superiors he never publicly admitted to being a member of the party.

A year before, with Communism coming under close scrutiny after the Nazi-Soviet Non-Aggression Pact, Halperin's embracing of the left led to his removal from the university faculty. Halperin loudly and falsely denied his membership in the party at the time of the investigation into his affairs, but the Oklahoma legislature was adamant and insisted that he be fired.

The university president, however, believed that Halperin wasn't a party member and arranged a fully paid year's sabbatical and a job with the newly formed Coordinator of Information in Washington. Donovan immediately made Halperin head of the Latin American Division of its Research and Analysis section. Three days after being hired by Donovan, Halperin was met in Washington by a man named Bruce Minton, one of the editors of the intellectual journal *New Masses* in *New York*. Through Minton, Halperin was covertly introduced to Zarubin, known to him only as Maxim, and was given the code name Stowaway, which both men thought suited Halperin and his position well.

The elevator reached the basement, and Halperin stepped out into the gloomy underground garage. As a division head, he had a choice parking spot close to the elevator, and a few moments later he was driving his six-year-old Chevy Master DeLuxe up the ramp to the Seventh Street exit.

He drove quickly but carefully, piloting the dark green two-door north and turning left onto K Street just below Mt. Vernon Square. From there he followed K Street all the way across the city to the ravine at Rock Creek, taking the newly built cloverleaf down to the Rock Creek and Potomac Parkway and heading north. He veered to the right, skirting the National Zoological Park, and eventually reached Beach Drive, following its snaking path along the tree-lined creek to Pierce Mill.

Only a few years ago the mill and its outbuildings had been rat-infested ruins, but a WPA project soon changed that, and with its overshot wheel and millrace back in operating order it was now a small tourist attraction for families looking for a cool picnic spot.

It was a pretty place, the mill set on the banks of the burbling creek in a small meadow, surrounded by mostly undisturbed woodland where dogwoods flowered in the spring and wildflowers bloomed in abundance through three seasons. Secluded footpaths wound through the forested areas and around the picnic sites with their fireplaces and rustic outdoor furniture. It was a perfect place for children to play while their parents relaxed, and it was just as perfect for spies.

Maurice Halperin followed his chosen footpath to the bench at the foot of a narrow, lonely ravine, a huge boulder looming over the pathway. The trees on either side of the ravine blocked the meeting place from view, and because it was almost always in deep shade the bench was rarely occupied. Maxim was already waiting for him, legs crossed, reading the latest copy of *Life* magazine, the cover of which depicted a woman with the unlikely name of Eros Volusia, a Brazilian dancer, leaning on a Romanesque column, dressed in a costume that appeared to be made entirely of beads. Had Maxim been carrying the previous week's edition of the magazine; Halperin would have kept on walking, knowing that danger was present or that one or the other of them had been followed to the bench.

Halperin sat down on the bench, reached into his jacket and took out a package of Old Golds. He turned slightly toward Maxim and shook a cigarette halfway out of the package. "May I offer you one?"

Ignoring the agreed-upon sign/countersign protocol, Zarubin flipped the magazine closed and stared at the voluptuous woman on the cover. "Do you really think she was born with the name Eros Volusia?"

"That's not the countersign," said Halperin, irritated.

"I'm not quite sure why we really need all of this cloak-and-dagger stuff."

"It's established procedure."

"And Iron Feliks, the man who invented it, is long dead. Comrade Beria has taken his place and cares for nothing except results."

"Still . . ."

"You put a great swot of geraniums on top of the building you work in and I understood what it meant. Don't be silly. I know who you are and you know who I am."

"All right."

"Fleming picked up a woman at the airport yesterday. A man arrived today. Presumably some of Mr. Donovan's new recruits."

"I wouldn't presume quite so much," Halperin answered. "The woman is a onetime press photographer named Jane Todd. She just arrived from New York after attending her sister's funeral."

"Why is Donovan interested in her?"

"It would appear that she comes with some experience. I'm not sure of what sort."

"Find out, please." Zarubin bent his head, took a last puff of his cigarette, then dropped it on the ground.

"I'll do what I can," Halperin said bitterly. "I'm not promising anything."

"What about the man?"

"A different sort of fish altogether."

"In what way?"

"Until a few days ago he was working in one of the Strategic Operations Executive training schools in England. Before that, he was involved in some very hush-hush operation involving MI5. That's where he knows Fleming from."

"What's his name?"

"Black. Morris Black."

"You seem to know quite a bit about them."

"I've been assigned to them. It would appear that they will be traveling south after they complete their training at the Farm."

"Where in the south?"

"Mexico."

"Specifically?"

"Mexico City."

"Any idea why?"

"I've been asked to prepare a brief for them on the Trotsky assassination. Both attempts."

The two men wearing casual shirts and pants stood a hundred yards away on the far side of the ravine, almost completely hidden by trees and underbrush. Both men were focused completely on the two men sitting at the bench under the looming boulder. One of the men was using a Bolex H-16 16mm movie camera with its three-lens turret set on the 50mm close-up size, while his companion had an expensive pair of Zeiss binoculars up to his eyes, a mechanical pencil in his other hand and a stenographer's notepad in his hand.

"What are they talking about?" asked the man with the camera.

"The two new people, the Brit and the woman. I can't tell the details, but we can pick it up later when we see the film. Something about Mexico and Trotsky."

"When they're done, you take the camera to the lab and get the reel processed. I'll follow Halperin and see where he goes. The boss is going to want to know about this PDQ."

"Gotcha."

The man continued to film and the other man continued to take down Maxim and Stowaway's lip-read conversation in shorthand. Ten minutes later, the meeting was over.

After their meeting at the Willard, Fleming had delivered Jane Todd and Morris Black to an elegant town house on the Thirty-third Street end of Dent Place, a one-block-long and clearly very exclusive address. The house had three floors plus a full basement that included a breakfast room, kitchen, and laundry. A dining room at the rear of the first floor overlooked a small back garden with a high brick wall surrounding it. The furniture and appointments were bland, neither masculine nor feminine, and the walls were painted a neutral eggshell white.

"If a house could be a hotel room this would be it," said Jane. She'd found the refrigerator in the basement and the pantry fully stocked, so she'd brewed them a pot of coffee, which they were now enjoying in the dining room. A single magnolia tree stood at the rear of the little patch of soil, its white blossoms lying around its base like a slowly yellowing shroud.

"Fleming mentioned that it was Donovan's place when he worked with the Department of Justice here some years ago," said Black. "He'd donated it to the cause. Visiting potentates such as ourselves."

"I don't feel much like a potentate," Jane grumbled. "For some reason I feel as though I've been handed a bill of goods."

"Bill of goods?"

"Lie. Bull puckie."

"Bull puckie?"

"Crap, shit, old man." She laughed, shaking her head. "Am I going to have to teach you how to speak American on top of everything else?"

Black smiled back. Jane was surprised at how nice it made him look, not to mention ten years younger.

"Perhaps I should be teaching you the King's English instead," said the detective. He turned the smile up a few degrees. "After all, we did invent the language."

"Yeah, but we won the Revolution in 1776."

"We tend to leave that out of our history texts," said Black. "At most it's referred to as a small colonial aberration."

Jane stared at her companion thoughtfully. "Do you really believe all of this stuff we've been handed?" Jane asked after a moment. She lit a cigarette and Black immediately followed suit.

"The bill of goods, you mean?"

"Yes."

"No. Not entirely," Black said, the smile slowly fading. "It's all too carefully put together, even Fleming being here. It's like a set piece for our benefit."

"You mean Fleming being your friend and all?"

"He helped me through a bad time—let's just leave it at that."

"Can I ask you a personal question?"

"Certainly not," Black answered, but the smile was back again.

"What exactly were you doing before you came over here?"

"Not to go into too much detail, but basically I was teaching soldiers how to react to interrogation by the Gestapo."

"Using your experience as a detective for Scotland Yard, right?" She shook her head.

He smiled. "Using my experience as a right bastard is more like it."

"And I was taking kiss-and-tell shots and occasionally shooting pictures of nitwit movie stars, usually the ones on the way up or on the way down."

"So why were we drafted into service for Mr. Donovan and Mr. Stephenson, is that what you mean?"

"Exactly."

"I have been wondering something of that sort myself," said Black.

"No offense, but we really are being a pair of yutzes— idiots—about all of this. I helped bring down an assassin a couple of years ago and that makes me a spy?"

"And I was a copper who found the wrong body at the wrong time, nothing more than that really."

"And now here we are in Bill Donovan's town house in Georgetown. I mean, when you get right down to it, what do they need us for? Us in particular?"

Black sat back in his chair, slowly smoking his cigarette and occasionally taking a sip from his coffee cup. He was staring up at some blank point in the ceiling, and Jane knew he had, for all intents and purposes, left the room. She let her eyes move over him like a photographer, picking up details. His clothes didn't quite fit him; his collars were a little frayed and loose around his neck and the suit was too roomy in the shoulders, while his white shirt belled out too much. The button cuffs on the shirt were as frayed as the collar, but she could tell that the shirt itself was an expensive one and the pen in his pocket was recognizably a Montblanc Meisterstuck. The watch he wore on his right wrist was a solid gold Rolex Oyster Perpetual. Scotland Yard copper or not, there was money somewhere in the detective's background.

He was wearing only one ring: a simple gold wedding band on the third finger of his right, not his left, hand. Didn't that mean he'd been married but was now a widower? His face looked a little drawn, but there were none of those chicken wattles hanging down and the faint lines around the corners of his eyes just made him look a little sad, not old. His hair was thinning up into a widow's peak, but it was still dark and well cared for. The only real flaw she could find was a faint nicotine stain between the index and second fingers of his left hand, below the knuckle.

"Well?" said Black, his voice bland. "What do you see?"

Jane flushed slightly at being caught out in her inspection. She cleared her throat and lit another Camel. She took a couple of puffs, organizing her thoughts. "Okay," she said finally. "You're in your early forties. You have very blue eyes, which is a little odd since I'll bet you're a Jew."

"What makes you think I'm a Jew?"

"Your name is Morris. Nobody except a Jew is named Morris, believe me. It's like there are no Jews named Christopher."

Black smiled. "Go on."

"You come from a wealthy family. You're recently a widower, but you still take care of yourself, which makes me think there's a bit of vanity going on, but not enough for you to buy your own clothes. Your wife did all your shopping for you, didn't she?"

"Yes." There was a faint hint of nostalgia in his answer, and Jane was almost sorry she'd said anything. "Anything else?"

"You're left-handed and you're not queer."

"How can you tell that?"

"You wear your Rolex on your right wrist. Only left-handed people do that, and you smoke with your left hand, holding the butt below the knuckle like a guy does, not above the knuckle like a pansy or a girl." She held up her own hand to show the position of her cigarette high above the knuckle. "How'd I do?"

"Extremely well. Bang on, as a matter of fact. Maybe you really are the sort of person to be in this business. You seem to have the properly suspicious turn of mind."

"Photographers are like detectives, I guess. They see a lot." She grinned at him. "You do me now."

"My age, maybe a little younger, not married but you like men. You were born in New York, but you've spent most of your time recently either in Florida or California. I'd be willing to bet California. You're a real blonde, not one out of a bottle, and you came from an extremely poor background, not a wealthy one. You're also extremely observant, as you just proved, and you can't sew worth a damn. How did I do?"

"How'd you know about California?"

"You told me."

"No, I didn't."

Black closed his eyes and concentrated. " 'I was taking kiss-and-tell shots and occasionally shooting pictures of nitwit movie stars, usually the ones on the way up or on the way down.' You've got a tan, but since there aren't too many nitwit movie stars in Florida, I bet on California."

"The blonde bit? There's usually only one way to prove it and we're not that close."

"The hairs on your arms are blond."

"That could be the tan."

"And so are those little soft hairs right at the nape of your neck." The detective reached out, his long fingers gently touching her.

She shivered slightly. This wasn't going the way she'd expected.

"You tried to fix the hem on your skirt. The thread is the right color, but the stitches are a little too far apart to be professional and the fabric is puckering a little."

"You're embarrassing me."

"I've got a frayed collar and cuffs and I need a haircut. No need to be embarrassed."

"Not married?"

"Intuition. You don't sound or act as though you've been domesticated. You do things your own way."

"You got that right. The poor childhood?" He was so close it was spooky.

"More intuition. You've got a tough edge to you they don't teach in expensive schools."

"You said I liked men. Maybe I'm a bull dagger." She smiled.

"She who shall remain nameless," said Black, smiling again. "I don't think so."

"But how can you tell?"

"You asked after Tom Barry. He told me about you when he got home from his time in America. He told me a great deal about you. As a matter of fact, it was difficult to shut him up."

"You cheated. You had inside information."

"That's what being a spy is all about." He laughed. "And all coppers have informers."

There was a long silence, and once again Jane found herself thinking about Thomas. Such a shy man, and there was no doubt in her mind that he and Sheila Connelly, the IRA woman, had been involved with each other, however briefly. Like a fool she'd never said anything to him about her own feelings and in the end he'd burst into that hotel room, probably saving her life, but also catching her virtually in flagrante delicto in an assassin's bed. Any possibility of romance between them vanished in that single instant, lost in a hail of bullets, a fog of smoke, and a sea of blood. She smiled sadly, thinking of him again, wondering how different her life and his life would have been if she'd simply told him the truth. Jane stared out at the magnolia tree. It was getting dark now and long shadows were tracing across the little garden as the sun went down. A small breeze blew up and the last of the blossoms fell from the tree.

"I don't know if it's my place to say this," said Black, his voice coming out of the semidarkness of the room, "but you should know that Thomas Barry loved you very much." Black smiled. "I can see why." He looked her over with frank interest.

"I loved him too," Jane answered quietly. "I loved him and I never said a word."

Chapter 5

The two men who had been watching the meeting between Halperin and Zarubin the previous day climbed down from the rusted, rattling twelve-year-old Ford Tri-Motor, swallowing hard several times in a vain attempt to get their hearing back. The flight from Laredo had been a bumpy one, and both men, to their embarrassment, had been violently ill. Stumbling down the rickety steps to the ground, they took deep breaths of thin, foul-smelling air. A huge dome of brown air stretched out over the entire city, and everything smelled like they were standing directly in the path of a diesel exhaust pipe.

The men were dressed entirely inappropriately for the sweltering heat, but both had worn suits in an attempt to disguise the fact that they were carrying very heavy armament. The taller of the two men, his hair almost white blond and thinning, was Trevor K. Harding. He wore a .45 caliber Colt Automatic pistol in a shoulder rig. Everyone in the office said the K was for Kraut because he actually looked like everyone's idea of a Nazi. The brown suit added to the look. The shorter one, with a round red nose, was called Sneezy because he looked a little like the Disney dwarf and always seemed to have a cold. He wore a blue suit and lifts in his Florsheims; his real name was Conrad Bonafontini. He preferred a Smith & Wesson Model 10 .38, since it weighed a lot less than the Kraut's Colt Auto and fit into a snap holster he wore at the base of his spine, even though it did act as a conduit for sweat dripping down between the cheeks of his ass. What it didn't do was sag down the left side of his suit jacket.

Sneezy and the Kraut went through customs formalities, showing perfectly authentic U.S. Treasury identification and paying five dollars U.S. *mordida*, or "bite," to the customs officer so there wouldn't be any long complicated forms in Spanish to fill out to get their weapons into the country. With their business done they left the terminal, found the Hertz booth next to the parking lot and rented the best car they could find on the lot, a dusty black 1931 Dodge DG four-door sedan with rusted-out running boards and no spare tire in the fender well. They were also obliged to fill up the tank at the Hertz pump, but since payment was in pesos, the blatantly inflated charge wasn't so difficult to bear. The Kraut got in behind the wheel, and Sneezy, taking a small hand-drawn map from his suit jacket pocket, climbed in beside him.

"Where to?" said the Kraut.

Sneezy pointed to a paved road that ran roughly southwest. "We go down this Avenida Morelos and then turn left about five miles along at Avenida Coyoacán."

"That's it?"

"According to the map."

"Seems too simple."

"You've been doing this too long," said Sneezy. "Sometimes things are just what they seem."

"Nobody listens to that Freud shit anymore."

"What's Freud got to do with it?"

"Sometimes a cigar is just a cigar, you know."

"Just drive the fucking car."

The Kraut started up the engine and crashed the big floor-mounted shift lever into gear. Lurching and grinding, they drove out of the parking lot. Soon they were lost in the fog of engine exhaust and the mad rush of automobiles, fuming moto-cyclettes and thundering trucks that streamed all around them. After a dozen wrong turns, the death of a chicken on a side street that required another dose of *mordida* and instant, raging headaches caused by the high altitude and the poor air

quality, they eventually reached Avenida Coyoacán and
headed south. Ten minutes after that, drenched in sweat,
they reached the small provincial town of the same
name.

"Did you ever take Spanish in school?" asked Sneezy
as they drove through the outskirts of the little town.

"Why would I take Spanish? Useless language. Everybody speaks American anyway."

"I took a language course first year at Yale," said
Sneezy. "Thought it might be interesting."

"Was it?"

"Interesting enough," Sneezy said. "You got to learn
about root languages and how one language can 'cover'
another when the first country is invaded. Coyoacán isn't
Spanish, at least I don't think. Maybe some Aztec mixed
in or something, but the word has something to do
with coyotes."

"Who gives a shit, Conrad?" said the Kraut. "We're
here to do a job, remember? When we're done, we drive
back to the airport and we get on the first fucking plane
back to the closest place they have fans in the hotel
rooms."

The Kraut rolled the Dodge into the Plaza Hidalgo
on the eastern side of town and pulled to a stop in front
of the ornate Casa de Cortes, once Coyoacán's town
hall. The square, like everywhere else in Mexico City,
was empty. The Mexicans, it seemed, took their Sundays
seriously. Sneezy checked the hand-drawn map again.

"Now where?" asked the Kraut.

Sneezy followed a lightly penciled line on the map.
"Seven, eight blocks from here. Nineteen Viena Street.
According to the diagram, we're supposed to use the
north entrance on Churubusco Street at the corner of
Morelos."

"Just get us there," said the Kraut.

"West out of the plaza," Sneezy answered, his tone a
little clipped. "Up Avenida Mexico, then veer right
when you see a sign that says Centenario. Got that?"

"Sure."

The tall blond man followed the directions given to
him by his shorter companion, and within a few minutes
of driving along the town's cobbled streets they came

within fifty yards of the house at 19 Viena Street. "That's Morelos, running at right angles to us," offered Sneezy. The Kraut just stared at Leon Trotsky's former residence. The street itself was treed, sun dappling down through the leaves, and looked very cool and pleasant. The compound, walled on every side with roughly made concrete lookout towers at the corners, was a fortress. At the corner of Viena and Morelos they could see a sky blue door set into the heavy concrete wall and, over the wall, the roof of what was probably some sort of guardhouse.

"Surprised they got at him. Place is like a fort."

"They tried once," said Sneezy, who had read up on the subject when he heard about their assignment. "Bunch of Stalinist types dressed up as Mexican cops got into the compound and opened up with a bunch of tommy guns last year. Got everything but Trotsky and his wife."

"I thought he was killed with an ice pick." The Kraut slipped the Colt out of its shoulder holster and took a dull gunmetal Maxim silencer out of his jacket pocket. He began screwing the silencer onto the end of the automatic.

"It was an ice *ax*," corrected Sneezy. "The guy's name was Ramon Mercador, although there's some people think that's a phony. He was screwing Trotsky's secretary, got so he could come and go as he pleased. Went into Trotsky's office one day and hit him with the ax."

"They hang him, give him a ride on old Sparky? Whatever they do down here?"

"He hasn't even gone to trial yet. They've got him in the city jail downtown. Whores, food brought in, liquor."

"Lucky boy. Who's paying the tab?"

"Lot of bribes, I think. There's no Russian embassy here, but lots of Reds around."

The Kraut put the silenced automatic on the seat beside him. Sneezy took out his S&W, checked the cylinder and dropped the gun into his jacket pocket. "Okay," he said. "Time to get this done and get back home like you want."

"You really think we're going to find anything?" said the Kraut.

"Honestly? No, not a chance. This whole thing is a wild-goose chase. Bet your ass the NKVD here had a dozen guys going through the place before the body was cold. We're just dotting i's and putting in the periods."

"I don't know about that," said Sneezy. "Why would Donovan be sending them to Mexico City if that was true?"

"Same reason as us. To say that he covered all the bases."

"Well, let's just go see anyway," said Sneezy. "Turn left on Morelos and pull in just before we get to the corner. That's the entrance we're supposed to use."

"Why that one?"

"It's the only one with a guard."

"I see."

The Kraut put the car into gear again and flipped down the signal lever, even though by now he knew it didn't work. He drove slowly down the tree-lined street, looking left and right as he went. There were only a few cars parked and none of them was occupied.

"Quiet," said Sneezy.

"So am I," the Kraut answered, reaching down and patting the heavy, flat weight of the Colt. A few seconds later he spotted the red door at the end of the wall and slowed even more. He found a parking spot only a few yards from the entrance and pulled into it, cutting the engine. He and Sneezy climbed out of the old Dodge and walked to the scarred red door, their weapons hanging loosely in their hands. Sneezy kept his concentration on the street, his eyes roving ceaselessly while the Kraut kept his eyes on the red door. If there was any problem, Sneezy would provide noisy and hopefully distracting cover, allowing them to get back to the car.

They reached the red door. Sneezy stood facing the street, watching carefully. There were no pedestrians and no visible movement in any of the parked cars. The Kraut hammered on the door with his free hand and waited. A full minute passed without any sound or movement from behind the door. The Kraut banged again. This time there was a muffled voice.

"No entrada."

"Now what?" said the Kraut, turning to Sneezy. "He's got to open the door."

"Mi hermano está enfermo," Sneezy called out.

"What did you say?"

"I told him my brother was sick."

"Jesus."

It worked. They heard a key turning in a lock and the door swung open a few inches. A man in a brown policeman's uniform peered out at them. *"Qué?"*

"Hola," said Sneezy, turning away from the street, smiling pleasantly at the man. The guard was fat with large sweat patches in his armpits, pitted skin, a heavy mustache and nicotine-stained teeth. His hair was thinning and slicked back with some kind of oil.

"Hola."

"Hasta luego," Sneezy said and gave the Kraut the nod. The Kraut lifted up the big Colt, put the end of the silencer an inch away from the bridge of the man's bulbous nose and fired once. There was a sound like a wet twig snapping. The entrance wound was the size of a nickel, ringed by speckled powder burns that matched the blackheads on the nose below the little hole. The exit wound was the size of a saucer and blew the back of the man's head off, little bits of skull clattering off the wall of the guardhouse at his back, blood and tissue spraying everywhere. As the dead man began to fall, the Kraut pushed him backward so he wouldn't sag into the street. He stepped over the body and through the doorway, Sneezy hard on his heels. Sneezy closed the door, and as he did so a second guard came around the corner of the guardhouse, this one stripped down to his undershirt, a bottle of Noche Buena in one fist, the other hand lost somewhere in the crotch of his uniform trousers.

"Alvaro?"

The Kraut didn't wait for introductions. He leveled the .45 and shot the man in the chest and in the head. The guard's left eye disappeared and a blood rose spread across the undershirt. He dropped, already deadweight, his bowels and bladder discharging as he slid to the ground.

"Stinks," said the Kraut. He eased past the freshly

killed guard and went around the side of the guardhouse while Sneezy waited. The Kraut reappeared a minute later.

"Anything?" asked Sneezy.

The Kraut shook his head. "Place is a pigsty. Looks like they live there. Little stove, food, couple of beds. Few dirty comic books. Some newspapers. There's a watchtower upstairs. You get to it by using a ladder. Crude."

"How old were the newspapers?"

"Yesterday's and today's."

"Probably started their shift Friday night or Saturday morning."

"You think?"

"Good chance. They said there were only two guards for the whole place. Caretakers really. I mean, Trotsky's dead. So what's to guard?"

"Let's not plan on sticking around too long, though."

"Agreed."

The two men went down a short gravel path that intersected with a longer one that led to the villa. They spotted a second tower at the far end of the high concrete wall, but they had been told that it was vacant, having once been a garage. The garden within the walls was an overgrown waist-high jungle of plants, ferns and vines, the only landmark being the hutches for Trotsky's beloved rabbits.

The villa itself was surprisingly small with a living room–library, a kitchen, Trotsky's study and bedroom downstairs and four smaller bedrooms on the second floor. Behind the villa and almost totally hidden by it was a small building that had once been the guards' and servants' quarters, but which eventually was used by Trotsky's grandson, Seva Volkov, and the other members of his family.

Inside, it was as they had been briefed; the villa resembled almost exactly the way it had been the day Trotsky had died, right down to the blood-spattered walls and an open book on the desk in his study with a pair of glasses resting on the pages, one lens cracked, the other completely smashed. Friends and followers had suggested buying the house from the government, which had taken possession of it in lieu of payment for the extensive security precautions they had put in place during Trotsky's time there. When and if the money was ever donated, the house and grounds would be turned into a museum commemorating Trotsky's life and work. So far the idea was still in the planning stages.

They worked as quickly as they could, going through everything in every room and even sometimes prying up loose floorboards. After more than an hour, they had found nothing.

"That's it. It's not here." The Kraut was standing in the middle of the living room on the main floor, surveying the wreckage created by their search.

"We haven't checked the other building."

"He wouldn't have kept it there. It was too valuable."

"Maybe that's what he wanted everyone to think."

"Oh, for Christ's sake," said the Kraut. "You could roll that one over forever." He shook his head, then lit a cigarette. "Besides, he would have wanted to get at it quickly if he ever had to run." He shook his head again. "No. It's not here. Probably never was."

"Not according to our information," said Sneezy. "Levitsky was in Tampico when the tanker from Norway arrived. He secretly gave it to the Kahlo woman, Diego Rivera's wife, and she handed it over to Trotsky on the train from Tampico to Mexico City. Levitsky got away before we could get to him. Disappeared."

"How can they be sure?"

"In the first place the tanker—*Ruth*, I think she was called—was one of ours, and in the second place, the Norwegian cop, Jonas Lie, was on our payroll."

"Well, it's not here now." The Kraut sighed.

"Which means it was sent somewhere else."

"You're always stating the obvious." The Kraut checked his watch. "Come on, let's get out of here. Maybe we can have a beer or two before we catch the flight back home."

The man and the woman observing the Kraut and Sneezy's movements from the shadows of the second watchtower at the far end of the garden saw the two men come out of the main door of the villa, walk down the steps and then along the gravel path to the exit.

The name on the man's Canadian passport was Nicholas Fisher, while the woman, supposedly his wife, was named Maria. Their cover names were Pair and Reef and both were longtime agents from the illegal NKVD *Rezidentura* in Mexico City. Both were armed and either one of them could have easily shot and killed the two Americans, but neither made a move. A few moments later they heard the sound of an automobile engine starting and then the grinding of gears as the Kraut drove the old Dodge away from the curb.

"They weren't carrying anything," said Maria Fisher in Kiev-accented Russian. "They didn't find it."

"One of them could have had it under his jacket."

"It doesn't matter," said the woman. "The customs officers on duty have been bribed. They will search our two American friends very thoroughly. If they have it, they won't have it long."

Chapter 6

Fleming picked up Jane Todd and Morris Black at six thirty the following morning, using the same nondescript brown car, but this time driving it himself. Dropping them off the previous afternoon, he had instructed both his charges to wear whatever they had in the way of comfortable "country" clothing on the following day.

They drove out of Georgetown and headed for the Francis Scott Key Bridge, crossing into Virginia. Fleming turned the car onto the George Washington Memorial Parkway, flicking the wipers on and off to clear the windshield of the early-morning mist that lay in tatters across the landscape.

"This isn't quite how it's done normally," said the British Naval Intelligence officer. "The average candidate gets a very cloak-and-dagger introduction. He's told to arrive at the Schools and Training Headquarters at Twenty-fourth and F Streets, usually at an even more ungodly hour than this. All smoke and mirrors, of course, supposed to make them take it all very seriously. They hand over their personal effects, change into army fatigues, and then they're told to pick a fictitious name from a list they're to use for the duration. After that they're loaded into trucks and spirited away. *Nacht und Knebel,* as the Gestapo likes to call it, Night and Fog. Meant to deter the peasantry from doing anything even vaguely un-Nazi."

"Knights of ghost and shadow," Black murmured.

"Pardon?" said Jane.

"The people who think up gambits like taking your personal things and making you choose a new name for yourself. That's what I called them. Knights of ghost and shadow, because that's the sort of wretched world they live in."

"Sounds like the title of a dime novel."

"I'm a little miffed," said Fleming. "I mean, after all, I'm one of those knights you're talking about and that's my wretched world you're talking about."

Black laughed. He took out a cigarette and offered one to Jane. "They'll never give you a gong, Ian. His Majesty doesn't like men who like women, and his wife likes them even less. Not to mention the fact that deep down you think it's all a game."

Fleming lit a cigarette of his own and blew smoke at the windshield. "That's what my dear brother Peter calls it," he said, "the Great Game."

Jane used her hand to wipe condensation off the window and stared out through the streaky glass. They were well out into the country now. Rolling hills, mist-filled dells and patches of dark, brooding forest that looked like something out of the Brothers Grimm.

"Mind if I ask a boring question?" she said.

"Bore away, my dear," said Fleming.

"Where exactly are we going?"

"Place called Ravenwood Run," Fleming answered. "A grand old plantation right out of Scarlett O'Hara and Rhett Butler."

"Ravenwood Run. Another dime-novel title," said Jane.

"You keep on bursting my bubbles," said Fleming with a mock pout. "I've always thought I'd be rather good at writing dime novels myself."

They turned to the west, heading even more deeply into the Virginia countryside, occasionally going through small villages and towns, most of them still shuttered and quiet, only a few farmers up and about, driving their cows to pasture.

"Pretty," said Jane. She turned and glanced at Black. He was sitting quietly, barely moving, staring out through the windshield, obviously deep in thought. In the end it was Fleming who spoke.

"Katherine is in Switzerland."

"Really?" said Black.

"I thought you might like to know."

"I was wondering."

"Working for Big Bill, just like she was in London."

"Yes."

"Been there almost since the last time you saw her," said Fleming.

"Um," Black responded. For a brief instant Jane thought about asking who Katherine was, then decided against it. Sitting beside Black, she could see the rigid cords of his throat and a small pulsing vein at his temple. Katherine was from his past, and from the looks of it Black wasn't enjoying his little trip down memory lane.

"Married," added Fleming. It sounded as though the younger man was doing some kind of morbid duty, filling in unpleasant blanks. His hands were gripping the steering wheel tightly enough to blanch his knuckles.

"Oh."

"Career diplomat. Plodding sort. You know the type."

"Yes."

"They have a child. Boy from what I understand."

Let's pray the woman didn't call him Morris, thought Jane.

"She liked children. Always wanted to have them," said Black.

"Called him Nicholas."

"Nice name."

"I thought so too," said Fleming, and the conversation ended.

They drove on in silence for another fifteen or twenty minutes, eventually going past a small, single-runway airport and through a village called Bailey's Crossroads.

"The people in the village have been told that Ravenwood Run is actually an army rehabilitation center. That's even what the sign at the main gate says. The villagers are all convinced that the place is full of raving lunatics. All the candidates have cover stories as well, to go with their false names."

"I'm not sure I get the point," said Jane. "We don't have cover names, we don't have cover stories and we're not dressed in army fatigues like everyone else. We're going to stand out like sore thumbs."

"I think that *is* the point," Black said before Fleming could offer his own explanation. "We're supposed to stand out, aren't we, Ian? Donovan thinks one of his Communist cuckoos might be in the nest at this Tara of his in the bosky countryside."

"Something like that."

"I'd like a better explanation before we get there," said Black. "We're the ones putting our necks in the noose."

"I wouldn't go quite that far."

"I know exactly how far people like Donovan are willing to go," said Black, anger like a dark undercurrent in his voice. "We're being set up like clay pigeons. I'd like to know why."

"Me too," Jane put in. "All this stuff about nooses and clay pigeons is starting to make me a little nervous."

"Do either one of you know who Ramon Mercador is?"

"The guy who ice-picked Trotsky in Mexico City."

"It was an ice ax actually," said Black.

"Pick, ax, it killed him."

"Yes, well, at any rate," said Fleming, "in forty-eight hours you'll be in Mexico City, interrogating the man."

"Really," said Jane. "Why?"

"Because we know for a fact that Levitsky, the man who actually shot the film, managed to get the film to Trotsky when he arrived in Mexico. That was the last anyone ever saw of him."

"What does Mercador have to do with it?" asked Black.

"The assassination was botched," said Fleming. "Mercador was supposed to use the pointed end of the ax, not the blade end. Trotsky was supposed to die instantly and silently. Mercador was supposed to retrieve the key that hung around Trotsky's neck on a chain, day and night, then slip away, then hand the key over to a husband-and-wife team of NKVD agents. He never got the chance."

"What was the key for?" Jane asked.

"That's what we want you to find out from Mercador." They turned slightly and Fleming eased down on the brake, negotiating a long winding hill with thick forest on either side.

Black spoke up. "Presumably you've primed the pump?"

Fleming nodded. "A few rumors have been spread. Most of the staff will know this is just a quick course for you before you go down south. It has also been rumored that you're the best 'Gestapo interrogator' in SOE, which is most of the reason you've been brought over. The assumption is that for whatever reason you'll be able to break Mercador."

"At which point your man at the school here does a bunk and leads us to the film."

"Something like that. Trotsky had a number of bodyguards, several of them American. We have reason to believe one of them worked for the NKVD, either out of Washington or San Francisco."

"And now you think he's working here?" Jane asked. "I'm surprised he'd be able to get a security clearance."

"All he'd need would be a degree from an Ivy League university." Fleming laughed. "Big Bill sees Hitler as the main threat. He doesn't mind the odd commie academic. For the moment anyway."

"Asking for trouble," said Black. "In the end, the world is going to find out that Stalin was the master and Hitler just a student."

"Well, for now we're allies," said Fleming.

"Except for the one who has that can of film," Jane observed.

"Exactly," said Fleming. "Except for that one."

They reached the bottom of the hill and Fleming braked even harder. On the left appeared a three-plank white fence with a metal gate. Parked just inside the gate was a dark blue Mercury station wagon with varnished wooden side panels. It looked brand-new. Beyond it a long, perfectly straight paved road cut through the trees. Jane could read the large black-and-white sign on the far side of the service road:

RAVENWOOD RUN REHABILITATION CENTER
NO UNAUTHORIZED ENTRY
DO NOT PICK UP HITCHHIKERS WITHIN ONE MILE

"Now that makes sense," said Jane. "Everybody in the area knows it's a loony bin and they put up a sign telling you not to pick up hitchhikers."

"Government efficiency." Fleming grinned.

He pulled in at the gate and waited. Jane noted that the gate was bound to the fence with a large linked chain with a heavy padlock. A tall man in a tweed jacket, corduroy pants and high-topped boots stepped out of the station wagon. He was carrying an open double-barreled shotgun casually across his arm and he was wearing a flat tweed shooting cap that matched his jacket. A second man in the car watched, neither of his hands visible.

"Looks like a bloody country squire," Black commented. "Is he really supposed to fool anyone kitted out like that?"

"I doubt it," Fleming answered. "They just want to keep down the military presence. Uncle Adolf hasn't come knocking at the American door yet."

The man approached the car and Fleming rolled down his window with one hand and fumbled for his identification with the other. As the window came down, the man outside snapped the shotgun closed.

"State your business, please."

Fleming handed out his identification card. "Bringing in two new recruits."

"Why didn't they come in with the others an hour ago?" the man asked. "In the trucks."

"Special orders."

"I don't like special orders," the man said. "I don't like Limeys either." He handed back Fleming's card and peered into the car. "You two Limeys as well?" he said, speaking to Jane and Morris Black.

"Break it up, Bruno," Jane said. "It's none of your business who or what we are, so take a pill and open the gate."

The guard stared at Jane, his mouth open to say something. He backed away from the car, took a large key out of his pocket and began unchaining the gate. He looked over his shoulder and Black smiled at her.

"Well done," said Black.

"Give him a little New York. Works all the time. They don't expect it from a girl."

The gate opened and they drove through, Jane waving and smiling as she went past the man with the shotgun, who was still staring at her. They drove down the long lane for at least half a mile and then they were suddenly out of the trees and driving through open, rolling meadowland. In the distance, backed by what appeared to be an orchard and a formal garden, they saw an enormous mansion, painted pure white, the only other accent being pale gray window frames. Jeffersonian columns ran along the hundred-foot-long front porch of the great house and Jane counted seven windows on each side of the black painted double front doors. A few men in army fatigues were clipping bushes in front of the house, and off to the left, following a gravel pathway, Jane could see a dozen men running to some sort of muffled cadence. She didn't see a single woman anywhere.

"Looks like a man's game," she said.

"We give the ladies an equal chance on our side of the Atlantic," said Black. "They've run tests and were quite disturbed when they found out that women could endure pain under torture somewhat better than men could."

"The same tests discovered that they lie a lot better as well," said Fleming.

"Of course," Jane said without batting an eye. "Comes from thousands of years of telling men what they want to hear instead of the truth."

"Donovan uses a lot of woman actually," said Fleming. "Mostly at Arlington Hall."

"What's that?" asked Jane.

"Cryptography section," Fleming answered. He threw a quick glance at Black but didn't say any more. Jane didn't miss the look.

"Another secret between the two of you?" she said. "I'm starting to feel left out."

"Some things we're not allowed to talk about," said Fleming. "Not until you're cleared."

"And he is?" said Jane, nodding at Black.

"He's got a higher security clearance than I do," Fleming answered.

He pulled the car up in front of the building and pushed the gear lever into neutral. "This is where we part company for the day," he said. "You'll be met inside by the director and then taken off to your various assessment points. Sometimes you'll be together, sometimes not. I'll pick you up here at six and we'll go back to Washington. I'll take you to Naylor's for oysters as payment for being clay pigeons."

"Does the director have any idea what's going on?" Black asked.

Fleming shook his head. "None at all. All he knows is that you're Donovan's pets for the moment."

"Anything special we should be looking for?" asked Jane.

"Somebody who asks too many questions," said Fleming.

"Or none at all," put in Black.

"That too," said Fleming. "And by the way, you *do* have cover names: Morris is Jack and you're Jill."

"How imaginative." Jane pulled down the door handle and climbed out of the car. Black followed, and before Jane closed the door she peered in at Fleming.

"Two dozen oysters and a lobster," she said.

"Done." Fleming grinned. She slammed the door and he crashed the car into gear and drove off.

Jane looked up at the looming, bright white façade of the mansion. She turned to Black. "Knights of ghost and shadow, *Nacht und Knebel.* I don't know if I'm cut out for this business. I can't tell who's lying and who's telling the truth."

"Assume everyone is lying," said Black. "It simplifies matters." He took her by the arm and they went up the front steps. Black opened the right-side door and they stepped through into the front hall. It was gigantic, with a massive chandelier hanging down from the upper story and a magnificent spiral staircase winding up the curving wall on the left. The floors of the hall were black, green-flecked marble and there were several large leather armchairs scattered here and there along with several free-standing ashtrays.

A tall man with close-cropped reddish hair wearing the uniform of an army colonel was sitting in one of the chairs closest to the staircase, smoking a cigarette. He stubbed it out as Jane and Morris Black came through the door.

"Jack and Jill, I presume?"

"Come to fetch a pail of water," Jane said tartly. The colonel didn't seem to appreciate her humor and indicated his displeasure by completely ignoring both the comment and Jane herself.

"My name is Colonel Watts," said the man, staring directly at Black. "I am the director of this facility and for the rest of your time here you will be under my orders. Our job here is to discover, if you have them, any special skills, unique abilities and individual talents that we may find of use.

"You must claim to have been born in some place other than your natural birthplace, educated in institutions other than those you attended, working at an occupation other than your real profession and living in a location other than where you reside. Let me warn you at this point that various members of the staff will, from time to time, try to trap you into breaking cover by asking casual questions about yourself when you are off guard. Do not be caught."

Black smiled. If it was anything like the SOE facilities in England they would have been under surveillance from the moment they arrived. Nothing would be as it seemed and no one would be who they said they were. The chances were quite good in fact that Watts was neither a colonel nor the director of the facility; it was far more likely that he was a psychologist or psychiatrist of some kind.

Watts began speaking again, clearly by rote; this was a speech he'd given a hundred times. "Normally your stay here would be three full days, but in your case we are under acute time pressure. Therefore every hour will be taken up by mental tests, psychological tests and physical tests. To estimate your ability to observe and draw correct inferences you will be placed in a room containing twenty-six articles of clothing, personal belongings, timetables and newspaper clippings. After studying these items for four minutes you will be taken to another room and given a questionnaire about the mythical person whose effects you have just examined: age, marital status, weight, color of hair, residence, occupation, and so on."

"Kim's game," said Black, knowing the interruption would annoy Watts during his droning dissertation.

"I beg your pardon?"

"It was in a story by Rudyard Kipling. Set in India. Baden-Powell used it in his Boy Scout manual, Tenderfoot to King's Scout."

Blood flooded into Watts's face and his lips thinned out into a scowl. "This is not a story or the Boy Scouts, Mr. Black, and it is most certainly not a game."

"Who's Mr. Black?" Jane asked innocently. "I thought he was Jack and I was Jill."

"Perhaps it's one of the diabolical traps meant to make us break cover," said Black.

"The two of you don't seem to be taking this very seriously."

"Maybe you're missing the whole point," said Jane sharply. "Maybe we've been sent here to test you. Maybe we're not who you think we are at all."

"This serves no purpose whatsoever," said Watts. "I have much more important things to do than trade jibes with either one of you. Other than your mental tests you will be given two physical objectives. One is the Brook Test, in which you must find the quickest and most efficient way to cross a small stream, and the other is a construction test."

"Are you kidding?" said Jane, looking down at the skirt she was wearing. "Not in these glad rags."

Watts pointed to a door on the far side of the entrance hall. "In the dressing room you will find two sets of fatigues. Put them on. Your individual guides will meet you on the front portico in five minutes." With that Watts turned on his heel without another word and trotted up the spiral staircase.

"Prig," muttered Black, watching him go.

"I was going to be a little more vulgar than that, but it wouldn't have been ladylike."

Black made a little bow in the direction of the dressing room pointed out by Watts. "After you, madam."

Jane returned a gentle nod and went to get into her army clothes.

A few minutes later they were standing on the columned front porch, waiting for their "guides."

"Well, there goes us sticking out like sore thumbs," said Jane, plucking at the too-large coveralls that had been given to her. Beside her Black was dressed in regulation olive drab fatigues without any rank or insignia of any kind.

"Oh, yes. We'll meld right in," Black answered, looking down at himself. "A 'Limey' and a woman in WAAC coveralls." He let out a small, tired laugh. "I can feel my thumbs beginning to ache already."

Black could see a couple of young men in military uniform, right down to their British-style soup-bowl helmets, jogging toward the mansion. "I think our Indian guides are arriving, Jill, my dear. Just remember what we're here for."

"Roger wilco," said Jane. Black gave her a curious look and then their guides were upon them. The two men were young, clean shaven and blank-faced. They could have been cut from a pattern.

"Jack, sir?" said one.

"So they tell me," said Black.

"And you'll be Jill, ma'am?" said the other.

"That's me."

"We're supposed to split you up for the day."

"Not very nice," said Jane.

"Prevents collusion. Probably Colonel Watts's idea."

"Colonel Watts?" asked one of the young soldiers. "There's no Colonel Watts on staff here."

"Oh, dear," said Black. "Here we go."

Chapter 7

Sunday, November 23, 1941
Fairfax County, Virginia

They completed their battery of tests, then, as promised, Fleming picked them up in front of the mansion at six sharp and drove them back to Georgetown. Both Jane and Morris Black changed into more reasonable clothes and then Fleming drove them across town to Maine Avenue and the Washington Channel, the city's working waterfront. Naylor's Restaurant was right on the pier, close to Seventh Avenue and the Potomac River Lines sightseeing boat terminal. It wasn't the kind of place Jane would have chosen—the whole area looked run-down and smelled of fish and brackish water—but the cars parked in front of the long, low, warehouse-style building were mostly late model and expensive and the customers at the bar just inside the front door obviously weren't hicks from the sticks.

The low-ceilinged restaurant was packed, but Fleming had reserved a window table that looked out onto the channel, giving them a pleasant view of the sunset over the trees and hillocks of East Potomac Park a few hundred yards away on the opposite side of the water. Fleming flagged down a passing waiter and ordered drinks for all of them.

"Thank God that's over," said Jane, dropping down into one of the padded captain's chairs at their table. She used the flickering candle to light a cigarette and let out a long sigh. "It was like being in a mental hospital and not being able to convince people you were sane."

"My sentiments exactly," said Black. "Particularly the so-called construction problem."

"That was the one with the giant Tinkertoys?"

The construction problem consisted of being shown into a large room empty of furniture, containing a pile of wooden blocks and half blocks drilled with circular holes and a stack of long dowels sized to fit the holes. There were also two men in the room, both wearing G.I. uniforms. When asked, they referred to themselves as Buster and Kippy. Jane's experience had been unpleasant but bearable, probably because having a woman to deal with caught the two G.I. tormentors off guard. Black on the other hand had been infuriated by them.

Both men were fat, wore glasses and smelled faintly of some sort of cheap aftershave. Within ten seconds of meeting them Black was privately thinking of them as Tweedledum and Tweedledee. Tweedledum had the flat accent of a Midwesterner and Dee was definitely from New Jersey.

"So," said Dee. "Whatcha in, the Limey navy? You look like one of them curly-headed navy boys all the girls are after. Or do you like boys better?"

"I don't have curly hair," said Black, examining the pieces of wood laid out in front of him, knowing that every second he wasted talking was coming off his ten-minute total.

"You must be in some kind of service," said Dum. "You guys are at war, aren't you?"

Black had come to the conclusion that no response was the best response of all. He kept his mouth shut and started fitting pieces of his oversized puzzle together. His silence did nothing to deter his two companions.

"You look healthy enough," said Dee. "You some kind of draft dodger or something?"

Dum stared at the pile of wood and Black's efforts to put it together. "What kind of work did you do before all this? It sure as hell wasn't in the building trades."

"Bugger off," said Black, allowing himself a moment to relieve his building tension.

"Bugger. That's, like, sticking your dick up someone's ass, right? You Limeys do that a lot I hear."

"Arse," Black answered, finishing the left side of the cube and bracing it with a longer dowel across the diagonal.

"Arse."

"As in arsehole."

"Nice mouth on you, pal," said Dum. "You don't have to be insulting, you know. We're only here to help."

"You haven't done a bloody thing."

"Well I never," said Dee. "First time anyone ever complained about me not working. I think I deserve an apology. What's your name anyway, or do I just call you Limey?"

Black continued to concentrate on putting the cube together. By his estimation he'd used up nearly all of his time.

"Hey, at least tell us your name," said Dum. The man was actually pouting. Black slammed a dowel into the cube, connecting another section.

"Call me Buffalo Bill."

Dee looked surprised. "You're a Limey and you know about Buffalo Bill?"

Black didn't answer. In fact he knew a great deal about the life and times of William F. Cody, and the old American West in general. His Shepherd's Market flat had a library full of history books on the subject.

Dum made a derisive sound in the back of his throat. "Better to call you stupid, pal. You can't even put together a kid's toy."

Black snapped in the last piece of dowel. "Go fuck yourself . . . pal." Black turned on his heel and started out of the room.

Dee looked at his wristwatch. "Two minutes over. You lose."

Black slammed the door behind him as he left.

By the time Jane and Black had filled Fleming in on the rest of their day the trio had gone through three dozen bluepoints, several Chesapeake Bay crabs and a Maine lobster apiece. They all had dessert and by the time they reached coffee and cigarettes the restaurant was rapidly emptying.

"What I want to know is, was the whole operation worth it?" said Jane. "That was a one-day course in how to be Mata Hari or the Green Hornet. It's not like Morris and I are going to be parachuting into Berlin anytime soon."

"In other words," said Black, "did the clay pigeons draw any fire?"

"Well," said Fleming, "not to mix metaphors, but we seem to have flushed our pheasant."

"Do tell," said Jane.

"Anyone want to hazard a guess?" Fleming asked.

Black spoke up, tapping his cigarette into the imitation ship's wheel ashtray in the center of the table. "I'd have said one of the staff members at the so-called Gestapo interrogation."

"The Stress Interview." Fleming nodded.

"Back in England we call it the third degree, actually." He shook his head. "But it was all too melodramatic. All that foolishness with the dark room and the spotlight, for instance."

"I'm surprised one of the quizzers wasn't wearing a monocle and speaking with an accent. 'Cross your legs, uncross your legs. Smoke, do not smoke. Zis is no joke, fräulein!'"

"And then telling you that you failed the test to see what your reaction would be," said Black. "I doubt anyone ever passes, do they?"

"No," said Fleming.

"Well, all I know is no one said a word about Trotsky, Mexico or home movies." Jane shrugged.

"I think I know," Said Black finally, stubbing out his cigarette. "Jane is quite right. No one really showed more than simple curiosity about us."

"So?"

"So by process of elimination it has to be Watts," said Black. "He was the only one who really seemed to know we were coming. He was waiting for us."

"Well done!" said Fleming, clapping his hands together. "Watts it is. Both Big Bill and I have been watching him for some time. Today our suspicions were confirmed."

"How?"

"He did a bunk, didn't he?" said Jane. "Took off."

"Quite right," said Fleming. "Within five minutes after leaving you, in fact. Sadly he managed to give us the slip. We'll catch him up eventually, though, never fear."

"What's the connection?" Black asked.

"His real name is James Quentin Maddox. He was a professor of economics at Yale before he signed on with Donovan's organization. A security check was done on him, of course, but at the time there seemed to be no connection between him and CPUSA."

"The Communist Party?"

"Umm," said Fleming. "As it turns out, when we dug a little deeper recently we discovered that one of his students was a young man named Robert Sheldon Harte."

"The name rings a very faint bell," said Jane. "He was a New Yorker, right?"

"Quite right. He was also a communist. When the FBI searched his apartment in Brooklyn, they discovered a poster of Stalin on the wall."

"Not a Trotsky follower then," said Black.

"So you'd assume." Fleming nodded. "But Harte was one of Trotsky's bodyguards and sometime secretary, translating things from English to Russian for Comrade Bronstein."

Black frowned and lit another cigarette. "A traitor, or an agent provocateur?"

"Once again, that would seem to follow," said Fleming. "But according to the so-called evidence you'd think he was actually a martyr. He was unaccountably kidnapped following the first attempt on Trotsky's life and then murdered. Shot in the head, once in the face, once in the back of the head, NKVD style, then covered with quicklime and buried in the basement of a farmhouse in the countryside."

"This was the first attempt?" asked Black.

"That's right."

"Then how could he be involved in the actual assassination?" Jane asked.

"Because the body they found in the basement wasn't Harte. It was established that he was murdered five days after the first attempt, May twenty-ninth. The body was discovered by the police on June twenty-fifth, almost a month later, yet Trotsky himself made a positive identification of the remains."

"Bollocks," said Black. "Even without being covered with lime, a month after death there'd be nothing left to identify. The body would have been utterly putrefied. Believe me, I've seen enough of them over the years."

Jane made a face. "Please. I just ate." She chewed on her lip for a moment, then turned and looked out the window at the blinking lights of a trawler as it came late into port. She turned back to Black and Fleming. "I don't get it. Why would Trotsky identify the body?"

"To save face," Fleming answered. "Heaven forbid that the great Leon Trotsky, father of the Russian Revolution, could be duped by a traitor. He even went so far as to put up a plaque to the young man in his garden."

"It still doesn't make much sense."

"It does if you accept the fact that the body they found buried in the basement wasn't this Harte fellow," said Black thoughtfully.

"Explain that."

"Harte's body is replaced by some other poor blighter's. Presumably someone of about the same size and weight. Harte's simulacrum is dead, ergo the real Harte is free as a bird." Black looked across the table at Fleming. "How long was Harte employed by Trotsky?"

"Eight weeks."

"Just enough time to acquire enough intelligence within the Trotsky compound. He's whisked away, supposedly kidnapped, then killed, for no particular reason that I can see . . . unless he was alive and sent back to whoever his NKVD contacts were with his inside information."

Jane stared at Black, impressed. "You're pretty good at this, aren't you?"

"He's very good at it," said Fleming. "Which is precisely why he's been brought over here, kicking and screaming all the way." Fleming took a long draw on his cigarette and let the smoke trail out through his nostrils. "We can assume that Harte was provided with one of those passports the Bolshies picked up during the Spanish War. God knows what name he's traveling under now."

"The only problem is, you've gone and lost this Watts, or Maddox or whatever his name is, and he was probably Harte's handler. It's all supposition. There's no way to prove any of it."

Fleming glanced at his watch. "There is, as a matter of fact. Either one of you mind a quick flight to New York? United has a flight at ten. If we catch it we can be there by midnight."

"Why New York?" Jane asked.

"We're going to do a little grave digging of our own."

Chapter 8

Emil Haas drove the plain gray BMW 315 through the night fog of Berlin-im-Westen, a large, dull district of stone buildings and rooming houses on the eastern side of the city. Haas, like the car, was unprepossessing, of average height and weight, wearing a suit the same color as the car and no hat to cover his thick graying hair. His eyes were a cornflower blue that was almost feminine, his nose was small and his mouth was a little too wide for any woman to call him handsome, but overall it was an interesting face and one that most people, men and women alike, found attractive.

By day Haas knew Berlin-im-Westen was a place of strange contrasts, alternating between the shabbiness of a slum and the rough energy of commerce. Most of the buildings were ramshackle old dwellings unconvincingly converted into storefronts—pawnshops, cheap Kinos that were really no more than peep shows, secondhand dealers in clothing and resale shops of every kind.

What few people he saw—invariably men except for the obvious streetwalkers—moved with their shoulders stooped and their faces well hidden beneath their hat brims. Whatever the truth of the world was, the führer deplored all vice and all those who indulged in it. To be caught soliciting a whore, or worse, a man-whore, was dangerous these days, especially in a place like this. In the darkness, lit only by bright windows and flickering electric signs, a man would sometimes hesitate before a window, ashamed and scared. As he heard the BMW's engine he would turn and walk quickly away, like a fish frightened from a baited hook.

The shops were ostensibly those of dressmakers, hatmakers and lingerie sellers. Most of these Haas knew had special cubicles in the rear for a broad assortment of homosexual acts for a broad assortment of prices. The cubicles and their occupants were advertised in the leading newspapers of the city in ambiguous but well-known terminology.

Haas turned down an unnamed alley and parked the automobile close to a bright green door with no indication of what lay behind it except a small peephole blocked by a sliding piece of metal, also painted green. Approaching the door, Haas saw that it was much heavier than it originally looked, the metal solid and studded with rivets all around.

He knocked lightly on the door and the peephole slid back. The porter's face, joweled and angry-looking, like a bulldog, peered out. The porter, whose name Haas knew was Trost, had a huge scar running across his cheek, raised from his puckered skin like a writhing, multisegmented worm.

The peephole slammed shut, followed by the sound of several bolts being drawn back. This place, the so-called Aryan Café, was Berlin's latest attraction, the ne plus ultra in *Folter Kultur*. The door opened and the porter stepped back, allowing Haas into a long, narrow corridor leading to a broad mahogany staircase sweeping steeply upward. Between the door and the stairs was a closet-sized booth, metal like the door, with a small thick window threaded with heavy wire with a narrow slot at the bottom. Sitting in the booth was a colored man, a rare sight in Berlin these days. The arrangements had been made the day before, and the colored man, who called himself Victor Hugo, was expecting him. Haas brought a thick envelope out of the inside pocket of his suit jacket and pushed it through the slot and into Victor's large hand, where it disappeared instantly.

"Room thirty-six," said Victor in Alabama-accented German. "It's all set."

"What's her name?"

"LuLu."

"Does she know she's being paid extra?"

"Yes. And she knows what you'll say."

"Good." Haas showed a feral smile. "If everything goes well there'll be a bonus in it for you."

"That's fine." Victor nodded. "Just so long as no one knows I was involved. Worth my job, or these days maybe even more."

"Don't worry," said Haas. "I'll keep you out of it."

"I always worry. That's why I'm still alive."

Haas climbed the staircase, stepping out of the way of a clutch of richly dressed people coming down. At the top of the stairs was a gathering of more of Berlin's pleasure seekers, most of them drinking champagne, their voices pitched nervously high as though they belonged in this place but were afraid to stay too long.

From other rooms off the stairway landing came the sounds of shrill talk and shrill singing as well as cigar smoke as thick as any London fog. Without pausing Haas went through one of the rooms to the right. It was full of men in evening clothes sitting at small tables, looking for drink and women, prostitutes soliciting business, gold diggers looking for generous "squarehead" sugar daddies, vamping demoiselles looking for their own victims and here and there the crooks and rouged dandies of the Berlin underworld, the so-called Robin Hoods of the Friedrichstrasse.

From the smaller dining room Haas stepped into the Banquet Hall, its draperies a fantastic Prussian blue with paintings on the walls showing men and women and children engaged in every sordid act imaginable. There were photographs as well, mostly of women in the nude, but of children posing as well. A few people were eating from the large buffet, but most stood against the walls and turned back the paintings and the photographs on hidden hinges, revealing small peepholes where patrons of the "café" could spy upon their fellow revelers.

Haas had seen all the place had to offer on previous visits. The first room showed a strange conglomerate of beautifully dressed women in gowns and underwear and lingerie of the finest materials. The women were made up and rouged like dolls, and only careful inspection showed that this was a metamorphosis worthy of a story by Franz Kafka, perhaps even imagined by him in a place like this, for these women were not women at all. They were men, displayed through the peepholes in their freakish makeup for prospective customers.

Haas, whose own sexual proclivities ran to the mundane, wasn't offended by what he saw. Over the past decade he'd seen an entire country succumb to madness, of which this place was only a small representation, and perhaps in its own way a healthier expression than the pounding, marching feet on the treeless Unter den Linden and the screaming hordes at the rallies in Nuremberg.

The next room was for various masochistic pleasures, and the third was for those who liked to inflict the pain rather than receive it. The room, Haas knew, was set up like a monstrous hospital ward complete with nail beds, drugs, racks, whips and chains of every kind, the patients screaming as the doctors did their pain-filled work.

Stepping through a pair of long black curtains, Haas found himself in the last room on the floor, a dark chamber lit only from above, spotlighting a perfect blond Nordic couple on a bed, performing relatively tame demonstrations of sexual relations. The couple looked very young, just barely adult.

From a phonograph in the center of the floor, the disk spinning madly, came the voice of a woman, smooth and silky, her velvet tones describing what every newly wed Nazi should do on his or her wedding night as the demonstrating couple did her bidding, following her words exactly. Haas passed out into a short corridor leading to a winding set of stairs to the floor above and eased out of the way and allowed two women to pass, both dressed in silk lingerie, one of them heavily pregnant and the other a hunchback. Haas knew from the rumors he'd heard that women like these fetched the highest prices in Berlin.

Haas moved slowly up the stairs, listening. There were eight or nine rooms on the upper floor, each one numbered, each with a red light above the door to announce whether the room was occupied. Haas heard all kinds of sound and movement on the other side of the doors, but he ignored them and continued the length of the passageway to number thirty-six.

Standing outside the door, he took a standard Parabellum pistol from its dangling holster under his arm. The only difference between it and the regular army-issue weapon was that the front sight had been filed off and the end of the barrel tapped for the first inch and a half. From his other pocket Haas brought out a short 1908 Maxim silencer and twirled it onto the end of the barrel.

Haas rapped on the door. "LuLu?" He paused. "You have a telephone call."

"Tell the person she's busy." The voice that replied spoke German with a heavy Polish accent.

"I'm afraid it's very important." Haas cleared his throat. "You will be reimbursed for your time, Mein Herr."

There was a heartfelt sigh and then the squeaking of a bed. Haas heard bare feet padding across the floor and suddenly the red light went off and LuLu opened the door. She tried to edge past Haas, but with his free hand he gently pushed her back into the room. The man in the bed, a look of irritation on his face, was a Pole named Juri de Sosnowski who had been "lucky" enough to have a German mother, which allowed him to be employed at the big Maybach automobile showroom on Luetzow Platz a block or so away from Abwehr headquarters on Bendler Strasse. He also had a flat just around the corner from the five joined town houses between 72 and 76 Tirpitz Ufer, where he regularly received super-classified operations reports almost as soon as they were typed up, provided by a very willing secretary from the General Staff Office.

"This isn't right," said LuLu, pouting, an angry expression on her face. "I was to get a telephone call."

"Just what in the devil's name is going on here!" demanded the Pole. Haas could see that Sosnowski was edging over on the bed to get his hand within reach of a jacket hanging over a chair nearby. Haas took out the Parabellum and shot LuLu first, since she was closest to him and probably had a knife hidden somewhere close by. The bullet took her full in the mouth, blowing through her teeth and exiting through the top of her spine by way of the neck. She made a small squeaking noise and slipped down onto the floor. Sosnowski lunged for his jacket and Haas shot him twice, once through the chest and once through the forehead. The wall behind the bed was sprayed with blood in a huge rosette pattern that also began to broadly stain the sheet. Sosnowski slipped over the side of the bed and crumpled naked on the bare floor. Staring down at him, Haas could see the large tempting organ that had initially seduced the secretary from Tirpitz Ufer.

He listened for a few long moments as he replaced the Parabellum in its holster. There were no sounds of alarm or fear, which was reasonable enough since the automatic pistol with the silencer made a sound no louder than the muffled squeals and moans and slapping sounds that came from the rooms all around him.

Haas flipped the switch beside the door and the light outside in the hall went on. The red light would give him more than enough time to get clear. He stepped out into the hall and paused, looking in both directions as he opened the cellophane on a fresh package of Junos. He lit one, then headed back the way he'd come, eventually reaching the bottom of the stairs that led to the front door. He stopped in front of Victor's booth.

"How'd it go?" said Victor.

"Fine," said Haas, "no problems so far."

"So far."

"Not quite done," said Haas. "A few loose ends."

He took out the Parabellum again, slipped the barrel and the silencer under the slot in Victor's bulletproof glass shield and fired three times, moving the weapon slightly from side to side, stitching across the black man's chest. Two of the shots hit Victor squarely in the heart and pericardium, flooding the heart cavity with blood, and the third shot blew a ragged hole in the man's right lung.

By the time Haas had fired the second shot, the bull-dog porter at the main door was already running forward, struggling to bring out his own weapon. Haas turned slightly and began to fire at the heavyset figure running toward him, picking chest and head shots until the man dropped to the floor six feet away from him, bleeding in several different directions. Given the man's size, Haas made the prudent choice. As he passed on his way out the door he bent down and put a single shot through the back of the porter's head. When he was done, he stepped out the door, climbed back into the BMW and drove off.

He made his way past the crowds of waiting young men outside the sooty old Alexanderplatz Station and crossed the Spree at the Kaiser Wilhelm Bridge, finally reaching the Tiergarten Station and Berlinerstrasse. He turned off the main thoroughfare and its spotlit Hakkenkruze banners, turning down to the Landswehr Kanal and the narrow street that ran along it, the Tirpitz Ufer. Reaching the row of elegant five-story town houses that ran from number 72 to 76, he pulled the BMW up onto the sidewalk on the canal side of the street and switched off the engine. He took out a large, white-enameled medallion identifying his car as an official vehicle, climbed out of the BMW, then locked it. Glancing at his watch, he saw that it was after one in the morning. Almost without thinking about it, his eye was drawn up to the fifth-floor window exactly in the center of the row of buildings. The window was dimly lit and Haas could imagine the man in the room within bending over some strange document, the room lit only by his plain old gooseneck lamp.

Haas crossed the empty street and ducked under a granite portico. He nodded to the pair of police guards who stood sentry at the door, then climbed two steps and entered the Fuchsbau—the Fox's Lair, as everyone who worked in the Abwehr headquarters called it. He stopped at the guard's cubbyhole and a weary night porter took his identification and then returned it with a stamped security pass. He bypassed the elevator and instead took the large, split staircase that curved up left and right to the mezzanine. He went down the dimly lit corridor on the left, then took several narrower flights of stairs to the high-ceilinged fifth floor and the large office of Wilhelm Canaris, chief of the Abwehr.

As predicted, the broad-shouldered, short little man was seated at his desk, poring over a document within a manila file folder with a bright red tab. Haas stood in the open doorway to the large room, waiting for a command to come farther. The office was as it always was, bare except for a pair of Japanese scrolls on the wall, a long black leather couch that was more for the use of Canaris's two dachshunds, Sepell and Sabine, than it was for the admiral, and a huge map of the world pinned up behind his desk. The large desk itself was barren except for the green gooseneck lamp and a trio of solid brass seated monkeys, one covering its eyes, the next its mouth and the third its ears. See no evil, speak no evil, hear no evil. Behind the desk, on a stand and behind glass, was a model of his old light cruiser, *Dresden.*

Canaris finally slapped the file folder shut and swore under his breath. He looked up and waved Haas forward. "Come in, come in." He pointed to the single chair across from his desk. "It's all been dealt with?"

"Yes."

"Good." Canaris pushed the file into the exact center of his desk. "One less leaking pipe in this old building."

Haas nodded. "But not the last."

"I'm afraid not," said Canaris. "I often wonder if it wouldn't be smarter to simply go out on the street and yell out every secret we have. We've been virtually emasculated in Mexico and the United States, and our agents in England have always been of questionable value, perhaps even compromised." He sighed. "Ah, well, I can always trust you, though, can't I, Haas?"

"Of course, sir."

"Then let me ask you a question, old friend."

"Certainly."

"What do you know about the Romanovs?"

Chapter 9

They reached LaGuardia just after midnight and found Detective Dan Hennessy behind the wheel of an unmarked dark blue Chrysler Saratoga fitted with a set of two-way radio whip antennas fore and aft that would have identified it as a cop car to any kid or crook in New York City. Seeing Jane, Black and Fleming coming out of the terminal, he climbed out of the big car and pulled open the rear door.

"Fancy meeting you here," said Jane, smiling at her old friend.

"You got some pull, girlie," the Irish cop replied. "Commissioner Valentine says to use his personal car, and I get an exhumation order within an hour of asking for it with no notification to next of kin." He frowned. "Rattling the police commissioner's cage and stealing his car, not to mention waking up a judge in the middle of the night to sign the order. I hope you know what you're doing."

"I don't," said Jane. "But these two do." She gestured toward Black and Fleming, who introduced themselves. "Just don't call them Limeys, they don't take kindly to it."

"Then I'll just be calling them English gentlemen," Hennessy answered, putting on a thick brogue that had nothing at all to do with being born and raised in Canarsie. Fleming and Black climbed into the back of the Chrysler, and Jane got in beside Hennessy. They took

the five-year-old Grand Central Parkway south, the
three lanes on each side of the grassy boulevard empty
at this time of night.

"What about the dentist?" asked Fleming.

Hennessy threw an irritated glance up at the rearview
mirror. "Don't worry, pally, he'll be there. Our friends
at the J. Edgar Hoover Benevolent Society will have
tracked him down by now. We're a little dim, us Mick
coppers, but we get the job done."

"You're on the outs with Maureen again, aren't you?"
Jane said. "Sleeping in the coop at Centre Street."

"What makes you say that?"

"Your pissy mood, Daniel." She grinned. "With you
it's either Judys or Jameisons."

"Sometimes it's both," he grunted. He glanced into
the rearview again. "Apologies, gentlemen, but I'm not
in the best of moods as it is, and digging up moldy
corpses after midnight isn't any sane man's fancy."

"Apology accepted," said Fleming.

Black nodded as well. "Perhaps you should try Bush-
mills instead."

"Protestant sludge," Hennessy said with a grin. "No
good Catholic would touch the stuff unless he had no
other choice."

After ten minutes on the GCP, Hennessy pulled the
Saratoga around the cloverleaf and put them on the Interborough, heading west, taking them deep into the
heart of Brooklyn. They left the Interborough at Highland Boulevard, the high brick walls of the huge cemetery on their right. There were iron gates at Conway
Street, but they were firmly padlocked, so Hennessy kept
on going, following the wall around to the main entrance
on Central Avenue.

"Good Christ!" said Fleming.

"Something, isn't it?" said Hennessy. The two men in
the backseat stared out the windows as they approached
the entrance. It was built of sandstone and carved like
something from an ancient temple site in India, complete
with stone minarets and carved figures, in this case various saints and angels rather than animals and naked
women. The entranceway was also massive, rising at
least three stories, pierced by two tunnel-like openings,

the left one with its iron gate open. Hennessy drove through and slowed as a uniformed cop stepped out from under the porch of a surprisingly modern-looking administration building and waved them to a stop.

The cop shone his flashlight in through the window. "You Detective Hennessy?" The uniform was young, barely old enough to shave.

"You're right about that, sonny boy, and if you don't take that fucking light out of my eyes I'll have you cleaning up horseshit at Pelham Bay!" The kid jerked back as though he had a fishhook in his collar and the light snapped off.

"Yes, sir!"

"Where are they?"

"Prospect Hill, plot sixteen, sir. Just behind the mausoleum on your left, sir." He dug into the flap pocket of his uniform and brought out a folded map, thrusting it in the window at Hennessy. The detective took it and tossed it to Jane.

"Prospect Hill?" said Jane. "Not much in the way of prospects here."

Hennessy put the car in gear again and slowly moved forward as Jane unfolded the map. The main roads of the cemetery were lit like city streets.

"Sounds like a bunch of neighborhoods in Boston," said Jane, reading from the map. "Hickory Hill, Tulip Grove, Greenwood Shade. Beacon Hill, Pleasant Hill, Oak Hill. Lots of Hills."

Fifty feet beyond the administration building rose a low hill thinly planted with trees and heavily planted with headstones. A one-lane pea-gravel roadway ran around the base of the hill. On their right was a sign that read CELESTIAL HILL #2 even though there was no visible hill. The stones here all had Chinese characters on them.

Coming around the wall side of the hill they saw their destination. Halfway up the low rise several lights had been set up and there was the sound of a generator running. Half a dozen men were gathered around a single grave site watching as two heavyset workers, already dug down to their waists, were digging up Robert Sheldon Harte.

They climbed out of the Saratoga and headed slowly up the hill, Hennessy and Jane in the lead, Fleming and Black behind them.

"We're going to need pictures," said Fleming.

"You should have brought a camera, then," Jane answered, looking back over her shoulder. Fleming reached into his pocket and handed her something that looked like a small silver ingot.

"A Minox Riga," she said, surprised. She'd wanted one of the little cameras since they were introduced in the United States two years before, but she'd never thought of a good enough reason to lay out the eighty bucks.

"F three-point-five with a fifteen-millimeter lens. Shutter speed from half a second to one one-thousandth. I'm particularly interested in his teeth."

"Do I get to keep the camera?"

"Yes," said Fleming. "I want you to take it with you to Mexico City. I'll give you some extra cartridges of film and the name of a place where the film you shoot tonight can be developed. It might be useful in dealing with Mercador."

Jane nodded. "All right." She took the subminiature camera and slipped it into the pocket of her now rather wrinkled blazer. She stared up at the group of men and the bright lights set up around the grave. Her seafood dinner began to protest a little, but she swallowed hard and kept pace with Hennessy.

They reached the top of the hill, the generator puffing and popping away, the two grave diggers still throwing up clods of earth. Jane tried not to think about her sister, but it was hard not to. She closed her eyes and took a deep breath of the cool night air. Including the grave diggers, there were seven men at the grave site and three men with her. Nine against one. There was no way in hell she was going to sick up in front of all that maleness.

The men around the grave were introduced. Two were uniforms, one was the local precinct captain for the district, while the fourth man was Dr. Potts, Robert Sheldon Harte's dentist, who was carrying a small black doctor's bag and scowling. The last man was an appropriately cadaverous figure dressed entirely in black whose name was Hiram Smelkhurst, one of the cemetery trustees, there to see that his helpless client wasn't put to any more distress than was necessary.

"Utter foolishness," said Potts, his hands jammed into his overcoat pockets. "Known the family for years."

"He's been going on like this for an hour," Morrison, the precinct captain, commented. "Sadly, there's no law against running your mouth in the middle of the night." He glanced at Jane. "Who's the bimbo?"

"The bimbo, as you call her, is with me, Captain," said Hennessy, his jaw tightening. "And she deserves a little respect if you don't mind."

"Sorry." Morrison grinned brightly. "I didn't know they were going in for carpet munchers downtown."

Hennessy looked ready to launch a fist into the man's face, but Jane knew how much damage something like that could do to his career, no matter how many strings he was capable of pulling. She put a hand on her friend's arm.

"Forget it, Dan. The mutt's probably a daisy himself and doesn't want anyone to know about it."

Morrison started to go red in the face, and Jane turned away to look at Harte's headstone.

Robert Sheldon Harte
April 12, 1915–May 29, 1940
Died for His Beliefs

Above the inscription was a deeply carved hammer and sickle.

"Only twenty-five," said Jane.

Fleming sneered. "If I'm right, the little bugger's already celebrated his twenty-sixth birthday. Probably somewhere in the Kremlin, being toasted by Stalin and Beria with some cheap Bulgarian version of champagne."

From deep within the hole came a hollow thump and then a scraping sound as the grave diggers cleared away the last of the earth from the top of the coffin. A few more clods of earth were tossed up onto the pile. Jane stepped forward and peered into the open grave. The two men were pushing a pair of worn canvas straps underneath the plain varnished box. When they were done, they flipped the four ends of the straps up out of the grave and climbed up themselves.

Morrison gestured to the two uniforms. "Jiggs, Kelly, grab an end."

The two men stepped forward and grabbed one end of a strap while the two others picked up the other pair. At a nod from one of the grave diggers the four men began to pull and step backward at the same time, raising the casket out of the ground with a faint sucking noise. Straining, they brought the box up to the surface, and then at another command from the grave digger they began shuffling sideways, bringing the casket to the far end of the grave, then lowering it to the ground.

Everyone instinctively moved back from the earth-clotted box except for Smelkhurst, who stepped forward and used some kind of universal key to undo the half dozen wing nuts that kept the lid screwed down. When he was done, he gestured to the grave diggers, one of whom stepped up and took a long-handled chisel out of the back pocket of his coveralls. Using the heel of his palm he rammed the thick blade between the lid and the casket proper, then pushed up, repeating the motion half a dozen times as he moved slowly around the casket.

"Done," he said. The second grave digger came around the other side of the box and both men grabbed the underlip of the lid and pulled upward. The top of the casket came off and they laid it aside. "All yours, gentlemen," said one of the grave diggers. He looked across at Jane and grinned broadly, showing a three-toothed gap in his face. "Lady."

Nobody moved, so Jane stepped forward, taking the Minox out of her pocket, cocking the camera like an automatic pistol to advance the film. She looked down into the coffin, bringing the viewfinder up to her eye, knowing that seeing the body in the coffin through the viewfinder of a camera would somehow reduce the horror a little.

But not much. What was inside the box was little more than a few bones swimming around in a gray-green gelatinous soup made up of rotted maggots and other insect castings mixed with rotted clothing, jutting sticks of reddish bone and a hank of hair to mark where the head had been. Most of the teeth had been eaten away along with the major part of the jaw and the skull itself. Gruesomely, winking brightly in the harsh white light from above, was the flashing shape of a gold molar.

The smell coming from the box was foul, but nothing more than that of some animal dead through the winter and revealed in the spring. Jane held her breath and clicked off one exposure after another, both close up and from a distance, panning from the ruined head down to the nonexistent toes to get a complete array of the casket's contents. Finally she was done, the camera empty.

"Are you quite done?" asked Potts, the dentist.

"Be my guest," said Jane, stepping back out of the way. Potts shuffled up to the coffin, glanced in and frowned.

"There is a great deal more decomposition than I would have expected."

"Jewish law forbids embalming," said Black.

Smelkhurst gave a somber nod. "Although the young Mr. Harte was not a regular practitioner of his faith, his father insisted on a traditional burial. As that tradition requires, the headstone was also kept covered for the requisite nine months. I must say we were quite surprised at the, um, decoration on the headpiece."

"Well, *this* damn headpiece is all wrong." Potts opened up his little black bag, pulled out what looked like an ordinary pair of long-nosed pliers and got down on his knees beside the coffin, first covering his mouth and nose with a handkerchief. He reached down with the pliers, dug around in the glutinous remains of the mouth and brought up the glittering gold molar. He held it up so everyone could see.

"What do you see?" he asked.

"A gold molar," said Jane.

"Third lower right, to be specific," Potts instructed. "The crown suggests that it was designed for a tooth with two roots rather than three."

"So what?" said Hennessy, keeping his eyes on the gold rather than the contents of the coffin.

"So what?" said Potts, indignant. "Because I was

Robert Sheldon Harte's dentist for the last ten years and
I certainly never put a gold third lower right molar into
the boy's jaw, or any kind of gold tooth at all, and I
have the X-rays in my bag to prove it." He used the
pliers to point down at the suppurating mess beside him.
Reaching into the bag again, he brought out a jeweler's
loupe, removed his spectacles and screwed the loupe into
his right eye socket. He held the tooth up to the loupe
and examined it for a moment, then popped the loupe
out and put his glasses back on. "The workmanship is
quite poor and the gold has a distinct red cast to it. I
would say the gold is Mexican. I saw Sheldon less than
two weeks before he went off on his adventures. There
was nothing wrong with his molars then. At any rate,
this is definitely not the remains of Robert Sheldon
Harte. That headstone is a fraud."

Chapter 10

Vassili Zarubin sat at the bar in the Falmouth Hotel Cocktail Lounge and listened to a tired-looking sextet trying to imitate Glenn Miller doing "In the Mood." Before that it had been ersatz Tommy Dorsey doing "All the Things You Are" and a very pale version of "Dream Valley" by Sammy Kaye. The four sleepy couples out on the small dance floor were mostly in their late thirties and dressed for a night out. Apparently in Portland, Maine, the Falmouth Cocktail Lounge was the best there was on a Monday night.

The Russian espionage agent scrubbed at his face with both hands, yawned and lit another cigarette. He waved a finger at the tuxedoed bartender and pointed to his empty glass. A few moments later the silent man appeared with a fresh Maker's Mark on the rocks and whisked away the empty all in one motion. Zarubin took a small appreciative sip and reminded himself not to drink too much; the night was far from over and he needed his wits about him.

Watts, his contact at Donovan's supposedly top secret training school in Fairfax, had called him at the embassy that morning, giving him the single code word Shakespeare, which meant that his cover had been blown and that he was in need of assistance. Zarubin gave the appropriate response and then hung up. From that point on everything became automatic.

Zarubin's response to Watts, or James Maddox, was

one of seven different possibilities. This particular plan, "Pencil," called for Maddox to fly out of Washington on the first available flight to either New York or Boston, whichever came first. A car would be waiting for him at both airports, which he would then drive north to Portland. When he arrived he was to book himself into one of the tourist camps on the outskirts of the small city. At midnight he was to drive into the downtown area, park in front of the Falmouth and wait for Zarubin to appear.

Immediately after receiving the call from Maddox, Zarubin had begun making his own preparations for the trip north; Maddox knew far too much, including the names of several other illegals within Donovan's group and more than one of Zarubin's people in New York. Worse, his capture could easily upset the trail he was following to capture the elusive Comrade Levitsky and his damning evidence.

He had to be whisked away before there was the slightest chance of his being quizzed. Only the day before he'd received a coded cable from London advising him that Morris Black, the ex–Scotland Yard detective who'd suddenly appeared with Fleming and the unidentified woman, had previously headed up the Interrogation Division of the SOE training school at Beaulieu Abbey.

Zarubin checked his watch. Ten to twelve. If he knew Maddox, the man's nerves would be wire taut and he'd be in place outside on Middle Street. The Russian shook his head—a nervous-looking man sitting alone in a car at midnight. The first policeman passing by would be instantly suspicious. He waved for the bartender again, paid his tab and drained away the last of the Maker's Mark. Taking a last puff on his cigarette, he stubbed it out in the ashtray and climbed off his bar stool. He shrugged on his overcoat and his favorite hat, a battered center-dent Panama. The little group squeezed onto the tiny bandstand did a jerky swing into Jimmy Dorsey's "Green Eyes" and Zarubin left the cocktail lounge with no regrets and a slight headache.

Stepping out in the cool night air, he saw a pair of headlights flashing at the end of the block. He walked down the sidewalk to the corner of Cross Street and the lights flashed again. It was Maddox, sitting behind the wheel of a big Roadmaster Trunkback in a nice unobtrusive banana yellow. He'd have to have a little chat with whoever had arranged that.

Zarubin opened the passenger-side door and slid into the car. Maddox looked as though he was about to have a heart attack. Beads of sweat glistened in the thinning hair at his temples and his face was the color of old cheese.

"You look nervous, Watts."

"Of course I'm nervous. They're on to me. It's all ruined."

The other man's voice was cracked and dry. Usually the epitome of enlightened superiority, he now sounded like his new persona, the fleeing criminal at his wits' end and terrified, willing to grasp at any straw.

Zarubin was unperturbed by the man's broken emotional state. He'd inherited this man from the previous *Rezident* and had never trusted his stability. "Tell me how you know this, but first tell me if you were followed at any time."

"No. I took all the usual precautions."

"You saw nothing out of the ordinary?"

"No. I did exactly what I was supposed to do. The first flight out was to New York. The car was waiting by the time I arrived and I drove the rest of the way."

Zarubin knew the first flight out was to New York because he'd checked it himself before leaving Washington. "And nobody followed?"

"No, I'm sure of it."

He was wrong, of course. Maddox had been picked up by two of Zarubin's own people even before he left the terminal at La Guardia. Had he been followed or otherwise interfered with, Zarubin's men would have dealt with the situation. As it was, they were now down at the boat, waiting with the woman.

"All right. Now tell me why you think they were suddenly 'on to you'?"

"Because the Englishman and the woman were all wrong. Since I've been there no one has ever taken a one-day course, and certainly no women. The only women in COI are secretaries and cryptographers. No one who'd need training for overseas assignments. They were sent in looking for someone. I couldn't take the chance."

"You don't think you acted a little precipitously? It might have been nothing. What do you Americans call it, 'a fishing expedition'?"

"I couldn't take the risk. I'm too high up in the party to be caught."

The possibility that anyone in the Communist Party of the United States, including Browder, its leader, was too high up was laughable, but as an NKVD asset Maddox was right. A problem, however, that was about to be solved by his swift removal.

Zarubin changed course suddenly. He didn't want Maddox to think too long or too hard. "The woman with this Morris Black, the Englishman. Do you have any idea who she really is?"

"No. Her accent is New York, but she was tanned, as though she'd spent time in Florida, or perhaps California."

"A professional. Police?"

"No, I'm almost sure of that."

"All right," said Zarubin. "It's none of your concern now."

"What's going to happen to me?" asked the frightened ex-professor.

"We're going to chop you up and feed you to Comrade Beria in little pieces," said Zarubin.

Maddox looked horrified, the cheesy caste of his complexion turning an almost pure white.

Zarubin clapped Maddox on the back. "Relax, old friend, a joke only."

"Not funny."

"No, perhaps not." The Russian took out his cigarettes and offered the package to Maddox. The man shook his head. Zarubin lit one for himself and blew a stream of smoke at the windshield of the big car. "It amazes me how you Americans can build such wonderful things as this automobile." He reached out and stroked the dashboard appreciatively. "Hopefully they will not build tanks so well, or aircraft when the time comes."

"We were talking about what was going to be done," Maddox snapped.

Zarubin reached into the deep pocket of his overcoat and brought out a medium-sized manila envelope folded over and sealed with a broad strip of masking tape. The Russian pushed his index finger under the flap of the envelope and tore it open. Inside was a Canadian passport in a stiff cardboard slipcase and a well-worn Buxton man's wallet. Zarubin held up the passport.

"A valid Canadian passport in the name of Philip Andrew Groman, otherwise known as Skip, and sometimes Skippy. It lists you as being born in Ottawa, the capital city. You are unmarried and your occupation is listed as schoolteacher. You teach at a place called Lisgar Collegiate Institute, a local high school. You are forty-one years of age, born March 11, 1900, which of course is your real age and real date of birth to keep things simple if you are ever questioned. Your address is 492 Somerset Street West, apartment six. Any mail sent to that address will be dealt with by our people there." He handed the passport to Maddox, who took it, flipping through the pages cautiously.

"The only stamp I have is for Southampton. Three or four times in a dozen years."

"You're not much of a traveler. Your father was born in England so you occasionally visit. "

"I don't understand."

"You will in a little while." Zarubin held up the wallet. "Philip Groman's wallet. In it an Ontario driver's license in that name with your Somerset Street address in Ottawa. Several business cards, an old ticket stub from the Capitol Theatre on Bank Street, a photograph of you with your sister Margaret. On the back it says 'Skippy and Bunny,' Meach Lake, 1936. Meach Lake is across the Ottawa River in Quebec. There is another photograph of a young man in a British army uniform from the Great War, presumably your father. In the wallet there is two hundred dollars in mixed U.S. and Canadian currency."

"Why both currencies?"

"Because you've been on a short visit to the United States and now you're returning home."

"To Canada."

"Yes." Zarubin sighed. "You will make your way to Halifax, where you will take a train to Montreal. From there you will get on the connecting Canadian Pacific transcontinental train for Vancouver. Once there you will board the Soviet freighter *Klara Zetkin* to Vladivostok and safety."

"A long journey."

"Better than spending the rest of your life in prison, or worse."

"Yes," said Maddox, his voice resigned. He slipped the wallet and passport into the inside pocket of his jacket. "What next?"

"The journey begins," Zarubin answered. He reached out and patted Maddox on the shoulder. "Be of good cheer, my friend. A hero's welcome awaits you in Moscow." Maddox smiled weakly and nodded. "Now," Zarubin continued, "drive down to the corner and turn right."

Maddox started the engine and did as he was told, turning toward the Portland waterfront. Following Zarubin's directions, the onetime university-professor-turned-traitor took a left again, rumbling over the two sets of railway tracks that ran down the center of Commercial Street. It was still bustling at this time of night as freighters unloaded cargo at State Pier, while at Central Pier a little farther on the trawlers of the Portland fishing fleet were preparing to go out on the next tide so they could reach their fishing grounds by early morning.

Zarubin told Maddox to leave the car at the far end of Portland Pier, and they climbed out into the night air, redolent with the smell of fish and a hundred other cargoes that had seeped into the cedar piles and the railway-tie underpinnings of the cobbled roadway. Of all the piers on the waterfront this one was still reminiscent of the city's past shipping glory, complete with crooked-roof ancient buildings with nets strung from their upper windows to dry and the dozens of ship chandlers and outfitters on the far side of Commercial Street.

Halfway down the pier they reached a set of stone steps that led down to the water, the lower half still slick and wet from the last high tide. At the foot of the steps a short stocky man wearing a dark overcoat waited. Behind him, shifting slightly against the rubber-tire bumpers at the foot of the steps, was a Chris-Craft cabin cruiser. The hull was white, the upperworks the standard Chris-Craft plain varnished wood. The name *Dawn Treader* was picked out in black and gold on the bow.

"We're going to Canada in this?" asked Maddox, surprised.

"Certainly," Zarubin said. "The ferries go from here to Yarmouth in ten hours. We usually do it in half that. We'll have you there by dawn and none the wiser."

"You've done this before?" Maddox asked.

"In both directions," Zarubin lied. "It's a perfect place to bring people in or take them out." He nodded across the water to a large boat docked a hundred feet or so away. "All we have to worry about is the *Algonquin*, the Coast Guard cutter. We could outrun her easily if necessary, but she's got so much territory to cover, it's unlikely we'll have to." The Russian gestured for Maddox to climb aboard, which he did, helped by a hand on the elbow from the still silent man in the dark coat. Zarubin followed him, the man in the coat cast off the aft and forward lines, and almost immediately the engine fired and caught and they began to move away from the pier. Ahead of them lay utter darkness, broken only by the regular sweep of the beam from Portland Head Light.

"You left that man on the pier," said Maddox nervously.

"He'll deal with the car," Zarubin answered. "Wouldn't do to leave it where it is. Not with New York plates."

"I'm cold," said Maddox. "Can we go into the cabin?" He inclined his head toward the closed doorway forward.

"Why don't we sit out here for a while?" the Russian suggested, guiding Maddox with a hand pressed on his back, gently pushing him toward a bench that ran along the port-side gunwale. Zarubin took out a yellow package of Sportsman cigarettes and lit one from a book of matches, cupping his hand over the fragile paper flame.

"I thought you smoked Camels," said Maddox. Zarubin smiled to himself. Maddox, like any animal in flight from a predator, had all his senses finely tuned.

"I like to change from time to time. What is it they say, variety is the spice of life?"

For the next two hours they sat side by side, Zarubin smoking one Sportsman after another, Maddox becoming more and more nervous with each passing mile. They were soon surrounded by darkness and even the faint lights of Portland were long gone, vanished somewhere over the stern of the *Dawn Treader*. The boat roared at full throttle, a frothing white wake marking their passage. The Russian enjoyed his cigarette for a few moments and then, without comment, reached into his overcoat pocket and brought out a large, and quite ugly, Polish Radom 9mm automatic. He laid it on the bench beside him. Maddox looked down at it as though he were staring at a snake about to strike. Zarubin shifted slightly in his seat and looked at his companion, lit now only by the burning end of his cigarette and the bright green port-side running light.

"What's that for?" Maddox asked. He looked around, but there was nothing to see except the dark rolling water and the black night sky.

"Do you know what your new friends are doing right now?"

"What new friends?"

"Fleming, Detective Black and his female companion, as well as half a dozen New York policemen." Zarubin paused, took a last drag on his cigarette and flipped the butt out into the darkness. "They are exhuming the body of Robert Sheldon Harte."

"Oh, Christ."

"Quite so. And as we know, when they open the grave they are going to discover that Mr. Harte is not buried in it."

"No."

"Mr. Harte was once your student. This is correct, yes?"

"Yes."

"And you were lovers, yes?"

Maddox looked stunned. "You knew about that?"

"Of course we knew," said the Russian.

Maddox looked down at the pistol resting between them. It was flat black and roughly made, the end of the narrow, tapered barrel taped for a silencer. "I'm sorry," he whispered.

Zarubin ignored the apology. "Mr. Harte was sent down to Mexico to infiltrate the Trotsky household. He was to gather as much information as possible, pass it on to Siqueiros, who actually organized the project, and then follow through with the kidnapping charade. He escaped from his captors."

"Yes." Maddox swallowed. "He told me he was afraid that he'd be killed, that he was no longer of any use except as a martyr."

"He was right." Zarubin nodded. He lit another Sportsman and inhaled deeply. The powerful engine thundered, sending its vibrations through the hull of the Chris-Craft as they continued east into the dark night. "He came to you after he escaped, didn't he?"

"How did you know?"

"The young man is many things—being a fool is not one of them. He knew we would be watching his apartment and probably his parents' house in Queens." The Russian paused. "You had some way of communicating with him, didn't you?"

"Yes."

"What did he tell you that he didn't tell Siqueiros?"

"He told him everything."

Zarubin picked up the Radom and caressed the American's cheek with it. "No, he left something out."

"I swear!" Maddox protested, flinching at the gentle touch of the gun. "You must believe me!"

"I did not get to my present position within the NKVD by believing people, Comrade Maddox. Everyone lies—it is a fact of life. Some lie more than others, and I can assure you, some lie much more poorly than others. People such as yourself." Zarubin sucked in a mouthful of smoke and pulled back the slide on the Radom, cocking it. "You were his lover, James. He told you everything. He even told you about the key Comrade Trotsky wore on a silver chain around his neck."

"You knew?"

"We only needed his corroboration."

"And when you had it?"

"We would have killed him."

"Then he was right."

"Yes."

"Dear God, this was not what I became a Communist for. There is no honor here. This is no people's government."

"Of course not." Zarubin wanted to laugh at this bit of ivory-tower naivete. "It is a system, like any other form of government, that's all. The rest is politics and power. Marx has been dead for a very long time, comrade. What he wrote in the Reading Room of the British Museum half a century ago has very little practical relevance today. Think of it this way: Comrade Stalin is not always right, but he is never wrong, and when he uncovers a hidden enemy, he has that enemy removed whether the person in question was really an enemy or not. It is an efficient and expedient method. If the person really was an enemy, then Comrade Stalin has succeeded, and if the person was not an enemy, he never really existed at all, do you understand?"

"You are justifying murder."

"Murder doesn't need justification, only rationale. Sometimes not even that." The Russian felt a faint touch of mist on his face. All the better to hide their progress.

"Are you going to kill me?"

"Why on earth would we do that?" Zarubin shook his head. "If we were going to kill you, we would have done so a long time ago, and we certainly wouldn't be going to all this trouble." He paused again. "A few more questions, though."

"Yes?" The man sounded exhausted and confused.

"The idea was for Mercador to get into Trotsky's study and kill him silently, then retrieve the key and leave with it, but he panicked and was caught. But he has managed to tell us that there was no chain around Trotsky's neck and no sign of any key."

"Perhaps he is lying."

"No."

"Then perhaps Trotsky hid the key after the first attempt."

"Possible. But where?"

"I have no idea."

"Perhaps he gave it to someone else."

"Again, I have no idea."

"Would your young friend know?"

"I doubt it."

"I'd like the chance to ask him myself."

"I don't know where he is."

This time Zarubin used the barrel of the Radom to tap Maddox on the side of the head, hard, but not hard enough to break the skin. "You're lying. He came to you for help and you gave it to him."

"No."

"I told you. If you cooperate, we are willing to overlook your small transgressions. You have been of great service to us in the past and we are grateful, but this is very important. I promise you, the boy will not be harmed, but it is paramount that we discover what happened to that key." The Russian could see the conflict on the man's face and understood it. Betray his lover and become a hero; remain silent and his likely destination would be the basement of the Lubyanka Prison on Dzerzhinskiy Square. Which was it to be, love or survival? The conflict resolved itself, and Zarubin saw the man's shoulders sag with relief.

"Santa Barbara. An old colleague at the state college owed me a favor and found him a job at the public library."

"Does he live by himself?"

"No. My friend took him in."

"Your friend's name?"

"Pelham. Rupert Andrew Pelham."

"Excellent." Zarubin put the Radom back into his pocket and patted Maddox on the shoulder again. "You did very well." The Russian stood up.

"You won't hurt him?" Maddox asked.

"Of course not," said Zarubin. "He never had anything to worry about. He should simply have come to you openly, and we could have solved the problem with ease."

"What will you do with him?"

"Send him on to Moscow if that is what he wishes." Zarubin smiled pleasantly. "Perhaps the two of you will be reunited."

"I'd like that," Maddox answered wistfully.

"For the time being, let's go into the cabin and I'll make us some coffee." He helped Maddox stand and keep his balance on the vibrating deck. "Perhaps I'll add some brandy to it as fortification against the cold." He pushed Maddox gently toward the cabin door.

As Maddox reached for the handle, Zarubin had just enough time to bring out the Radom again. He held it by the barrel and brought down the heavy butt of the gun on the back of the American's skull. Maddox dropped to his knees, groaning, and Zarubin struck him again. He hit him a third time and Maddox slid down to the deck, silent. The Russian tapped on the cabin door.

A few seconds later a slim, good-looking woman named Guadalupe Gomez appeared on deck. Gomez, who traveled under a number of assumed identities, was Cuban by birth but had spent most of her formative years attending various schools in Moscow and elsewhere in the Soviet Union, including the infamous English School. She was wearing deck shoes, a pair of corduroy men's trousers and a heavy navy blue sweater. Over her shoulder Zarubin could see Tuzov, one of his New York illegals, seated on a high stool at the helm of *Dawn Treader*, manipulating the small wheel and staring into the darkness ahead. The woman closed the cabin door and looked down at Maddox.

"Is he dead?" She spoke in Russian, but there was definitely something else in the accent.

"I have no idea." Zarubin shrugged. "Does it matter?"

"Not really. Help me with him."

Together they dragged Maddox to the stern, then balanced him on the transom so that his head dangled over the rear of the boat.

"Did you get what you needed?"

"Yes." Zarubin nodded. "The young man is in Santa Barbara."

"Is he to be killed?"

"Eventually. Interrogated first."

"You wish me to do this?"

"No," Zarubin said. "I'll deal with him myself, I think. The weather will be warmer too." He smiled. "I could use a little sun. Besides, at the moment I have another, more urgent task for you." He reached into his overcoat and took out the Sportsman cigarettes and the book of matches. He slipped them into the side pocket of Maddox's jacket. As the woman dragged Maddox higher up onto the broad transom, the onetime academic began to groan again.

"He's still alive," said the woman.

"Then we should be quick about it." Zarubin looked out over the water. "How far out are we?"

"Sixty-five, seventy miles. Bangor is due north from this point."

"The tide?"

"Rising. He'll be taken by the currents of the Fundy bore if we're lucky. Fifteen-foot tides at Sandy Point on the Canadian side. Moving at twelve knots."

"And if we're not lucky?"

"He washes up on Cheney Island. I studied the charts carefully, as you requested. I can't see that makes any difference, not in the shape he'll be in." She shrugged. "They'll simply assume he fell off one of the ferries. It has happened a number of times in the past."

"I suppose you're right." Zarubin helped shift Maddox even farther until his head was actually in the water and they were holding him by his lower legs.

"A little more," said the woman.

They both shifted their grip to Maddox's ankles, letting him slide down farther. Suddenly a stuttering howl erupted from the engine as the twin propellers bit into the American's skull, turning his head to ruin. Together they pulled up on Maddox's heels a little, lifting the remains of his head away from the propellers.

"There are sharks in these waters as well, I think," said Zarubin.

"Blue sharks, mako, porbeagle and threshers." The woman nodded. "I checked."

Earlier that day she'd purchased an 8½-inch Don Carlos fish-gutting knife from one of the chandlers on Commercial Street in Portland. She took it out of the sheath on her hip, ripped open Maddox's shirt and then plunged the knife into his belly, just above the pubic bone.

Angling the blade slightly, she sliced up through the

belly and the heart, ending at the base of the man's throat. Viscera, blood, fecal matter and bile poured out of the man's body, tumbling down over what was left of his head. Zarubin and the woman let go of the American's heels, and he slid overboard, swallowed up almost instantly by their wake. The woman had sliced open Maddox so neatly there wasn't a trace of blood showing anywhere except on the blade of the knife, which she threw overboard into the darkness.

"I doubt if he'll last long," said the woman.

Zarubin stared into the darkness, following the foaming line of their wake. How easy it was to make someone vanish, as though they'd never existed at all. No one to care for the passing of a nonexistent soul. He smiled a little at that. Not that any good Communist even believed in the concept of such a thing.

"So where do I go next if it's not to be this Santa Barbara place?"

"You're bound for Mexico," said the squirrel-cheeked man.

Chapter 11

After leaving the cemetery in Brooklyn, Jane Todd and
Morris Black just managed to catch the Eastern Airlines
sleeper flight to San Diego, and after a four-hour layover
they boarded an Aeronaves de Mexico flight into Mexico
City. By the time they arrived the day was gone, and it
was all they could do to stay awake on the taxi ride from
the airport on the eastern edge of the city to the Regis
Hotel on the Avenida Juarez, supposedly Mexico City's
version of Fifth Avenue in New York.

Someone at COI had booked adjoining rooms for
them, and after signing in they crossed the modern lobby
and had a late dinner in the Salon de Don Quijote, an
enormous, nearly empty dining room decorated with
massive wall panels in encaustic tile depicting the salient
episodes in the life of Don Quixote, the Man of La Mancha, as well as more scenes of daily life in medieval
Spain. The effect was almost overwhelming.

"I'm not sure I can eat with all these visions of Don
Quixote staring down at me." Jane was trying to work
her way through a pair of enormous loglike burritos
smothered in some kind of stringy cheese. Eventually
she gave up and concentrated on an equally large bowl
of pozole, which turned out to be a mixture of grits,
broth and unidentifiable meats and vegetables. The only
thing she was sure of was that it had a lot of chili
peppers.

"I'm not even sure what I'm eating," said Black, poking at something the waiter had called a *tamal*. "It would appear to be some sort of curry wrapped in a banana leaf."

They both gave up on the meal after a few minutes and settled for a Mexican version of crème caramel and coffee. The coffee, when it arrived, turned out to be a pot of hot water, two cups and a jar of Nescafé.

"Perhaps we should consult with someone the next time we order a meal," Black said dryly. "We're obviously not doing this right."

"I'm too tired to care very much at this point." Yawning, Jane lit a cigarette and leaned back in her chair. "I'm just glad to be sitting down without the whole room vibrating."

"Try a flying boat over Iceland." Black winced, thinking of the icy cold. "Cure you of airplanes for good." He pulled out his tin of Senior Service and popped it open. There was only one left. "My last link to the old country," he said, lighting it. "I shall have to start smoking American cigarettes now, I suppose."

"Could be worse." Jane laughed. "Have you ever tried Mexican tobacco? Someone offered me something called a Faro once. I think the word means 'Light,' because the package had a lighthouse on it. I thought I was going to choke to death."

"Perhaps it's time we gave it up," Black said.

"Not on your life, pal. Besides, four out of five—"

"—doctors recommend Camels."

Jane yawned again, covering her mouth with her hand and closing her eyes for a few seconds. She'd slept on the plane, but only lightly, and her sleep had been full of dreams. Dreams of her sister and the dark hell of the hospital on Welfare Island. Dreams of the killer John Bone, her brief lover and the man she'd killed from less than ten feet away. Dreams of the explosion that had almost killed her and dreams of Bone again, at the World's Fair in Flushing, standing in the flatboat, hidden by the shadows of the bridge above him, his rifle aimed at the king and queen, all of them mixed into a single unraveling nightmare that never seemed to end.

She opened her eyes and found Morris Black staring at her intently. The first thought that came into her mind was that he was about to make a pass. The second thought was that she didn't think she'd mind if he did.

"What are you staring at?" she said lightly. "Do I have a chili pepper caught between my teeth or something?"

Black smiled. "I thought you'd fallen asleep for a moment there."

"I almost did."

"I was also wondering what brought you to all of this."

"I thought we were supposed to keep secrets, not tell them."

"I don't like secrets," said Black. "In fact, I abhor them."

"And you're in the spy business? Tell me another one!"

"I beg your pardon?"

"It means I don't believe you."

"It's quite true," Black answered, tapping his cigarette on the edge of a cut-glass ashtray. "I spent most of my career unraveling secrets, not keeping them, or worse, defending them."

"You were a cop."

"Detective."

"So how did you get to be a spy?"

"Believe it or not, that's a secret," he said, laughing bitterly. "I'd be thrown in jail for the rest of my life, or put up against a wall and shot, if I told you."

She looked mildly shocked. "You're kidding. That must be some secret."

"It is." Black nodded. "And knowing it is what turned me into a spy and stopped me from being a policeman."

"I am not an adventurer by choice, but by fate," said Jane.

"Pardon?"

"Vincent van Gogh said that. In a letter to his brother."

"You like van Gogh?"

"He reminds me of me." Jane nodded. "I like to look forward, not back. I guess you could call it curiosity."

"Didn't do much for poor Vincent. Lost an ear, as I recall."

"I think he thought it was probably worth it," said Jane. And suddenly she found herself thinking about those intimate few moments she'd spent with John Bone and she felt the color rising in her cheeks.

"A penny for them."

"What?"

"Your thoughts. You're blushing like a bride."

"It's nothing. Just thinking about something I probably shouldn't be thinking about."

"You never did tell me what brought you into all of this," said Black.

"Circumstances. A twist of fate, like your big secret. Even though I don't really believe in fate."

"*Ca ira,*" said Black.

"Excuse me?"

"I'm trading you, quote for quote. It's French—it means, roughly, 'It will go its way.' Fate, that is. Spoken by your man Benjamin Franklin when he was United States ambassador to France. He was speaking about the American Revolution, but it applies to most things, I think."

Jane ran one hand through her hair and brushed invisible crumbs off the front of her blouse. "Like Trotsky getting an ice ax in the back of his head. Never occurred to me that I'd ever have anything to do with that, but here I am. And you as well. A long way from England."

"How true." Black smiled.

The waiter appeared and looked silently down at their barely eaten meals. He shook his head, said something under his breath and began gathering up the dishes. He turned and left them alone again. Jane looked around. They were the only ones still communing with the Man of La Mancha. Somewhere, faintly, she could hear the sound of dance music led by a wailing clarinet. Not as good as Benny Goodman, but not bad.

"I haven't gone dancing in a long, long time," she said quietly.

"I hope that's not a suggestion," said Black. "Not that I wouldn't mind dancing with you, but I can barely put one foot in front of the other as it is."

"No suggestion," Jane answered, shaking her head wearily. "I've probably forgotten how anyway." She listened for another moment. "Just brings back memories."

"For me as well," said Black, and Jane saw a quick, deeply sad expression cross his face and then cloud over with something else. "Oh, what the hell." He reached out a hand across the table. "Care to dance, madam?"

Jane accepted the hand and came around the table. Black led her out onto the dance floor and into the small spinning circle of a dozen or so couples. His hand went around her waist, fitting comfortably just at the base of her spine, and they began to sway together. For such an apparently shy man his moves were surprisingly smooth and practiced.

"You've done this before."

"My wife, Fay, and I used to go dancing all the time."

"You don't talk about her very much."

"No," said Black.

"I'm sorry," Jane whispered softly. She knew Black's wife had died from cancer a year or two before and it obviously still pained him. It suddenly occurred to her that dancing together was breaking some kind of trust. She stopped in the middle of the floor but Black urged her on.

"Don't be sorry. I'm enjoying myself. Please."

And so they kept on dancing for a while longer. The music ended finally and Jane realized how lost in the dancing she'd become. They stood together, still touching for a moment, then stepped apart, slightly embarrassed, and returned to their table. Jane offered him a Camel. They both lit their cigarettes and Jane saw that Black's hand was nervously shaking.

"What about tomorrow?" she said to break the silence.

"The meeting with Mercador. Then I'd like to get a look at Trotsky's place afterward."

"We just waltz in?"

"Fleming's thought of everything. We pick up the documents we need at state police headquarters in the morning."

"What time?"

"Eight."

"Then perhaps we'd better get some sleep."

Black took out some of the American money Fleming had given him and dropped it on the table. "That should cover it."

"It certainly should," said Jane. "The bill is for fifty pesos, not fifty dollars." She picked up three of the five ten-dollar bills and handed them back to Black. She pushed back her chair and stood up, suddenly feeling the full force of her tiredness catching up with her. She closed her eyes for a second and suddenly felt as though she was rocketing backward on a freight train. A moment later she felt a hand on her arm. It was Black.

"Are you all right? You looked as though you were about to faint."

"I'm okay. I just need to get some sleep."

"Come along then," said Black. "I'll tuck you in."

"I wish," Jane muttered softly.

"Pardon?" said Black.

"Nothing."

The big yacht stood out beyond Long Cay, her running lights off and any interior lights blacked out by heavy curtains. She stood easily at anchor; the night air was calm and so was the sea. Once every eight seconds the beam from the Hog Island Light swept across them, but too high to detect their presence.

Two men stood on deck above the companionway ladder that had been let down to accommodate their guest. The man on the left, tall, imposing and perhaps a little too heavy for his expensively cut New Bond Street suit, stared through a pair of binoculars at the small darkened wharf at the entrance to the conch fleets' harbor at Arawak Cay. At the end of the harbor was the fish market, and even from a mile away he could smell the sweet-rot odor of the conch, their meat removed and their beautiful shells tossed aside, later to be collected and polished up for the rich American tourists who sometimes spent weekends here.

The man's name was Axel Wenner-Gren, a multimillionaire and the owner of the yacht, the *Southern Cross*. The tall, thin man with a bullet head and grim expression standing beside him had several names, spelled in several different ways; the present one, complete with title, was Count Anastase Andreivitch Vonsiatsky. He professed to be from the Russian royal family but was actually a captain in the Polish army who had fled in 1919 from the Bolsheviks. He had made his way to America in the early twenties, became a naturalized citizen in 1927, and then married the mutton heiress Marion Ream. He established the All-Russian Fascist Party in Thompson, Connecticut, which was odd since neither the so-called count nor his wife were Russian. The only thing really dangerous about him was the amount of money his wife had and her enthusiastic agreement with her husband's cause—to bring back the Russian monarchy, with the help of the Nazis if need be.

"She's late," said the count.

"She's always late."

"She should have more discipline."

"You're not talking about some farm girl here, Anastase Andreivitch. She is the key to our project."

"The key is her husband," snapped the count. "He is the one with the position and the power."

"If he had such position and power why did he wind up in such a godforsaken place as this?" Wenner-Gren answered. "A lump of coral inhabited by a few thousand *svart apa* who climb trees and cut down coconuts for a living. No. We will give him the power, and it will come through her. He has the brains of one of his wretched subjects, which is to say none at all."

A dark, nondescript car drove slowly down what was officially known as West Bay Street but which the locals called Beach Road, really no more than a rutted track of crushed stone. The car was an old Ford or Dodge, covered in dust like everything else on the island, driving on what the Americans would call the wrong side of the road. Its headlamps were out and so were its sidelights. Two passengers could just be seen inside—a thin, elegant woman behind the wheel and a slight, well-dressed man sitting ramrod straight on the seat beside her, looking directly forward, never turning his face left or right. It was a handsome face and had all the properties you'd expect to see on the profile of a man portrayed on a coin or a banknote, or possibly a postage stamp.

The vehicle slowed in front of a large Victorian house

that belonged to one of the few black doctors on the island, then turned and went down a short angled road leading to the docks. It came to a stop and then its headlamps, pointing out to sea, flashed three times in quick succession.

The man and the woman got out of the car. The woman handed the keys to the man, who unlocked the trunk, revealing four identical expensive-looking medium-sized cloth-sided suitcases. The man and the woman each took a pair of the suitcases and walked down to the dock. They went all the way to the end and put the suitcases down carefully. In the middle distance they could hear the sound of a launch approaching over the small sounds of the water. The man was almost gagging on the smell of the place, but the woman appeared not to notice. As the launch appeared out of the darkness she put her hands on the man's shoulders.

"You'll be all right without me, David?"

"I only wish that I was going with you, doing my bit, don't you know."

"I'm afraid it would be noticed rather quickly, sweetie pie." She smiled. The launch pulled in to the dock. Two men in striped matelot-styled naval sweaters were on board. One jumped up out of the boat and tied up, then began loading the suitcases.

"I suppose you're right," said the man she called David. He let out a little theatrical sigh. "I shall very much miss our games though."

She put her hand on his cheek, stroking it gently, the way you'd settle a dog. We'll play again when I return," she said. She looked down and saw that the two men were ready, one waiting to hand her down into the boat, the other behind the wheel. She turned back to her companion. She noticed that his puppy eyes were filled with tears.

"I never meant it to be this way, you know."

"I know, dear, I know," she soothed. "Let Mommy go now and I'll make it all better when I get back." She smiled. "At least no one will be suspicious if I come back with a bit of a tan." She pecked him on the cheek, squeezed his hand, then turned away quickly and let the waiting sailor hand her down into the launch. She sat down beside her suitcases as the man cast off the lines and climbed back into the boat. Engine burbling, the launch backed away from the dock. The woman waved and the man on the dock waved back. The boat swung around and headed out to sea. The man kept waving long after he could no longer see the launch or its phosphorescent wake, tears streaming down his face.

"I never meant it to be this way at all," he whispered, but no one answered on the gentle breeze, bringing him nothing but the scent of gutted fish and rotting conch.

Chapter 12

Wednesday, November 26, 1941
Mexico City

Choosing the slightly less exotic Quick Lunch room for their morning breakfast, Jane Todd and Morris Black filled up on scrambled eggs, bacon and fried potatoes, then set out to find Manuel Durantes, one of the half dozen or so assistant managers at the hotel, who promised to find them a rental car within the hour and to have it waiting in the large parking lot across the street. He also gave them directions down Avenida Cinco de Mayo and to the National Palace.

Both Jane and Black were exhausted and soaked with sweat after the half-mile walk, breathing hard in the thin air. Jane was beginning to think hard about quitting smoking before they were halfway to the palacio, and she was a confirmed abstainer by the time they reached the busy plaza at the end of the avenue. Even at this early hour it was filled with tramcars rattling around their rails in circles as they either began or ended their passage up or down any of the ten major streets that emptied into the plaza. There were scores of taxicabs and private vehicles and hundreds of tourists taking pictures and other pedestrians dodging the nonstop honking traffic as they tried to reach the broad stairs leading up to the entrance to the block-long sandstone red building.

The palace was just that, a palace, and housed the presidential offices and the presidential residence as well. The main floor was divided up into scores of rooms and halls, including the national museum, which occupied one entire wing of the building. The upper floors were given over to the bureaucracy of the state, a maze of rooms and halls that would have been impossible to navigate without the help of a uniformed guide who took them to the part of the building occupied by the offices of the state police. Jane gave the man a five-dollar bill and promised him a second one if he stuck around for the return trip to the front door.

It was a complicated business even though Fleming and Donovan's people had already cleared the path for them. Prior to Trotsky's murder, being a communist in Mexico was of no great consequence, but after the uncovering of a huge spy and smuggling ring run by the Nazis' Abwehr in 1939, the police were more suspicious, particularly so following Trotsky's assassination. The question of why a pair of noncommunists, one American and one English, should be interested in Trotsky's house as well as the man who murdered him was even more suspicious.

Nevertheless, they were eventually given the documentation necessary to visit both Ramon Mercador and Trotsky's house. Captain Morales, the official who stamped the documents after more than an hour, also suggested they visit a man named Dr. Alfonso Quiroz Cuaron, one of the psychologists who had eventually cracked the protective façade of lies and disinformation Mercador had erected to disguise his real identity. As it turned out, Dr. Cuaron lived only a few blocks from the Trotsky house in Coyoacán.

"I want to see Mercador first," said Black.

"Of course," said Morales."

This time Black removed twenty dollars from his wallet, slipped it across Morales's desk and waited. The man smiled. "Gracias, señor." He turned to the old-fashioned candlestick telephone on his desk and set up the interview with the prisoner, explaining the situation in machine-gun Spanish. A moment later he hooked the phone and smiled benignly across the desk, his hands clasped in front of him.

"He has been removed to the penitentiary. They will have him ready for you." He kept on smiling. Jane and Black thanked him and then left his office. Morales

waited for a few moments then picked up the telephone
again and placed another call.

Returning to the hotel, Jane and Black discovered an
enormous twenty-year-old Pierce Arrow out front.
Under the dust and dirt it had once been blue, but now
it was gray brown with rust red showing in patches here
and there. The canvas tonneau cover was torn in several
places, and the flat front windscreen had a large star-
shaped crack on the passenger side that looked suspiciously as though it might have been created by a bullet
passing through the glass. The leather upholstery, a
dusty green, had been patched at least a score of times.
Behind the wheel, dressed in what might have once
passed as a chauffeur's uniform, was a man who had to
be no more than fifteen or sixteen. Standing proudly
beside the car was the assistant manager, Durantes.

"It was occurring to me," said Durantes, without pre-
amble, "that if you are not knowing Mexico City well,
perhaps a car with a driver would be of more use to
you."

"Is he old enough to drive?"

Durantes spoke proudly. "He is my son, Cesar, and
he has been driving an automobile since he is twelve
years old."

"Well, at least he can see over the steering wheel,"
Black commented.

"Your car, Señor Durantes?" Jane asked.

"My son and I share ownership. It was left behind
some years ago by a guest who was forced to leave
quickly." Durantes shook his head sadly. "Romantic en-
tanglements, I think. At any rate, he could not pay his
bill, so the car was left in the parking lot for some years.
It became an eyesore and Señor Meza, the general manager, asked me to remove it. I asked him if I could have
the automobile and he had no objection, so now Cesar
drives and I keep the vehicle in working order."

"We're going to need him for most of the day."

"Thirty-five pesos and whatever gratuity you see fit,"
Durantes answered promptly. He cleared his throat.
"You of course would be responsible for the petrol,
yes?"

"Sure," said Jane. "Give him ten dollars, Morris.

That'll cover the tab for now." She stepped up to the rear door, and Durantes hustled forward, opening it for her.

Cesar turned around in his seat and smiled. He looked a lot like his father except for the fact that he had no detectable facial hair whatsoever. Jane doubted that he was fifteen or anything close to it. "I am your cho-fair, madam. I will take you to anyplace you wish to go."

"Great," said Jane. "I've never been cho-faired anywhere before."

Grinning, Black climbed into the front seat beside Cesar. He showed him the slip of paper Captain Morales had given him with the address of the penitentiary on it. "You know this place?"

"Yes."

Cesar put the car into gear seamlessly, let out the clutch, then went into a swinging turn that completely ignored the traffic moving in both directions. He spun the wheel and laid his hand to the horn, bullying his way into a wide and completely illegal U-turn, taking them east.

"Was that entirely necessary?" asked Black.

"No, señor," answered Cesar. "But exciting, no?"

"Yes," said Jane, sitting close to the door, clutching at the armrest.

"You know it is a joke, I hope?"

"What is?" Black asked.

"That they call the penitentiary the White Palace." He laughed. "It is not what those inside call it."

"Oh?"

"No, señor. My father tells me that when it was built, almost fifty years ago now, it was pure white because the inmates kept it so. But there is a slaughterhouse on one side and an army shooting range on the other. Between and behind there is a sewer plant. The place is so dirty now they call it the Black Palace. It smells very bad as well."

They drove for twenty minutes into the eastern outskirts of the city and eventually reached the prison. Cesar was right. It was almost the spitting image of Mountjoy Prison in Dublin, except much larger. A giant two-story octagon with spokes like wings leading into a central hub. Jane could hear the dreadful screaming of the sheep and cows being slaughtered in the abattoir on the left of the prison and the crack of rifles firing from the army installation a hundred yards to the right. The air smelled of blood and death and fear, topped off with the wafting scent of human waste and animal shit.

Cesar pulled the large car into a space to one side of the main entrance. He pulled a lime out of his shirt pocket, rolled it in his hands for a few seconds, then poked a small hole in it with a penknife he carried in his trousers. He squeezed juice into one hand and rubbed the juice under his nose.

"I will stay in the car if you don't mind. They say it stinks even worse inside." He leaned back in the driver's seat, yawned and closed his eyes. Jane and Morris Black climbed out of the car and made their way to the door set within the tall iron front gates. A uniformed guard appeared, looked at the document from Morales for a moment, then ushered them inside. They crossed a triangular courtyard, both of them well aware that they were being watched from the small barred windows all around them, and then they were inside the prison itself.

Cesar was right; the smell within was even worse.

They were met by another uniformed guard, who took them along a short passageway and then into a room divided in two by a heavy wire barrier. There was a table and chair on one side of the barrier, and two chairs and a table on the other. There were no windows, only a narrow door on the far side of the barrier with another uniformed and armed guard standing beside it, his arms crossed over his chest. Sitting at the table was a muscular-looking man who appeared to be in his late twenties or early thirties with dark hair, a strong chin and long, almost pendulous ears. He wore heavy tortoiseshell spectacles, and his eyes were dark and intelligent. The clothes he was wearing looked unwashed but expensive. Black reached into his jacket pocket and took out a small notepad and a pen he had brought with him from the hotel.

"You call yourself Jacques Mornard and say you are the son of a Belgian diplomat?" asked Black, speaking English.

"That depends on who is asking," answered the man in the same language. There was a faint Spanish accent to his words.

"My name is Morris Black," the detective answered truthfully. "I am here at the request of the Mexican government."

"The Mexicans hate the British."

"Not like me." Black smiled.

"What makes you different?"

Black switched into Russian. "Because I can get you things, you young idiot," he said. "I can't get you out of here at the moment but I assure you that I can make your life in this place much easier than it is at present." Mercador's jaw dropped. Fleming had given Black an extensive file in Washington and the onetime Scotland Yard detective knew far more about the young assassin than Mercador thought.

"Who are you?" Mercador hissed. His Russian was as good as Black's and perhaps learned at an earlier age.

"A friend," said Black.

"The woman?"

"Also a friend." Under the table Black moved his foot gently against Jane's shoe. She smiled at Mercador. Mercador smiled back a little nervously.

"How do I know this is true?"

"Why would I lie?" He continued to smile. "We went to the same schools in Moscow, my friend. I owe my allegiance to the people at Dzerzhinskiy Square, not the king of England or that plump little turtledove he married."

"Maybe you just want to get information from me. To find out things."

"Mornard, Frank Jacson the Canadian, Vandendreshd—I know all your names. Also the name of Leonid Eitington, your case officer, who is also the longtime lover of your mother, Caridad Mercador. You think I would know that if I was not of the Brotherhood . . . Ramon?" The Brotherhood being common slang for the NKVD. Black smiled and Mercador's eyes widened behind his thick glasses. "That is your real name, isn't it? Ramon Mercador?" said Black calmly.

"I have told no one that!" Mercador whispered. "Not

even that idiot psychiatrist they made me speak to and do silly puzzles for."

"Dr. Cuaron," said Black with a nod, still speaking Russian. "A Republican fool." With a large enough bribe Stephenson's people had managed to get a copy of Cuaron's analysis of Mercador, and the doctor was by no means a fool. Cuaron said that it was likely that other than as an information conduit to the members of the first team sent in to kill Trotsky, Mercador was simply trying to guarantee himself a place in history. It was a question of ego. Taken away from his father at an early age, a rootless traveler with his mother, Mercador had been a blank slate, a perfect tablet for the NKVD to write on. It was also clear to the doctor that Mercador, a trained mountaineer, had been in a state of utter terror when he attacked Trotsky, since he used the wrong end of the *piolet,* or climber's ice ax, in his bungled attempt. Had he used the pick rather than the ax end Trotsky would have died instantly and Mercador could have escaped. More importantly to Black, it would have given the young man the time he needed to get the film.

All of this, Black knew, was the essence of a successful interrogation—to know more than the subject expected you to know, and to reveal your knowledge at the appropriate moment, making it seem as though you knew far more than you really did. It was a classic Gestapo tactic and almost always worked. It was simply a matter of taking your subject where you wanted him to go and make him think it was his idea all the time.

"Well," said Black, smiling. "You were caught but you will be given a hero's welcome back in the *Rodina.*" He purposely used the word for Motherland rather than simply Russia.

"I am no hero," Mercador answered, but it was clear that he appreciated the comment. "A real hero would have escaped, or killed himself before being captured."

"From what I hear you had no time at all, and no weapon for that matter," Black added. He grinned as he said, "Since it was buried in the back of Comrade Trotsky's head."

"I had a knife in my jacket and an automatic pistol

in my boot." Mercador shrugged. "But you are right. There was very little time before the guards came."

"Certainly not enough time to find the film."

Mercador looked up at Black sharply, his eyes suddenly filled with suspicion. "You know about the film?"

It was Black's turn to shrug. "Of course. That's what it was really all about. The killing of Comrade Trotsky was only necessary because of it. Or did Comrade Eitington and your mother tell you the assassination was an end in itself?" Black paused for a long moment. "Or can't you remember?"

Dr. Cuaron had made one thing abundantly clear in his report. Whatever faults Mercador had did not lie with his memory. He spoke several languages perfectly, a single reading of a note or a letter could be read back hours later without hesitation. He had total recall, a photographic memory.

Mercador's chest puffed out with self-importance. "I knew what I was there to do. I would have found it."

"You didn't know where it was hidden?"

"No. The old man only mentioned it once. He made a joke and said that it was somehow fitting that his own life was protected by Christ's resurrection." He shook his head. "We were having a picnic in the gardens with several other people from the villa. He was drunk. I never understood what he meant and I didn't want to show too much interest." He shook his head. "I'm sure it was in his study somewhere. He would have kept it close by, I'm sure."

"He never mentioned it again?"

"Never a single reference. No."

"Oh, well," said Black. "I suppose it doesn't really matter." He slipped back into English, glancing at Jane as he did so. "Now then, let us get down to the matter of what you think you might need in the way of . . . creature comforts during your stay in this so-called palace."

They spent the next ten minutes or so discussing cigarettes, liquor, women, money and the various methods of passing messages back and forth, all of them made up by Black on the spot. When Mercador finally had a real visitor with his best interests in mind, the young man was going to be grievously surprised.

Jane was silent all the way back to the gates. Once outside they both lit cigarettes and walked toward the car. "Well, that was an education," she said. "I barely understood a word."

"A confused young man," said Black. "What we used to call a bit of a booby back when I was at school."

"Your basic pawn?" asked Jane.

"Something like that." They reached the car and Black opened the door.

"Anything at all worthwhile?"

"A clue perhaps," he said quietly.

"All that for one clue?"

"One clue's better than none, don't you think?"

They climbed into the car. Cesar woke up from his catnap and let out a jaw-cracking yawn. Jane shook her head; how he could sleep in surroundings like this was beyond her.

"Onward, Cesar," said Black. "Next stop—Coyoacán, if you please."

"Not a problem, señor." The young man smiled, started the engine, and a few seconds later they were heading away from the prison and back into Mexico City.

Half an hour later they reached the quiet suburban village.

"You know where the house is?" Black asked Cesar.

"Of course. Everyone here does. It is on Avenida Viena."

"Can you find it?"

"Certainly, señor. The main entrance is on Morelos Street."

"Then take us there."

"*Sí*, señor."

Five minutes later, the boy had navigated his way through the twisting streets and they found themselves at the red door in the high wall around the Trotsky house. Morris Black rapped loudly on the door, but after a long minute there was no response at all. Jane now had her Leica slung around her neck and the Minox ready in the breast pocket of her blouse.

"Hello?" Black called. "We have a pass from Captain Morales from the Palacio Nationale!" Still nothing.

"Hear that?" Jane asked.

"What?"

"Listen."

From behind the door came a buzzing sound, fluctuating, rising and falling in intensity.

"What is it?"

"Flies, I think." Jane said. "Maybe we should just leave well enough alone. Last time I opened a door like this, it blew up in my face." Unconsciously she fingered the long scar at her temple, hidden by her hair.

"I'm going inside."

"I don't suppose you brought a gun or anything?"

"I didn't think it was necessary."

"Let's hope you're right."

Black tried the latch on the large metal-clad door and was surprised when it opened under the pressure of his thumb. "It's open."

"Horses and barn doors," Jane commented.

"Pardon?"

"Trotsky's dead. Nothing left to guard but old mistakes."

"Aren't we looking for the film? Or at least the key the old man was wearing before the first attack?"

Jane shrugged. "Then open the door."

Black did so and the two of them slipped through the narrow opening.

"Oh, shit," Jane said. Directly in front of them, the back of his head propped at an impossible angle against the wall of the guardhouse, was a fat man in uniform with pitted skin and nicotine-stained teeth. Dozens of flies were congregated on his tongue, moving in and out of his mouth like coal miners hard at work, and around the hole in the bridge of his nose. The man's gun was still in its holster. A dozen feet away to the right was a second body, this one wearing uniform trousers and a grayish undershirt. He had been shot in the left eye at close range, and he had emptied his bowels and bladder when he died. His weapon was also in his holster. In his hand was a broken bottle of Noche Buena beer.

"Caught them by surprise," Black commented.

"Surprise is one word for it," said Jane. "Who?"

"Someone who was looking for the same thing we are. Russians, maybe even the Germans if they know the film exists." He looked down at the dead bodies in front of him. "I'm not sure about any of this anymore."

"What about the guns?"

Black leaned down, popped open the shoulder holster of the guard nearest him and pulled out an American Eagle 1911 .45 automatic. He dropped the heavy gun into the pocket of his jacket

"Now what?"

"We search the house."

"What's the point? Someone's been here before us. Whatever was here is gone."

"No," Black said. "There's something here."

Over the century's span of the London Metropolitan Police, usually referred to as Scotland Yard, the Criminal Investigation Division had employed literally hundreds of detectives, almost all of them at least competent, some of them extremely good and a very few exceptional. Black was considered to be one of the exceptional ones. Most of his colleagues put it down to what was quietly referred to as "the Sight" around the Yard, an almost supernatural ability to see beyond the evidence to something else, a point in time where a theoretical leap beyond logic could bring you closer to a crime's resolution than a hundred interviews. Anyone who believed in such things at the Yard knew that Morris Black had the Sight in greater abundance than any detective, past or present.

They went through Trotsky's villa quickly. Black barely paused as he went from room to room, virtually striding through without much apparent interest in his surroundings. He stopped briefly to examine the blood spatters on the wall by Trotsky's desk and the smashed eyeglasses, but nothing more. The place had obviously been ransacked, right down to torn-up floorboards. Every room had been searched as thoroughly as possible.

"What did I tell you?" Jane said. "Someone's gone through this place with a fine-tooth comb."

"They didn't find anything," said Black as they made their way back to the overturned living room.

"How can you be sure?"

"Because there's no end to the search."

"I don't get you."

"If you look and you find something, there is a moment like Archimedes—'Eureka.' I have found it! Unless by some incredible fluke that which is discovered is in the last possible place to search."

Jane looked around and saw what Black meant. The entire place had been gone through, everything and everyplace. Nothing had been overlooked. "And that means they didn't find what they were looking for?"

"It means more than that. This place has been searched more than once. The first time was calm and careful. Somebody went to the trouble of putting Trotsky's glasses back on his desk. The second was more reckless, as though they didn't have much time."

"But nobody found anything?"

"They may have found a lot of things," said Black, "but they didn't find what they were looking for."

"The film."

"Or the key."

"Okay, we've searched now. That makes three sets of people who've gone through the house. What now?"

"Mercador's clue."

"What was it he said?" Jane asked.

"The irony of the film being protected by Christ's resurrection."

"I haven't seen any crucifixes anywhere."

"In the house of a Communist like Trotsky? Doubtful, especially since he was born a Jew."

"Then what's the joke?"

"Trotsky wasn't known to have much of a sense of humor, so it's probably a bad one," Black answered. He stared blankly out the nearest window and into the gardens.

"The Resurrection is Easter," said Jane. She smiled broadly. "Didn't I read somewhere that Trotsky was passionate about raising rabbits?"

Black spun on his heel. He grabbed Jane by the shoulders and pulled her into a bussing kiss on the mouth. "Bloody good!" he crowed. "Our Red friend hid the damn film in his rabbit hutches!" He released her and headed for the stairs. "Come on!" Jane stood for a moment, two fingers up to her lips, then followed him as he went down the steps two at a time.

There were six empty hutches, side by side, wire boxes on high wooden legs fitted with simple wire doors. Troughs hung from the side walls of each hutch to provide food and water. Rabbit pellets had fallen freely down through the wire floors and piled up beneath the hutches, where the rotting fecal matter had half composted into earth, aided by a variety of nasty-looking beetles, centipedes and worms.

After ten minutes of searching, Jane and Black could find no conceivable hiding place for either a reel of cine film or a key on a silver chain.

"That's it, then." Black lit a cigarette and stood staring at the hutches. "I was so bloody sure."

"I still am," said Jane. She looked around until she found a wide stick and began pushing apart the foul piles beneath the hutches. Before long Black found his own stick and joined her, plunging it into each pile, spreading the material around as widely as possible. They found what they were looking for under the center hutch. Jane came up with it, a small flat key dangling from a filthy silver chain.

"Well, well, well," she said, "the proverbial needle in the haystack."

"No wonder it was never found." Grinning, Black took a handkerchief out of his jacket pocket and cleaned off the key and the chain as best he could. He threw away the handkerchief, then dropped the chain and the key into the water in the birdbath behind him, rinsing off the last of the shit. Jane took out her pocket pack of Kleenex and dried it off. They stood there in the hot morning sun examining their find.

The key was unburnished gray, three inches long with four flat notches along the blade of the metal. The only mark on it were the letters FNB/V engraved on the side.

"Safe-deposit box?" asked Jane.

"I'd say that's likely. The question is, where?"

"Maybe Mercador knows."

"If he does, it's unlikely he'll tell us, and I think the chances are reasonably good that our interview with him will be recorded. The Mexicans are sure to be interested."

"Why?" Jane asked. "What do they have to do with it? To them it's just a murder."

"The Mexicans have been secretly selling petrol to the Nazis for several years."

"I didn't know that."

"It doesn't matter. I think our best bet is to get this key back to Washington and put the whole thing back where it belongs—in Donovan's hands."

Chapter 13

The Cuban-born NKVD agent Guadalupe Gomez, traveling on a doctored Greek passport that identified her as Alexandra Kalinos, sat in the second-floor bedroom of the house directly across the street from the Trotsky villa on Morelos Street. She had arrived in Mexico City at almost the same time as Morris Black and Jane Todd and had wasted no time checking into a hotel. Taking a taxicab to Plaza Hidalgo, she had walked with her bag to Morelos Street and followed it until she reached the house opposite the red door marking the entrance to Trotsky's former residence.

There had been lights on in the house across from Trotsky's, and she found two people in residence, a manservant who let her into the outer yard and the owner of the house, an old widower. The manservant had been easy. As a rule Gomez kept an eight-inch section of sharpened coat hanger up the sleeve of her blouse for such occasions. With virtually no effort at all she'd managed to slide the weapon out, palm the tape-wrapped end and shove the point into the corner of the man's eye, letting the point slide along the bone to the superior optic fissure and from there into the brain. At that point she moved the wire quickly back and forth as though she were scrambling eggs and doing precisely that to the man's brain. He was dead in seconds. She dragged him off to one side of the path, roughly hiding him under a bank of shrubbery.

Taking the short winding path up to the front door, she entered and dropped her bag in the living room, searching through the house until she found her quarry, the old man. Looking through his mail later that night, she discovered that his name was Rafael Torres, a retired jeweler with a married daughter living in Vera Cruz who operated a small jewelry booth at the Hotel Imperial with her father as silent partner.

She'd found Torres in his study, asleep in his chair with the radio on. She simply slit his throat with her pocketknife and left him seated where he was. From there she found the second-floor bedroom that looked out onto the street, returned to the living room and fetched her bag. From it she took the broken-down M91/30 sniper rifle and PU scope she had been supplied with by Zarubin and reassembled it. Then she sat down to wait, keeping the shutters partially open and the curtains drawn, leaving a gap of only an inch or so.

The targets had arrived less than an hour ago, the sound of their vehicle bringing her out of her light, catnapping sleep. They left a young man at the wheel of the old Pierce Arrow and went in through the red door. Zarubin had briefed her on what they would find once they arrived, but they didn't reappear immediately. Gomez returned to Torres's study, placed her required telephone call, then returned to the bedroom, hefting the familiar weight of the rifle in her arms. The man and the woman remained hidden from view for the next half hour, finally reappearing shortly after ten thirty. Just as they came through the red door, Gomez heard the first police sirens in the distance. She put the rifle to her shoulder and her eye to the sight. Squeezing the trigger, she shot through the windscreen of the car, choosing a safe body shot that pierced the young driver's chest. She pushed the bolt of the rifle forward, then pulled it back, managing to get a second and then a third shot off, trying for the man and woman, but both of them ducked down behind the protective body of the car. Not that it mattered, since the point of the exercise was simply to keep them where they were until Morales arrived.

*   *   *

Jane was moving toward the car when she suddenly saw the windscreen explode and the terrible spray of blood erupt from Cesar's chest. The young man shuddered once, then slid sideways, dead, on the seat. Black grabbed her by the arm and harshly yanked her to the ground as the sound of the first shot blasted in her ears, followed by the hammering of the second and third shots into the wall behind her. He dragged Jane into the protective shadow of the Pierce Arrow and pulled the big automatic out of his jacket pocket. In the distance Jane could hear the odd, ululating sound of the European-style police sirens.

Another shot splintered stone in the wall behind them, and Jane pushed herself even closer to the side of the car. "What the hell is happening!"

"We're Judas goats!" Black answered as another shot slammed into the metal cladding of the door. He fired back blindly, the big semiautomatic bucking in his hand.

"Speak English, for Christ's sake!"

"It's a setup!" The detective put an arm around her shoulder and pushed her around him so the mass of the twelve-cylinder engine block would be between her and the shooter. Using his heels, he pushed himself along the sidewalk, dragging himself toward the passenger-side door. In the distance the sirens were getting closer with each passing second.

"What setup? Who?"

"Our Captain Morales is involved. I can tell you that much," said Black. "Why else would the police be so close?" Black reached up with one hand and pulled down on the door handle. "Not to mention the fact that he was the only one who knew we were coming here."

"Unless you count the professor or whatever he was."

"I don't think so." Another shot rang out, this one striking the opposite door of the car. Black pulled open the passenger door and slithered into the car on his belly, keeping as low as possible. Jane heard the sound of the ignition key and then the starter button engage. The engine fired up instantly. Black appeared a few seconds later, dragging the body of Cesar Durantes by the collar of his shirt. Jane was horrified.

"What are you doing?"

"Clearing the way," Black grunted. He managed to get the body out of the car and eased it down onto the sidewalk. "When I give you the word, I want you to get behind the wheel and be ready to go at a moment's notice. I want you to angle the car to the other side of the street. It will increase the angle of fire and give us a better chance." The sirens were very loud now, no more than two or three blocks away. Another shot smashed into the side mirror of the Pierce Arrow, sending shards of glass and metal in all directions.

"Why don't *you* get behind the wheel?"

"Because I can't bloody drive!"

Jane stared at the body on the sidewalk. In death the young man looked no more than a child. "We can't just leave him here!"

"He's dead. He's past caring," Black answered. "On the count of three."

"What?"

"One, two, three!"

Black pulled back the heavy slide of the automatic pistol, jerked himself up into a standing position and began to fire, aiming upward at the house across the street. He glanced to his left, saw that Jane was at the wheel of the car, and threw himself into the front seat. "Now!" he yelled. "Drive!"

Jane lifted her foot off the clutch and jammed it down onto the gas, swinging the big wheel to the left, swerving over to the other side of the street and the protective foliage of the trees lining the cobbled roadway. Their speed increased as the engine roared, Jane pushing through the gears as quickly as she could. Black pulled himself up into a sitting position just as Jane reached the corner and careened into the heavy traffic on Rio Churubusco Avenue. Looking to his left, Black saw that the leather of Jane's seat was a sticky mass of blood. The sound of the sirens was fading behind them, but the bullet-riddled car and the nonexistent windscreen would soon attract the wrong kind of attention. The street they were on was actually a broad boulevard, with mature trees running down a parklike grass median.

"We can't stay in this thing much longer," Jane said, reading his mind. "We have to find another car."

"Turn off the first chance you get."

A few seconds later Jane spotted a break in the boulevard, swung across both lanes of traffic and hurled the big car down a narrow side street. A block farther on Jane spotted a large green-and-white sign that read PEMEX, the name of the government petroleum monopoly.

"Is that a gas station?"

"Looks like it," said Black.

"I've got an idea."

Jane wheeled the big car onto the gas station lot, which was sandwiched between two warehouses. There were two ball-topped pumps, the pumps green, the balls white, and behind them an ancient-looking garage with a rusting, corrugated metal roof. Several old cars were parked against the warehouse wall on the right, and both of the sliding doors on the garage itself were open, the work bays empty. A fat man in an undershirt and a straw hat was sleeping in an old car seat, a section of newspaper keeping the sun out of his eyes.

Without being asked, Jane drove directly into one of the empty service bays and both she and Black climbed out of the car. Using greasy canvas straps riveted to the bottoms of the garage doors, the detective pulled both of them down. The doors, like the roof, were made from corrugated metal that had once been painted green like the pumps, the remains of the paint now eaten away with surface rust. Going through the garage into the connecting office, Jane looked around until she saw a rack of keys, each set marked with a paper tag and a scrawled license number. By this time the fat man had awakened and came storming into the office, screaming at Jane in Spanish. She ignored him until he made a grab for her, at which point Black pulled the automatic pistol out of his jacket and pointed it at the man. He had no idea if there was any ammunition left but it seemed to do the trick.

"Parada," he said, assuming that it meant stop, since the word was on most street corners in red. Black moved the pistol a little closer to the man's bulbous nose.

"Sí." The man stepped back, raising his hands over

his head, smiling and showing off a set of tobacco-stained teeth.

"Turn that sign around," Jane said to Black. She pointed at the hanging sign on the door leading out to the lot. Black edged around the fat man with his hands up and switched the sign from *Abierto* to *Cerrado,* then pulled down a faded green roller blind. Jane waved her hand toward the rack of keys. *"Donde está il llave de Chevrolet?"* The man glanced at the gun.

"I didn't know you spoke Spanish," said Black.

"I don't." She pointed. "The word's painted on the rack. *Llave.*" She turned back to the fat garage owner. "Chevrolet!"

"Cinco," the garage owner said nervously. He made a fist with one hand and then opened it.

"Five," said Black.

"Sí, sí!" said the man, turning toward the detective. "Fife."

"We'll need something to tie him up with and to gag him as well."

"We're stealing a car presumably."

"Right."

"Excellent idea." Black handed the gun to Jane, turned around and went back into the garage. Keeping the gun on the man, Jane slid over to the rack of keys and took down the fifth set.

"Sí?" asked Jane, dangling them in her hand.

"Sí," Said the fat man, nodding vigorously, his smile threatening to dislocate his jaw in his eagerness to please.

Black found a skein of copper wire, a pair of pliers and a roll of wide silver plumber's tape. The fat man's face fell. Jane gave the gun back to Black, went behind the small office desk behind her and rolled out a wooden chair on wheels.

"Show him you want him to hold out his hands," she said.

Black put his wrists together, demonstrating what he wanted the garage owner to do. He obeyed, sweat rolling freely down his cheeks now, the black hair at his temples wet and lank. He blinked nervously, looking back and forth between Jane and Black. Jane pulled a four-foot length of wire and snipped it off. She wrapped the fat man's wrists with it, tightly enough to make the Mexican wince. When the man's hands were secured, Jane took one end of the roll of silver tape and began wrapping it around and around the man's head, being careful not to cover his nostrils. When she'd gone around a dozen times, she ripped off the tape end.

"That should do it," she said.

"I wonder what the Spanish word for sit is?"

"Point your gun at the chair," said Jane. "He'll understand that."

Black pointed his gun at the chair, but the man didn't move.

"Sit!" The man looked at Black, obviously terrified now. *"Idioto!"*

"Wait," said Jane, "you'll give him heart failure." She took the man's bound wrists and led him to the chair, gently pushing him down into it. The Mexican dropped down heavily and the chair half spun around. He desperately tried to look over his shoulder at his armed captor, and when Black turned the chair around there was a widening stain on the lap of the man's trousers.

"He's wet himself."

"Good," said Jane. "Means he'll stay put and not try to escape."

"We can only hope."

Jane got down on one knee and repeated the binding process with the copper wire, tying the man's feet together tightly. Then she went to the front door leading out onto the lot and rattled the knob. *"Llave!"* she ordered. *"Donde está el llave de porto?"*

The garage owner nodded down toward his trousers.

"What did you ask him for?" asked Black.

"The key to the door. If someone comes along trying to find our friend here I think we want the door locked."

"Good idea," said Black. Wrinkling his nose, he went behind the man in the chair, reached down into his pocket and pulled out a pair of long old-fashioned keys tied together on a loop of the same wire that bound his hands and feet.

"Sí?" asked Jane. The garage owner nodded.

"Let's get him behind the desk, then lower him down onto the floor, keep him out of sight," said Black. Jane nodded and they rolled the chair and its heavily breathing contents to the back of the office. Jane helped lower the garage owner to the floor. The two headed for the door, but Black put a hand on Jane's shoulder.

"We need a map, unless you have an idea of where we're going."

"Cuernavaca," said Jane. "I saw a brochure at the hotel this morning. It's the closest big town to Mexico City. We can hide out there until we figure out how to get out of this mess."

"All right," Black responded. "But you can't go out on the street looking like that."

"Like what?"

"Your blouse is covered with blood."

"Oh, Jesus," she whispered. "I almost forgot." She rubbed a hand across her forehead. "Poor Cesar."

"It wasn't your fault, or mine," said Black quietly. "And it could just as easily have been you or me." The detective glanced around the office and spotted a moth-eaten navy blue cardigan hanging on a nail. He took it down and handed it to Jane. She looked at it for a moment, sighed and slipped it on. The sweater was ridiculously large, but at least it covered the blood. They stepped out of the office, and Black closed the door, locking it with one of the silver keys.

"Which automobile?"

"The green Chevy," Jane answered, leading the way to the parked car. It was a large square four-door touring car, the rubber on the running boards rotted through to the metal and one of the bug-eye headlights cracked. The windshield was filthy with old bugs and dried mud, and the spare tire was missing from its place in the driver's-side fender. Jane unlocked the car, eased behind the wheel and plugged the key into the slot on the dashboard. She pressed the starter button and the engine coughed to life. "Get in," she said to Black. He did so, gingerly closing the squeaking door.

Jane put the car into gear and slowly drove over to the pumps. She got out quickly, put the nozzle from one of the pumps into the car's tank outlet and wound up

the meter. She switched it on and gasoline began to fill
the tank. While it was filling, she took a rag from a rack
between the pumps, dipped it into a galvanized bucket
of grimy water and did her best to clean the windshield,
managing to remove at least some of the dirt and petri-
fied bug matter. She went back to the pump, waited until
gasoline began to spill out onto the dusty ground at her
feet, then switched off the meter and hung up the hose.
As she climbed back in behind the wheel and slammed
the door, a pair of state police cruisers roared past the
gas station, sirens moaning.

"That was a near thing," said Black.

"Miss is as good as a mile."

Jane put the car in gear again and they headed back
out onto the street. Looking into the rearview mirror,
she checked to see that everything appeared normal at
the gas station behind her. "Siesta time," she said, nodding to herself, pleased. She drove off the lot and onto
the narrow street.

She eventually found a sign for Highway 9 and an
arrow pointing to Cuernavaca. Soon they were driving
through a heavily populated and clearly very poor district that seemed to be given over to small manufacturing concerns. Ten minutes later, the landscape changed
dramatically as they reached the broad streets and attractive homes of the Loma de Chapultepec, one of
Mexico City's wealthiest suburban "colonias." By now
they were well away from Coyoacán and there was no
sign of the police. Eventually the colonia gave way to
open, hilly farmland, filled on either side with fields of
the spiky maguey plant, used for making the rough,
working-class liquor known as pulque. Dotted among the
maguey were pepper trees, cacti, melon patches and
truck vegetables. Above it all was a perfect azure sky
made pale by the burning sun.

"What did you mean when you said we'd been set
up?" Jane asked, keeping exactly to the speed limit and
checking the rearview mirror every few seconds.

Black cocked a thumb and forefinger, making a shooting gesture. "Those shots were fired from the villa across
the road from where we were. The upper floor. The only

person who knew we were going to be there was Morales."

"The state police?" Jane frowned. Somehow it didn't seem possible.

"No, I don't think so, at least not officially. I think Morales is bent. On the jake."

"Jake?"

"Take, as in taking bribes."

"On the pad, you mean."

"Yes."

"Who's doing the bribing?"

"Someone closer than we think, I'm almost sure of that."

"Why?"

"We appear. Watts or whatever he calls himself disappears. Think about it. We flew from Washington to New York for the exhumation. Who the bloody hell knew about that?"

"Fleming?" Jane's frown deepened. "Surely not him. I thought you two worked together or something."

"We did, and I find it hard to believe as well. The only other people who might have known are Donovan and that other British person, whatshisname?"

"Stephenson. William Stephenson. But they just hired us, for Christ's sake," Jane continued. "Now you're saying they're trying to kill us? Where's the sense in that?" She dropped down a gear as the highway began to climb. The fields had slipped away, replaced by dense stands of pines. The air coming in through Jane's partially opened window was also a great deal cooler.

"I don't think the objective was to get us killed," said Black. "Whoever was firing that weapon knew precisely what he was doing. Cesar was killed with a single shot to the chest. I counted half a dozen rounds fired after that, all of which missed."

"We were being pinned down on purpose."

"I think so. Cesar dead, those guards we found."

"That's crazy. Those guards had been dead for at least a couple of days. I've covered enough crime scenes to know that. And if we killed Cesar, what did we do with the rifle we shot him with?"

"Of course it's crazy, but it would have had us tied up with the police for God knows how long. Out of the way."

"Out of whose way?"

"Whoever ordered Cesar's killer to fire on us."

"This is all going around in circles."

"For now we've got to concentrate on getting away from Morales and his people."

"And how do we do that?" Jane asked. "That fat guy we left in the garage is going to get loose eventually, or someone's going to find him. Every cop in Mexico is going to be looking for us. This car is going to turn into a death trap if we don't do something about it pretty soon."

"We'll think of something."

"I just did," said Jane, pointing to an open meadow on their left. She slowed, struggling with the wheel, taking the old car across the highway, where she drew up at a roughly painted sign beside an open gate.

AIRPLANE RIDES
CONDUCIRA AEROPLANO
FOR TOURISTS
POR TURISTAS
$40
(PESOS)

Resting on the grass a dozen yards away, a very run-down aircraft sagged on its undercarriage. The body of the aircraft had been bright red at some time in the past, but the old Shell Oil identification could be seen quite clearly through the thin coat of paint. At some later date the plane must have been used for crop dusting because Jane could see the thin metal tubes and nozzles bolted to the underside of the nearest wing. There were long streaks of oil and exhaust on the cabin, and the underside of the wing and the tail of the single-winged aircraft was coated in oily filth. There was also no visible antenna running from the head of the cockpit back over the fuselage, which probably meant there was no radio. From the looks of it, the *aeroplano* wasn't *conduciri*ng many *turistas* these days, even though forty pesos was a perfectly reasonable price.

"Dear God," said Black, staring through the windscreen at the machine in front of him. "What on earth is that?"

"Sweet deliverance," said Jane. "Give me twenty simoleons and don't let the guy who owns that thing see your gun."

"Simoleons?"

"Bucks, dinero, dollars." She shook her head. "I'm going to have to hire us a translator." She put the car in gear and drove through the open gate and onto the meadow.

Chapter 14

A man wearing brown dungarees and a navy blue pull-over sweater was lying under the wing of the airplane, his head pillowed on a rolled-up leather jacket that looked as old and grimy as the plane itself. He had a battered tan fedora pulled over his eyes and a pair of lined flying boots on his feet. As Jane pulled up beside the wing, the man stirred, tipped back the fedora and got up, ducking out from under the wing, blinking and yawning in the bright sunlight.

Jane got out from behind the wheel of the Chevrolet and pulled her own sweater tighter around her so the pilot wouldn't notice Cesar's blood, now drying to a deep brown. Black got out of the car on the other side, keeping his right hand in the pocket of his jacket.

"Por favor," Jane began.

"Relax, I'm an American," said the man, grinning. He was fox-faced, his cheeks bony, his nose and chin sharp. His skin was deep brown and weathered, his lips cracked by too much exposure to the sun. He swiped off his hat and ran one hand through thick, slightly reddish brown hair. His eyes were the most extraordinary color of blue Jane had ever seen, bright, laughing and as full of youth as Cesar's had been, set in the face of a man who had seen and done far too much. "Name's Lindbergh, believe it or not. Arnie Lindbergh. No relation, of course, or I wouldn't be lying on my kiester in the middle of a Mexican beanfield, would I?" He wiped his right hand on the thigh of his dungarees and offered it to Jane. She shook it.

"Pleased to meet you, Mr. Lindbergh."

He smiled. "If you want to be formal, it's Lieutenant Lindbergh, but I'd be obliged if you'd call me Arnie. I'm not the stuffy type." He picked up the leather jacket and shook it out. Jane could see gold wings stitched onto the chest and a circular patch on the shoulder that had a laurel wreath wrapped around the Roman numeral IX.

"Lieutenant in what service, if you don't mind me asking?" said Black.

"Ninth Aero Squadron, U.S. Army Signal Corps, out of Camp Kelly, Texas, to France via Winchester and Grantham, England, flying Sopwith Scouts. Called us the Night Watch in Vavincourt. We flew the Breguet fourteen. Specialized in night recon." He paused. "You're a Limey, right? How about you?"

"Runner for the Cherryknobs. Motorcycles."

Jane gave Black an odd look. Arnie Lindbergh laughed.

"Military police. Boy, I remember you guys. See those funny red hats coming into the pubs after hours and you knew the jig was up."

"How'd you wind up here?" Jane asked.

Arnie shrugged. "They disbanded the squadron. I wanted to go back to Texas, but there wasn't a whole lot of work. Wound up flying for Shell Oil." He patted the side of the old plane fondly. "That's how I inherited Gertie here. When Mexico nationalized all the oil companies a few years back, Shell pulled out overnight and here I was. Bought the plane from them for a dollar 'cause they didn't want to haul it back to the States. I went into crop dusting for the big pulque plantations. When the plantations started getting broken up, I took out the dusting tanks and started flying the *turistas.* Which is what you people are, I'm guessing."

"Newlyweds," said Black quickly.

"That right?" said Arnie. "Well, in that case it'll be thirty pesos instead of forty. How's that for a deal?"

"Fine."

"Then climb in." Arnie made a sweeping gesture, bowing low, then gave Jane a hand up on the step into the aircraft. There were two seats up front and two behind. The front seats were faced by two large wooden steering wheels exactly like the one in the Chevrolet, and both places had identical foot pedals. Jane noticed there were fewer instruments on the dashboard of the plane than there had been in the Chevrolet. The windscreen was divided into three sections, and the seats behind each had their own window.

Arnie climbed in and dropped into the left-hand pilot's seat. Black clambered in after him, closing and latching the hatchway. It smelled like a combination of insect spray and kerosene.

"Stinson Detroiter," said Arnie, patting the nominal dashboard. "First diesel airplane ever built, so smoke 'em if you got 'em. You'd need a blowtorch to set fire to Gertie. Also the first electric starter." Arnie pulled out a pair of knobs on the dashboard, threw a single toggle switch, then turned the big white starter knob to the right. The engine coughed, died, coughed, then caught, the propeller jerking, then spinning madly as the engine spooled up, sending deep, shuddering vibrations through the plane.

"What's Gertie's range?" Jane asked, raising her voice over the bellowing howl of the engine.

" 'Bout seven hundred miles, you want to pray real hard," Arnie yelled back. "Hang on." He set his feet onto the pedals, then hauled back on the single tall throttle lever. Instantly the airplane jerked forward and began to gain speed as they roared down the meadow. Looking between Arnie's and Morris Black's shoulders, Jane was horrified to see that the meadow canted to the left less than two hundred yards ahead of them, the ground leaning down into a narrow, ravinelike valley. Fifty feet on from that a line of tall pine trees loomed like a green cliff. Jane could see Black's shoulders stiffening, and she gripped the back of Arnie's seat, digging her fingers into the old cracked leather.

"Relax, ma'am," said Arnie. "Gertie and I have been sweethearts for a lot of years now. We know each other pretty well."

As the meadow began to tilt away, Arnie simultaneously pushed his foot down on the left pedal and pulled back on the wheel. Almost magically, engine screaming in protest, the Stinson seemed to leap into the air. Hitting the right pedal and pulling back the wheel even more, Arnie used the slump in the landscape to give him instant altitude and enough room and acceleration to get them over the trees by what seemed to be a matter of a few feet. Arnie leveled off. "Anything special you want to see?"

"What's north of here?" Jane asked, leaning forward in her seat and speaking directly into Arnie's ear.

"Other than Mexico City?"

"Other than Mexico City."

"The Altiplano Centrale, the Central Plateau, the Sierra Madres."

"Beyond that."

"Cost you more than a few pesos," Arnie answered. "Gertie's easy on fuel, but not that easy."

"How about a few hundred dollars?" said Jane. She glanced to the right and caught Black's eye. He nodded briefly.

Arnie reached his left hand into the canvas chart pocket on the pilot's door and brought out a massive Smith & Wesson .44 caliber revolver that looked older than he was. He thumbed back the hammer and aimed the huge old gun at Morris Black's temple, the muzzle less than an inch away from his skull.

"How about a few answers?" asked Arnie. "But first I'd appreciate it if your husband, so-called, would very slowly take his right hand out of his jacket pocket and drop whatever it's holding onto the floor. Immediately or sooner if you don't mind."

The Scotland Yard detective did exactly what he was told, moving extremely slowly.

"What if I told you I had a pistol like that and it was aimed at the small of your back?" said Jane.

"Well," said Arnie, his gun hand steady, "I'd say, number one, it'd be a matter of who shot quickest, me or you, number two, whether my hand might spasm and shoot this fellow even if you did get off a round first, and number three, even if you shot first and my hand didn't clench up, just who the hell do you think would fly Gertie?"

"He makes several valid points," said Morris Black. "The last being the most telling."

"Shit" was all Jane could say.

"So how about you tell me what this is all about?" Arnie asked. "You two aren't newlyweds, are you?"

"I'm afraid not," said Black.

"Cops after you." It wasn't really a question.

"He is a cop," Jane offered.

"Not around here he's not."

"It's a long story."

"We talking the Federales here, or some kind of small potatoes?" asked Arnie. "Soon's you drove up I knew there was something out of whack with the two of you. No *turista* badge on the windshield and that old piece of tin you were driving wasn't from any rental garage I know about. You need special plates."

"Shit," said Jane again.

"Rough mouth there, lady."

"She's from New York," said Black, as though that explained everything.

"And it's not small potatoes."

"So it is the Federales."

"The state police."

"That's what I said."

"Bad trouble."

"I'm afraid it couldn't be much worse," said Black.

"If you knew we were lying, why did you take us up?" Jane asked.

"Idle curiosity," said Arnie. "That blood on your blouse, ma'am?"

"Yes."

"Not yours."

"No. Not mine. A young man's."

"You or hubby here do the shooting?"

"No."

"Any reason I should believe you?"

"Reasons, no proof."

Arnie turned to Black. "You really a Cherryknob?"

"Corporal. Spent a great deal of time in Belgium directing traffic."

"You're a real cop now?"

"Was."

"Dearie me, now that sounds like another long story."

"You have no idea," Black answered, grimacing. Even from the rear seat, distracted and frightened as she was, Jane could see a terrible dark look cross Black's features. Death, pain, madness maybe? Was it nothing more than the face of war or was there something more to it than that?

"Well," Arnie drawled, "we hold our breath we can just about make Brownsville." He paused. "That's on the assumption that you'd like to get across the border undetected, as they say."

"You're not going to turn us over to the police?" said Jane, astounded.

"Now why would I go and do a thing like that?" Arnie answered, equally surprised. He turned and gave Jane a broad smile. "It's not like I'm absolutely lily white when it comes to slipping across the line."

"You're a smuggler?" asked Black.

"A small businessman making his way through an uncaring world is more like it. Not to mention the fact that we were allies during the last war, and right now I'm ashamed that we haven't come to your aid sooner." He took one hand off the wheel and patted Black on the shoulder. "Just doing my bit for my English friends, and here's hoping I can fool them into thinking I'm young enough to fight again, even if you people do serve your beer warm."

Chapter 15

Emil Haas sat at a small sidewalk table outside the Café St. Michel, ignoring the grimly cold weather and the late-afternoon traffic on the famous boulevard for which the café was named, keeping his attention on the rue de la Huchette instead, particularly on a tall, narrow four-story building halfway down the block, Le Panier Fleuri. Ostensibly a flower shop squeezed in between a news-agent and a dry-goods store, Le Panier Fleuri was the only enterprise of the three that seemed to be flourishing under German occupation. Le Panier was what the French called a *lupinar*, or rabbit hutch, the Germans called *das Bordell*, and Americans called a whorehouse.

Haas had been sitting at the table for almost an hour, freezing his knackers off, sipping some ghastly wartime excuse for coffee and reading a reasonably current copy of *Time* magazine given to him by Canaris's props department. The magazine offered him instant cover at the café, as did the U.S. dollars he had used to pay the proprietor, Monsieur Trevise, putting the man eternally in his debt since any kind of hard currency was almost impossible to get in Paris these days. In his heart what Haas really wanted was a *Braunschweiger* sausage sandwich and a stein of Löwenbräu.

Keeping his eyes looking over the top of the page as he leafed through the magazine, Haas was finally rewarded by the sight of his quarry emerging from the front door of Le Panier. The man was well dressed, if a

little old-fashioned, in his early sixties, and bore a striking resemblance to the late King George V of England,
who had in fact been his cousin, as had Tsar Nicholas
II before his untimely murder twenty-three years previously. The man was Boris Vladimirovich Romanov,
Grand Duke of all the Russias, and his particular favorite at Le Panier was an eighteen-year-old woman named
Bibi, who was perfectly happy to do anything the old
Russian wanted, even some of the stranger vices he occasionally requested.

Since Le Panier was also a designated brothel for use
by any German officer above the rank of *Leutnant*, it
came as no surprise to Haas that Bibi also worked for
both the Abwehr and the Gestapo. Thus, for every cou-
pling in her small room the young woman was being
paid three times: once by the client, once by Lieutenant-
Colonel Rudolf, head of the Abwehr in Paris, and once
by Walter Boemelburg, the Parisian Gestapo chief. The
French, if nothing else, were enterprising in the face of
defeat.

As Vladimirovich jauntily made his way down the
sidewalk, then crossed the cobbled street, Haas dropped
another dollar on the table and got to his feet, rolling
up the magazine. He put it into his jacket pocket and
took a package of American Old Gold cigarettes out of
his shirt pocket and tapped one out into his hand.
Reaching Vladimirovich, Haas paused.

"I wonder if you might have a match, Toverishch Vladimirovich?" Haas asked in fluent Russian, purposely
using the Soviet-adopted word *Tovarishch*, which was
certain to offend if not actually frighten any right-
thinking tsarist. It stopped Grand Duke Boris dead in
his tracks. When he replied, it was in French.

"I beg your pardon?" he said mildly. Yet a nerve in
his cheek twitched, betraying him.

"A match, Your Highness," said Haas. "For my cigarette." He lifted the cigarette in his hand. "Would you
like one?" He took out the package and offered it to
the frightened man standing less than two feet away.
Hand shaking, Vladimirovich took the package and
shook one out. He reached into the pocket of his own
jacket and took out a slim gold lighter that had almost

certainly been made or at least cased by Fabergé, the Russian imperial jewelers. He lit Haas's cigarette and then his own.

"Keep the package," said Haas, this time speaking in flat, Midwestern English.

The Russian put the package into his pocket along with the lighter. Cigarettes, especially American ones, were virtually impossible to get in Paris, like almost everything else.

"Who are you?" Vladimirovich asked, also speaking English.

"Perhaps we should walk as we talk," Haas said, taking the grand duke by the elbow.

The Russian shook him off. "I'm not going anywhere with you!"

"Yes, you are," Haas responded. "And keep your voice down," he added quietly. He reached his hand into his jacket pocket and half revealed a tiny Mauser m1910 vest-pocket pistol. It was only a .25 caliber, but it was capable of a great deal of bodily harm at close range. "Come along," said Haas. He gripped the man's elbow again, turning him around and heading him toward rue des Deux Ponts, a hundred yards away.

"What do you want?" Vladimirovich said, voice tight. "There's a police station just along here, you know. All I have to do is shout."

"The two fat *flics* in there have been drinking cheap wine for most of the day," said Haas. "They'll be half asleep by now. I could put a bullet in your ear and be sitting in a pew at Notre Dame before anyone noticed."

Vladimirovich looked around wildly. The narrow street was empty. There was no one to come to his aid. "You're a *Chekisti*, aren't you?" said the man. "You obviously know who I am."

"I'm not anything of the sort," Haas answered, laughing. "But I do know who you are." They reached the tiny little police post. "Down here," Haas ordered. He guided Vladimirovich down a tiny alley on the left. A small metal street sign was riveted to the wall of the police building: RUE DU CHAT QUI PÊCHE. Street of the Fishing Cat. Local mythology had it that a hundred years or more ago the Seine, which lay at the end of the street, had regularly flooded in the spring, sending the overflow up the alley, where cats would come and paw the river carp out of the rising water.

Their footsteps rang and echoed in the narrow confines of the little street. "Are you going to kill me?"

"Not if you tell me the truth."

"The truth about what?"

"You'll find out soon enough."

They reached the end of the alley, which emptied out on the Quai St. Michel. Somewhere nearby Picasso had his studio. Haas smiled, thinking about the mad Spaniard. To the prudish führer he was a man as decadent as the Aryan Café in Berlin, and just as dangerous.

Haas led Vladimirovich across the quai and they sat down on a bench looking across to the Île de la Cité and the Conciergerie. "Somewhat like the Lubyanka, don't you think?" said Haas, referring to the NKVD prison housed in the basement of their headquarters in Moscow's old State Insurance Building on Dzerzhinskiy Square.

"I don't know what you're talking about."

"Of course you do." Haas laughed again. He flipped his cigarette butt over the iron railing in front of them and out into the turgid waters of the river.

"Why don't you just tell me what you want?" said the grand duke. Even under threat he still had the arrogant bearing of a prince.

"First I'll tell you what I know."

"As you wish," said the Russian. "After all, you are the one who has a gun."

"You are Grand Duke Boris Vladimirovich, one of Tsar Nicholas the Second's four first cousins. With the death of your brother Kyril a number of years ago, you are now the eldest of the remaining Vladimirovichi. There are also the children of Grand Duchess Zenia, the eldest of which is Feodor, or Theodore, as they call it in English. I believe he lives in England but recently went to America because of the bombing."

"He is only forty or so. My age gives me the more direct claim."

Haas ignored the comment. "The only other remaining surviving male close to the tsar was Grand

Duke Dimitri, the son of Nicholas the Second's youngest uncle, Grand Duke Paul." Haas shook his head. "A grand number of dukes, I'm sure you'll agree." He smiled at his play on words. The grand duke did not.

"Is there any point to this lecture concerning my family tree?"

"Certainly."

"Then perhaps you might do me the kindness of getting to it."

"Again, certainly." Haas nodded. "The point is simply this: under the Russian imperial rules of succession and under the old Salic Law, the crown is only passed to males, through males, until there were no males left."

"You continue to tell me things which I already know."

Haas ignored the terse interruption. "When the tsar died and neither a son nor a brother was available, the eldest eligible male from the branch of the family closest to the tsar would succeed. In the case of Tsar Nicholas, this was your elder brother Kyril. Since your brother is now dead, this means that you are next in line to become tsar emperor of all the Russias."

"History," said the grand duke. "And unlikely to be repeated under the present regime in my country."

"Perhaps not."

"What is that supposed to mean?"

"You have spent the larger part of your life playing the wastrel, 'Russia's Greatest Spender.' There are some people who think that you are only playing a part. They think that you would do almost anything at all to regain the throne of imperial Russia."

"Now who is the fool?" the grand duke asked. "I am an old man with few illusions left. Do you really think I have the means necessary for such an end?"

"To regain the throne and title of tsar emperor you would need an enormous amount of money, a great deal of which is being held in a number of foreign banks simply because those banks have chosen to agree to disagree. To claim the money you must have indisputable proof that the tsar and his family are in fact dead."

"Something which it is patently impossible to do."

"I asked you to be truthful," said Haas.

"You accuse me of lying?"

"Of course," said Haas. "Everyone lies. Isn't it a lie when you visit a slut like Bibi at the Panier Fleuris?"

"It is discreet."

"It is wise. You know as well as I do that if your wife discovered your infidelities, not to mention some of your more outlandish 'requirements,' she would divorce you without a second thought. She might do worse. That kind of humiliation might cause her to do violence." The threat was clear.

"Get on with it!"

"In the winter of 1925 you and your wife the Grand Duchess Zinaida traveled to New York. While there you had a brief meeting with a man in your suite at the Ritz Carlton Hotel. The man's name was Alexander Mikhailovitch Levitsky." Haas let it sit for a moment, then spoke again. "He showed you a piece of film."

"Milyj Kristos!" the grand duke whispered.

Chapter 16

Colonel Stewart George Menzies—his last name pro-
nounced Mingus for some perversely British reason lost
in the mists of Scottish Highland time—took a staff car
from his offices at MI6 in Broadway Buildings to Piccadilly and Bond Street, stepping out into the full dark of
the evening. There was a light raid on tonight, a few
dozen bombers toppling what small buildings were still
left standing in the East End after the blitz of last year,
the crumping sound of the explosives like distant, grumbling thunder. Menzies nodded to the pair of top-hatted
porters standing guard at the front door, then went to
the desk and identified himself as a member of Whites
and a guest of Robert Lockhart. He purchased a packet
of Sullivan cigarettes from the clerk behind the desk and
asked if Lockhart was in.

"Yes, Colonel. He's in his rooms. Top of the stairs. . . ."

"I know the way." He dropped a few pence in the
small tin tray at the end of the desk and went up the
gloomy carpeted stairs to the second floor, turning left
and walking to the end of the hall. He knocked on a
door marked 8 and waited. He heard Lockhart's voice
telling him the door was unlocked and Menzies let himself in. The flat was relatively small, but it seemed to
suit Lockhart perfectly, at least when he was in town
and not out standing up to his hips in the Itchen or the
Avon trying to land himself a trout or two. There was

a full bathroom, a small cell-like bedroom and a larger living room looking out over Piccadilly that Lockhart had transformed into an office, complete with half a dozen bookcases, a large desk in front of the window, a smaller table for his typewriter and several institutional-looking file cabinets. The only concession to company or the pleasure of it was a small leather couch and a matching club chair set before a gas fireplace full of cast-iron logs.

Lockhart looked more like a country squire than he did a diplomat, let alone a spy, which of course is what he really was, and if he did look anything like a spy it was one of the old sort, Richard Hannay from *The Thirty-Nine Steps,* searching out secret codes and the kaiser's submarines whilst wearing tweeds, smoking a pipe and fly-fishing in between bouts with his adversaries. The man was in his mid-fifties, square-faced with brownish red hair and a pale complexion. While in Malaya trying to make his fortune in rubber he'd contracted malaria and had been left in perpetual bad health, especially his heart and circulation.

He got up from behind his desk and crossed the room to shake Menzies's hand. The two men, only a few years different in age, couldn't have been more different in bearing. Lockhart was slightly stooped and inevitably looked tired and slightly rumpled. Menzies, even when not wearing his Guards uniform, had the look of a military man, his back straight, his eyes bright and his expression invariably cold and removed.

"Drink?" asked Lockhart.

"Please."

Lockhart went to a small cupboard by the fireplace and removed a pair of glasses and a bottle of fifteen-year-old Highland Dalwhinnie single malt. He put the glasses down beside the club chair and poured two inches into each of them, neat, without soda, water or ice. He handed one glass to Menzies and sat down in the club chair, Menzies opposite him on the couch. Menzies sipped and smacked his lips appreciatively.

"That's extremely good Scotch."

"I've become a bit of an expert over the years."

"That and fishing."

"Without women in my life what else is there?" Lockhart laughed.

"The day there's no women in your life is the day they lower you into the ground, Mr. Lockhart."

"They do make life more interesting."

"And more dangerous."

"Are you putting yourself in the way of telling me something I should hear?" asked Lockhart, his voice drifting home to a faint memory of its original Scots accent.

"It would appear that our Russian friends have taken the bait."

"You have some information concerning the film?"

"Black and the American woman appear to have found something at the Trotsky estate in Mexico City."

"Found what, may I ask?"

"The key Mercador talked about."

"You're sure of this?"

"Not entirely. The Russians set a trap for them. It would appear they were aided by at least one member of the local state police."

"The trap was unsuccessful?"

"Yes. They seem to have escaped. We have no idea where they are at the moment, but they'll turn up eventually."

"Do they have any idea what they're after?"

"Only in general terms, only what we and our American counterparts have told them." Menzies handed over his empty glass and Lockhart filled it again. Menzies lit one of the Sullivans he'd purchased at the desk. He offered the package to Lockhart, who declined with a wave of his hand.

"What about the king?"

"The king?" said Menzies. "For God's sake, man, I haven't even told Churchill about any of this."

"They'll both have to be told," said Lockhart wearily, leaning back against the comforting leather of the heavy chair.

"Not until a number of problems have been worked out. According to our friends at Coutts and at the Bank of England, there is the small matter of three hundred million pounds. Three hundred million pounds that is no longer covered by specie or anything else at either bank. We are speaking of fraud here, Lockhart. Fraud and complicity in the de facto assassination of a head of state, condoned by a head of state. If any of this, and I mean *any* of this, gets out to the public it will make the duke of Windsor's abdication from the throne seem like a garden fete." He paused. "There is another, perhaps more personal question which must be dealt with."

"Yes?"

"Your relationship with Moura Budberg."

Lockhart bristled. "She is a friend."

"You no longer have an intimate relationship with her?"

"I don't see how that is anyone's business but my own."

"It is most definitely my business if she is an active agent for the NKVD."

"That's never been proven."

"The only way to prove it would be by public tribunal," Menzies responded. "A trial. Your name would almost certainly come up. You might even be called as a witness."

"Testifying to what?"

"Testifying to her confession to you that she was in fact in the pay of the NKVD."

"As she was during her relationship with Gorky and also with the esteemed Mr. Wells. She confessed the same thing to them. It is something she does to get sympathy, nothing more."

"It has also been recently suggested that you yourself may well have been recruited by the NKVD."

Lockhart stared wide-eyed at the man across from him. "You say this sipping my single malt, in my rooms?"

"I'm merely saying what is being bruited about by people within my office." Menzies paused again. "You are aware of Wells's accidental meeting with her?"

"No."

"He was entering Russia to interview Stalin. She was

in the process of leaving, even though he'd told her a number of times that if she went back she would be killed."

"Claptrap," said Lockhart.

"I'm afraid not. I checked. Wells was quite right. Miss Budberg, or Countess, if you believe what she says, has applied for and been given free passage into the Soviet Union on a number of occasions over the past fifteen years. She travels in and out of Russia as though it had been fitted with a revolving door."

"Are you really saying that I'm a spy for the NKVD?" Lockhart laughed, his head tilting back. After a few moments the laughter ended and he leaned forward across the small space separating them. "In case you've forgotten, Menzies, after being thrown out of the bloody country I was tried in absentia and convicted of concocting a conspiracy to assassinate Lenin himself. They had a name for it. They called it the Lockhart Plot. I was supposed to have been in league with that lunatic you once employed, Sydney Reilly. What did the press call him? Ace of Spies? After the trial I was sentenced to death."

Menzies let out a long sigh and swallowed the rest of his drink. "The facts are these, Lockhart. You were a British consular agent in Russia in 1917 when you met Moura Budberg, of which you knew nothing other than the fact that she was mistress to Maxim Gorky and that she had confessed to him that she was an agent for the NKVD. Nevertheless you initiated an affair with her. An affair which has continued into the present. There is some small circumstantial evidence that you were in fact recruited as an agent of the NKVD, and most telling of all, Lockhart, you were aware that there was cine film in existence showing the assassination of the entire Romanov family, yet you never said anything about its existence until you discovered our interest in it. You must admit, keeping such a secret does rather raise one's suspicions."

"I simply didn't want to cause embarrassment," Lockhart said gruffly.

"Embarrassment to whom?"

"The crown for one. Your office for another."

"My office?"

"Reilly told me that SIS had been charged with developing a rescue mission for the tsar and his family, but they were too late."

"Sadly, Mr. Reilly, being among the dead, cannot corroborate your story."

"Presumably the PRO could confirm his orders."

"You know as well as I do that any such orders would be under one-hundred-year seal, even if the Foreign Office 'Pickers' haven't gone through them pruning history back to a safe level."

"You're speaking of a distant past," said Lockhart wearily. "A time when things were very different than they are now."

"Adultery, treason, deceit, subterfuge?" Menzies shook his head. "Very little has changed, Lockhart, if anything."

"You're an intelligence officer, Menzies. You deal with those things all the time. In point of fact they are the bread and butter of your business."

"I expect better from those I work with."

"Why? We're all of us human." He laughed. "There's no honor among spies any more than there is honor among thieves; if you believe otherwise you are a fool." Lockhart shook his head again. "And what does it all mean in the great scheme of things?"

"In the great scheme of things, probably nothing," said Menzies. "In the real world it means that two people are now being used as bait and will possibly die because of your libidinous excesses with Miss Budberg, your little Russian tart, not to mention any pillow talk of official secrets she was privy to."

"You are perilously close, Colonel."

"To what?" Menzies snapped. "Offending you? Offending Miss Budberg's so-called honor? A Mata Hari willing to fornicate for her supper?"

"What," said Lockhart angrily, "are you trying to say?"

"I'm not saying, Lockhart, I'm telling. You are on notice as of now that Miss Budberg is under twenty-four-hour surveillance by both our people and by Special Branch. Any contact you have with her, either in person or by telephone, will be duly noted."

"You have a listening watch on her telephone?" said Lockhart, astounded.

Menzies climbed to his feet. "And on yours," he said, and left the room.

Arnie Lindbergh landed the Stinson at sunset on a field just outside the little village of Jaumave and refueled. There were two other planes on the field, both of them crop dusters, and no sign of police. Lindbergh bought some roughly made sandwiches and beer, and then they were on their way again. By midnight they crossed high above the town of Aldamas.

"How far to the border now?" Jane asked.

"Thirty miles. 'Nother twenty minutes." Arnie yawned.

"Think you can stay awake that long?" asked Morris Black. "You've had four bottles of beer by my count."

"I could fly Gertie blind as well as blind drunk," said the flier. "You just make no never mind about that, my Limey friend."

"Anybody likely to stop us?" asked Jane.

"There's a Federale post at Ciudad Camargo—that's about four, five miles from the river."

"The river?" said Black.

"The Rio Grande, my friend. The border."

"Will they know about us?"

"By this time?" said Arnie. "Sure. Not that there's much they can do about it. They're supposed to work with the Border Patrol in Rio Grande City to keep the wets out, but mostly they just take some *mordida* to look the other way."

"Wets?" asked Black.

"Wetbacks. Beaners. Call 'em what you want. Mex farmworkers. Come up here during picking season. More of them over to California."

"No aircraft?"

"Few trucks and a big jail when the Border Patrol kicks 'em back after the picking. Steals what money they can find, then sends them home. More *mordida*."

"Strange system," murmured Black.

Arnie grinned, his face lit by the glow from the instruments. "I believe you folks in England called it droit de seigneur or something. You got the peasants working for peanuts and you got first crack at the best-looking women."

"Touché." Black smiled.

"What happens after we land?" said Jane. "Are we going to have any trouble with the Border Guard?"

"Won't even know we're there," Arnie answered. "We go in dead stick."

"Sounds ominous," said Black.

"In case you hadn't noticed, I've had Gertie climbing ever since we hit Los Aldamas." As if to demonstrate, the pilot pushed in the wheel slightly, leveling them off. "We're at just under ten thousand feet. 'Bout three minutes from now you'll see a few lights down there on the left. That's Comales. From there on I cut the engine and we glide over the border like a big old bat. The airport in Rio Grande City is a good five miles north of town. Closed this time of night. Nobody's going to know we're there except for Postie."

"Postie?"

"As in deaf as one." Arnie grinned. "Ever since he got back from France. He was artillery. Blew both his eardrums standing beside those howitzers all day. Now he runs the taxi service from the airfield into town or anywhere else you want to go. He'll take you to Brownsville."

"Then what do we do?"

"There's a train in the morning. Take you to Dallas. From there you can go anywhere."

"What will you do?"

"Sleep in Gertie for the rest of the night, then head out sometime before dawn."

"Back to Mexico?"

"Yup."

"What about the car we stole?" asked Jane. "It's still parked in your beanfield. They'll have found it by now. The police will know you flew us across the border."

Arnie reached into the side pocket of his door again and withdrew the old .44 caliber revolver. He handed it to Morris Black.

"What am I supposed to do with this?"

"Aim it," said Arnie. He took hold of the barrel of

the gun and brought it up to his temple. "See?" He smiled. "You held a gun to my head and that ain't no lie." He took the gun back from Black, used his knees to keep the wheel steady, then shook out the cylinder, emptying the bullets into his hand. He pushed open his window an inch and tipped the shells out into the dark, roaring wind. They tinkled against the side of the plane, pulled along by the backdraft, and then they were gone. "Emptied out the gun when you left me. Damned humiliating."

"Will they believe you?"

"I'll do a little palm greasing and then suggest that maybe they should see how much they get for the car. They'll forget all about me."

Jane peered out the window next to her. Far below she could see a pale wash of light and what appeared to be a fair-sized lake. "Is that Comales?"

"Yep," said Arnie. "Time to keep our voices down." He twisted the starter to the off position and pushed in the throttles. The engine coughed once or twice, backfired noisily and then fell silent. It was an eerie sensation, gliding through the darkness in silence, and Jane felt an uncomfortable lightness in the pit of her stomach. It was like riding a down elevator with no bottom. A few minutes later she saw the broad silver ribbon of the Rio Grande and then the lights of the town on the U.S. side.

Starr County Airport was just where Arnie said it would be and so was Postie, asleep at the wheel of a two-decades-old open-sided Ford station wagon that looked as though it might have started life as a military ambulance. Postie was a small redheaded man with a perfectly round face, pop eyes and freckles. According to Arnie he could read lips perfectly as long as you were looking straight at him.

"He just looks dumb as a post," said Arnie, "which is the other reason for him being called that."

"What's his real name?" Jane asked.

"Ignatius Loyola Kiddler," Arnie answered. "His daddy used to be a priest according to him."

Morris Black paid Arnie and they said their goodbyes, Jane giving Arnie a hug and a kiss on the cheek for all his help. Then they climbed into the back of the station wagon and Postie drove across the bumpy road that led out to the narrow highway.

"You've been quiet," said Jane as they reached the paved road. In front of them Postie was driving at a steady twenty-five miles per hour, both hands gripping the wheel, looking forward as though his neck was locked in place. It was late, but the night was still warm and Jane felt relaxed for the first time since she'd watched Cesar die.

"I've been thinking." Black lit a cigarette and stared out at the dark, flat landscape.

"A penny for them, then."

"We were set up."

"You said that before."

"We were set up long before we went to Mexico. We were set up right from the beginning. We were sent to Mexico to fail, perhaps even to die. We've been lied to from the start. By our own people."

"You really believe that?"

"Yes."

"Okay, say you're right. What are we going to do about it?"

"We're bloody well going to find out why."

Chapter 17

Saturday, November 29, 1941
Washington, D.C.

After being dropped off at the terminal in Brownsville, Jane Todd and Morris Black took a brand-new Texas, New Mexico, and Oklahoma Coach bus to Dallas, and from there, through a series of exhausting connections, they finally arrived in Chicago with just enough time for Black to place a trunk call to Fleming in Washington before they boarded the 20th Century Limited. For the first time since their headlong flight from Mexico the two finally began to relax, and they spent most of the twenty hours on the train sleeping. In their upper and lower berths. Arriving in New York, they barely paused for a meal before climbing onto yet another train and heading south to the nation's capital.

In Washington Black called Ian Fleming and agreed to meet with him at the Hay-Adams English Tap Room and Grill later in the day. They spent the morning buying new clothes and arrived at the hotel half an hour before the appointed time. They booked a day room, dropped off their purchases, then went to the restaurant. They found a booth in the rear of the grill, ordered something to drink and settled back to wait for Fleming.

"What if it's him?" Jane asked, sucking the froth off the top of her glass of Schlitz. "Fleming, I mean. What if he's the leak?"

"I don't think so," Black answered, shaking his head. He would have given anything for a room-temperature pint of Fuller's, but he contented himself with a small sherry instead.

Jane lit a cigarette. "Why not? Because he's one of your own?"

"No. Because he has nothing to gain. The cloak-and-dagger part of it is his sort of thing. Rather runs in the family, actually. His brother Peter has something to do with Intelligence himself. Far East, I think. He might be telling a few tales out of school to Godfrey at Naval Intelligence, but he's not a Red, I assure you. Drives a Bentley Touring Car and has all his books bound in black leather with gold-stamped titles on the spine and his family crest on the front. Not the sort of behavior that would appeal to Uncle Joe and Comrade Beria down in the dungeons of the Lubyanka."

"Then who?" Not that she expected any real answer; it was a question they'd asked each other a hundred times in the past few days.

"At first I thought the only people it could be is the Russians. On the face of it they're the only ones who stand to gain."

"And now?"

"Now I'm not so sure."

A dark-haired figure appeared out of the gloom, dressed in an expensive-looking suit and smoking a cigarette.

"So tell me about Mexico," said Ian Fleming, sitting down in a seat facing them. A waiter appeared almost instantly and took his order for a martini, and Fleming went to great pains to request that it be shaken and not stirred. Jane smiled to herself. Black was right—the darkly handsome man across from her was far too much of a pompous ass to be one of Joseph Stalin's secret henchmen. She took another sip of her far more plebeian Schlitz and puffed on her cigarette.

"We were set up," said Black.

"So you suggested when you called from Chicago."

"The only people who knew we were there were you, Donovan and Stephenson," said Jane bluntly.

"So you think I'm a suspect?"

"Black doesn't, but I'm not convinced."

"Good for you. Never rule someone out just because you know each other." The waiter arrived with Fleming's martini on a tray. He set it down in front of the Intelligence officer and waited while Fleming took a judicious sip. He nodded and the waiter withdrew. "On the other hand," he continued, "you shouldn't just jump to conclusions. You're forgetting the clerk who managed to get your traveling money, the administrative assistant who cobbled together your airline tickets, any number of other people within COI or British Security Coordination. There's also the very real possibility that your Mr. Hoover may well have had the town house in Georgetown wired for sound." Fleming paused. "Which is precisely the reason I suggested that we meet here."

"Doesn't say much for your ability to keep a secret," Jane snorted. "In fact, it sounds more like you're all spying on each other more than you are the enemy."

"I'm afraid you may well be right." Fleming nodded. He finished his martini, speared the onion with his swizzle stick and looked around for the waiter. Spotting him behind the bar, he gestured for a refill and turned back to Jane. "It does say something for the British Old Boys network, however. Most of our best people went to school together, or know someone who went to school or worked with the candidate in question. You Americans haven't had a decent intelligence organization since the days of Benedict Arnold and your Revolution."

"On the other hand, we did catch him."

"Touché." Fleming smiled. "But you still haven't told me very much about your escapades down south."

"As I said, someone set us up."

"The newspapers said there were two murdered policemen and a young man dead as well. He was referred to as the driver of your getaway car."

"He was just a boy," said Jane. "An innocent bystander. In the wrong place at the wrong time."

"The policemen?"

"Already dead, and for some time by the look of them." She made a sour face. "Long enough for the flies to have found them."

"We were shot at from a reasonably long range," said

Black. "Almost certainly someone using a high-powered rifle. The policemen were killed by a revolver or automatic pistol, not to mention the fact that they were protected by a high wall. The whole story is absurd. A cover-up."

"I'm almost sure it was connected with Mercador," said Jane. "The man they have in prison for Trotsky's assassination. They didn't want us talking to him so they tried to get us out of the picture."

"Then why didn't they just kill this Mercador fellow?" said Fleming.

"He's far too prominent and the Communists have a lot of friends in Mexico," said Jane. "Including their el presidente or whatever they call him."

Fleming's second martini arrived. He lit another cigarette and waited until the waiter had gone before he spoke again. "You're probably right." He nodded. "I asked your FBI friend Foxworth to do some checking for me. According to him a woman traveling as Evangelina Herrera flew into Miami from Havana a week ago, then flew onward to Boston. This was only a few days before our dear Professor Maddox did a flit and we went on our grave-digging expedition. The passport eventually came up as stolen, but by then it was too late. From the description we think it was an NKVD agent named Guadalupe Gomez. She was probably the one who shot at you. According to her file she does her best work with long guns."

"A woman?" asked Jane.

"Equality of the sexes in Stalin's empire, or so they say," Fleming answered. "It makes quite a lot of sense actually; most people would never expect a woman assassin."

"What about Maddox?" Black asked. "Do you have a line on him yet?"

"Odd that you should phrase it that way." Fleming made a small laughing sound, far back in his throat. "A little macabre actually. He was picked up in a net in the middle of the Bay of Fundy by a Canadian halibut fisherman. Bit of luck there, I think."

"Not for Maddox," said Jane.

"Quite." Fleming nodded. "He'd been gutted and most of his face had been chewed off, most likely by a propeller from a boat."

"You're sure it's him?"

"Yes. That's what I meant by luck. He hadn't been in the water long enough for the sharks to get at him, or for his fingerprints to be ruined. It's him."

"Murdered?"

"Without a doubt. He had a great deal of false identification on his person. Supposedly he was a Canadian named Groman. None of it checked out. His address in Ottawa was an empty apartment. Frankly I don't think he was ever meant to be found. He was interrogated and murdered."

"The Bay of Fundy?" Jane asked, frowning.

"That's right."

"The closest American port of any size would be Portland, right?"

"Yes."

"Which isn't too far from Boston."

"Umm."

"You think it was this Gomez woman?"

"We think she was part of it. Donovan has a theory that Maddox running was just an excuse for them to get rid of him before he turned. They were planning it even before you two came on the scene."

"They?" Black asked. "Gomez and who else?"

"Fellow named Vassili Zarubin. Chief of NKVD operations in the United States, sometimes called Squirrel Cheeks behind his back because he has a faintly rodent look about him. Very smart, very methodical. Made his way up the Stalinist ladder by turning in his superiors until there weren't any left."

"He was running Maddox?"

"Almost certainly."

"Anyone else in Donovan's Swiss cheese of an organization?" asked Jane.

"Yes. His sources of information are far too good to have all come from someone like Maddox. In the first place the professor didn't have the access and in the second place he was a homosexual. Zarubin wouldn't have trusted him. Too vulnerable to have played a senior role."

Jane took another sip of her beer and lit a cigarette. She pulled herself up against the back of the leather banquette of the booth and let out a small, frustrated sigh. "Let me see if I've got this straight. Donovan wants us to get hold of the film because he wants to help his pals in England, but his operation has a Commie spy in it who a) either already has the film or b) knows where it is. Stephenson's bunch wants the film because they don't want their man Lockhart exposed, because that would embarrass the king of England, and the Russkies want the film because they don't want to be embarrassed either, which seems a bit silly if you ask me because I don't think anything could embarrass Stalin, and all the Romanovs in exile want the film because that way they could get all the money, which is a billion or so dollars."

"Very succinctly put." Fleming nodded, sipping his martini.

Black pinched the bridge of his nose between thumb and forefinger, wincing slightly, his eyes closing briefly. "All of this on the word of a woman who seems to have rutted her way through half the British and Russian intelligentsia. The word is bollocks. It's been the better part of twenty-five years, Ian. Secrets don't stay secrets for that long. I'm beginning to wonder if the film exists at all. If it did, somebody would have seen it by now."

"Someone has." Fleming shrugged.

"Do tell," said Jane.

"Yes, please do."

"Miss Budberg, of course," said Fleming plainly. "The man who shot the film, Levitsky, showed it to her."

"Her again," said Jane.

Black snorted. "She lied to Maxim Gorky, she lied to Lockhart and she lied to Wells. Who's to say she's not lying about this?"

"That's what we thought the two of you could find out for us."

"How?"

"By talking to her."

"According to Wells she's still in England."

"Mr. Wells is wrong. Miss Budberg, referring to herself as the Countess Moura Zakrevskaia Benckendorff, is presently living in Los Angeles. The Bryson Towers,

I believe. Some sort of posh apartment building." He handed Jane a slip of paper with the address and phone number on it.

"And just how in hell did she get to Los Angeles?" Jane asked.

"Without much difficulty, it would seem. She flew to Dublin and then on to Lisbon via Aer Lingus. From there she took the Pan Am Clipper to New York."

"What lunatic gave her a visa?" Black asked.

"All very much on the up and up. The Yanks had no reason *not* to let her into the country. She's supposedly acting as an advisor on a film they're making in Hollywood based on one of Gorky's works."

Black reached into the pocket of his jacket and removed the key he and Jane had discovered in the manure pile beneath the rabbit hutches at Trotsky's villa. It was about three inches long, flat, with a place on the bow where a number had been stamped but filed off and the letters FNB/V engraved along the side. The Scotland Yard detective pushed it across the table to Fleming, who picked it up and examined it in the dim light.

"The key to a safe-deposit box?"

"Presumably."

"We think the FNB probably means First National Bank, but the V is anyone's guess." Jane shrugged. "First National Bank of Vainom Kug for all we know."

"Vainom Kug?" said Black.

"Place in Arizona. Something to do with ducks, or silver mines. Came across it in a *National Geographic* article a while ago."

Fleming stared at the key in his hand. "You found this in Mexico City?"

"Yes."

"Who else knows about this?"

"Just the three of us," said Jane. "Morris and I think it should stay that way, at least for the time being." She paused and smiled blandly across the table. "That way we can keep track of who's lying to who."

"Whom," Fleming corrected.

"Who's on first," Jane responded. Fleming gave her an odd look. "An old joke." Jane waved a dismissing hand. "The point is, Morris and I know perfectly well that Donovan and Stephenson and probably Foxworth are using us as a lure. We put our heads in a noose so you can follow all the little Commie roaches that come out of the woodwork looking for this piece of film Miss Budberg has been whispering about. You say she's a Russian spy, but she could just as easily be working for you as well. It's not like she's the most faithful woman in the world. Maybe she's collecting a paycheck from Donovan too."

"The ultimate agent provocateur," put in Black. "Working for and against all sides at once."

"There is some corroboration to her story. Miss Budberg informed us that she wasn't the only one to have seen the film."

"Who else?"

"The Grand Duke Boris Vladimirovich Romanov."

"One of the pretenders?" Jane asked. "Like this Anna Anderson woman?"

"No," said Fleming. "*The* pretender. He's officially next in line to become tsar. And to get his hands on all that money."

Black laughed. "Good bloody luck to him!"

"Grand Duke Boris was a great traveler before the outbreak of hostilities. He came to New York in 1925 and was visited by Levitsky in his hotel suite at the Ritz Carlton. While Levitsky was there, the grand duke sent out for a film projector. The connection is clear."

"And circumstantial," Black responded. "They could have been viewing old home movies for all you know."

"Unlikely and you know it, Morris."

"You say this story comes from the Budberg broad?" asked Jane.

"Yes."

"Anybody back her story up?"

"The concierge at the Ritz Carlton at the time and the bellman who brought the projector up to the suite."

There was a brief silence. "How come you think it was this Levitsky mook?" Jane asked.

"Good question," said Black.

"The FBI has a running file on Grand Duke Boris. He was being watched, closely. When Levitsky went to the front desk the person on duty asked for his name so he could be announced. He told the desk clerk his name was Alexander Levitsky. It's in the special agent's notes, and consequently it's in the grand duke's file. They had no idea who Levitsky was at the time." Fleming paused, smiling coolly. "They still don't, as a matter of fact."

"So we talk to Countess Bugaboo, she tells us where to find Levitsky and he hands over the film?" said Jane. "What about the safe-deposit key we found?"

"A print? Who knows?" Fleming shrugged.

"You're making this sound pretty damn easy," Jane said skeptically.

"Budberg will cooperate," said Fleming. "If anything, she's a survivor. She won't be heading back to Russia anytime in the near future, and London's no fun with bombs falling all over the place. Donovan could have her thrown out of the country anytime he wanted and the same goes for Stephenson. Wells and Lockhart would have a fit, I'm sure, but he could have her visitor's visa revoked with a snap of his fingers."

There was another short silence. Black sighed. "We'll need some money."

"Already taken care of." Fleming reached into the inside pocket of his jacket and took out a thick business-sized envelope and handed it across to Black. He in turn handed it to Jane, who dropped it into the new shoulder bag she'd just purchased at Garfinkel's. At the same time she took a small pad out of the bag and a tiny, half-sized ladies' pencil. She scribbled something on the pad, tore off the sheet and folded it, putting the sheet back in the bag.

"Just a note to myself." She smiled. She took a last swallow of her beer. "So now what?"

"Donovan wants to talk to you first thing Monday; then you'll fly out to Los Angeles on an overnight that evening."

"Fine by me." Jane nodded. She smiled at Fleming. "You go buy the tickets, Morris here can find us a hotel room and I'm going back to Garfinkel's to return this bag. I also have to buy a few ladies' unmentionables." She lifted up the exquisite Italian Bojola purse, which Black had characterized as being a suitcase on a strap. He also knew that it had been love at first sight for Jane and the bag. He gave her an odd look, but she cautioned him with a short, almost imperceptible shake of her head.

"Why do you need a hotel room?" Fleming asked.

"You said it yourself: Donovan's place is probably being wiretapped by the FBI, or by Donovan himself." Jane grinned. "Maybe both."

"All right." Fleming nodded. "Dinner?" He looked at the Omega he wore on his wrist. "It's four now. How about drinks at the Mayflower at six thirty? Seventeenth and L. That should give us all plenty of time."

"Fine," said Black. He stood up, and as Jane brushed past him, he felt her right hand go into the pocket of his jacket for a few seconds. She threaded her way between the tables of the grill and then she was gone.

"Seems to be in a bit of a rush, don't you think?" asked Fleming.

"A woman of great decisiveness," Black answered. Not to mention a woman with something on her mind, he thought.

"Bloody suspicious too, if you ask me. All these Yanks seem to be the same."

"Tough, single-minded and stubborn?" Black said. "I can think of worse personality traits for a nation."

Black waited until Fleming was a few steps ahead before he took the folded piece of paper from his pocket— the note Jane had torn from her pad. Keeping the note hidden in his palm, he read it quickly.

Bar at the Willard.
Fourteenth and F
6:00 sharp.

The detective crumpled up the piece of paper and dropped it into a sand-filled pedestal ashtray as they went out through the doorway. There was a large placard on an easel outside the door reminding everyone that there would be a special Thanksgiving party the following evening and free cranberry cocktails served. Reaching the lobby, Black looked around casually and saw that Jane had already vanished.

* * *

Grand Duke Boris Vladimirovich Romanov stood on the curved balcony of his top-floor suite at the Los Angeles Biltmore Hotel, smoking a Lucky Strike cigarette in his ornate silver-and-ivory Fabergé holder and staring down into Pershing Square, ten stories below. The rectangular park was a grotesquerie that even the French could not have come up with, a collection of trees from all around the world, planted together for no good reason, sprinkled with statuary ranging from half a dozen cupids apparently suffering from dropsy to a gaunt and extremely depressing figure of a Great War American doughboy staring balefully down at the pigeon droppings covering him. On his single tour through the park Romanov had seen everything from ragged, jobless and sniveling bums, lonely tourists looking for someone to talk to, and a wild-eyed Bolshevik in a worn black suit babbling almost incoherently about the wrongs of the Forgotten Man and the sins of the Demon Rich. The grand duke quickly fled back to the creature comforts of his suite at the Biltmore—which, oddly enough, was being paid for in full by Admiral Wilhelm Canaris and the Nazi Abwehr.

It was all surreal. Emil Haas had made his requirements and his threats equally clear. The German spy was already aware that the grand duke's cousin, Feodor Mikhailovich, was in the market for the Yekaterinburg film, and he, the grand duke, was to use any means possible to convince the younger man to purchase the film on the Third Reich's behalf. Should he not be able to convince the young Prince Feodor, he and his family would be summarily imprisoned in one of the new concentration camps being built in Poland. According to their information, the film was either in the possession of onetime NKVD agent Moura Budberg or she knew where it was and was willing to auction off the information. The grand duke had not really ever had a choice in the matter and he agreed on the spot.

From that point things moved quickly. The grand duke was put on a military flight to Berlin, transferred to a Lufthansa diplomatic flight to Lisbon, and then transferred again to a Pan American Airways Clipper flight to Bermuda and onward to New York. From there

he'd taken a series of miserable and exhausting flights
to Los Angeles, where he was to meet his young cousin,
Prince Feodor. In all the trip had taken five grueling
days and the grand duke's mood was foul. To deal with
one of the Grand Duchess Zenia's Mikhailovich off-
spring was bad enough, but to do it at the behest of the
Nazis was almost unbearable. He'd been many things in
life, but never a friend to those inhuman savages.

He heard a faint tapping at the door to the suite and
went back inside. He crossed the plush sitting room and
went down the short hall to the door. Opening it he
found himself facing a man in his early forties with thinning hair and a rather dull expression on his face. He
was wearing an expensive-looking suit, and when he shot
his cuffs the grand duke could see that his shirt was
monogrammed with his initials in gold and the Romanov
crest in black, red and yellow. To the grand duke's experienced eye the fabric of the shirt was a very high quality
cream-colored silk.

"Feodor," said Boris Vladimirovich.

"Prince Feodor Mikhailovich Romanov, sir."

"As I said," the grand duke responded, "cousin
Feodor." He opened the door wide and stepped aside,
gesturing for the younger man to enter. He then closed
the door, stepped around his cousin and led him back
to the sitting room. Warm air was blowing in from the
open doors out to the balcony. The grand duke pointed
to a green velvet-covered club chair. "Something to
drink, Feodor?"

"No, thank you," said the exquisitely dressed man
with thinning hair. He sat down, looking uncomfortable,
as though the green of the chair might be clashing with
the pale cream of his shirt. Which it was. The grand
duke went to the bar on the far side of the room and
poured himself a large Scotch, neat. He took a swallow,
then turned back to his cousin.

"Feodor . . ."

"Before you begin, let me make one thing clear," said
the young Mikhailovich. "I am here only because my
mother, the grand duchess, asked me to come. I have much
more pressing affairs to attend to, I can assure you."

"I know all about your relationship with that Polish

buffoon in Connecticut, what's his name? Vonsiatskoy, Vonsiatsky?"

"He is not Polish. He is Russian like you and me, and he is a count."

"He is married to a woman who inherited a pig farm, I believe."

"She is as committed to the cause as the count."

"That cause would be the All-Russian Fascist Party, I presume?" said the grand duke. He had been fully briefed on the subject by Haas.

"Yes," Feodor snapped, clearly irritated. "He will raise an army in our homeland and I will be restored to my rightful place as tsar." He started to rise from the chair but a word from the grand duke sat him down again.

"You're going off to buy the Yekaterinburg film, I suppose."

"What?" The word was almost stuttered.

"A countess this time. Who is really an NKVD agent named Moura Budberg."

"What are you talking about?"

"The reason for your presence here in Los Angeles and the reason I've come all the way from Paris by a very roundabout route to speak with you."

"You're not making sense. The countess is a patriot, as I am."

"Of course, of course. You're going to try and purchase the film with the help of your count and his pigheiress wife. You and Vonsiatsky and the other bidders are supposed to meet her in Honolulu. The two of you are leaving on the Matson Line SS *Monterey* tomorrow evening."

"How do you know all this?" Feodor whispered.

"Because, you little idiot, I have been told all this!"

"Who by?"

"The Abwehr in Berlin. They wish you to use Vonsiatsky's money, and even some of theirs if necessary, to purchase the film for them."

"And why would I do that?" Feodor asked. "And why are you doing this for them?"

"They have put me under threat. And my family."

Feodor shrugged and shot his cuffs again, his thin chest puffing out. "That is no concern of mine."

The grand duke sighed. He thought about Haas and the Nazis and Admiral Canaris and wondered whether they really were an unstoppable force destined to rule the world. At the moment it seemed likely. What was that old quotation? "All evil needs to triumph is that good men do nothing." Something like that.

"Feodor, it's not as simple as that."

"Clean up your own mess, cousin. Not that I would have expected anything less from a Vladimirovich."

"Stupid and rude. Much like the rest of your family," said the grand duke. Before Feodor could speak out the grand duke continued. "You have six brothers and sisters as I recall."

"Yes."

"Living in England?"

"Some of them are here. The younger ones are with my mother."

"Do you think the führer is going to invade England?"

"Eventually, of course. Hitler is many things but he is not a fool. England must fall."

"And when it does?"

"What do you mean?"

"Have you ever heard of the Black Book?" asked the grand duke. He barely paused. "No, I can see that you have not." He took out a cigarette and screwed it carefully into the end of his holder, then lit it with a large silver Ronson that sat on the bar. "The Black Book was developed by the SS and the Gestapo. It lists everyone in England who might be a real or political threat. Those people are to be arrested as soon as England has been conquered. Some will be sent to camps, some will be put under surveillance, some will be tortured for information and some will simply be murdered out of hand. Your mother is listed and so are your brothers and sisters. They are listed among those who will be killed."

"You're lying," said Feodor. "There is no such book."

The grand duke pulled open a drawer below the bar and took out a Bible-sized volume bound in black imitation leather. There was a gold swastika stamped into the cover. The book was almost two inches thick, the pages a pale blue color. He tossed the book to Feodor, where it landed in the man's lap.

"Look under R, for Romanov," said the grand duke. "And then listen carefully to what I have to tell you."

Chapter 18

After leaving the two men in the grill, Jane slipped off to the day room they'd taken and quickly packed the two newly purchased Streamlite overnight cases with their new clothes and toiletries. Ten minutes and a twenty-cent cab ride later she was at Union Station, and a few minutes after that she was at the Pennsy counter buying two tickets on the seven o'clock Trail Blazer to Chicago. She dropped off the suitcases at the baggage office, then caught another cab, this time to the National Press Building at Fourteenth and F Streets, directly across from the Willard Hotel. She took an elevator up to the ninth floor and the private office of her old friend and colleague John Franklin Carter.

Carter, in his mid-forties, wrote a syndicated column called "We the People" and had once been a speech-writer for Vice President Henry Wallace, then secretary of agriculture. Before that he had been a practicing jour-nalist for *Liberty, Time,* and most prominently the *New York Times,* which was where Jane had met him back in the early thirties.

Carter, one of seven children born to an Episcopalian minister from Fall River, Massachusetts, was a Yalie and had gone to school with the likes of Steven Vincent Benét, Thornton Wilder, Archibald MacLeish and Henry Luce, but he never pretended to any kind of superiority, intellectual or otherwise, and was just as happy shooting pool with Jane and her friends from the *Daily News* and the other city rags as he was hobnobbing at the Rainbow Room with poets who wrote for the *New Yorker*.

Stepping into the large office, Jane found the man behind his desk machine-gunning away at a decrepit old Royal, one of the few journalists she knew who touch-typed like a secretary. He had an ancient, fuming Kay-woodie clamped between his horsey teeth and still looked like everyone's idea of a small-town librarian: thinning dark hair behind thick glasses in plain, tortoise-shell frames and a large, kipper-style bow tie in bright red against a plain white shirt and striped suspenders. A pinstripe suit jacket was draped over the back of his high-back leather chair and an idiotic Tyrolean hat complete with feathered plume sat on the desk. The hat was a decade out of style, but Carter insisted that it had been given to him by the prince of Wales, now the duke of Windsor.

He looked up as Jane came into the room, popped the pipe out of his mouth and grinned, pushing himself away from the typewriter. Jane glanced around the big windowless room. The walls were covered in framed photographs of Carter with celebrities and pundits ranging from Gandhi to Gurdjieff and Hemingway with a tarpon to J. Edgar Hoover with a tommy gun. There was even one that Jane had taken herself of a broadly smiling Carter with his arm around Gloria Swanson's waist while Sherman Billingsley, the owner of the Stork Club, stood on the other side with his arm around the actress's shoulder.

"Still got your trophy wall, I see," said Jane. She dropped down into a red leather chair in front of his desk and lit a cigarette, dropping the spent match into the freestanding ashtray beside her. The ashtray was filled with quartz sand that looked as though it hadn't been cleaned in years. The container itself was made from the dull bronze casing of a howitzer shell from the Great War.

Carter relit his pipe and stared at her across the desk, eyes blinking slowly behind the thick lenses of his eye-glasses. "I don't see any scars," he said after a moment.

"Scars from what?"

"From that little accident you had a year or so ago."

"You heard about that?"

"I tend to hear about my friends having their dark-rooms blown up by pipe bombs," he answered.

"Hardly page-one stuff."

"I hear about everything," said Carter, leaning back in the chair. "That's my job."

"I never thought about you as a gossip columnist." Jane laughed. She leaned over in her chair and examined the photograph on the wall closest to her. It was an austere photograph of the present pope, Pius XII, hands clasped in pontifical seriousness, big hooked nose pointing at the prayer book in front of him on a reading stand. The inscription in ink on the portrait read: *To Jay Carter, a Good Friend of the Church and a Good Friend of Mine, Eugenio Maria Giuseppe Giovanni Pacelli/Pius XII.* The lower third of the photograph, which included the papal signature, was embossed with a Vatican seal just in case no one believed the signature.

"I bet Louella doesn't have one of those," she said.

"Louella Parsons is a vindictive power-hungry impossibly vain fat bitch," said Carter.

"Well, isn't it a good thing you're not opinionated or anything?" Jane said.

There was a short silence and Jane watched as the smile on Carter's face stiffened slightly. Playing pool a few years back was one thing, but here he sat a syndicated columnist whose time was valuable. Maybe too much power did that to you, just like it had to Louella Parsons, now universally hated from one end of Los Angeles to the other, a dark presence hanging over Hollywood like the black cloud hanging over that sad-looking character in the *Li'l Abner* strip.

"Are you here to reminisce?" he asked finally, his tone flat. "Or do you have something specific in mind?" The columnist tapped his pipe out in the sawn-off bottom of a shell casing of a smaller caliber than the ashtray Jane was using.

"What if I was here to give you a story. A big story?"

"Are you?"

"Maybe."

"Depends on the quid pro quo, I suppose."

"Something like that," said Jane.

"I'd have to know a little bit about the quid before we got to the pro quo."

"Hypothetically, what if I told you I found the key to a safe-deposit box under a pile of rabbit droppings in Leon Trotsky's garden?"

"I'd say the pipe bomb did more damage than you thought."

"I'm serious."

"But hypothetical."

"For now." Jane nodded.

"What's in the box the key opens?"

"Hypothetically it might be a reel of film that shows the entire Romanov family, including the tsar, being assassinated."

"Interesting, but not earthshaking." Carter reached into the right pocket of the jacket hanging over his chair and pulled out a leather tobacco pouch. A faint apple-and-rum odor wafted into the room. He began pressing wads of damp-looking tobacco into the bowl of the Kay-woodie. Interesting but not earthshaking, he'd said, but she'd seen something in his eyes that said it meant something more to the man across the desk from her. She stubbed her Camel out into the sand of the howitzer shell.

"What if I told you a senior British diplomat at the time was somehow involved, on behalf of the king?"

"Bruce Lockhart?"

Jane was surprised. "How did you know?"

"Read a little bit of history sometime, kiddo. The Lockhart Plot is famous."

"The Lockhart Plot was supposedly a conspiracy to assassinate Lenin."

"It was anything the Reds wanted it to be, including some kind of plot between the tsar and the king of England to band their resources and friends together and 'wipe out all the Jew conspirators,' Lenin, Trotsky, Zinoviev and all the others."

"So the film's a myth?"

"Promulgated by that idiotic Budberg woman. She tried to peddle the same story to me a week after she got off the boat in New York. She even tried Winchell and he usually bites at anything, but not this."

"You know about *her* as well?"

"Everybody does, at least in this town. She pretends she's a Russian spy so she'll be invited to parties. She's eaten out at tables halfway round the world on those old stories. Trouble is, she can never prove any of them. It's all just gossip and innuendo, and no matter what some people might think, I'm *not* a gossip columnist."

"Donovan thinks she's got something."

"Wild Bill?" Carter laughed. "You're not working for him now, are you?" He paused. "You don't seem his type somehow—no Ivy League degree, for starters."

"Let's just say I fell into the job."

"Like the thing with the pipe bomb."

"Something like that." She watched as the journalist took a match out of a small pewter holder on his desk. "It seemed like a good idea at the time."

Carter put the fresh match to his pipe, blew out a huge cloud of smoke and settled back in his chair. "Let me tell you something about Washington, kiddo. This place is full of spies—Wild Bill's just the newest one on the block. We've got Free French spying on the Vichy French, usually in restaurants. We've got Germans sniffing around Baltimore Harbor. We've got the Russians snooping everywhere. We've got the Brits with their silly Passport Control Office as a cover for the other Bill and his bunch, and then we have our own people spying on each other."

"I think I'm being used as bait," Jane said flatly. "I've already been shot at. I'm in way over my head, but I don't know if I can get out."

"We're back to pipe bombs?"

"Something like that."

"You'd better tell me about it." Carter sighed. He reached into his jacket and pulled out a Parker Vacumatic and took a pad and a bottle of Waterman's blue-black out of his desk drawer. He sucked up enough ink to fill the pen and they began.

An hour later, Carter had it all. Jane finished up by repeating Black's theory about the money.

The columnist nodded. He'd written half a dozen pages of small, neat script, but now he stopped and put the top back on his pen, putting it gently down on top of the pad. "He's probably right." Carter pursed his lips and used one hand to adjust his large, floppy bow tie. "I once even heard a rumor about a shipload of Russian bullion that came into Canada on the West Coast. Seventeen tons, I think, all of it hidden in ammunition boxes. It was supposed to go by train to the Bank of Canada in Ottawa, which is the equivalent of the Bullion Depository at Fort Knox. Except the Canadians say it never got there. It's like Moura Budberg, your Russian countess. It's all rumor and gossip. Wisps of fog you can never quite get your hands on."

"That person in Mexico wasn't firing wisps of fog, Jay."

"Trotsky's been dead less than a year. It's still a volatile situation. I think you may just have been in the wrong place at the wrong time and got caught in someone else's cross fire."

"Maybe," said Jane. She checked her watch: five thirty. She stood up, using one hand to wave away the cloud of mixed pipe and tobacco smoke that had clouded the room over the past hour or so. "Or maybe there's something to all of this."

"I still don't quite know what you want me to do about it." Carter shrugged his narrow shoulders.

"You've got connections, high and low. There's a big fat leak in Donovan's bunch and I want to know who it is. I'd also like to know what happened to Trotsky's bodyguard, Harte. He wasn't in that grave in Brooklyn, so where the hell is he?"

"I'll see what I can find out," said Carter. "But I'm not making any promises."

"I don't want promises, just a few answers," Jane responded. "And I wanted someone I trust to have all the details, just in case . . ." She left it dangling.

"I understand," said Carter. He stood up behind his desk. "Just be careful, Jane."

"I will," she answered. "Thanks for letting me bend your ear."

"No problem," he said. "Keep in touch."

Jane gave him a smile, turned on her heel and left the office. Carter waited for a moment, then sat down in his chair again. Instead of getting back to the typewriter, he picked up his telephone and dialed a number he knew by heart. It was answered on the second ring, the voice calm and slightly nasal.

"White House switchboard. Who, may I ask, is calling and how may I direct your call?"

Chapter 19

A light snow was falling, and the clock on the twelve-story tower of Chicago's Dearborn Station on Polk Street read exactly seven p.m. as the Atcheson, Topeka and Santa Fe's crack passenger express, the Super Chief, left the pink granite terminal and began to move west on its thirty-nine-and-a-half-hour journey to Los Angeles. Most of the passengers barely noticed the gentle tug as the train began to move, thumping through the complex throat of the station's approach tracks and then coming out into the cool air of the early evening.

The train was made up of two engine units painted in the Santa Fe's traditional scarlet and yellow livery. There were no coaches, only Pullman sleeping cars, their interiors finished luxuriously and equipped with every modern amenity. Each streamliner car had a name, inscribed on panels on either side of the car as well as on the broad metal bars across each door leading to the next car in the train. Using Fleming's money, Jane had thrown caution to the winds and booked herself and Black into double bedroom D in Oraibi—which contained six double bedrooms, two compartments and two drawing rooms—roughly in the middle of the train and only one car away from the diner.

While Jane used a tube of Ipana and the brand-new Dr. West Miracle Tuft she'd bought at the Fred Harvey newsstand in the station, Black pulled his armchair close to the window and watched as the Super Chief crossed the X's of the huge switching yard beyond Dearborn Station, heading southwest. As they rumbled over the train bridge that crossed the foul-smelling Illinois and Michigan Canal in the industrial wasteland around Thirty-first Street, Black saw a dozen slipways running off the main canal, scores of barges piled high with lumber moored neatly, waiting for their inland cargoes to be offloaded and taken to the harbor.

Jane came out of the tiny bathroom, the tip of her tongue testing her freshly brushed teeth. She stopped when she saw Black, his nose virtually pressed up against the glass of the window as he peered out into the gathering darkness. "You look like a little kid."

"I always dreamed of this," the detective answered without taking his eyes off the passing scenery. "Riding a transcontinental train into the American Wild West and beyond. I used to read books about it. Wild Bill Hickok, Jesse James, Buffalo Bill Cody. Sitting Bull and Geronimo."

"Cross the mighty Mississippi and all of a sudden there's a bunch of Indians whooping it up, wearing warbonnets and paint, shooting arrows at the train."

"And every horse a pinto," said Black, smiling up at her. "The first cinema I ever went to was showing *Riders of the Purple Sage*."

"You had it bad," Jane said. "Getting back to the present, Sheriff, look across the corridor and you'll see the Chicago Sewage Canal running along on the other side of us." She laughed. "Good thing this train's got air-conditioning."

"You're putting a blight on a child's fantasy."

"I was never very good with kids," she drawled.

Black sat back in his chair and regarded her seriously. "I would have thought you'd be rather good with children."

"Too late."

"Not possible."

"It is for this old horse," said Jane.

Something in her expression stopped Black from continuing the conversation. "I'm sorry," he said. "I didn't mean to intrude on your personal life."

"No apology necessary." She stepped over to the

other armchair, sat down and lit a cigarette. "My old man worked for the railroad. Nothing as exotic at this—he was a switcher in the Brooklyn Yards. He died in the war, 1917. Gassed at Passchendaele. My mother died a year later during the influenza epidemic."

"You were orphaned."

"I was eighteen and I had a feeble sister, Annie, to take care of. I went to work for New York Central as a telegraphist. It didn't last more than a year or two. I had to put Annie in a hospital. I worked as a copy girl at a newspaper for a while and then I saved up enough for a Speed Graphic and went to work as a press photographer."

"We've established that you're not married, but you must have had offers."

"God no! All I do with men is make mistakes." She laughed, then stopped abruptly, suddenly remembering that Black had been recently widowed. "I never really had the time. Always too busy," she added quickly. She took a drag on her cigarette, watching as the little fan fitted into one corner of the small room sucked up the smoke, pulling it back through a small ventilator grille.

"I wonder where we are now," Black murmured, turning his attention back to the window. It was getting darker by the minute and more difficult to see anything but the sweep and blur of lights.

"Glenn," said Jane, "according to the little sign we passed. Some kind of switchyard with all the tracks. That must be Midway in the distance, with all those lights."

"Midway?"

"Busiest airport in the world," said Jane, "or so they say."

Half a mile away Black could see the lines of colored runway lights and then the blinking navigation lights of aircraft taking off and landing. There seemed to be dozens of planes, all in motion at once. "It's a wonder they don't run into each other all the time," he said.

"I don't really trust them," said Jane. "Take a train and have an accident at least you've got a chance of surviving. Same with a boat. There's lifeboats and life jackets and at least I can swim. No way can I flap my arms and fly."

"I'm afraid I tend to agree." Black nodded. "Is that why you got us tickets on the train?"

"I got us tickets on the Super Chief because I don't trust Fleming or any of the other dumb bunnies I've met on this little expedition. He won't even miss us really until sometime tomorrow and by then it'll be way too late."

"You don't think he'll figure it out?"

"There's half a dozen different airlines we could take and three or four ways of getting to L.A. by train. He'll have the stations there covered, but I can get around him on that. Los Angeles is my turf, or at least it was until a week or so ago. I don't think they have the manpower to cover everything."

"Even Mr. Hoover's people?"

"Mr. Hoover's people couldn't find their willies with a flashlight."

"I'll take your word for it," Black said, flushing slightly. They were on the outskirts of the city now, picking up more and more speed. The diesel engine's triple horns blasted out a long, moaning warning note as they approached each level crossing.

They sat silently for a long moment, staring out the window rather than at each other. Jane stubbed out her cigarette and thought about lighting another, realizing that it would make her look both unladylike and nervous. She *was* nervous and right this second the last thing she wanted to feel was unladylike. Mind you, she thought, it was probably unladylike for her to be thinking the thoughts she was thinking, let alone feeling the physical sensations she was feeling—a soft liquid feeling somewhere down low as though her legs would turn to water if she tried to stand up, and that familiar tingling sensation directly under her stomach.

She wondered if Morris was thinking the same sort of things; he had that glazed look guys got when they were thinking rude thoughts, but he was a Brit and they were about as poker-faced as the Chinese. On the other hand, they said that people on the lam usually got hot for each other. To hell with it. She knew perfectly well she should stop thinking about it unless she was going to do something about it. One thing she was sure of was that Morris wasn't going to make a pass at her.

"Anyone ever call you Moe? Or Morrie?" she blurted out lamely. So much for her intestinal fortitude.

"No. Never," he said, turning away from the window. "Either Morris, or just Black."

"Which do you like better?"

"It depends on who's saying it." He was actually smiling now. She was making progress.

"Me."

"Well, we are partners in crime so I suppose that makes us closer than most," Black said. Jane smiled back. Definite progress. *Partners in crime.* "I suppose I could let you call me by the nickname I had when I was in school."

"Which was?"

"Conker."

"Conker?"

"A conker is a dried-out chestnut. You drill a hole in it and pass a string through, then knot the end. You go around challenging other boys to play conkers. You whirl your conker around, and he whirls his around, and you try to hit the other boy's conker with yours. If his shatters, you win; if yours shatters, he wins. Every boy in England has a conker at the right time of the year." His voice sounded very nervous and he was blushing furiously, as though he was trying to avoid a single second of silence in the compartment.

"So how come you got the nickname if they were so common?"

"I was playing once and by accident hit myself on the head with my own conker. Knocked myself unconscious. I was ten years old at the time. The name stuck until I was twenty. When I was eighteen I thought I was going to be Conker Black for the rest of my life."

Jane tried to imagine whispering Conker in the dark and just couldn't picture it. She tried not to laugh but a giggle slipped out. Black's blush darkened.

There was a sudden rapping on the door and Jane almost leapt out of her shoes. She stood up and opened the door. It was a porter, dressed in a white jacket.

He stepped into the compartment. "My name's Eli.

I'm the night porter for this car. Thought I might come in and put down the beds if you've a mind to turning in a little early." He glanced at Black and smiled. "How many beds you want made up, by the way?"

"Two," said Black quickly. Now it was Jane's turn to blush.

"Two it is then," said Eli.

"But not right now. I mean . . ." The sentence dangled.

"Just let me know when you want it," said Eli pleasantly. "Super Chief aims to please." He tipped his hat and stepped back out of the room. Black stood up, moving awkwardly with the sway of the train.

"Look, I didn't mean to . . ."

The car lurched as they went across a switch and Black was thrown forward, almost knocking Jane over. She put her hands up onto his chest to stop his fall. The touch lingered. Black pulled back as though he'd been burned. Jane reached out and took his hand. It was warm and dry, his fingers long and powerful, like a pianist's.

"Come on," she said. "Time for us to get something to eat." She grinned. "Maybe they'll have a turkey dinner for Thanksgiving."

Chapter 20

Emil Haas sat alone at one of the two-seat tables at the head end of the Cochita dining car, his back against one of the ornately engraved glass partitions as he perused the extensive menu. The Americans really were extraordinary. Their British allies were living on turnips and tea, the French were being shipped off to work camps all over the Reich, and here they were serving Boneless Rocky Mountain Trout (10 oz.), *sauté meunière* chicken pies, calves liver, top sirloin *au jus*, shrimp cocktails, half a dozen different kinds of wine and desserts that included everything from freshly baked peach pie to strawberry shortcake. They even had a four-course Thanksgiving dinner with pumpkin pie for the holiday. If Hitler went even more insane than he already was and declared war on these people, they'd throw up barricades of lamb chops and New Potatoes *persillade* to fight behind.

The German eventually chose the twelve-ounce broiled sirloin steak with french fried onion rings and the Louisiana-style tossed salad with shrimp, all of it washed down with a half bottle of burgundy, followed by lemon sherbet and freshly brewed coffee. As instructed he wrote down his order on the guest check, which was promptly picked up by a black porter whose name was Ira. The porter brought over a chilled glass of tomato juice and dinner rolls and butter to satisfy any peckishness he might be feeling. Haas broke open one of the still warm, yeasty rolls, buttered it and sat back in his chair.

His recent arrival in America had been relatively easy to accomplish. First he flew from Berlin to Occupied France via military transport. Since Spain was supposedly a neutral country, as was Portugal, Haas then flew on to Barajas Airport just outside Madrid in what appeared to be a Cruz Roja Espanolas, or Spanish Red Cross, aircraft but which was actually a Luftwaffe courier plane painted in the appropriate livery. From there it was a simple task to fly from Madrid to Lisbon in a German-made JU52 transport left over from the Spanish Civil War that was now operated by the state-owned Lineas Aeras Espanolas. From Lisbon he took the regular Pan American Clipper to Bermuda and then on to New York.

The German's shrimp salad arrived, as did the bottle of burgundy, which turned out to be a very pleasant 1938 Bouchard Pommard. Ira poured a glass for him without any of that absurd French pomp and let him be. Haas took a judicious sip of the wine, then began to eat his salad.

When he'd arrived in Washington, Haas had discovered that the German embassy was a pigeon-stained redbrick nineteenth-century horror on Massachusetts Avenue, complete with stubby parapets like a dwarf Rhine castle and endless amounts of rusting cast-iron ornamental railings, with red, black and white Nazi flags flapping wherever there was a place to put them. The place was a horror, and so were the people inside it.

At least it had been easy enough to track down his quarry. He was told almost instantly about the two newly minted OSS agents on the run and presumably returning to Washington. Tailing them from the train station had been a simple task to accomplish, and almost immediately they'd met with Fleming, Admiral Godfrey's liaison from British Naval Intelligence. Acting purely on instinct, he'd followed the woman after their brief luncheon at the Hay-Adams, first to the Pennsylvania Railway ticket counter, where she'd purchased two tickets to Chicago and inquired about the Santa Fe Super Chief schedule. She'd gone to the National Press Building, then come across the street to the Willard, where she met with her companion, the man Canaris's analysts in Oster's Research division, IHWest/Abteilung Z at the Tirpitz Ufer, had identified as Detective Inspector Morris Black, previously of Scotland Yard and presently working in one of the espionage schools of the Special Operations Executive in the south of England. According to the research people it was this same man, in conjunction with operatives from MI5, who had exposed the agent known as the Doctor in London less than a year ago.

Not wanting to take any chances, Haas decided to get one step ahead of what was clearly a very dangerous and intelligent man and flew to Chicago on the last Eastern Airlines flight out. He'd purchased a roomette ticket on the Super Chief and waited in Dearborn Station until he saw his quarry arrive and board the train before boarding himself. According to his information, Black and the woman had almost certainly found something of interest at the Trotsky villa in Mexico City that was now leading them west to Los Angeles.

The dining car steward brought Haas his steak, poured him another glass of wine and then withdrew, moving through the crowded dining car with a graceful sway that matched the lurching movement of the train exactly. Using the steak knife Ira had provided, the German spy carved out a minuscule bite, stabbed a small onion ring and popped the combination into his mouth. He glanced out the darkened window as the train roared through the little village of Kinsman, the name board on the tiny station an unreadable blur. He was staring at his half-seen reflection in the night glass and pondering the fact that he had less than forty hours to find out what it was that Black and the woman had discovered and then dispose of them when the couple appeared at the corridor end of the dining car and handed the chief steward their reservation card. The pair looked either nervous or guilty. Perhaps both.

Keeping one eye on them, Haas continued to eat. Three or four minutes later an elderly couple occupying two of the four seats at the table directly across from him paid their bill, stood up and left the dining car, banging into tables and once into Ira as they stumbled toward the opposite end of the car. A few seconds later Ira stepped up as gracefully as a dancer, used a small stainless-steel device like a miniature carpet sweeper to clean up the old people's crumbs, and had the white linen tablecloth cleaned and relaid with cutlery and crystal in under a minute. Ira stepped out of the way, and the chief steward, two menus under his arm, led the Scotland Yard detective and his female companion to their places at the table.

Haas checked the lovely Tutima Fleiger wristwatch with alligator strap he'd been given on his last birthday. From the time he sat down to the arrival of his steak had been eleven minutes. He could probably count on that much time if not a little more—say, fifteen or twenty minutes from arrival to completion of their meal at the very least. This was the last call, and the stewards wouldn't mind if their patrons lingered over drinks or coffee at the end of the meal.

He took two five-dollar bills from his wallet, dropped them on the table and made his way out of the dining car. The chief steward's back shielded him from Detective Black's view as he slid past. Reaching the small, waist-high counter the chief steward usually stood behind, Haas quickly checked the top reservation card. The car number was 305 and the room assignment was bedroom D.

The bedroom on a Budd Streamliner was six and a half feet wide by eight feet across. Included in this space were two fold-down beds, two collapsible armchairs for use during the day and a small toilet cubicle. The sink and potable water supply were built into one side of the toilet cubicle on the outside, and the stainless-steel sink folded neatly down out of its recess to reveal the hot and cold water taps as well as the drinking water spigot. The narrow steel door to the outer corridor could be locked from the inside by sliding in a recessed bolt, but the door could not be locked from the outside. This meant that when the occupants were visiting the dining car or the observation-lounge car, their bedroom was left open. When the door was opened from the outside, it opened into the compartment rather than outward into the corridor.

Reaching the door of bedroom D, Emil Haas looked up and down the corridor to make sure he was not being observed. Although he knew that both Black and the woman were in the dining room, he took no chances. Reaching into his jacket pocket, he took out a brass, steel and Bakelite folding knife he'd purchased in a pawnshop on Canal Street in Manhattan.

He had the little .25 caliber Mauser in his suitcase, but on the off chance he was ever stopped in the street, he didn't want to be found with a pistol in his possession. The folding knife had a four-inch stainless-steel blade that Haas had sharpened to a razor edge. The toffee-colored Bakelite body of the instrument had a photo-etched depiction of the Trylon and Perisphere with the words NEW YORK WORLD'S FAIR down the side. Nothing more than an innocuous souvenir from the festivities in 1939. The German agent took a deep breath, used his thumb to pop open the blade, ensuring that it was locked, then pushed down on the door handle. It opened and he pushed it rapidly inward.

The swinging movement of the door caught the two men already in the bedroom completely by surprise. The taller, blond man was trying to jimmy the lock on an imitation leather suitcase while his partner, six inches shorter with a bulbous red nose, was doing the same with a smaller bag of the same type. The taller man spotted Haas, eyes widening. He dug under his jacket, scrabbling for the large automatic he kept holstered at his armpit. Barely pausing, Haas stepped fully into the room, swinging the door shut behind him and lunging forward over the short man's back, sliding the blade of the knife deep into the back of the taller man's neck. He withdrew the knife, used his free hand to pull back the shorter man's head by the fuller hair in the center of his scalp, then swung the innocuous little weapon up, planting the blade into the exact center of the man's eye, popping it like a ripe grape as the point slipped in through the right orbit of the man's skull and sliced two and a half inches into his brain. The two men were dead in less time than it would have taken to say their names. Both dropped awkwardly to the thinly carpeted floor. Haas wiped the blade of the knife on the back of the shorter man's suit jacket. He noted, approvingly, that there was very little blood. Haas folded the knife closed and slipped it back into his pocket.

He began going through the men's clothing. According to his wallet, the taller of the two men was named Trevor K. Harding and he was an investigator for something called the State Department Investigation Bureau, which Haas had never heard of. He carried a .45 caliber Colt Automatic pistol in a left-handed shoulder holster, indicating that he shot right-handed. He wore a Lord Elgin watch with a solid gold rectangular case on his left wrist and a small ring on the third finger of his right hand with a small enameled shield and the Latin word *Ver-It-As*. A Harvard Law School ring. The second, shorter man had the same sort of identification, but in the name of Conrad Bonafontini. He carried a Smith & Wesson Model 10 in a slip holster tucked into the back of his belt and hidden by his suit jacket. Bonafontini also wore a Harvard Law ring, although neither man quite looked the type. Not that it mattered. Trevor and Conrad had revealed themselves as players in the game when they stepped into bedroom D and had suffered for it. They were almost certainly looking for the same thing as Emil Haas: the Romanov film.

Without wasting any time, the Abwehr agent used his folding knife to cut open the two small suitcases, satisfying himself that neither contained the elusive film. The beds still hadn't been let down, and there were few places anything could be hidden except for the narrow locker on the left of the door and the shoe compartment above it. Both were empty. There was nothing in the narrow toilet cubicle. He checked his watch: He'd been in the bedroom for six minutes, and he knew nothing more than when he'd entered. He had changed the playing field, however. Black and the woman would be confronted by the two bodies when they returned to their compartment, and what they did in response to finding a pair of corpses in their room would decide Haas's next step.

Methodically he stripped the two men of their wallets and the identifying rings they wore. No sense in letting Black and the woman know who the men were. He dropped the wallets and rings into the pocket of his jacket, to be disposed of later. That done, he eased open the door and looked up and down the corridor. Empty. He slipped out into the corridor and walked back two cars to his own compartment in the Albuquerque. He carefully washed his hands in the small sink, dried them, ran a comb through his hair and stepped out of the bedroom. Turning left, he went back one car into the tail end observation-lounge car to see how events unfolded. Ordering a Scotch and water, he sat down on one of the comfortable banquettes and lit a cigarette.

Chapter 21

Their Thanksgiving dinner went by in a haze for both of them, incipient exhaustion after their headlong escape, first from Mexico and then from Washington, tempered with relief at having managed to actually accomplish the maneuver. All of this was complicated by the fact that there was definitely some kind of undeclared situation rising between them and the tacit understanding that the means to resolve it were only just down the corridor.

Both Morris and Jane made a courageous attempt to finish their meal, from the complimentary glass of tomato juice all the way down to the pumpkin pie. The waiter came by asking them if they wanted coffee or a liqueur and both Morris and Jane answered no almost as one voice. Black paid and they headed back to their compartment. Reaching the corridor, they were left with the problem that the two of them couldn't reach the bedroom side by side, meaning that one of them would have to lead the way. In the end, working on the same rule that applies to who goes first in a movie theater, Jane went on ahead with Black a few steps behind her. They passed two couples on their way to the dining car and Jane was mortified, sure that the couples knew exactly where she and Morris were going and precisely what they were illicitly going to do there. Gritting her teeth, Jane continued on; a little bit of mortification never hurt a girl and it wasn't as though she'd been raised a Catholic.

It suddenly occurred to her that as a Jew Morris might be breaking some holy rule or something but she didn't really care. She didn't think Morris did either.

Jane reached the compartment, took a deep breath, and put her hand on the door. Black covered it with his own.

"Look, Jane . . . I'm not very good at this but . . ."

"Bad form to tell a girl you're no good before the event. Just relax." She smiled. "I'm as nervous as you are." She pulled open the door and stepped inside.

The closer man was lying on his back, his left eye already filming over, his mouth open and his tongue lolling back into his throat like a fat, darkening slug. His right eye had collapsed in on itself, leaking a trail of blood and clear tissue down his cheek.

Jane felt her turkey dinner rising in her throat in a sour rush of bile, but she managed to keep it down. She grabbed Black by the sleeve of his jacket, pulling him into the compartment and jerking the door closed. She twisted the locking knob below the handle and sagged back against the metal wall.

"Good Christ," said Black, staring down at the two men and the spilled contents of their suitcases. Jane pulled one of the two armchairs away from the bodies and dropped down into it.

"Who are they?"

"They were looking through our things." The detective bent down and quickly checked the pockets of both men. A packet of Lucky Strikes, a Ronson lighter and some small change in the clothing of the shorter man as well as a .38 caliber pistol in a worn holster clipped to his trousers at the small of his back. There was a through ticket to Los Angeles in his inside jacket pocket. The taller man had more spare change, no cigarettes and his own ticket. Both tickets were for the same compartment in Iselta, located toward the head end of the train. The taller man had a .45 caliber automatic pistol in a sling shoulder holster hidden by his jacket. He had been stabbed once in the neck. The spinal ganglia at the base of his skull had been severed, killing him instantly.

"Both armed, both without any kind of identification, both killed very professionally."

"I don't get it."

"They were going through our things. They were interrupted and they were killed. Left for us to deal with."

"Russians?"

"I don't know."

"They don't look like Russians."

"What does a Russian look like?"

"Not that well dressed, for one thing," said Jane. She pulled cigarettes out of her bag and lit one, her hand quivering. "Shit," she whispered. "Shaking like a leaf."

"Quite rightly so." Black knelt down and flipped back the short man's jacket. "Brooks Brothers. New York."

"Pretty high-toned for a Russian." Jane took a deep drag on her cigarette. "Donovan's people, keeping tabs?"

"Or your Mr. Hoover's FBI."

"Not my Mr. Hoover." Jane shook her head. "Right now I don't think it matters much anyway. We've got two dead bodies in our bedroom; that's going to take a lot of explaining." She glanced at her watch. It was just after nine. "The porter's going to be coming around to put down the beds any minute."

Black frowned. "What's the next stop on the line?"

Jane turned slightly and pulled the full schedule out of the leather pocket on the wall behind her. She flipped through the pages until she found what she was looking for, running her finger down the list. "Galesburg."

"What time?"

"Ten o'clock. According to this the train stops for fifteen minutes."

"After that?"

"Nothing until Kansas City. Two forty-five in the morning." She moved her finger across the schedule. "Almost five hundred miles from Chicago."

"And Galesburg?"

"One hundred and seventy-seven miles."

"How long would it take us to get back to Chicago?"

"Greyhound it might be six or seven hours unless you got an express. You could drive it yourself in three and a half, maybe four."

Black gestured at the bodies on the floor of the compartment. "Whoever did this is still on board the train."

"So the sooner we get off the better, is that what you mean?" She was still staring down at the two dead men, horrified.

"Yes," he uttered slowly, a sick look on his face.

"Then what?"

"Presumably we could get a flight to Los Angeles."

"If these are Donovan's boys, or the FBI, they'll be watching the airport."

"Perhaps you can suggest something else," said Black. "If so I propose you do so as quickly as possible."

She gestured at the corpses. "One way or the other we have to hide the bodies. Once the porter puts down the beds, no one is going to bother us for the rest of the night. It might be smarter catching that flight out of Kansas City rather than Chicago. Less likely to be spotted."

Black thought for a moment, then nodded. "All right," said the detective, "I defer to your better grasp of American geography."

There was a hard rap on the compartment door and Jane let out a startled yelp.

A muffled voice from the corridor announced, "Porter. Put down your beds?"

Black stared at the door in dread. Jane answered, trying to make her voice light. "Can we have another few minutes, Eli?"

"Yes, ma'am. You take your time."

"Thank you." Jane held her breath. They both heard the sound of the porter moving down the corridor to the next compartment. Jane stabbed out her cigarette in the narrow steel ashtray riveted to the wall close to where the lower bunk would rest. "So how do we manage this?"

Black nodded to himself. "We'll prop the bodies in the toilet stall. I'll be in there with them. You head for the bar car. If the porter wants to come in after he puts down the beds, I'll tell him it's occupied. We'll meet in the bar."

"Okay. I'll tell him to do our beds next on my way out."

"That would be lovely," muttered Black. He bent down and began shifting the deadweight of the short man's corpse.

* * *

The thing Vassili Zarubin enjoyed most about the United States was its slow but steady corruption of the entire world's culture, beginning with her food, and usually for a remarkably low price: the hot dog in a bun, sold at every baseball game and once a very different concoction sold on the streets of Frankfurt; lox on a bagel with cream cheese, which no Jew except one from Brooklyn would so much as look at; the pizza slice, stolen from the Sicilian workingman's lunch bucket; and the french fry, picked off the plates of Parisian gourmands having their *bifteck bien cuit avec pommes frites*. And these things in front of him, thin squares of sizzling fried meat garnished with onions fried along with them to the point of being caramelized, daubed with liquid mustard, then garnished again with round slices of pickle and packed between two fluffy halves of a puffy white bun—nothing at all like the things sold in Hamburg, their city of origin. On the other hand, perhaps he was thinking all this because there was no food of any kind available in the perfection of the Soviet Union these days.

He sat in the tiny shiny interior of the White Castle restaurant at the bottom of State Street in Santa Barbara, between the railroad tracks and the beach, and bit into the last of his three burgers, augmenting the meat packet with the fries in the box on his left. On his right was a bottle of Coke with a straw floating around in it, which he took occasional sips from. The Coke was thick as blood, sweet as candy and ice cold. His old grandmother, tasting it, would have choked loudly and died screaming. So would the great Comrade Stalin, and perhaps that was what Uncle Joe feared: that it would be things like hamburgers, hot dogs and Coca-Cola that would insidiously convert the world rather than his stern and steel version of Marxist-Leninism.

Zarubin turned on his stool and glanced out the window. It was just past seven in the evening, and the sun was nothing more than a few purple and orange streaks on the Pacific horizon above the Channel Islands a few miles offshore. To his left he could see the occasional flare of the lighthouse at Santa Barbara Point.

It had been a simple, easy day. First a shower in his motel room at the Ocean Palms only a few blocks away down the beach, then a drive around the city in the rental car from the airport to acclimate himself, including a visit to the public library on Anacapa Street, where Harte supposedly worked, as well as the state college campus where Rupert Pelham worked, according to the late Professor Maddox. Finally he'd gone on a leisurely drive up to have a quick look at his objective, a small house in the foothills just off Stanwood Drive. He was back by one in the afternoon and had more than enough time to take in the double feature showing at the Fox-Arlington farther up State Street: *The Wolf Man* with Lon Chaney and Bela Lugosi followed by *Man Hunt*, with Walter Pidgeon playing a big-game hunter who tries to assassinate Hitler and then has the tables turned on him. He took a last bite of his hamburger, crunching through a thin slice of acidic pickle. Zarubin wondered if Hitler would have a screening of the film in his aerie in Berchtesgarten.

Zarubin lit a cigarette and drank from his bottle of Coke. How much would it take to give up the workers' paradise of the Soviet Union and the potentially fatal climb up the rickety NKVD ladder of success that could have you falling into the basement dungeons of the Lubyanka? Behind the high Kremlin walls Comrade Stalin and his cronies were in a constant frenzy of list making, counting and recounting their enemies, sending them to the gulags or to the mental hospitals or simply burying them in the ground. How much would it take for him to give all that up for a few hamburgers at White Castle and a job threading the film projector at the Fox-Arlington motion picture theater? Or one of those little houses up in the hills, a car of his own to drive and a job teaching elementary Russian to the children at the college. All of that in such nice weather by the sea. My God, he could even take up sailboating if he wished.

In the end, of course, he knew he would not, for he didn't care who governed. Vassili Zarubin loved the country itself. A hard country, to be sure, but a people as hard and as loving as the land with a history stretching back to the beginning of time. Cossack blood still sang in his veins after a thousand years, always reminding him of who he was and where he came from, a legacy the Americans could never understand. Cowboys and Indians, Pilgrims and plantations indeed. A dozen Stalins and Lenins and Trotskys could come and go, just like the dozen tsars who came before them, but the *Rodina*, the Motherland, would go on forever.

He brushed the maudlin Russian thoughts from his mind, stubbed out his cigarette and climbed off his stool. Enough of this. He was in California for the time being, and he had a job to do.

The Russian spy climbed in behind the wheel of the rented dark blue Hudson Six, started it up and pulled out onto State Street. Heading back toward the harbor, he followed the beach, then turned again, this time to the left onto the Coast Highway, moving along to Salinas, then beginning his climb into the foothills along the Sycamore Canyon Road.

Chapter 22

Professor Rupert Andrew Pelham's house was located high in the heavily treed foothills at 122 Crest Road off Stanwood Drive, just below the Sheffield Reservoir, one of Santa Barbara's most important sources of fresh water. The area was only sparsely populated, but it was a favorite among Santa Barbara's "artistic" community, mostly for its privacy and isolation.

According to the administration office at Santa Barbara State College, Pelham taught both English literature and American history and had done so for the past seven years. A quick check by telephone with his own people in Washington revealed that while not an active member of CPUSA, Pelham had been an "adjunct agent," code-named Whitefish, for the International Liaison Department since 1936. The ILD was made up of hundreds of men and women who had wanted to be members of the Communist Party but instead became so-called sleeper agents, ready to be used at a moment's notice and with no possibility of their affiliations being recorded by the FBI or any other agency. It was, in effect, a covert amateur spy ring, and while it couldn't be trusted, its members were there to serve whenever necessary.

Easing the Hudson up the winding narrow line of Sycamore Canyon Road, Zarubin eventually reached the top and swung the heavy car north on Stanwood Drive, riding the upper ridgeback of the foothill with the Los Padres National Forest on his right and the twinkling lights of the city of Santa Barbara now far below him. He kept a careful watch and a few minutes later reached the turnoff for Crest Road and turned left, one foot hovering over the brake as he rode the steep, narrow road downward in a series of S turns without benefit of guardrail or signpost.

He finally reached his destination and pulled the car off onto the side of the road, the passenger side brushing against the thick stand of trees beside it. He'd checked earlier in the day and knew that there were only two other houses on this part of Crest Road, the nearest one several hundred yards away. It was unlikely that his car would be spotted.

Before he got out from behind the wheel, he took out the government-model Colt he'd picked up at Tembler Arms on D Street and checked the magazine again, even though he knew the weapon was fully loaded. The laws were comically lax about such things in the capital city. A weapon could be carried concealed if the cartridges were kept separately, and having a fully loaded weapon in the glove compartment of your car was deemed to be part of your residence and therefore not concealed. Not to mention the fact that a search warrant was needed to look for any weapon, concealed on your person or otherwise. He could have used the Radom but in this case thought it wiser to use a domestic firearm. He dropped the pistol back into the pocket of his jacket, climbed out of the car and locked it behind him.

Pelham's house was half screened by more fir trees at the top of a curving, gravel-covered lane. The house itself was small, really no more than a cottage. It was a plain clapboard stained a deep brown with a roof of cedar shakes, all of it blending into the slope of trees rising behind it. Cozy enough for two people, and quiet. Nothing but wind in the trees and maybe some raccoons up here.

Zarubin approached the house without any particular care; he wasn't trying to sneak up on them, after all. Since Maddox had become fish bait before he'd had time to warn his friend and his ex-lover, they had no idea of his fate, and no reason to question Zarubin's motives for seeking them out.

Zarubin paused at the foot of the path and lit a Camel.
The Russian walked up the path and saw a Thanksgiving
wreath on the door. Very festive. He rang the bell. Somewhere from deeper inside he could hear Glenn Miller
doing "Chattanooga Choo-Choo," which he seemed to
have heard a thousand times in the past few weeks. There
was no answer to the bell, so he rapped his knuckles
across the wood instead. Someone turned down the music
and a few moments later he could hear soft slippered footsteps whispering toward the door. The porch light went
on above his head and the door opened. The man standing there was wearing a red silk bathrobe, smoking a pipe,
and had dark hair and tortoiseshell glasses. His cheeks
were pinched and his Adam's apple seemed too large.

"You must be Professor Pelham."

"I am," said the man. "Who might you be?"

"A friend of Mr. Whitefish," Zarubin replied, smiling
pleasantly as the blood drained out of the chicken-
necked man's face.

"I'm afraid I don't know any Mr. Whitefish."

"That's not how you're supposed to answer."

"I don't know what you mean."

"You're supposed to tell me something about the
weather."

"I still don't know what you're talking about."

"Tired of playing the game, Professor?"

"Game?"

"The spy in the house of love. The young revolution-
ary who's not so young anymore." Zarubin kept smiling.
It wouldn't be the first defector he'd had to deal with in
the face of the American cornucopia and all it had to
offer. Comrade Stalin was fine when it came to philoso-
phy but not so capable when it came to the necessities
of life. Toilet paper and razor blades, for example. How
long would a revolution last if the comrades couldn't
keep their bums clean?

"I'm really afraid I don't know what you're going on
about," said Pelham, trying to push the door closed.

Zarubin stuck his foot in the crack. "Enough, Professor. I'm beginning to get a little irritated and I've come
a long way."

"For nothing, I'm afraid."

"No. For Mr. Robert Sheldon Harte, late of New York City and before that Coyoacán, Mexico. The villa of *Tovarishch* Lev Davidovich Bronstein, a Jew from Yanovka better known to us all as Leonid Trotsky."

"I don't know anyone by the name of Harte."

"You really must stop playing games, Professor. I'm not here to hurt you or your young friend. Quite the contrary."

"This is really becoming quite ridiculous, Mr. Zooboorin, is it?"

"Zarubin."

"Quite ridiculous. You make it sound as though I might be a member of your Communist Party, which is certainly not the case."

"One last chance, Professor. I'm going to walk away and leave you on your own. Pretend that I never met you or knew you. Pretend that you know no one named Robert Sheldon Harte and are not in fact offering him aid and succor. I will, in a word, leave you to your own devices."

"That sounds like an excellent idea. Why don't you do that?"

"You think it would give you enough time to run, or to send Harte on his way, send him to another so-called safe house, but you would be wrong, Professor. In a day or so someone will appear at your door, or at your office at the college, and there will be no introductions at all. The person will shoot you in the chest and in the face, probably with a 7.62 Tokarev pistol, which has a clip of eight rounds, enough to churn your brains into butter, Mr. Professor of English and History." He had a brief and somewhat gory image of the young and deadly Guadalupe Gomez dropping in on Pelham for tea. It was not a pleasant thought.

"You are threatening me? In my own house?"

"I am not threatening you, Professor. I am simply telling you what will happen. And as a good Communist the fact of this being 'your' house should be of no importance to you."

Rupert Pelham stared at him, goggle-eyed through the lenses of his spectacles, blinking like an owl. He said nothing.

"I cannot stand out here all night, Professor," said Zarubin, a weary sigh in his voice. He reached into his pocket and took out the Colt, pulling back the slide to jack a round into the barrel. "If you don't let me into your house in a very few seconds, I will use my own gun to turn your brain into pudding myself. Please make up your mind." He aimed the gun directly at Pelham's upper lip. The professor took a step back, and Zarubin took a step forward, entering the house and closing the door behind him. He put the Colt back in his pocket.

"Thank you."

There was a foyer with a flight of stairs directly ahead and the entrance to a living room on the left. To the right were a pair of half-open pocket doors leading into what appeared to be a study. The walls of the foyer were painted a rusty orange color and the lights were wrought iron hanging from sconces around the walls. A larger version hung from the ceiling like a chandelier in the shape of a wheel, set with candles, except that the candles were actually flame-shaped electrical bulbs.

Pelham led Zarubin into the study and told him to wait there. There was a scalloped ceiling with mahogany strips, bookcases along two walls crammed with volumes, a bar, a large fireplace with a wrought-iron grill around it and large windows on either side of the fireplace. A man's room, yet designed with a subtle feminine hand. Pelham was almost certainly a homosexual, which probably explained it.

Pelham returned a few moments later with a very apprehensive young man. Robert Sheldon Harte was in his early twenties and a little fey-looking, not at all the type you'd expect to find hired as a bodyguard. He had dark hair, dark brown eyes and high cheekbones. He was wearing a poorly fitting brown suit. He sat down at the far end of the red leather couch, keeping as distant as possible from Zarubin. Pelham went to stand in front of the fireplace, hands behind his back.

"Who sent you?" he said finally.

"I sent myself."

"Someone told you Robert was here."

"That was Professor Maddox."

"Jimmy wouldn't do that!" Pelham blurted.

The blood seemed to drain out of Harte's face. "Did someone hurt him?"

"No," Zarubin lied. "He was interrogated."

"By whom?"

"The FBI. A man named Percy Foxworth."

"And he told the FBI about us?"

"Not in so many words. Your code names only."

"Then how did you find us?"

"I was the one who gave you the code names in the first place."

"How did you know he'd talked?"

Zarubin gave an uninterested shrug. "We have people in the Bureau. We were told almost from the time he was arrested and taken in for questioning."

"I can't believe he would compromise us," Harte whispered. He stood up and went to the bar. He poured himself a large Scotch with no ice. He drained it and refilled his glass, this time spritzing it with a splash of soda. He went back to the couch, turning the glass around and around in his hands, staring down into it as though the liquor was a crystal ball.

"It still doesn't explain your presence," Pelham insisted. His brow was furrowed and he looked suspicious.

"Think of me as your guardian angel." Zarubin smiled. "And I wouldn't mind a drink myself. Bourbon if you have it."

Harte put his own glass down on the coffee table and went around to the bar. He poured three fingers of I.W. Harper over ice into a heavy crystal glass, then brought it to Zarubin. The Russian sipped appreciatively; to him all Russian liquor tasted the same—like gasoline. The American stuff had much more flavor. He smiled to himself. Maybe he was being converted to the West after all.

"I'm waiting," said Pelham, his voice crisp and pedantic. Zarubin could imagine him in a lecture hall, hands wrapped around a pointer like it was a rapier.

"Professor Maddox is in custody and he continues to be interrogated," said Zarubin. "I don't doubt that they will next resort to drugs."

"He doesn't know anything!" said Harte.

"He knows enough. He knows why you were sent to Trotsky. What your mission was."

"Robert's mission is none of your concern."

"Of course it is, since it was I who devised the mission in the first place."

"He was handled by Maddox."

"And Maddox was in turn handled by me, as is every single active agent in the United States, yourself included. We are all aware that Mr. Harte was infiltrated into the Trotsky household to discover the whereabouts of the film handed over to Trotsky by Alexander Levitsky when Trotsky arrived in Mexico."

"There was no such film in Coyoacán," said Harte firmly.

"I am aware of that, comrade. There was, however, a pair of keys to a safe-deposit box. The box was opened either by Diego Rivera or Frida Kahlo on one of their trips to Los Angeles or San Francisco. It is our opinion that the film was removed to this safe-deposit box and the keys returned to Trotsky. He kept one of these keys around his neck and hid the other."

"I don't see the point of any of this or what it has to do with either me or my friend Robert." Pelham's arms were now folded aggressively across his chest in a most irritating way.

"Comrade Harte has one of the two keys. Presumably it was given to him by Trotsky."

"He did nothing of the sort!" Pelham blustered.

"Of course he did. It's the only explanation."

"Explanation for what?"

"Mercador, the so-called Trotsky assassin, had a second agenda. It was his job to take the key that was hanging on a chain around Trotsky's neck. Señor Mercador has been interviewed most strenuously about this. According to him there was no such key."

"Why would Trotsky give it to Robert?"

"Because he trusted him. Because he knew that Robert would do as he was told."

"And what was that?"

"Follow orders."

"Such as?"

"When the time came, your young charge would hand over the key to the appropriate person."

"Who?" said Pelham belligerently.

"Levitsky," said Harte, his voice quiet. Both men turned to him. Pelham took a step away from the fireplace, a look of concern on his face as though the young man had just said something terrible.

"The man who shot the film in the first place?" said Zarubin.

"He entrusted the film to Trotsky, for his protection," Harte explained. "With Trotsky dead that is no longer of any importance obviously."

"So he wants the film back?"

"Yes." Harte nodded. "That was the agreement."

"What agreement?"

"The agreement between Siqueiros and Levitsky."

Zarubin stared at the young man blankly. He was conversant with the convoluted conspiracies and Machiavellian plots within and without the Kremlin, but this bordered on the insane. David Alfaro Siqueiros was the artist-activist accused of making the first machine-gun attempt against Trotsky in Coyoacán as well as kidnapping and supposedly murdering the man seated beside him on the red leather couch. "Siqueiros is a confirmed Stalinist," said Zarubin.

"Of course." Harte nodded. "He would hardly have attempted to assassinate Comrade Trotsky otherwise."

"Of course," Zarubin said, bemused. The fact that this conversation was taking place in a well-to-do American seaside town like Santa Barbara was even more surreal.

"In fact, the entire thing was arranged by Rivera and Frida, close friends of Siqueiros."

"An attempt to murder their friend *Tovarishch* Trotsky?"

"Precisely. Until that point no one had taken the possibility of an assassination attempt seriously, especially President Cárdenas. This was to spur him into action."

"People were killed," said Zarubin.

"We all must make sacrifices for the revolution," Harte responded blandly. A true believer to the core, Zarubin thought. He'd wear a bomb strapped to his chest or walk through fire to reach his holy Socialist objective.

"So you took the key with you when you were 'kidnapped'?"

"And the film." Harte nodded. "I placed the reel in the safe-deposit box and retained the key. I have yet to meet with Levitsky."

"And when you do?"

"I will give him the key and he will make the film public."

"Accomplishing what? Beyond embarrassing various governments?"

"It is concrete evidence that the tsar and his family are all dead. There can be no usurpers to the throne of Russia or any question of a government in exile. All monies once held by the imperial treasury will now belong to the Union of Soviet Socialist Republics." The boy's voice had risen by a full octave and had achieved a strident tone Zarubin was used to hearing on one of the Bremen shortwave propaganda stations that carried Lord Haw-Haw.

"I'm not quite sure what Señor Siqueiros got out of all this."

"Financing for his friends, the mine workers and their union. Siqueiros was in no position to sell the film or give it any kind of provenance. Levitsky obviously was. They struck a deal."

That was more like it, thought Zarubin, though he doubted any of the mine workers would see much of the money. Even Stalin called the Mexican mural painter more than half a gangster.

"Where is the key?"

"I have it," Harte answered.

"I know that," said Zarubin, "but where do you have it?"

"Here," said Harte. He reached below the collar of his shirt and extracted a thin silver chain. There was a flat pewter-colored key threaded onto the chain.

"To what bank?"

"Don't tell him, Robert," Pelham interjected. He took another short step toward his young friend.

"The First National Bank in Ventura."

"Ventura. It is a small place down the coast toward Los Angeles, yes?"

"Yes."

Zarubin nodded. He'd seen it on a map, perhaps thirty or forty miles south of here.

"How many keys are necessary?"

"One," Harte answered. "And the correct name of the keyholder."

"Don't be a fool!" screamed Pelham. "Once he knows, he'll kill you! He'll kill us both!"

"You're being far too melodramatic about this," said Zarubin calmly. "I have no intention of killing anyone. I just need the information. It is your duty to give it to me." He paused. "Now, the name."

"Bronstein. Lev Bronstein." Of course, what else would it be? Levitsky's little joke: Trotsky's birth name.

"When were you to meet?"

"I had a number to call. In Ventura."

"Levitsky lives there?"

"I think so."

"What is the number?"

"Main 2457."

"The address?"

"South Laurel Street, 218. By the railway tracks and the harbor."

"Fool," Pelham whispered.

Harte turned on his friend, his face twisted. "He is my superior, not you! You talk about the revolution, but you do not live it!"

Pelham slumped down in a brightly decorated wooden chair close to the fireplace, a flush burning across his cheeks. Both of them were right: Harte was a fool and Pelham was nothing but a fellow traveler, a dilettante who talked about the proletariat but drank expensive Scotch.

Zarubin took a long, satisfying swallow from his drink. He had almost everything he needed now. "Levitsky has had the film for a great many years. Why dispose of it now?"

It was Pelham who answered, not Harte. "No one was interested twenty years ago. King George might have been embarrassed, but he had no direct involvement in the tsar's death and the death of his family, and by their dying he managed to avoid giving them refuge in England. Both he and the government feared his presence might incite a Bolshevik-style revolution there. The Germans might have wanted it because the kaiser was the tsar's cousin as well."

"Ancient history."

"Of which the present is a result," snapped Pelham. "History is a river, comrade. It flows like water, and the past is always before us as the present quickly runs into the future."

"You're speaking in riddles."

"A very plain truth. There is a great deal of money at stake. Money and power. The death of the tsar put that fortune in play. It still is. Levitsky's film has the power to change that."

"You think Levitsky is doing it for money after all these years?"

"He has no other reason and he is no fool. The world is about to fall into the abyss of total war; there will be no time at all for his little film after that happens. The film will go to the highest bidder. He doesn't care which group of madmen he sells it to." Pelham shook his head wearily. "He sees his moment and he intends to seize it."

"Then I suppose I should seize mine," said Zarubin. He stood up, reached into his pocket and took out the Colt Automatic.

"Are you going to kill us now?" asked Harte. His voice had something close to expectation in it.

"Of course not," said Zarubin, smiling down at the young man.

He turned and pumped three shots from the weapon into Pelham's chest before the man had done more than half rise from his chair, his right hand coming up in a vain attempt to stop the bullets, one of which tore through the palmar muscles of the hand before continuing on to the professor's face.

Zarubin then turned, leaned down and used the thumb and forefinger of his left hand to squeeze the cheeks of Robert Sheldon Harte's face together, forcing his mouth open, ignoring as best he could the young man's soft doe eyes, wet with fear, tears threatening to spill down his cheeks. With the lips and teeth parted Zarubin fired a single shot into the young man's brain, killing him instantly and opening up a messy exit wound in the back of his head that sprayed the back of the couch and even up to the ceiling seven and a half feet above his head, discoloring the pale yellow plaster with gray and red and showers of faint pink. Before it began to drip down on them, Zarubin quickly wiped off any fingerprints on the Colt with one of the throw pillows, then pressed the gun into Harte's dead right hand, pointing it in the general direction of Pelham's body.

He forced the trigger down, firing the weapon again. The bullet struck a large watercolor painting, which turned out to be by none other than Frida Kahlo. There was a certain irony in that, and Zarubin smiled. Killing a painting by the woman who had purportedly been Trotsky's mistress for a time. All that done, he carefully unclipped the chain around Harte's neck and slipped it off.

Leaving the gun in Harte's dead hand, he stood back to examine the scene. Pelham by the fireplace, Harte on the couch. A lovers' quarrel perhaps. Harte tiring of his pedantic old lover, looking for excitement elsewhere. Threatening to leave? Harte finds a newer, younger lover among Pelham's students? All possible. If the police ever saw it as anything more than a simple pansy slapfest that went too far, they wouldn't find much else. Harte was living under a different name, and Pelham had no direct connection to CPUSA or any other Communist organization.

One last detail, even though he didn't really think the question of fingerprints would ever become important. He wiped down his own glass, left Harte's where it was and then carried the bourbon across to Pelham's chair. He wrapped the man's hand around the heavy crystal, then let it drop. The half-filled glass dropped to the floor, the booze and ice cubes spilling out onto the Chinese art deco carpet. Zarubin took a last look around. Nothing seemed out of place. If things went according to plan, he would have the film within the next day or two and be on his way back to Washington.

The winner, as he always knew he'd be.

Chapter 23

Jane Todd and Morris Black arrived in Kansas City at two thirty-five a.m. and got off the Super Chief without incident. There were no local police or FBI agents waiting to arrest them as they left the train and no sign at all that the two dead men had been found stuffed into the toilet cubicle of their bedroom. If they were lucky, the bodies wouldn't be discovered until late morning or even early afternoon. By then the barman and the steward serving in the lounge car might remember the two passengers who'd stayed up all the way to Kansas City, but by then it would be too late.

They made their way through the high-ceilinged domed concourse of Union Station, stepped out into the chilly early-morning darkness and managed to find a cab. They asked their sleepy driver for a good hotel, and he took them to the Continental on Baltimore Street. Both the cocktail lounges were closed, but the coffee shop was still open. They ordered an early breakfast, and after asking the waitress Jane managed to find a brochure for Transcontinental and Western Airways on a rack by one of the lounge cloakrooms. According to the TWA schedule there was an early-morning flight leaving the recently improved Municipal Airport at six a.m. scheduled to arrive in Los Angeles ten hours later at just after two in the afternoon West Coast time. With time on their hands they ate slowly, then ordered more coffee and lit cigarettes. Any thoughts of romance had vanished, at least for the moment.

"Bodies are starting to pile up, Morris." Jane shook her head wearily. "Maddox, Cesar Durantes, the two Mexican cops, two more guys on the train, not to mention the attempt to kill us at Trotsky's villa."

"I still think that was a ruse," Black answered. He took a sip of his coffee and scowled. "Too hot," he muttered. He dragged on his cigarette, inhaling deeply, then letting the smoke drift slowly out through his nostrils. He tapped the cigarette nervously on the edge of the little tin ashtray in the center of the table. "None of it fits," he said after a moment.

"Fits?"

"A crime is a series of facts. A fight between a husband and a wife. The wife goes to the kitchen, fetches a butcher knife and sneaks up behind her husband while he's listening to the radio. She stabs him in the back and he falls forward, dead as mutton, the tea spilling all over his lap. She goes upstairs to the bathroom, draws herself a hot bath, climbs into it and slashes her wrist from remorse. Any copper coming onto a scene like that could read the facts like a book. Neighbors heard the fight, there's a knife missing from the set in the kitchen, the radio's still on and there's a tea stain on the dead man's lap and on the carpet, and the wife is upstairs in the tub with the water all gone nasty and the knife on the floor where she dropped it. All facts that can be matched to evidence."

"What are you getting at?"

"We don't have facts. We have suppositions, theories, directions to investigate, but none of it adds up."

"Maddox thought he was going to be found out so he ran. His masters decided it was too risky to let him live."

"A theory. All we know for a fact is that Maddox ran when we showed up and that they fished him out of the Bay of Fundy or whatever you call it a day or so later."

"He was Harte's lover."

"Once again no facts. We have no evidence. We also don't have Harte. Why wasn't he in the grave? Presumably because he's still alive. But if he's left alive, why did they kill Maddox?"

"Well," said Jane, "at least we know why Cesar died. Wrong place, wrong time."

"I doubt that's the reason." Black sipped the coffee, then took a longer swallow.

"You think he was killed on purpose?" said Jane. "Why the hell would anyone want to kill an innocent kid like that?"

"Because somebody connected directly to us had to die. The two Mexican policemen inside the compound weren't enough. Eventually it would have come out that they were dead long before we arrived in Mexico, let alone at the murder scene."

"That still doesn't explain Cesar's death."

"According to Fleming this Guadalupe Gomez woman is a crack rifle shot. Cesar was struck square in the chest at a relatively high angle, and through the glass of the automobile's windscreen. A difficult shot but easily made by someone like her, but she misses you and me completely. I don't believe it."

"She murdered him just for the sake of doing it?"

"She murdered him because a murder was necessary. Think about it. We heard police sirens within a few seconds of the first shots being fired. That means the police were called, or somehow knew about the situation before the incident began. It was meant to slow us down, take us out of the picture."

"By who?"

"The same people who killed Maddox. Most likely at the order of this Zarubin fellow, the NKVD agent."

"And the two men on the train?"

"God knows," said Black. "Your guess is as good as mine. You seem to think they weren't Russians."

"Not dressed in Brooks Brothers, and besides, their teeth were too good."

"I beg your pardon?"

"Brooks Brothers and good dental work don't add up to people from Eastern Europe, and they were both wearing rings on the third finger of their right hands."

"I didn't notice either one of them wearing a ring," said Black.

"They weren't." Jane grinned. "But they had been. You could see the marks and the short guy had some tan. You could see the white spot on his finger. Whoever took their wallets took their rings."

"Why?"

"Because the rings identified them somehow. West Point gives rings to its graduates, so do the Naval Academy at Annapolis and some of the major universities. They do that at the University of Moscow or whatever the Reds call it?"

"Probably not."

"There you go."

"But hardly fact." Black smiled. "Just one more theory to add to the rest."

"The real question isn't who they are anyway," said Jane. She lit another cigarette off the butt end of her previous one. "The real question is how they knew we were on that train. Nobody knew about that. Not even Fleming. He was expecting us to meet with Donovan the following day, then fly out to Los Angeles that evening."

"It has to be the Russian again," said Black. "It can't be anyone else."

"But that's the whole point," Jane responded. "If the two guys on the train aren't this Zarubin guy's people, then it can't be Zarubin who followed us."

"Which brings us back to Donovan."

"I've thought about that too," said Jane. "Maybe he kept a permanent watch on us, independent of your friend Fleming."

"Fairly Machiavellian, don't you think?"

"Machiavellian times. And anyway, who else could it be?"

"Hoover."

"That's what you said on the train."

"It makes a certain amount of sense. Hoover doesn't like Stephenson or his British Security Co-ordination mob very much, and there's no love lost between him and Donovan either."

"Which leads us to another problem," said Jane.

"Which is?"

"If they were Hoover's boys, and they were snooping through our things looking for some clue about what we were up to, then who came along out of the blue and killed them?"

*   *   *

The man drove the dark blue Mercury Town Sedan up Connecticut Avenue in the gathering dawn, heading for Chevy Chase. Normally he would have been driving one of the Bureau cars, but this visit to the director was a particularly sensitive one so he was driving his own car instead. He was dressed in a plain dark suit, a white shirt and a plain navy blue tie. The shoes on his feet were black Florsheims and his dark hair was short and neatly combed. He had also taken particular care in showering, shaving closely and trimming his nails, before picking up his passenger at National Airport, well aware of the director's germ phobia and his very clear-cut attitudes concerning dress and personal hygiene. Edward A. Tamm was officially the assistant director for criminal investigations at the Federal Bureau of Investigation as well as being the unofficial head of the newly revived General Intelligence Division. He had joined the FBI eleven years before after graduating from Georgetown University Law School. He was thirty-seven years old.

The man in the front passenger seat was a dozen years older with a drawn basset-hound face and eyes a shade of gray that matched his three-piece suit. He wore an old but recently blocked snap-brim fedora. His name was J. E. Connelly and he was one of the director's "Specials" who went back even further than the creation of the Federal Bureau to the time when the director was head of the original General Intelligence Division of the Justice Department, most often known then as the Red Squad. It had been officially disbanded in 1920 after a series of political debacles, but the director had revived it, using the war in Europe as his excuse and the Hitler-Stalin Nonaggression Pact as his rationale, painting a picture of a nation rife with plots and spies, both Red and Nazi. Connelly had not spoken a word to Tamm since he'd been picked up at the airport.

The younger man flicked the signal lever down and swung the wheel of the big car onto Thirtieth Place.

"Park the car," said Connelly. His voice was worn and raw as though he smoked too many cigarettes but Tamm hadn't seen him light one since they'd left the airport. Obediently he pulled the car over to the curb and parked.

"The director's house is at the far end of the block."

"I'm aware of that," said Connelly. "People have a tendency to note down license numbers. I don't want yours being jotted down." Connelly climbed out of the car before Tamm could answer. The younger man thought he was overdoing it a little, but Connelly was clearly the man in charge and Tamm wouldn't have it any other way, especially if Connelly was the bearer of bad tidings. The director might not actually shoot the messenger, but he was more than capable of exiling the poor bastard to a field office in Omaha. He climbed out of the car, fetched his worn, government-issue briefcase from the backseat and locked the car door. He adjusted the holstered .38 Smith & Wesson on his hip and did up both buttons of his suit jacket. He risked a look in the side mirror, smoothed back his hair at the temples and followed Connelly up the shadowed residential street.

The house at 4936 Thirtieth Place NW was a two-story brick on a half-acre lot. It had a mansard roof with slate shingles and a single chimney, but the overall style was Colonial Federal. The director had purchased the property shortly after the death of his mother, Alice Hoover.

The two men turned up the front walk. As Connelly pressed the small lighted buzzer, Tamm noted that, as usual, all the Venetian blinds on the front windows of the house were closed. There was a brief pause and then the front door opened. Annie Fields, the Negro live-in cook and housekeeper, stood in the doorway. She was dressed in a colorful print dress covered by a white apron. She stood aside and the two men entered the house.

"He's in the study," she said.

Connelly nodded and finally removed his hat. He headed past the colored woman to the carpeted stairs and headed up, with Tamm following. The area around the bottom landing was cluttered with small tables and antiques, most of them Oriental, while the wall all the way up to the first landing was covered with photographs, including a large autographed one of the president. On the first landing was a gilt-framed oil painting of the director in a stern, almost grim pose, his positioning giving the impression of a much taller man than he really was. There was also a bronze bust of him on a small cherrywood table.

Along the walls of the upstairs hallway there were literally dozens of drawings, etchings and cartoons, all of them depicting the director, usually with an exaggerated bulldog chin. Interspersed among these were more photographs of Hoover, these showing him with a variety of Hollywood celebrities from Barrymore to W. C. Fields. Notably missing from the pantheon of actors and actresses was Charlie Chaplin, who the director had almost single-handedly had thrown out of the country.

The door to the director's study was closed. Connelly knocked quietly and received a one-word response:

"Come."

The older man opened the door and entered, followed closely by Tamm. The room was large, two walls papered with more photographs, these of the director playing golf and tennis with notable sports figures going back to the mid-twenties. There was one wall with a large draped window while the fourth, like his fifth-floor office in the Justice Department Building, held a huge map of the United States flagged in red, showing every one of the FBI field offices, headquarters marked with a gold star. Lines of thread connected the field offices to Washington. All roads leading to Rome.

There were several Persian carpets on the cherry floor, a long leather couch under the map and two leather armchairs in front of a large antique oak desk. Seated behind the desk in a leather armchair of his own was the director, John Edgar Hoover. He gestured toward the two armchairs with a wave of his hand and the men sat down, Tamm holding his briefcase on his lap, Connelly his fedora. The only light in the room came from a simple green gooseneck lamp on the desk, throwing a puddle of light on several file folders covered by Hoover's small, clasped hands.

Hoover was scowling, his usual expression and one beloved by political cartoonists for the better part of twenty-five years. "Well?" he said to Connelly.

"We've lost Harding and Bonafontini."

Hoover's lips twitched but other than that his expression remained the same.

"These were the two you had following the Limey and the woman?"

"Yes, sir."

Tamm knew who both men were: the Kraut and Sneezy, both members of the supposedly mythical "Squad," commissioned to mete out extreme and terminal justice on people deemed deserving of it by the director. He also knew that they were under the unofficial or "blue memo" orders of the man sitting in the chair beside him.

"Where?"

"They were found on the Super Chief, sir, en route to Los Angeles, jammed into the toilet facility of our targets' compartment. They were discovered just outside of La Junta, Colorado, when the steward went into the room to make up the beds."

"They were traveling in the same room?"

"Harding and Bonafontini, sir?"

"Don't be a fucking idiot. The targets." Not for the first time Tamm found himself wondering how such a supposedly pious and sinless man in public could curse like a longshoreman in private.

"Yes, sir."

"Were they screwing each other?"

Tamm gritted his teeth and forced himself not to laugh. The Kraut and Sneezy? That was ripe.

"I have no idea, sir," said Connelly.

"Find out. It could be important."

"Yes, sir."

"Who killed them?"

"I'd have to say the Russians, sir. It's the only thing that fits. We also have some evidence that Zarubin is no longer in Washington. He managed to slip his tail, sir." Connelly paused. "A day or so later they found that professor floating in the ocean with his face half gone."

"Donovan's runner?"

"Yes, sir."

"Commie?"

"Presumably. From what I understand that's half who he hires."

That's a boy, thought Tamm. Tell the man what he wants to hear.

"You think it was Zarubin?"

"Could have been, sir. It fits."

"Could he have been on the train?"

"I believe so."

"The targets?"

"Long gone. Probably Kansas City. Flew out to Los Angeles."

"Who's our man out there?"

"Jack Tollett, sir."

Tamm nodded to himself. Jack Tollett was another one of the old boys from the Red Squad days.

"Watching the Budberg slut?"

"Yes, sir. As you requested."

"Fucking Red cunt. I'd have her thrown out if I could, but it might upset our Limey friends. Get that dyke bitch in the White House all in a tizzy."

"Yes, sir."

"Did I ever show you the drawings I have of her? The ones I got from W. C."

"Yes, sir. On several occasions. Very droll, sir."

"Aren't they just?" Hoover took a little breath and let it out with a strange puffing noise, half through his ruined, almost flat nose, half through his small pursed lips. The story was that he'd broken his nose when he was hit by a fly ball playing college baseball but Tamm knew better; working as a drugstore delivery boy when he was a kid Hoover had tripped on a cracked sidewalk. No college baseball team would have had him anyway, especially not as an outfielder; he was far too short.

"Budberg," said Hoover.

"Yes, sir."

"No sign of any activity?"

"Not yet."

"I want that film."

"Yes, sir. We'll get it, sir."

"Icing on the cake. I'll put that son of a bitch into a hole that smart-ass cocksucker will never climb out of. You know who I mean."

"Yes, sir," said Connelly. Tamm wasn't a hundred percent sure, but he presumed Hoover was talking about his archenemy, Wild Bill Donovan. Donovan had been his putative boss at the attorney general's office after he went off to war and became a hero, complete with the Congressional Medal of Honor, while Hoover stayed home on a deferment. The animosity was almost all Hoover's and didn't seem to be based on much more than Donovan's relatively patrician background and the fact that he'd gone to a better law school—Columbia versus George Washington University.

The director turned his gaze on Tamm. Shiny, wet little raisins in a blob of dough, thought the young man. Donovan looked like a hero, tall and handsome, while Hoover looked like the people he took such pride in arresting, jug-jawed thugs with beady eyes and five o'clock shadows.

"So you think it was the Reds who killed our two?" said Hoover.

"I suppose it's possible. I doubt it though. They didn't have any reason to."

"Reds don't need a reason. They got that fucker Stalin."

"Nevertheless, sir—"

"Don't give me ten-dollar words, Tamm. I want answers." The director paused, puffing on his cigar. "You know what I think, Tamm?"

"No, sir."

"I think it's the fucking Limey and the broad."

"He's a cop."

"He's a fucking Limey and he's a fucking Jew, which probably means he's a Red as well. I've seen the surveillance pictures. The girl wears goddamn pants all the time. She's a goddamm Red dyke."

"I suppose it's possible, sir."

"Damn right. Dollars to doughnuts they were the ones that did it. Harding and Bonafontini got caught with egg on their face and the Limey and the broad killed them. And goddamn it, Tamm, if they didn't do it they are involved somehow, I promise you that. Some kind of Limey conspiracy Churchill and fucking Roosevelt have cooked up to get us into this fucking war."

"What about motive, sir?" said Tamm.

"They're going to get the film for themselves. Blackmail Donovan and that other Limey, Stephenson, with it. Maybe even turn them into double agents."

Tamm thought about Wild Bill Donovan being turned by a news photographer and a Brit cop. It was silly. Not for the first time Tamm wondered if his boss might be just a little bit addled in the head. Maybe a lot addled. He'd heard some stories.

"Do you want them picked up, sir?" asked Connelly. There was an eagerness in his voice that Tamm didn't like. Connelly was from the old "pistol-whip them until they talk, and after they talk bury them in a New Jersey dump" school.

"No. Not yet," said the director. "Follow them to Los Angeles. If they seem to be getting away from you, then take them, but not before. I want to squeeze the Limey until all the juice runs out of him." He stared at Tamm with his frog eyes. "That was humorous, Agent Tamm. Limey. Lime. Juice."

"Yes, sir."

"That's fine."

It was a dismissal. The orders had been given, the meeting was over.

Chapter 24

Vassili Zarubin sat in the window booth of Townsend's Café sipping a cup of morning coffee to go along with his two eggs sunny-side up, bacon crisp, white toast and pan fries. The whole meal was making him feel as American as all the men in the café with him, most of whom seemed to be dressed as businessmen or laborers. The two white-aproned waiters and the fat man named Billy who stood behind the counter working the grill seemed not to differentiate between their clientele, a man in paint-splashed coveralls sitting on one of the swiveling chrome-and-red leatherette bar stools at the counter being served before a well-dressed man in a suit who sat with several of his friends in a booth.

The restaurant had many of the small so-called juke-boxes, one for each booth and one for every two bar stools on the counter. When one person had made his choice and deposited his money, that song would be heard in all the jukeboxes in the café. They were presently playing something by Bill Bradley and his Orchestra titled "Scrub Me, Mama, with a Boogie Beat," which Zarubin didn't understand at all, even with his excellent command of the English language, but which the other people in the diner seemed to be enjoying immensely. As far as he could tell, the lyrics told the story of how everyone was going uptown to hear a washerwoman clean her clothes in a particular tuneful way. In Russia Comrade Beria would no doubt have a bullet put in the back of Mr. Bill Bradley's neck, although Zarubin himself found his left leg bouncing lightly beneath the table in time to the music.

The Russian mopped up the last of his egg yolk with a piece of toast just as one of the aproned waiters appeared and topped off his coffee. Then he took out a Camel and lit one, his attention now focused on the building kitty-corner across the intersection of California Street. The building had just opened its main doors. The structure dominated downtown Ventura, a four-story construction of Renaissance Revival brick and granite complete with high curved windows, twisted columns and frolicking, artfully draped cupids dancing over the large entranceway.

The entire main floor was given over to the First National Bank of Ventura. He'd walked past the building earlier in the morning and knew that the upper floors contained the offices of accountants, oil companies, lima bean and fruit exporters, customs brokers, and most of all lawyers, two full floors of them, including one company taking up the entire third floor, Benton, Orr, Duval and Buckingham, which Zarubin presumed accounted for all the suits present in Townsend's Café that morning. Almost on cue a dozen suited individuals dropped money on their tables or places at the counter, got up and left the narrow little restaurant. Vassili checked his wristwatch: precisely nine a.m. He himself was wearing a pair of off-the-rack rayon slacks, a plain white Van Heusen shirt with a striped Arrow tie, a tweed jacket and a very ordinary pair of Nettleton loafers. The sort of outfit no one remembered at all, which was precisely the effect he was looking for.

Zarubin stubbed out his cigarette and dropped three dollars on the table, securing it with his half-empty water glass. He edged around the table, sliding out of the booth, and pushed open the glass door. It was a perfect day, bright cloudless sky, a light breeze and the temperature in the mid-seventies. Early winter in California. He checked for traffic, then crossed over to the bank and went inside.

The interior of the bank was as ornate as the exterior with decorative moldings, a box beam ceiling, marble floors and mahogany counters. Potted palm trees were scattered around the perimeter of the large room, and all the brightwork above the counter was highly polished brass. There were half a dozen tellers already hard at work as well as several desks for loan officers and one that had a triangular plaque that read: SAFE-DEPOSIT BOXES. Vassili crossed over to the safe-deposit desk under the bland, uninterested eye of an armed, uniformed security guard and sat down. The woman behind the desk was in her late thirties, her hair dark brown with flecks of gray and pulled back into an efficient bun. Zarubin did a quick check, upgrading her age into the early forties by the lightly spotted, slightly arthritic look of her hands and the faint skein of crow's-feet at the corner of each eye. She wore no rings on her fingers, although she'd allowed herself a single string of nicely matched cultured Add-A-Pearls, probably one of the iridescent spheres for each intolerable year she'd worked at the bank. She was wearing a checked American Golfer dress with a high collar that was several years too young for her. She left him sitting for a long minute, pretending great interest in the ledger she was leafing through, then looked up at him.

"Yes?" Her voice was a little on the rough side, as though she smoked too many cigarettes or maybe had one too many sherries when she went home to her lonely house each night. The tone was considerably more pleasant than he'd expected.

"I'd like to rent a safe-deposit box."

"Certainly," she said, and smiled. She really was quite attractive. She held out one hand across the desk. "I'm Miss Kristensen, by the way."

"Pleased to meet you," said Zarubin, taking the hand. It was smooth and warm. He could detect a faint brush of perfume coming from her wrist. Something very subtle and elegant. She had an expectant look on her face and for a moment he was confused.

"Oh, yes," he said finally. "Andy Pelham. Just moved down from Santa Barbara." After killing both Pelham and Harte, he'd gone through the house carefully, picking up anything he thought might be useful, including Pelham's wallet and passport, which appeared to have

never been used. Miss Kristensen went into her desk
drawer and brought out a gray metal box about seven
inches long and four inches deep. She produced a key
from one of the pockets of her dress, opened the box
and withdrew a blank card.

"Can you spell the name?" she asked. Zarubin did so
and the woman printed it neatly on the card.
"Occupation?"

"Shipping," said Zarubin, remembering the board full
of company names at the side entrance to the building.

"That's interesting," she said, looking up at him and
smiling.

"It can be," he answered. "Mostly it's just paperwork."

"Like banking," she answered, and they both had a
little laugh. "Address?" she asked.

"It's 540 East Santa Clara. Apartment eleven. The
Medwick."

"That's just a block or so from here," she said.

He nodded. "Down toward the harbor. It's just temporary until I find a house."

"We do a lot of real estate transactions," said the
woman, her smile broadening. "I've just got my license.
Maybe I could look around for you."

"I've never heard of a woman real estate broker."

"More and more of us every day."

"Let me think about it," said Zarubin. The last thing
he wanted in Ventura was a house, but it was in his best
interest to keep the woman happy. "Let's get the safe-
deposit box rented first."

"Fine," she said, her tone cooling slightly. "How large
a size would you be needing? We have three."

"The smallest," Zarubin answered.

She made a tick on the card. "For how long? The
shortest term is one year."

"I'll take that."

Another tick. She made two little X marks on the card
and handed it across to him. "We'll need a password
there, printed please, and your signature below it."

"Password?"

"Yes. It's part of our procedure at the bank. We check

your signature and we check your password. Then we give you access to the box."

"What if I forget the password?"

"Choose something simple." She handed him her pen, a slim Parker Debutante with transparent bands through it so you could see the state of the ink supply. He wrote in the word Harte and then signed his name as Rupert Andrew Pelham. He handed the card and the pen back to Miss Kristensen. She looked at the card. "Interesting password."

"My mother's maiden name."

"Well, I guess you won't forget that." She was smiling again.

Or the name of a man you've recently murdered. He smiled back. "I take back what I said about lady real estate agents."

"Oh?"

"Why don't we have dinner tonight and discuss it?"

She sat back in her chair, the smile stiffening slightly, but not by much. "Are you making a pass at me, Mr. Pelham?"

Zarubin was vaguely aware what a "pass" was, but he wasn't about to test his command of American vernacular.

"I don't think so," he said, smiling. "I think I'm asking an attractive, newly licensed real estate broker out for dinner to discuss business." He paused. "And it's not Mr. Pelham. It's Andy."

"Now I know you're making a pass . . . Andy. And I accept. Why don't you pick me up here around six? There are plenty of good restaurants in the area."

"Perfect," said Zarubin.

"The box is ten dollars a year."

"Fine." He took Pelham's wallet out of his back pocket, took out one of Pelham's tens and handed it across the desk. Miss Kristensen scribbled out a receipt and handed it to him along with the key. He dropped it into his pocket and stood up, still smiling even though he knew the whole thing with the password could ruin his careful plan. It had never occurred to him.

"Six o'clock," he said.

"Six it is, Andy," the woman answered. "And I'm Karen."

Vassili Zarubin kept smiling. Truly, America was a land of opportunity.

Chapter 25

Their movements after leaving the Super Chief had been complicated, done mostly at Black's request. He knew perfectly well that there was no love lost between Stephenson and Hoover and he assumed the director's bullyboys would be waiting for them when they reached Los Angeles. In light of this he consulted with Jane and the schedules and discovered that the flight available to them stopped to refuel in Salt Lake City. Arriving there, they got off the plane and found a small freight and cargo company that was flying to Red Bluff, California, just over the Nevada line. From there they found a second freight company with a flight down to Bakersfield and hitched a ride, even though the pilot said his boss didn't like it when he took passengers. Something about insurance. Black made the doubts go away with a hundred dollars of Fleming's money. It was two in the afternoon by the time they arrived. The airport was a modest collection of two-story white stucco buildings, a few small hangars and a single runway, but it was big enough to have a Hertz desk and a café. Jane rented them a Chevy Super DeLuxe and then, famished, they both went into the café. Morris ordered toad-in-the-hole with chips, which had the waitress's eyebrows arching until Jane explained what chips were and described the concept of frying eggs inside a piece of toast. Jane had a cheeseburger.

"I'm probably worrying for no reason," said Black,

carving up a rubbery egg and spearing a few french fries on his fork, "but better safe than sorry."

"You're probably right." Jane shrugged. "Hoover's little boys can't cover every airport and bus station around, but they could cover L.A. National and United in Pasadena as well. And they'll probably be watching Budberg, you know."

"We'll cross that bridge when we come to it," said Black. He mopped up a suspiciously orange pool of yolk with some toast and washed it down with the last of his coffee. "Ready?"

"When you are."

They paid the waitress, went out into the blistering heat and climbed into the Chevy. Black helped Jane pull the roof of the car back into its slot behind the rear seat and then they were off. Jane went down the dusty dirt road and turned south on Highway 99, following the arrow-straight stretch of asphalt down the San Joaquin Valley, aiming for the rising peaks of the Tehachapi Mountains and their final destination.

Two and a half hours later they were in Los Angeles. Jane stopped at a pay phone and made reservations for them at the Del Capri Motor Hotel on Wilshire. Twenty minutes later they had reached their new temporary home. It was four thirty in the afternoon.

"It's eight bucks a night, single," said Jane as she rolled the rental car to their appointed slot in front of the door to their rooms. "But the coffee shop is good and so is the bar." It was also conveniently close to the Russian princess cum NKVD agent and literary lover, Moura Budberg, who was less than a mile away on the edge of Beverly Hills. They climbed out of the car, retrieved what little luggage they had from the trunk of the Chevy, and Jane handed Morris Black his key. She looked at her watch. It was moving toward dusk but the air was dry and warm, nothing like the bone-chilling cold of Washington or the damp chill of New York at this time of year. She was beginning to think she'd made a mistake bartering for a ticket to the European war zone. California had some very tempting assets.

"I want to get cleaned up and put on some fresh

clothes," said Jane. "Why don't you call our Russian friend and set up a meeting for around six?"

"All right." Black nodded. "You have the number, I presume?"

"Granite 87791. Think you can remember that?"

"Of course." He parroted the number back at her. They separated, Jane going left, Black going through the door to the right.

Morris Black closed the door behind him and let out a long breath. He put his suitcase down and looked around the room. It was remarkably close to how he'd always imagined an American motel room would be. There were two double beds with a small night table between them, the beds covered by hideous flower-patterned and quilted coverlets made from some bright yellow fabric.

The headboards were also padded and quilted with the same cloth, and the yellow on the walls was accented by a slightly less garish shade. There was a large Spanish-style wooden chest at the foot of each bed that matched the night table and two chests of drawers in the same style. Everything was alike and there was two of everything with the exception of the night table.

The window, which looked out onto the pool at the far end of the room, was covered with the same fabric as the beds. Between the chests of drawers was a connecting door to Jane's room, which was bolted. He leaned toward the door and could hear the faint sound of a shower running. He sat down on the edge of one of the beds, lit a cigarette and smiled. He hadn't had a proper bath since leaving England, only showers, just like the Americans.

His mind was suddenly wiped clean and filled with the startling and uncomfortable image of Jane in the shower. He tried to brush it from his thoughts but the image refused to remove itself. Ever since they'd met he'd found himself drawn to the woman; to her obvious intelligence, her forthrightness, her laughter and her healthy good looks. She was the fantasy New York girl he'd always imagined in his life, smart, but without the upper-class associations he'd always felt with Katherine, the only other American woman he'd known. He smiled again and yawned. His mother would have been polite to Katherine had they ever met, but she would have taken Jane to her heart. He laughed out loud. Knowing his mother, she'd probably have taught her how to make a good Jewish meal, from herring to macaroons.

In the background he could hear the sound of the shower stopping. She'd be stepping out into her room now, wearing nothing but a towel. . . . He stopped himself. Every time they came even close to intimacy it seemed to lead to some ghastly horror, like discovering the two bodies on the Super Chief. He looked at his watch instead. Time to phone Moura Budberg, not to think about the naked woman in the next room.

He picked up the telephone on the night table and began to dial. It didn't take him long to realize that he couldn't dial out directly from the room. He heard a very tinny woman's voice in his ear instead.

"Switchboard."

"I beg your pardon?"

"What I said, pal. This is the switchboard."

"I'd like to reach a number, please."

"Sure, pal. Give it to me."

"Granite 87791."

"Sure, pal. Just give me a second."

"Take as long as you'd like," said Black.

"Right. Hang on."

Black hung on. He could hear the mechanical sound of a telephone being dialed, then a strange metallic noise.

"Hello."

"There you go, pal."

Suddenly, a little faintly, he could hear the ringing of a telephone. It was picked up on the third ring. Another woman's voice, this one very slightly accented.

"Granite 87791."

"I'd like to speak with Miss Moura Budberg." He refused to use the idiotic title she'd given herself—Countess Moura Zakrevskaia Benckendorff or whatever the hell it was. She didn't seem to mind at all.

"You have an English accent," the woman said with a little laughter in her voice. "You must be MI6."

"I've heard you referred to as an agent for the NKVD," countered Black.

"Pah," said the woman, laughing out loud now. "A story to tell at parties. It excites young men." She paused. "Older ones too, for that matter. They always seem to think they're saving me from a fate worse that death."

"And were they?"

"Only from boredom," the woman replied.

She's flirting with me, Black realized. It was either a natural talent or a skill she'd developed to the point of being an art. No more than a whisper, but she could probably raise your body temperature simply by being in the same room with her. She'd told at least three of her lovers that she was an agent for the Soviets, vaguely denied it to Black a few seconds ago, and now he was starting to doubt his own information, not to mention the file he'd read about her. He tried to shake the feeling off by bringing things back to the business at hand.

"Aren't you afraid the FBI might be listening? They may well be tapping your telephone line."

"I'm quite sure they are," said the woman. "As well as the British Secret Service, which I happen to know has several operatives in Los Angeles, almost certainly Colonel Donovan's apparat and probably my old friends from Dzerzhinskiy Square as well."

"You don't mind them listening to your every word?"

"The idea is quite terrifying. That fat little bulldog Mr. Hoover would have me arrested in a minute."

"I'm not sure I understand."

"Mr. Hoover and Mr. Donovan and whoever is running the NKVD in the United States may well be listening to the telephone in my apartment. They may even have microphones behind every painting on the walls of my bedroom, but they will hear nothing slanderous, seditious or salacious, I assure you."

"I still don't understand."

The Budberg woman sighed. "They may be tapping the telephone line in my apartment. They are not, however, tapping *this* telephone line." She waited to see if Black would understand what she was saying. He did.

"You have another apartment in the building."

"Well done, Mr. Englishman. Very convenient as well. Right across the hall from the one I openly rent but which I do not occupy."

"Expensive."

"I have a great many resources, Mr. Englishman, financial and otherwise."

"Nevertheless, it's devious enough for Mata Hari."

"Pah," said the woman. "A highly overrated amateur at best."

"You're sure this number isn't tapped?"

"Quite sure. I have a friend at one of the movie studios—a gaffer, I believe he is called. He moonlights for people like myself. There is a device attached to my telephone which I believe he described as being a voltmeter. Apparently there is a certain amount of electricity flowing through a telephone line, enough to carry the voice and make the bell ring. If one taps into the line, the amount of the current is slightly drained, which shows up on the voltmeter. My gaffer friend also arranged for an extension from my formal apartment across the hall."

"Ingenious," said Black, meaning it.

"I thought so." She paused. "What exactly can I do for you, Mr. Englishman?"

"My associate and I would like to have a preliminary meeting with you."

"When?"

"This evening if possible. Seven?"

"Fine, but there is one thing you should know before you make your visit."

"Tell me," said Black: And she did.

Chapter 26

Bryson Towers was a narrow fourteen-story paean of praise to the art deco era when radios looked like rocket ships and buildings looked like radios. The concrete was stained a pale ochre color and decorated along the top floors with dark bas reliefs of modernistic, industrial-looking human figures and motifs. The penthouse floors were decorated with more Edward Hopper–style men and women with bulging muscles and things that looked a lot like electrical coils.

At seven o'clock a Ford delivery van drove up in front of Bryson Towers, parking on the street rather than under the cloth canopy of the building, which would have blocked any cabs or limousines delivering people to the apartment house. The truck was painted a dark blue and the name Star Catering was written across the side in gold script.

A man and a woman climbed out of the van, the man dressed in full evening dress, the woman in a black-and-white French maid's outfit replete with silk stockings and high-heel shoes. They went around to the rear of the delivery van, and the man pulled open the double doors and climbed in. He let down two metal rails, forming a ramp from the rear of the truck to the ground, then proceeded to roll out a pair of large delivery carts covered with white linen cloths. The man pushed the rails back into the rear of the truck and closed the doors. He then pushed the larger of the two delivery carts up onto the sidewalk, down the broad walkway leading to the main doors of Bryson Towers, followed by the woman pushing the second delivery cart. They went through the doors and disappeared.

The two caterers were met at the door by the uniformed doorman, who asked them where they were delivering to. The man in the evening clothes said the delivery was for the Countess Moura Zakrevskaia Benckendorff and also informed the doorman that the hors d'oeuvres were getting cold and that surely the doorman didn't want to risk the countess contracting food poisoning from overheated caviar. He also slipped the man ten dollars, at which point he led them over to the brass-doored elevators, which were surmounted by the same sort of bas reliefs as the outside of the building. He used one white-gloved finger to press the UP button, and the doors opened to reveal another man in uniform, this one extremely old, dozing on a small leather-covered stool.

"Wake up, Sizlack."

The old man blinked and smacked his lips a couple of times. "What?" he said blearily.

"Twelve."

"What?"

"Twelve," said the doorman. He turned to the man in the evening clothes. "Joe's a little hard of hearing." He leaned into the elevator. "Take these nice people up to twelve." He added loudly, "The countess."

"Sure, sure," said Joe.

The two caterers rolled the carts into the elevator cage, filling it with an assortment of complicated cooking odors. Joe pushed the door-closing button, shifted his motor lever to the right, and the elevator began to rise.

Joe's nose twitched. "Smells good."

"That it does," said the woman in the maid's outfit.

"Got any extras maybe?" Joe asked, lifting a bushy gray eyebrow.

"No," said the man in the evening clothes.

"What about you, girlie?" Joe said with a leer. "You got any extras of your own you might like to give an old man?"

"Bet he doesn't talk to the tenants this way," said the woman.

"No," the man with her agreed.

"Can't blame a guy for trying," said Joe. "Didn't get much for the first sixty-two years of my life, so you might call this a last-ditch attempt."

"Good-looking guy like you, Joe?" said the maid. "Can't believe you weren't a hot catch in your time."

"All I ever caught was malaria and yellow fever digging that son-of-a-bitching Panama Canal and the syph, the drips, and a bad case o' crabs from the fucking prossies in fucking gay Paree during the big war, *pardonnez* my French, girlie." As he apologized, he gave the woman in the maid's costume a quick up and down over again. The woman laughed, reached down and hiked up her skirt a couple of inches, doing a quick back and forth like a chorus girl. Joe's eyes almost dropped out of his head.

"You've made an old man's day," said Joe. They hit twelve and the grizzled elevator operator pulled back the lever and opened the doors. The man backed out with his cart first, followed by the woman. "Last apartment on the left," said Joe.

The woman twitched her backside more than was entirely necessary as she headed away, figuring it was the least she could do for an old soldier, and it wasn't until they reached the apartment door and knocked that they heard the elevator door clang shut behind them.

The door opened and the two caterers found themselves facing a woman in her forties, dressed in a long silk gown, huge white flowers on a shimmering black background. She had an oval face, huge brown eyes and a largish nose all topped by a dark bobbed hairdo. Not beautiful perhaps, but certainly striking. She ushered the two caterers into the apartment and shut the door behind her. The caterers rolled the carts into the middle of the dining room, where Moura Budberg gave each of them a twenty-dollar bill.

"Thank you," she said. "You've been a great help."

"No problem," said the man. Budberg guided them back into the foyer and let them out of the apartment. By the time she'd returned to the dining room, Morris Black and Jane Todd had rolled out from their constricted hiding places under the draped carts.

"Bloody hell," said Black, stretching, his limbs making small cracking sounds. "I was beginning to cramp up permanently. About to turn into the ruddy hunchback of Notre Dame."

"Ah, my poor Quasimodo. Perhaps I can massage those shoulders of yours." Moura Budberg stepped toward him, but he raised a hand and glanced at Jane.

"I'll be fine." He'd noticed that the woman's accent had changed completely. On the phone it had been faintly European, perhaps Czech or Hungarian. Now it was West End well-educated London, a perfect match for Black's own speech. Jane was already giving her a skeptical look.

"Did you see why all this was necessary?"

"Sure," Jane answered. She had lifted the cloth covering her cart a little as they were being unloaded from her old friend Aldo's truck. "A dark blue Dodge and the white Mercury. Two guys wearing hats in the Dodge, so they must be FBI, two more in the Mercury who look like they might be Russkies."

"Very good," said Moura Budberg. "I agree with you about the men with hats, and the two men in the Mercury are Alexandrovichi. Local White Russians who think the tsars will rise again."

"You don't sound very positive about the idea," said Jane.

"Just realistic. Stalin will not live forever but there are plenty to take his place, and when they are gone, plenty more behind them. It is a very rich country to pillage if you have the stomach for it, or the madness."

"Comrade Stalin has enough of both," said Black.

"Quite so." She smiled. "Perhaps we should be on a closer basis now that we have met."

"Doesn't make sense until you know what kind of snake you're dealing with," said Jane.

"I am a snake?"

"You might be." Jane shrugged. "According to what I hear, you've got a fair number of men charmed right out of their little minds, just the way a cobra hypnotizes its prey."

"A little melodramatic, don't you think?"

"I like melodrama," said Jane. "I'm a sucker for movies with Greta Garbo in them."

"She was very good in *Anna Karenina*," answered the Budberg woman dismissively.

"Perhaps we should get down to business," said Jane.

"No. First I will show you around my home." The Budberg woman smiled. "It is the European way of things."

Black was astonished. The British accent was gone, replaced once again by the Eastern European but not quite Russian accent she'd put on previously, as though she was changing clothes. He knew from her file that the woman's spoken Russian wasn't very good either, and as far as written language went her skills were well below par. Odd for a woman who was supposed to have been born and raised in Russia as well as presuming to have a successful career as Maxim Gorky's translator. The file had held the facts, but the reality of seeing the woman in action was quite disconcerting.

Jane nodded. "Lead on, Countess."

The living room had a faintly Oriental look to it with lacquered beams set into the plaster of the ceiling and a Chinese scholar screen and scholar's bench in front of the fireplace. A pair of identical dark green leather couches with channeled backs faced each other across another carved scholar's bench that acted as a coffee table, and the narrow-planked white birch floor was covered by a huge but plain Japanese carpet in taupe with a wide black border.

The paintings on the walls were about as far from Oriental as you could get: What appeared to be a Rembrandt portrait or something very much like it hung on one wall and a massive Phillip Ferdinand de Hamilton hunting scene of bizarre-looking dogs, a pair of hooded falcons and a brace of very dead and exceedingly ornamental pheasant adorned another. In the hallway leading to the bedroom there was another portrait like the possible Rembrandt, this one of a seated woman in a dressing gown who was feeding a parrot.

The bedroom itself contained a Constantin Brancusi oil-on-board portrait signed and dated 1918 and an etching that had to be by Picasso showing a very odd-looking woman with a nose like a carrot and huge crying eyes. In the dining room, filled with more Oriental and art deco furniture, there was another Dutch Master of ships at anchor by Jan van de Cappelle. On the other side of the eighteenth-century Italian cherry table there was something that advertised itself as a Claude Monet, *Sailboats at Argenteuil,* painted in 1882.

"Very impressive," said Black as they came back into the living room.

Very expensive too, thought Jane. She almost asked which one of her lovers was paying the tab but kept her mouth shut.

The countess, as they now seemed to be calling her, smiled possessively and gestured toward one of the long leather couches. On the end tables were large, gleaming crystal ashtrays. Jane lit a cigarette without asking if she could as the countess sat down opposite her two visitors.

"Now can we get down to business?" asked Jane. "Or are there some more European things we have to do first?"

"My, you are very American, aren't you? No niceties." The British accent was back, flattened out a little as though she was practicing an American persona.

"I don't feel much like a nicety these days," Jane answered. "I've been shot at, had dead bodies left in my train compartment, been forced to run for my life in a crapped-out old airplane and just now I had to get one of my old friends from the movie business to sneak me in here crouched down in a catering cart. We're here about the Levitsky film."

"Of course you are," the countess responded brightly. "Rudely or otherwise."

Black lit a cigarette of his own. The countess reached into a red lacquered box on the table, withdrew a black cigarette with a gold tip and inserted the golden end into an ivory holder she took from the same box. She leaned across the table expectantly and Black lit hers as well.

"One thing we'd like to know is the part you're playing in all of this. From what I can tell, you were the one who began spreading the rumor that the film was being offered for sale."

"Aigee told you that?"

Who the hell was Aigee? thought Black, and then it struck him. Aigee was H. G. She was back in her Russian mode. "You mean Mr. Wells."

"Of course."

"I don't see that the source is relevant at the moment," Black said.

"Unless you really are a Red spy," said Jane.

The accent seemed to become thicker, more Russian. Even the words became stilted, more theatrical. "But of course I am a Red spy, as you call it, my dear. I have never said I was anything else, not for many years. I have even told your friend Detective Black this. A story to be told at parties."

"I'd still like to know what your role in all of this is."

"There are a number of people who want my friend Alexander Mikhailovitch's little film. There is not one of them who trusts the other, thus I am here."

"You're a friend of Levitsky's?"

"We have come to know each other."

"He asked you to be his broker in this?"

"He suggested it."

"Do you know who the other parties involved are?"

"I have some idea."

"Some of them seem to be shooting at us," put in Jane. "Friends of yours?"

"How unfortunate that you are being fired upon," said the countess, smiling benignly in Jane's direction. She reached out and tapped the end of her cigarette into an ashtray on the Oriental coffee table, then sat back, curling her legs up underneath her. Jane had a strong urge to reach across the coffee table and rip the cigarette holder out from between the woman's Max Factor lips. It didn't take any woman's intuition to know that this little viper lied as easily as she breathed.

"The FBI doesn't want the film," said Black. "I seriously doubt they're in the running."

"They'd like it if they could get it for nothing, I assure you." Her bombing run was dead on target.

"So that leaves us the Reds, the Whites and maybe even the Krauts," said Jane.

"You have evidence the Nazis are interested?"

"No, but it makes sense. Anything the Brits want that bad and the Reds are gunning for would interest Uncle Adolf, don't you think?"

"I never really thought of them as players in the game."

"If the film actually shows Lockhart in attendance at the assassination of the tsar and his family, it would be extraordinarily embarrassing for the royal family, especially at this particular moment in history. It would be proof positive that the king had abandoned his cousins to a gruesome death. Hardly the stuff of patriotism." Black paused. "That's Mr. Wells's position at any rate, which I suppose would also be the position of his friends, including people like Hoare and Beaverbrook. It would be a disaster for Churchill since Lockhart still works for the Foreign Office."

"Poor Aigee," said the countess, tapping the ash off her cigarette again. "Such a worrier."

"War has changed, madam," said Black. "Battles can be won or lost on the basis of world opinion, not just bombs and bullets."

"Bombs and bullets have as little to do with war as world opinion, Detective Black. Wars are fought and won on the basis of politics and money, which are often the same thing. The United States will enter the war when it becomes politically somewhat more expedient than it is at the moment, and when it suits their financial situation."

"This is a great conversation here," Jane cut in sourly. "Solving the world's problems over a coffee table. What we want to know is what we're getting into here and if anyone's going to be firing any more bullets at us."

Black interjected, "And does the film even exist."

"Certainly it exists." The countess sniffed loudly.

"Where is it?"

"In a safe place, I assure you."

"How do we get it?"

"By paying a great deal of money to Mr. Levitsky for the privilege."

"You're telling me this is going to be some sort of auction?"

"Something like that."

"When?"

"Five days. Saturday, December sixth."

"Where?"

"You will be informed well in advance and told the rules of play."

"This is no game," Jane said crisply. "And we're not playing."

"Don't quibble about words," the countess said, then added, "*Zadnitza tupoj*."

"And if the film isn't worth buying?" Jane asked, ignoring what she assumed was an insult.

"Then feel free not to buy it," snapped the countess. She stood up and crossed the room to where a telephone rested on a table near the window. "Now shall I call you a taxi?"

Black stood up and went to the large front window. The green two-door sedan with the large aerial he'd seen on their arrival was still there. "Presumably that vehicle is always parked in front of your building?" he asked the Budberg woman.

"The green one or the blue one?" She shrugged. "It's usually one or the other. I presume it's Mr. Hoover's young men. There are always two in each car."

"What's around back?" Jane asked.

"A hill. A path. The next street."

"They'll have someone there," said Black, shaking his head. He glanced down at the green car again. The passenger-side door was opening and a young man in a gray suit stepped out. He glanced up at the building and then started walking across Wilshire. "I think we're about to have company."

"I told my friend Aldo to say if anyone called they were supposed to say one of their trucks had been stolen. I didn't want to get him into any trouble."

"Well, they must have called."

"What do we do now?"

"I rather think the direct route is best," Black answered. He gave Moura Budberg a chilly smile. "And I wouldn't want us to discommode our host."

"I suppose I should return to my own apartment to greet our friend when he arrives," said Budberg.

They said a brief good-bye to the Russian woman and

stepped out into the hall. There was only one elevator in the building and the indicator light said it was on its way up. Jane and Morris Black headed for the fire stairs, taking them two at a time. They reached the bottom and paused in the main floor stairwell. The steps continued down one more flight.

"He's going to knock on her door and find out we're not there pretty quick," said Jane.

"Give me a minute or two," said Black. "I'm going to look for the basement exit. After two minutes, step out of the stairwell, cross the lobby and step outside where the other man can see you. Keep his attention on you."

"Then what?"

"When you see me coming cross the street, lean in through his window as though you want to talk to him. Show him as much of your . . ." He flushed slightly.

"Cleavage?"

"Um, yes," said Black. "As much as you can."

Jane adjusted her bra slightly and undid two buttons, her breasts almost popping out of her dark-colored blouse. "How's that?"

Black stared. "Quite lovely as a matter of fact."

Jane leaned over and gave him a peck on the cheek. "What a Romeo."

"Not bloody likely."

"Get going," Jane said. "We may not have much time."

"Quite right," said Black. He took a last look at her and headed down the last flight of steps to the basement.

Jane stayed where she was and began to keep a silent count as the seconds winked by. She had a fair idea of what Black was going to do and realized how mad it was, both in the execution and the aftermath. She shook her head, grinning as she continued to count off the seconds. And he'd seemed like such a levelheaded fellow when she'd first met him, a little shy, a little reserved, the methodical cop plodding along, doing his job. But there was more than met the eye—during the interrogation of Mercador he'd been a lying son of a bitch, playing the role of an NKVD officer down to his socks. At the Trotsky villa he'd drawy fire without a thought for himself, and when they'd discovered the two bodies on the Super Chief he'd treated it like an everyday occurrence. Not to mention the fact that aside from his thinning hair and being a little on the scrawny side he was also sexier than hell, especially with that accent, which she'd always been a sucker for. . . .

Before she got too deeply into that particular line of thinking, the little voice in her head reached the count of 120. Two minutes was up and it was time to go onstage. She adjusted her blouse, wished she had a couple of linen napkins or at least a few Kleenex to stuff into her bra, and stepped out of the stairwell and headed across the lobby. The uniformed doorman was following every step and was right there to open one of the double glass doors. She stepped out of the shadows of the awning that ran out to the sidewalk and posed for a few seconds until she was sure she'd caught the FBI agent's undivided attention. She headed across Wilshire, moving directly toward the car, swinging her can a little, but hopefully not making it look too much like a bad vamp. She reached the car, leaned over and stuck her head in through the open window, balancing her melons on the edge of the opening.

"You looking at something, Mr. FBI man, or you just being patriotic waving that flagpole in your pants?"

"I don't know what you're talking about, lady."

"About being FBI or the state of your notion?" She smiled. Pretty soon she was going to run out of Mae West lines from *My Little Chickadee*. There was a clicking sound as the Mexican semiautomatic was cocked. The agent jerked his eyes away from Jane and looked across at the passenger-side door. The pistol was being poked through the open window by Morris Black.

"Take out your weapon, slowly," said Black, "and put it on the seat beside you."

The young man hesitated, focused on the gun in Black's hand, and then did as he was told. His weapon turned out to be a standard-issue Smith & Wesson .38 Police Special with a four-inch barrel. He laid it on the passenger seat, his eyes still on Black.

"Get out of the automobile. Leave the key in the ignition," said Black.

"Fuck you," said the FBI agent.

"Commendable courage," said Black. "But pointless. I *will* shoot, you know."

"You don't have the pills for it, pal. None of you Limeys do."

"Really?" said Black. "Well, think about this. I won't shoot you in the head, or the chest, or the pills, as you call them. I'll shoot you in the knee. You'll walk with a limp for the rest of your life and your career as a heroic G-man will be over. How does that sound?"

The man stared at him. Jane reached out and pulled the door open. The man hesitated for a single second and then stepped out of the car. Jane swung in behind the wheel and slammed the door as Black got in on the other side.

"Drive," said Black, and Jane drove, leaving the unfortunate and unarmed FBI agent standing in the middle of Wilshire Boulevard, watching them go.

Chapter 27

Monday, December 1, 1941
Ventura

Vassili Zarubin continued to thrust for as long as he could but eventually gave up the ghost, slithering out from between the strong thighs of Miss Karen Kristensen, the safe-deposit officer at the First National Bank. As well as the sweat he had worked up over the last hour with her in the bedroom of her little house off Pico Street, he was also slick with her fluid, glistening from his navel halfway down to his knees, his still-thick organ wet with her, his dark pubic hair matted. He had never expected to find her either so passionate or so well versed in such intimate matters, and he'd long ago realized that he was not the seducer but the seduced. The woman with the strong thighs and the expressive mouth and tongue had done things to him he would never have believed possible. In comparison to the women of his own cold land, she was a wonderful, furnace-hot dream come true. Not to mention the interesting meal prepared for them by what appeared to be the entire Soo Hoo family at the Chinese Gardens Café on Main Street.

Vassili was reasonably sure he hadn't shamed himself as a lover. She had moaned sincerely as he entered her even though he knew perfectly well he was no more than a little larger than average, and she had climaxed at least twice, her voice ringing out so loudly that it occurred to him her neighbors might think she was in desperate straits and call the police. At one point her own ministrations had made him feel as though he was about to pass out, and the two ejaculations he had experienced had been enormous. The tables had certainly been turned. At the end of the evening he had been sure that she would be in his thrall and now it seemed that it was the reverse. To repeat his recent experience he knew he would do virtually anything she wanted.

"That was wonderful," he said, still panting. He crawled up the bed and dropped down beside her, his head falling back against the pillow. She turned on her side and he could feel the whole length of her pressed up against him. Her body was powerful and fit, her breasts large and heavy, her legs long and her hips almost as lean as a boy's. Ridiculously he felt himself beginning to harden again—ridiculous because he simply didn't have the physical energy to repeat his performance, at least not for a few more minutes.

He felt her move even closer, throwing one leg over his, pressing her soaking sex against his thigh, moving in a gentle rhythm. The mixture of the woman's perfume and her own rich musk was intoxicating. To break his own concentration on the sensations she was raising in him, he reached out to the night table and picked up his cigarettes. He lit one and dropped back against the pillow again.

"I'll have one of those," said Karen. She made a little laughing sound deep in her throat. "Since you seem to be taking a break." Vassili handed her the one he was smoking and lit a second one for himself.

"You saved an old lady's life."

"Old?" he said. "You're not old."

"When you haven't had a man for the better part of a year you start to feel old, believe me."

"I'm surprised to hear you say that."

"Don't be. Ventura doesn't have a lot to offer in the way of interesting men, or at least single ones." She took a drag on her cigarette and blew smoke rings up at the dimly seen ceiling above the bed. "Most of them come through the bank one way or another, either asking for loans or cosigning for them. Every businessman in the city has walked by my desk over the last eleven years."

"That's how long you've been with the bank?"

"That's right."

"I'm surprised you're not the president," he said.

"If I'd let myself be screwed by that shit Dorfman in Loans, or old man Mason, I probably would be by now. Amazing how many of my coworkers were so solicitous of my physical needs after Clancy died."

"Clancy?"

"My husband, Ray Clancy." She took another drag. "I went back to using my maiden name."

"I hope he died in bed with you," said Zarubin. "He would have been halfway to paradise already."

Karen leaned over and bit him gently on the shoulder. "You're sweet," she said softly and then sighed. "The truth is, he was a cheating son of a bitch who I probably would have killed myself if he hadn't done it on his own, drunk as a skunk in his car on the way back from a card game in Oxnard. That's what his friends said anyway. Only trouble was, he wasn't alone in the car. One of the town pumps was with him, and she died as well. It was never official, but they tell me her head was crushed on the steering column, and when they dragged the bastard out of the wreck his fly was unzipped and his dick was hanging out. Not that it was much of a dick when you get right down to it." She reached over Vassili with her free hand and squeezed his half-hard organ. "Not like yours, Mr. Mary Sunshine."

"You're going to make me blush," he said, trying to sound shy. She reached over him again to tap her cigarette into the ashtray on the bedside table, her big firm breast pressing against him. Her touch made him even firmer and she helped him along, squeezing him and slowly moving her fist up and down on his shaft.

"You're just about ready to go."

"My brain agrees with you, my body doesn't."

"Could have fooled me," said Karen, squeezing him a little harder. He gently removed her hand from his organ.

"Nature calls, I'm afraid."

She released him, and naked he climbed out of bed, went out the door into the hall and crossed to the bathroom. He closed and locked the door, then tried to make water, which was virtually impossible in his present condition. He put down the seat and sat down on the toilet, tucking his organ uncomfortably between his legs while it slowly detumesced and tried not to think about the job he'd come to do. If Moura Budberg's information was correct, the Americans, the Brits, the Alexandrovski and maybe even the Germans would all be vying for Levitsky's mysterious film. He wanted more than the film; he wanted Levitsky himself. Even after more than twenty years Stalin still wanted the man's head on the end of a stick, and Zarubin was bound and determined to deliver it to him. Beneath him he felt himself begin to shrivel, and after a few moments he urinated, still sitting down.

He stood up, flushed, then washed his hands. There was only one toothbrush in the little porcelain rack at the sink, so he wet his finger and squeezed a blob of Karen's Listerine Tooth Paste onto the tip of his finger and went over his gums and teeth with it.

When he returned to the bedroom, she was sitting with her back up against the padded headboard, her thighs open, wiping herself off with a tissue. It was a remarkably intimate sight for a man who was used to taking his pleasure with women who rarely removed their nightdresses, and he stood for a moment, watching her.

"Like what you see?" she asked finally, looking up.

"Very much."

"Me too," she answered. "Even though you don't quite look as dramatic as you did a few minutes ago." She grinned. "But I can fix that." She wadded up the tissue and threw it onto the night table. "First I want to know exactly who you are."

"You know who I am," he said pleasantly.

"I know you told me your name was Andy Pelham and I know you told me you were in the shipping business, but I don't believe you." She paused. "And I'd rather you didn't lie to me again."

"Why don't you think I was telling the truth?" Zarubin asked. His little pocket pistol was in his jacket, which was hanging over the chair, but he wanted to hear her out first.

"Well, first of all you're too smart to be in something

like shipping. There's something about you. People in the shipping business are like dull razor blades. They cut, but they leave a lot to be desired."

"And the name?"

"In the first place you don't look like an Andy, and the driver's license you showed me was from Santa Barbara. You could run a shipping business out of Santa Barbara just as easy as Ventura, and the final thing is, you don't make love like somebody named Andy who's in the shipping business. Call it woman's intuition, or maybe I'm just smarter than you thought I was." She waited. "So? Who are you?"

He stalled. "How does somebody in the shipping business make love?"

"Like every other businessman. Businesslike. Get your clothes off, get your dick in, get it off and get it out. Have one last drink and say good night."

"Sounds boring."

"It *is* boring. And you haven't answered my question. Who are you? Not just some slick passing through and looking for a little tail, I hope."

Zarubin didn't really know what she was talking about, but it didn't sound very positive. He shook his head.

"Then what?"

"What do *you* think?" he said, trying to buy some time.

"If I knew, I wouldn't be asking." She remained exactly as she'd been when he walked into the room, open and vulnerable, completely without inhibition. He thought about the kind of life she must have led working at the bank all those years and wondered if that might not be the answer. After all that boredom and unchanging routine without relief, she would want a little excitement, close enough to the truth to be believed.

"Have you ever heard the name Leon Trotsky?"

"Sure. The Commie who got an ice ax in the head last year in Mexico."

"He also has a safe-deposit box in your bank."

"You've got to be kidding me."

"Not at all. In your records it will be under the name Lev Bronstein."

She tried to think, pushing out her lips. "It doesn't ring a bell. We've got more than three hundred boxes, though. I can't put a face or a name to all of them."

"The Commies have been trying to get their hands on the contents of that box for the better part of five years now."

"What's in it?"

"Documents. Important ones." He went to his pants, which were neatly folded over a chair in one corner of the room. He took out the key on the silver chain he'd retrieved from Harte and held it up in the dim light.

"That's one of our keys," she said, surprised.

"Trotsky's key. Lev Bronstein's. The only problem is, I don't know his password."

"You still haven't answered my question."

"I work for an organization called the Co-ordinator of Information. COI. My boss is a man named William Donovan."

She straightened up from the wall. "I've heard of him."

"We need to get the contents of the box before the Communists do."

"What are the documents about?"

He had sunk the hook. He could get her to help him. "I'm afraid I can't tell you."

"Can you tell me your real name at least?"

"I'm not supposed to."

"But will you?"

"For you, yes."

"Well?"

He tried to think of a name she would like, one that would appeal to this strange woman.

"Daniel," he said quietly after a long moment. "I can't tell you the rest. It would be too dangerous for you to know."

"Daniel in the lions' den," she answered softly.

"It looks that way at the moment."

"Maybe there's something I can do to help."

After one more dance in the safe-deposit officer's bed, Vassili Zarubin showered with his new friend, dressed and had a cup of freshly percolated Chase and Sanborn in Karen Kristensen's spotless kitchen, where they developed their plan of attack. By the time they had finished their coffee and climbed into Karen's high-sided white 1936 Nash 400 coupe it was nine o'clock and darkness had completely fallen. With her high beams on she drove down the gentle hill on Church Street. She traversed the town, finally swinging the Nash into the alleyway that ran behind the First National Bank Building.

"You're sure you want to do this?" asked Zarubin.

"I'm sure." Karen nodded. She pulled out the parking brake and got out of the car, Zarubin getting out on the other side.

"Don't the police patrol the alleys?"

"Sure," Karen said, "and they all know my car. I've been known to work late. Nobody's going to get suspicious."

She locked up the car and they went down the alley to a narrow metal door. Karen brought a ring of keys out of her purse, chose one and deftly placed it into the lock. The door opened and she stood aside, ushering Zarubin into the back foyer of the bank. She came in behind him and locked the door behind her before stepping across to a gray metal box mounted on the wall. She used a second key from her ring to open the box, reached in and pulled down a single lever, exposing a brass timer with a white enamel face that registered twenty-three seconds out of sixty.

"Anyone entering the bank after hours has got one minute to get the box open and pull down the switch to turn off the exterior alarm after opening the door, or all hell breaks lose. The police station is less than a block away. Probably why this place has never been robbed."

Well, thought Vassili Zarubin with a sudden chill, there is always a first time. He'd never had sexual relations with an American woman who wasn't being paid for it, and he'd most certainly never robbed a bank before.

"Come on." Karen led him down a short, dimly lit hallway. She opened another door and Zarubin stepped out into the bank, which was flooded with light. The venetian blinds on the front windows were closed. She crossed to her desk with Zarubin on her heels. Seating herself at her desk, she opened her left-hand drawer, pulled out her gray box of file cards and used another one of her keys to open it.

"Baker, Bellman, Berman, Betinski—he's a strange one, Polish, I think. Here we go. Lev Bronstein, M34. M stands for Medium, our midsize box." She wrote the number down on a slip of paper and put the box away, then stood up again. "This is pretty exciting for someone like me."

Vassili nodded. It wasn't exciting for him; it was just nerve-racking to the point of nausea. If he was caught now, it wouldn't be long until he was on his way home to Moscow, and within five minutes of his arrival he'd be in the back of a big old Zis 44 prisoner bus on his way to Beria's chamber of horrors, or perhaps one of those insane asylums Beria was beginning to favor.

Keys in hand, Karen crossed the marble floor of the bank and went down a flight of steps to the lower level, Vassili very close behind her. Using yet another key, she unlocked a steel gate, opened it and turned to the right, where she stepped through into the safe-deposit-box area. Zarubin stood by, feeling cold lines of sweat trickling down from his armpits. The safe-deposit room, with a smaller annex equipped with a viewing table off to one side, was only a little bigger than a prison cell at the Lubyanka. Karen checked the piece of paper in her hand, crouched down on her haunches and finally found the one she was looking for.

"Give me your key," she said, holding up her hand. Zarubin handed it to her, chain and all. She fit her own key into the lock on the left and Bronstein's key into the lock on the right. She turned them both and then slid the box out of its niche. Smiling proudly, she handed the box up to Zarubin.

"I'll just wait outside until you open it," she said.

"Okay."

"This was pretty easy, wasn't it, Daniel?"

"Pretty easy." He felt as though he was going to throw up. "I'll just be a minute."

"Now that the alarm is off, take your time," Karen answered. She threw him a big smile, turned on her heel and left the room.

Surreptitiously Zarubin gave the box a little shake. Something metallic shifted inside. He sighed gratefully, then took the box into the little annex. He threw open the lid of the box and stared inside. Resting on the bottom of the box was a small metal can about seven inches across. A strip of gummed paper with a Russian inscription in ink was pasted over an old-fashioned Kodak label.

Dom Chegyaiihoro Nazhayehud
The House of Special Purpose

Vassili Zarubin lifted the can out of the box. A second piece of tape had been used to seal the two halves of the can together and then been shellacked over. The shellac had long since cracked and yellowed. The paper had also been slit, as though by a thumbnail or a pocketknife. Heart falling, Zarubin twisted the two halves of the flat can open to reveal its contents. The shellac on the paper tape cracked and crumbled, a small piece of it drifting down into the safe-deposit box.

The can was empty. The film was gone.

"Blyad'!" he cursed softly.

An hour later, the telephone rang in Moura Budberg's bedroom. She was reading a copy of Vladimir Nabokov's *Mashenk'a,* or *Mary*, his first novel in Russian. The newly released *The Real Life of Sebastian Knight*, his first novel in English, lay on her bedside table. She was intending to compare the level of his writing in both languages. At the sound of the telephone ringing she turned the book over in her lap and picked up the receiver.

"Yes?"

The man who responded did so neither in Russian nor in English. Instead he spoke fluent and cultured Swedish. Moura Budberg responded in kind.

"Levitsky emptied the box. The film is gone."

"When?"

"According to the files at the bank, it was several weeks ago."

"Anything else?"

"Levitsky's house in Ventura has been ransacked. From the contents of his refrigerator it appears likely he has not been in residence for some time." There was a pause. "A body was also discovered in his house. A woman. Fresh."

"Who?"

"Someone named Kristensen. An officer at the bank."

"Who did it?"

"Probably Zarubin."

"How did he find out about the safe-deposit box?"

"His contact in Donovan's organization, or one of them at least, was found dead. No doubt he gave up Pelham and Harte."

"Have you tried to contact them?"

"Of course. No response so far."

"Perhaps you should check."

"Perhaps you should check, madam. It is much too dangerous for any of our people to get involved."

"This changes everything."

"I don't see why. The venue remains the same. It has to for reasons you know quite well. There were enough questions in the Canal Zone as it was. I had to bribe everyone in sight and a few who weren't. Get the necessary parties here and do it by the fifth. This thing must be done by the sixth, no later."

"I'll call you when I've made arrangements."

"Please do."

The telephone went dead in her hand. She took a drag on her cigarette and thought about the people she would have to call. She smiled bleakly around the ivory cigarette holder. There were worse places to be than Hawaii in December.

Chapter 28

Commander Ian Fleming, acting alone and without any authority from either Donovan, Stephenson or his own boss, Admiral Godfrey of Naval Intelligence, met Jane Todd and Morris Black at San Francisco Municipal Airport shortly after nine.

Jane was wearing a short-haired brown wig barely showing under her service cap. She was wearing the complete uniform of a navy nurse, right down to the half-length dark blue cape. Black, his eyes half hidden behind a pair of smoke-tinted spectacles, was sporting a mustache and wore the blue uniform of a lieutenant commander in the United States Navy, complete with three stripes on the cuff of his jacket and an officer's dark peaked cap. They both knew that it was unlikely anyone would notice that the eagle on his cap insignias had its beak pointed to the left, rather than the right, and Black didn't intend anyone to get close enough to see the Dental Corps insignia that had come with the uniform from the wardrobe department at Metro. The naval getups had both come from the Wallace Beery clunker *Thunder Afloat,* which had been released a year or so before.

"My, don't we look dramatic," Fleming said with a smile. "I almost didn't recognize you."

"Good," said Black. "We recently pirated an FBI vehicle and held one of their agents at gunpoint. I don't think we're in Mr. Hoover's good books."

"Been busy by the sound of it," Fleming said. "Look over my shoulder and you'll see two men on the bench over there. One of them's reading a newspaper; the other seems very interested in his fingernails."

Black looked and so did Jane. The two men might just as well have had FBI stenciled in blue paint on their foreheads. "They're not paying any attention to us," said Jane. "I guess the disguises worked."

"Let's not test that theory too strenuously," said Fleming.

After gathering up their bags, they stopped briefly in the coffee shop of the Mission-style terminal building.

"Who knows you're here?" asked Black.

"Officially? Not a soul. As far as anyone in Washington is concerned, I've done a bunk."

"Unofficially?" asked Jane. The Harvey's waitress brought them coffee and a Danish for Jane, who was ravenous after the two-hour flight up from Los Angeles.

"Unofficially Stephenson knows. I had to tell him or Godfrey would have had me cashiered the minute I set foot back on British soil." He paused and lit a cigarette from his case. "And quite rightly too," he added, puffing out a cloud of smoke.

"What did you tell him?" Jane asked warily.

"Very little. He didn't want to know, when you get right down to it. It's more what he told me."

"Such as?"

"Apparently the two men on the train with you were FBI agents, but not on the regular roster. Donovan thinks they were part of an old Red Squad that was disbanded in the twenties and just reorganized a year or two ago."

"Going through our luggage?"

"Yes. Hoover doesn't like Stephenson much and he absolutely loathes Donovan."

"I'm getting rather tired of playing politics, Ian." Black sighed. "We were brought over here for a reason. I'm beginning to think it was all a sham. There's more going on here than meets the eye, isn't there?"

"It's possible. I'm not privy to all the secrets of Colonel Donovan's motives any more than I am of Mr. Stephenson's, our so-called Quiet Canadian. What I do know is that we tracked down the young man Harte and his minder in Santa Barbara. Both of them are dead. Murdered, but made to look like a suicide. Add to that the fact that our Mr. Zarubin of the Washington NKVD has also disappeared and so has our erstwhile friend Popov."

"Who?" asked Jane.

"A double agent," Fleming explained. "A Slav of some sort who went to work for Canaris and the Nazis, then turned himself over to our people in London."

"I'm not quite sure what any of all this has to do with your precious film," said Jane.

"There was enough evidence in the house Harte was murdered in to tell us what bank that key of yours is for. The First National Bank of Ventura. It turns out there was a box there registered in the name of Lev Bronstein."

"Trotsky's real name," said Black. "Cheeky of him."

"The only thing in the box was an empty film can. There was a label on it: The House of Special Purpose. The house where the tsar and his family were allegedly murdered. There was also a small house ransacked in the town, probably the same night as the box was broken into. A dead body was found in the house; the woman who was in charge of safe-deposit boxes at the bank." Fleming gave Jane a quick embarrassed look and then turned his attention back to Black. "She was autopsied. There were signs of very recent sexual relations. There were also more signs of such activity at the woman's house."

"Any idea who was banging her?" asked Jane flatly.

Fleming cleared his throat. "She was seen with a man in a local restaurant early that evening. The Chinese Gardens Café. The contents of the woman's stomach would also seem to verify that she had recently eaten Chinese food."

"Who was the man?" asked Jane.

"From the description it sounds very much like Vassili Zarubin."

"So he killed Harte and his minder as well as the woman in Ventura?"

"It looks that way."

"Then who killed the two FBI agents on the train?" asked Jane. "He couldn't have been in two places at once."

"We have no idea," Fleming said. "He's still at large."

"Along with Zarubin?"

"Yes."

"So what are we supposed to do now?" asked Jane.

"That's up to both of you. You can withdraw from the assignment or continue."

"That sounds like a trick answer," said Jane.

Black made a snorting sound. "This is where I stepped onto this wretched roundabout two years ago." He looked at Fleming hard. "How much choice do we have in this matter?"

"That's hard to say. Neither of you has any official capacity in this situation at all. There is no record of Detective Inspector Black's flight to the United States, nor of his leaving the Special Operations Executive training school at Beaulieu Abbey. As far as United Air Lines is concerned, the return portion of the ticket purchased on Jane's behalf by Mr. Noel Busch was simply left unused. After the funeral of your late sister you simply disappeared."

"And if I reappear again is up to me, right?"

"Something like that."

"What exactly are we supposed to do?" asked Black. "Other than be taken for fools?"

"According to what you told me on the telephone about your meeting with Miss Budberg, and her follow-up phone call, you are now legitimate aspirants to the ownership of Mr. Levitsky's film. At one point it seemed to Colonel Donovan and Mr. Stephenson that we might simply, er, appropriate the footage, so to speak. It now seems that such an event is unlikely, so we wish you to take part in the auction for it." He reached into his inside jacket pocket and withdrew a business-size buff envelope. "To that end I have here a draft drawn on the Westminster Bank in London in the amount of two hundred thousand pounds."

"And if the price goes above that amount?" said Black, secretly stunned by the amount.

"You have the promise of matching funds from Colonel Donovan's people."

"This whole thing has been moved to Hawaii," Jane said.

"So you said." Fleming reached into the pocket of his jacket and took out a blue, white and red ticker folder with the familiar winged world symbol of Pan American Airways printed on it. He handed the folder to Black. "Two tickets on the Honolulu Clipper, as requested." He paused. "They were hell to get, believe me. Everything's booked solid for the holiday season. Even the Matson Line ships are all filled right up until Christmas and New Year's. Bloody lucky you two are."

The agent on the bench reading the newspaper got up and went to the bank of telephone booths on the far side of the terminal while his companion kept his eye on the entrance to the Fred Harvey's café across the concourse. The first agent dialed the director's private office number. It took him a few minutes to place the call but he was finally connected and introduced himself.

"I'm at San Francisco Airport, sir."

"What of it?"

"We've been following the Brit."

"I know that. Fleming?"

"Yes, sir. We've been discreet. I don't think he's noticed us, sir."

"Why don't you get to the point?" said Hoover testily. "You followed Fleming. He's at the airport. Presumably he's going somewhere."

"I'm not sure if he's going anywhere, sir. But he did meet with two naval personnel a little while ago. They're in the Fred Harvey's here."

"What naval personnel?"

"A lieutenant commander and a nurse, sir."

"How can you tell she's a nurse?"

"She's in uniform as well, sir. My sister's a nurse so—"

"I don't give a shit about your sister."

"Yes, sir."

"You think it might be Black and that woman?"

"We only have a few surveillance photographs, sir. It's hard to say."

"If it is they'll probably go to ground somewhere."

"Well, that's what I was thinking, sir. Do we stick with Fleming or follow the other two?"

"Split up. One of you follows Fleming, the other keeps on the two navy types."

"Yes, sir."

Hoover hung up without saying anything else. The agent walked back to the bench and told his partner the score.

Chapter 29

Thursday, December 4, 1941
San Francisco

Their conversation done, Fleming caught the next United Air Lines flight out of San Francisco to Washington, D.C., and Jane Todd and Detective Inspector Morris Black caught a cab. They drove along Highway 101 North, taking the South San Francisco turnoff and entering the city on Third Street. The cabdriver was young, Chinese and talkative. The taxi itself was a bright yellow Dodge. The meter was huge and ticked away like an alarm clock.

"Come a long way?" he asked, glancing up into the rearview mirror.

"Los Angeles," said Jane.

"Sounds more like New York to me."

"Does it really matter?" asked Black.

The driver shrugged. "Not to me, pal. Just trying to make conversation. Make the trip a little more interesting."

"Why would knowing where we come from make the trip more interesting?" asked Jane.

"Well, you come from New York, that's interesting. Your friend, he sounds English. Me, I never been anywhere. Never seen anything except Chinatown." He let out a bubbling laughing sound. "That's a joke by the way."

"What's your name?" asked Jane.

"Chu," said the young man. "Most people call me Chewie, sometimes Chuck. I like Chuck."

"You don't have any Chinese accent," said Black.

"Why should I? Never been to China." Chuck made the laughing noise again. "You got any Chinky Chinamen in England, mister?"

"A few Chinese. Mostly in Limehouse. A few in Gerrard Street."

"Eat Chinese food a lot?"

"Some."

"Better here in San Francisco."

"Better on Mott Street." Jane laughed.

"That in New York?"

"Sure is. Best chop suey in the world."

"Know what chop suey mean in Chinese?" asked Chuck.

"Do tell."

"Nice way to say it would be 'leftovers.' The literal translation is probably closer to 'garbage.' When the whites in New York and here in San Francisco first started thinking that eating Chinese was exotic, the people running the restaurants needed to serve them something that wouldn't make them sick when they found out what it was, like chicken feet or pig intestine, so they made up the whole idea of chop suey."

"You've spent some time out of Chinatown," said Jane.

"Physics Department at the University of California," he answered proudly. "I work with Professor Lawrence at the Radiation Laboratory."

"Fascinating," said Jane, not understanding what on earth he was talking about.

"Interesting stuff," said Chuck. "Going to change the world one of these days. Sooner than you think maybe."

"I'll bet." Jane looked out the window. It had been overcast at the airport; here it was rolling, dense fog. The city was packed in cotton wool.

"You think we're going to be able to fly out of this?" she asked Black.

"I don't know."

"Flying the Clipper?" said Chuck. "No problem, folks. No matter what kind of fog, they can see the tops of the pylons on the Golden Gate, so that's what they aim for. Sometimes they go over, sometimes under."

"How very comforting," muttered Black.

"Any reason anybody be following you two?" asked Chuck as they made their way through the city.

"Not that I know of," said Black. "Why?"

"Well, there's been a cab on our tail all the way from the airport. My cousin Moe. That's Chu Yen Mo, but we just call him Moe, like one of the Three Stooges, you know."

"You're sure?" said Jane.

"You bet. Not that I blame him, you two are quite the pair."

"What's that supposed to mean?"

"The uniform's all wrong. Cap badge has the eagle pointing left when it should be right, the cuff insignia is dark yellow, not real gold braid, and he doesn't have a white cover on the cap. Plus I can see the cement gluing his mustache on."

"What about me?" said Jane.

"Hair's brown but you've got blue eyes and the hair on your arms is a lot lighter. Shows up against your tan, and you didn't get that in New York."

"Smart boy."

"You good guys or bad guys?" asked Chuck.

"Depends on how you look at it," Jane answered, glancing at Black. "Yesterday we stole an FBI car and held one of their agents at gunpoint. All in a good cause."

"Well, hell then," said Chuck. "Let's lose him."

"How?"

"Watch."

They were on Mission at Sixteenth Street. Chuck found a hole in traffic and made a screaming turn left on Sixteenth, narrowly missing a big International Harvester open-sided Coca-Cola truck that sent crates of soda spilling off onto the street, covering the asphalt with a foaming tidal wave of crates, soda and broken glass. Their physicist driver put the taxi into a bootlegger's turn and jammed on the brakes. Suddenly they were facing in the opposite direction and found themselves nose to nose with the other cab. Chuck jumped out of the car and his cousin leapt out of his cab. Behind them the Coca-Cola delivery man was staring at his ruined load as it ran off in thick rivulets toward the storm sewers.

The two young Chinese men stood together in the middle of the street, blocking traffic and screaming at each other, shaking their fists in each other's face. This went on for half a minute and then, as suddenly as it began, it was over. Chuck came trotting back to the cab, climbed in and gunned the engine. A few moments later they'd turned off onto a narrow side street. Jane looked back through the rear windshield. There was no sign of the other taxi.

"What the hell was that all about?" she said.

"Only way to talk to him up close, tell him the situation," Chuck answered.

"Sounded like you were screaming at him," said Black.

"I was." Chuck grinned. "You speak Chinese loud enough everyone thinks you're fighting."

"What did you say?"

"I told him to take his passenger for a ride. A long one."

"You give him a reason?" Jane asked.

"Don't need one," said Chuck with a laugh. "I'm Moe's cousin. His passenger's a *gwai lo,* no offense."

"Gwai lo?" Jane asked.

"Round eye," Black responded.

"Hey!" said Chuck. "Pretty good for a white man!"

They reached the bridge approaches at Fifth and Bryant, and Chuck handed the quarter toll to the uniformed man in the booth. They reached the ramp, slipped into the traffic stream and headed out over the suspension bridge that crossed half the bay.

A few minutes later, after an uneventful, foggy trip, Chuck took the exit ramp off the bridge just before the roadway dipped down into the tunnel under Yerba Buena Island. He drove around the perimeter of the Naval Reservation to the causeway connecting Yerba Buena to the artificially created Treasure Island, recently home to the Golden Gate International Exposition, which had run in tandem with the 1939 New York World's Fair. Half the buildings had already been demolished and the place had a run-down, almost desperate feeling to it, especially wreathed as it was in shroudlike rags of fog.

"Doesn't make the future look too bright, does it?" said Jane as they made their way through the old walkways and thoroughfares of the ghostly site.

"You think there's going to be a war?" asked Chuck, easing off on his speed as he drove across the exposition site.

"There already is a war," said Black, ice in his voice. "You're just not fighting it yet."

"Yeah, there's going to be a war, Chuck. Our own war."

"Well, I'm ready," said the Chinese taxi driver. He let out his strange laugh again. "So is Professor Lawrence, if what I hear is true."

The taxi turned in between two hangarlike buildings, and Jane and Black caught their first glimpse of the Honolulu Clipper moored to a long concrete pier. He pulled up beside half a dozen other Yellow Cabs and helped his passengers fetch their bags from the trunk.

The Clipper was bigger than the Sunderland Black had flown in—the wingspan a full 152 feet across with a fuselage 106 feet long. It was the largest airplane ever made in the United States, and one of the three largest in the world. It could carry seventy passengers on daylight flights or forty on overnight flights with sleeping berths.

A pair of stewards in white jackets were waiting on the pier beside a wide, floating gangway that led up at a slight angle to the hatchway door. One of the stewards took their bags and went nimbly up the gangway while the other man checked their tickets.

"We'll be taking off soon," said the steward on the pier. "You can go aboard any time you like."

"Thank you." Black turned to pay off the cabdriver, but Jane had already taken care of it.

"Good-bye, you two," said the young man. "Wish I was going with you."

"If you only knew, my lad," Black muttered. But he managed a wave as well. Letting Jane lead the way, he went up the gangway, ducking his head as he went inside.

The interior of the big airplane was surprisingly roomy and well lit. There was a small entrance vestibule with a set of metal stairs leading up to the flight compartment and the bridge, with a large hatchway to the left leading into several passenger compartments that ran the length of the aircraft. The fabric-covered walls were a pale cream color, the carpeted floors were a dark green and most of the seating was in deep "Pan American Blue" decorated with a pattern of stars.

They made their way down a short corridor with the galley on their left and the men's room on their right, went through another open hatchway and found themselves in the first of several passenger compartments fitted out with very modern-looking aluminum-framed chairs and writing desks.

There were three small windows on either side of each compartment covered over with venetian blinds, and like the train compartment they'd briefly shared on the Super Chief, the ashtrays were mounted on the bulkheads in several convenient positions. There was a Pullman-style berth that pulled down from the outer bulkhead, and a second berth beneath it created by a removable section that combined with the lower bulkhead seats.

As they made their way through the first two compartments looking for their seats, both Jane Todd and Morris Black noted that the passengers seemed to be almost evenly divided between uniformed naval personnel and people who were clearly going on a holiday excursion. The naval men, all petty officers, sat together talking quietly while the others seemed to be in a much more festive mood, consulting brochures, looking out the windows and chatting happily. The noncoms saluted Black as he went by and Black stiffly saluted them in return, hoping he was doing it correctly.

They passed through the dining lounge, which was divided up into a number of both large and small booth-style dining areas with a central aisle to provide easy access from the galley, and then stepped into the third passenger compartment, which was already almost full.

Their seats were on the port side and looked out on the foggy bay rather than the steel and concrete pilings that surrounded the artificial island. Directly across from them on the other side of the compartment two men sat facing each other. Both were dressed in dark blue suits, appeared to be in their early thirties, and had briefcases on their laps. They were neither naval-looking nor festive. Jane wondered if they were more FBI. Doubtful, unless they'd booked onto the flight for some other reason than the pursuit of Jane Todd and Morris Black.

Suddenly, one at a time, the massive 1,500-horsepower Wright Cyclone engines began to turn and fire, the giant propellers whirling, dissipating the fog that lay around the mooring and the pier. Even with the sound of the engines steadily beginning to increase, Jane could hear someone yelling instructions, and then they began to edge away from the pier in a slow arc to the left. As they moved, the engines took on a deep-throated tone, and a few moments later they headed around the lee side of the man-made island and motored into the much choppier waters of San Francisco Bay.

Spray started to splatter against the windows, and the hull of the aircraft began to rock back and forth slightly, like a ship at sea. Jane took a quick look at their friends on the opposite side of the compartment, but if they were feeling any fear, they weren't showing it. Both men could have been cut from stone.

The tone of the engines became more strident, and the beat of the water against the hull became a little more violent. The sounds from the other compartments began to die off, followed by complete silence throughout the aircraft except for the faint rattle of crockery coming from the forward galley.

Even if the day had been clear and bright, the lashings of spray against the windows would have made the view impenetrable. Jane noticed that Black's fingers were gripping the armrests of his chair so tightly his knuckles had gone white, and then she noticed that she was doing exactly the same thing.

She hadn't done a lot of flying in her life, but it was comforting to know that if you were going to spend twenty hours in the air over the largest ocean in the world, at least you were doing it in an airplane that was built like a boat. On the other hand, how far could an airplane as big as a house glide before it dropped out of the sky like a rock?

She blanked the thought out of her mind, and then, with a sudden freeing lurch, they were airborne. The spray was torn away from the windows and the fog broke on the bay just in time for her to see the bleak pile of rock that was Alcatraz and then they were climbing even farther upward, the bright, newly painted towers of the Golden Gate Bridge passing under their wings and the deep blue emptiness of the Pacific Ocean ahead of them.

Jane felt the tension go out of her fingers and watched as Black loosened his own hands.

"Amazing," she said. "I could almost do that all over again."

"It was exciting, wasn't it?" said Black dryly. "The last time I did something like that, it was pitch dark and the bloody airplane didn't have any windows."

A faint musical note pinged on the public-address system, as though someone had struck a triangle, and then the steward announced that those who smoked could now do so and that coffee was being served in the dining lounge if anyone was interested. Jane and Black immediately lit up, climbed out of their seats and headed forward.

As they passed, Jane checked their two fellow travelers again. Neither one was smoking and neither seemed to show any inclination to get up and go to the dining lounge. They remained exactly where they were, dull-eyed and expressionless, the blinds shut over the windows beside them.

Jane and Black went through the open hatchway and stepped into the dining lounge. People were beginning to filter into the nicely decorated room from both fore and aft, but they managed to find a small table and a pair of seats in the corner.

"What do you think of our two stony friends?" Jane asked.

"I'm not sure," Black answered. "They certainly don't seem to fit in with the rest of the passengers."

"You think they're following us?"

"Possible," said Black as the steward appeared to take their order. "But there's not a hell of a lot we can do about it now, is there?"

"No, I suppose not."

"Then," said Black, smiling, "I propose that we forget about everything we've been thinking about for the moment and simply enjoy the ride." The steward took their order for coffee and whatever pastry was on hand, and turned to the next table. "Honolulu holiday." Black grinned. "Sounds like one of those idiotic short subjects they show at the cinema in the dead of winter. If only I could send postcards to all my old friends at the Yard."

Chapter 30

At eight thirty a.m. Hawaiian time, the Pan American Airways Honolulu Clipper reached landfall, coming in on its approach directly over the northern tip of the island at Kahuku Point, gathering a few appreciative waves from early-riser golf fanatics playing through the eighth hole at the Kahuku Public Golf Course.

They continued south, losing altitude all the way, crossing the Territorial Forest Reservation that covered the spine of the island with a thick green coat, then passing over the pineapple plantations at Wahaiwa, dropping even lower as they made their final approach above the sugarcane fields on the outskirts of Pearl City and then over Pearl Harbor itself, its three peninsulas jutting out into the dark water, all of them pointing toward the runways of the Ford Island Naval Air Station and the narrow neck of the approach to the harbor. The passengers on the Clipper had a brief, impressive look at the hundreds of ships moored in the deep-water, protected anchorage and then they were out over the open seas again beyond the Barbers Point Lighthouse.

A few moments later the Clipper seemed to lean over on its starboard wing, heeling at a steep angle as it turned back toward land, following the visible lines of rolling surf that had been beating against the volcanic island for an eternity. Once again they were over the bottleneck of the entrance to Pearl Harbor, losing height at an almost alarming rate, heading for the smallest and most eastern of the three peninsulas of land around the perimeter of the harbor.

Suddenly the Clipper seemed to plummet from the sky, and Jane felt her stomach drop. Without any hesitation whatsoever the pilot slid the huge transoceanic aircraft down onto the water, threading an invisible needle between the row of anchored tenders on one side and the heavily treed finger of land on the other. A shudder ran through the floor beneath Jane's feet and they were down, the sound of the engines instantly dropping away. The outer engines stopped altogether, the big props slowing and then stopping, while the inner engines were throttled back as they headed for a long dock that jutted out into the water. The pilot swung the Clipper hard to starboard, edging them toward the dock, and through the dripping, spray-drenched window Jane could see half a dozen men in PAA dark blue coveralls. From somewhere in the forward section came the sound of a bulkhead door being cranked opened, and suddenly the interior of the aircraft was filled with the perfumed air of Hawaii. They had arrived.

Ever since getting up for breakfast an hour or so before landing, Jane had noticed Black's progressively darkening expression, but so far she'd said nothing. In the short time she'd known the detective from Scotland Yard, she'd learned to recognize that the growing thundercloud expression was a reflection of his way of thinking through a problem.

They lined up in the central aisle to disembark, their two stone-faced watchdogs a few passengers behind them. Jane exited first, stepping onto the blunt stabilizing winglet that kept them from capsizing on landing and from there onto a square floating canvas-covered platform and finally the dock itself. They were greeted by a dozen or so pretty young women dressed in long grass skirts and rather skimpy tops made out of woven straw handing out wreaths of fresh flowers and saying aloha to each passenger.

As Jane received her flowers, the woman placing the lei over her head and onto her shoulders pressed a small folded piece of paper in her hand. Jane closed her fist over it, then continued up the dock to solid ground. She waited for Black under a stand of palm trees on the edge of the water screening the small wooden Pan American Airways administration and baggage building.

A few yards up the path was a large gravel parking lot where half a dozen Chevrolet Master DeLuxe twelve-passenger limousines stood waiting, their blue and white Pan American livery gleaming brightly, their spoked white wheels and whitewall tires freshly washed. The drivers, all in Pan American uniforms, waited beside their vehicles, standing at attention while behind them and off to one side stood two battered-looking Plymouth PDs, complete with broad running boards and bug-eye headlights in front of their boxy flat-roofed bodies. For their age they looked well cared for, and both had been recently painted a bright crimson color. The name Two Bit Taxi Company was written neatly on each of the front doors in a yellow as bright as the red. Both of the drivers were sitting on their respective running boards, one reading a copy of the *Honolulu Advertiser,* the other smoking a cigarette, eyes closed, head back against the door of his taxi as he tried to snooze. Both men appeared to be Eurasian, their skin a faint tan color, their eyes almond shaped, their hair jet black.

A light wind ruffled the fronds of the palms above her, and Jane shivered slightly, squinting out into the harbor itself, staring at what appeared to be hundreds of ships. It was a strange sight, so many massive and overwhelmingly powerful instruments of war basking so peacefully in an island paradise of palms and beaches and bright blue, cloudless sky.

Jane unfolded the note in her palm.

Wenner-Gren.
Richard Shivers, SAIC FBI
Dillingham Transportation Building
Take the one with the broken headlight.

It was written on an old typewriter whose keys hadn't been cleaned in ages. Black stepped off the dock and walked up the path to where she was standing. He looked wretchedly uncomfortable with the lei around his neck and pulled at it every few seconds like a too-tight tie. He stopped beside her and lit a cigarette.

"Me too," she said. Black handed her the one he'd just lit and lit a second cigarette for himself.

"What have we got there?" he asked.

"Note. Apparently from the special agent in charge here." She handed it to him and he read it. Jane turned and looked at the Two Bit taxicabs. The one on the right with the driver reading the newspaper had a piece of heavy black electrical tape crisscrossed over the left headlamp. Most of the passengers from the Clipper flight were climbing into the complimentary limousines Jane had read about in the brochure she'd read during the flight. They'd go to the Pan American Hotel in Pearl City first and drop off any passengers continuing on to Manila or Singapore, then take the rest of the passengers to whichever hotel they'd booked, most of them on Millionaires Row in Waikiki, either the Ala Moana or the pink wedding cake of the Royal Hawaiian. Suddenly the driver of the other Two Bit taxi flipped away the butt of his cigarette and opened the rear door of his old car and ushered in a middle-aged couple. Their two watchdogs were now standing on the edge of the parking lot, desperately trying to look anywhere but at Jane and Morris Black.

The Scotland Yard detective folded the note neatly and put it into his pocket. "What do you think?" he asked quietly.

"Some kind of trap maybe, but I don't think so."

Black shrugged. "Maybe the taxi's been sent to take us out into the cane fields and chop us into little bits."

"You're listening to too much *Inner Sanctum.*"

Black frowned. "I beg your pardon?"

"Oh, forget it." Jane waved away the comment. "You're never going to figure out Americans."

"One certainly hopes not."

"The point is, the FBI could have picked us up a long time ago, and this guy knows Wenner-Gren's name."

"Which could simply mean the note was passed along by Wenner-Gren to lure us away into the cane fields."

"Scaredy-cat," Jane scoffed. "Wait here." She walked over to the parking lot and approached one of the limousine drivers, who was about to climb behind the wheel of his glistening vehicle. The man was very large and his chauffeur's cap barely fit over his boulder-sized skull. His smile was friendly enough as she approached though.

"Looking for a ride, lady?"

"Just the answer to a question."

"Shoot."

"Where does the FBI hang out in Honolulu?"

"I think it's called the Dillingham Building."

"Who's Dillingham?"

"One of the Big Five."

"Five what?"

"Five big *haole* families that stole Hawaii. They still own half of Honolulu and most of Waikiki on top of that."

"Where is it?"

"Bottom of Bishop Street at Ala Moana. Across from the Aloha Tower."

"Thanks."

"No problem, sistah. Anything for a cute little *puka* like you." He grinned and eased himself behind the wheel of the Master DeLuxe. Jane went back to where Black was standing.

"Well?"

"I'm a cute little *puka*, whatever that means, and it looks like this Shivers person is sending us to the right place."

"As long as he's the right person."

"Cute. You go get the bags and I'll bag the taxi."

The driver took them up the narrow peninsula with its small neat fields, palm-lined streets and large, expensive-looking houses, finally reaching the main highway and heading along the coast toward the city. He was skinny, round-faced, half Chinese by the looks of him and wore a ragged, sweat-stained straw hat set down squarely on his forehead. As they drove, he alternated between eating MoonPies, drinking RC Cola from a bottle he held between his legs and smoking Camels. Unlike the taxi drivers mentioned in Jane's brochure he was any-thing but communicative, not saying a word for the entire trip. It took them half an hour to reach the downtown area. In the distance Jane could see a tower close to the harbor, where a large liner was moored.

"Is that the Aloha Tower?"

The driver nodded and took a bite from his third MoonPie, washing it down with the dregs of his bottle of RC Cola. They reached Bishop Street and turned left, pulling up in front of a large, mock–Italian Renaissance four-story office building with a red tile roof. The main floor seemed to be encircled by a stone-arched arcade. Jane realized that from one side of the building, at least on the upper floors, you'd be able to see anyone arriving at the dock beyond the Aloha Tower.

"This it?"

"Eight bucks."

"Little high, isn't it?" Black commented.

"Not high. Eight bucks," said the driver. "It's always eight bucks."

"What happened to Two Bits?" asked Jane.

"Died behind the wheel of one of his own boilers. Fell asleep at the wheel."

"I don't understand any of this," said Black.

"Two bits is a quarter. Twenty-five cents. I thought it was the fare, but apparently it was the owner's nickname. Give him the eight dollars and let's get out of here."

"Not until he takes out our bags." Black reached into his European-sized wallet and neatly extracted a five and three ones. "The bags," he repeated. Grumbling under his breath, the driver climbed out of the taxi, went around to the rear of the old car and pulled their two new suitcases out of the trunk, setting them down hard on the sidewalk in front of the building. Jane got out, and the Scotland Yard detective finally handed over the handful of bills, which the driver carefully counted.

"No tip?"

"Oh, bugger off, mate." Black picked up both bags and walked briskly under the shadow of the arcade and disappeared through the main entrance. Jane gave the driver a friendly shrug and the man scowled and muttered something under his breath.

Jane went after Black, finally catching up to him just as he reached the main doors. "I guess he doesn't like the navy."

The main floor was a gigantic lobby with an art deco ceiling painted with a variety of transportation motifs that went from ships and steaming railroads to thundering trucks and a strange-looking barge fitted with a steam shovel that seemed to be dredging out Pearl Harbor, complete with monster dreadnoughts she was sure had never been part of the U.S. Navy. The floors were polished marble and rang like hammers as they walked across them. A cool cross breeze was created by the high windows set into the arcade arches, and the temperature of the floors made things even cooler. They found a brass-doored elevator etched with more trains, ships, and even a few aircraft as well. On the glass-covered directory beside it, the Federal Bureau of Investigation was listed as being on the second floor. Jane pressed the appropriate button, the doors slid open and they went up.

Almost the entire west wing of the second floor was given over to the FBI, including a large central room and half a dozen smaller offices on the perimeter. As Jane had suspected, the main room looked out over Ala Moana Boulevard and down to the Aloha Tower and the docks. She grinned, spotting a large telescope mounted on a tripod near one of the windows.

The main room was furnished with an assortment of wooden government-issue desks and rows of green filing cabinets. A scattering of plants was dying on windowsills. There were maps pinned up here and there, plus a blackboard. Across from a reproduction portrait of President Roosevelt was an equal-sized portrait of the Boss, J. Edgar Hoover himself. There wasn't a single person at any of the desks. Distantly Jane heard a door creak close and a few seconds later a narrow-shouldered man in shirtsleeves with a striped tie loosely knotted at his neck appeared. He was wearing glasses and a worried expression, and his dark hair was thinned back in a widow's peak. As he came forward, he managed a smile and extended a hand.

"I see the fleet's in." He smiled. "Hi, I'm Dick Shivers."

Black took the hand and shook it. Jane thought the name sounded like an unfinished newspaper headline: DICK SHIVERS, COLD SNAP COUNTINUES. She kept herself from smiling. Black put down the suitcases.

"Sorry to catch you before you got to your hotel, but I thought it was advisable." Shivers looked around the empty squad room. "Usually the joint is jumping, but I've got everybody gone home or on assignment. I thought we could do with some privacy. Coffee?"

Black opened his mouth to turn down the offer, but Jane beat him to the punch. "Sure. Sounds good."

"Follow me."

Shivers led them to his office, which was equipped with a desk, a chair behind it and two wooden armchairs for guests. An old Remington typewriter was set on a small table at right angles to the desk. Probably the one Shivers used to type the note. He also had a big West Bend vacuum coffeemaker and coffee-making paraphernalia on top of yet another trio of government-issue green filing cabinets. Shivers took their coffee orders, poured and charged with milk or sugar or both and handed cups around. Over Shivers's shoulder Jane could see the Aloha Tower out the window. She took a sip of her coffee, then stared down into her cup, amazed.

"That's incredibly good," she said.

Black took a sip of his own and nodded. "Very nice."

"Kona," said Shivers. "Just about the best-kept secret in Hawaii. We don't export too much."

"I'll take ten pounds," said Jane.

"Not before we find out what Special Agent Shivers wants," said Black, smiling benignly.

"Look," said Shivers. "I got a call from one of Hoover's boys saying you'd been seen at San Francisco Airport and to keep an eye out for you. Which I did, you have to admit."

"How come you didn't arrest us?" asked Jane.

"Hey, the director doesn't read any of my memos or warnings, so why should I listen to his? Plus I was curious."

"About us?" said Jane innocently.

"Holding a gun on a federal agent, impersonating members of the United States armed forces. I gather you've stepped over the line before that."

"I suppose you could say that," Black answered.

"What I want to know is why. I'm up to my ears in spies here and all I get from the beloved director is, 'Leave it to Naval Intelligence,' who—pardon my French, lady—don't know their asses from a hole in the ground."

"I thought that's what they say about the Bureau," Jane responded.

"Ha-ha," said Shivers. "I'm not kidding. This place is crawling with Jap spies, not to mention a few Germans and even the odd Russian, and I'm supposed to sit around and do nothing, pardon my French again, with my thumbs up my ass."

"From our information a pair of your old Red Squad pals tried to kill us on the Super Chief," said Jane.

"Not my old pals, and you can ask anyone you want, there's not much love lost between me and the director either."

"Why are you telling us this?" asked Jane. "From what I hear you don't lip the big G-man unless you're looking for a job in the sewage-treatment business."

"I've reached the point where I don't care. There's a war coming with the Japs and everyone knows it, and the son of a bitch has me counting up the nisei in the islands so we can have lists when we intern them."

"Nisei?"

"First-generation Japanese. Born here. U.S. citizens."

"Intern them?" asked Black.

"Already building camps in Colorado and California."

"Jesus," Jane whispered.

"Why are you so sure war's coming?" asked Black.

"We call it traffic weight," said Shivers. "We've got phone taps on everyone and the cable companies as well. The Japanese consulate has sent about ten times more messages and phone calls in the past ten days than it has in the past six months. Something big's coming and soon, and I can't do a damn thing about it."

"I still don't understand why you're telling us."

"I've got my sources," said Shivers flatly. "Donovan's bunch and your friend the Limey in New York have operations with more holes than a tea strainer. We've been following the Budberg woman around just like your people have, and now she turns up here with this Wenner-Gren character, the duke of Windsor's bosom buddy, not to mention half the known Nazi sympathizers in the Western Hemisphere, a Russian prince who claims he's the old tsar's nephew and another Russian lunatic named Vonsiatsky all holed up on Howard Hughes's old yacht, which is berthed down at the Yacht Club, pretty as a picture."

"Isn't there some kind of unofficial ban on him docking in any American port?" Black asked.

Shivers nodded. "This is a territory, though, which means the paperwork takes forever, not to mention the fact that he's muddied the waters by deeding over the boat to this Budberg woman for the time being, and there's no ban on her. Wenner-Gren's home port is Nassau, so there's really no way we can touch him . . . or his guests."

"Isn't Vonsiatsky the one who married the heiress and lives in Connecticut?" said Jane. "I saw something in *Life* about him. Like an American Mussolini or something."

"That's the one. Marion Ream, trust funds and a Pierce Arrow. He wears black uniforms and shaves his head."

"People take him seriously?"

"He's got a lot of money, and she backs him a hundred percent."

"You think he's involved with all these others?"

"He's on the boat, isn't he?"

"Point." Jane nodded. She lit a cigarette. Shivers got up and pulled open the window behind him, letting the fog of smoke dissipate. He sat down again.

"What do you want us to do for you?"

"You're obviously going to get invited on board the *Southern Cross*. You wouldn't be here otherwise. I want to know what happens on board."

"We have our own allegiances," said Black. "You aren't one of them."

Shivers made a snorting sound. "We're on the same side, pal, and you know it. I don't want to see England strangle to death and neither do you. The only thing that's going to save your ass is the Yanks getting into the war." He paused. "Like last time."

Morris bristled. "I think you'll have your hands full out here . . . pal."

"Maybe, but Hitler and Tojo are allies. Japs get into a war with us, Adolf's not going to have much of a choice."

"I'm surprised you don't have someone on board yourself."

"I did. He's disappeared. That's another reason I want to know what goes on. Harming a federal agent is a top-end crime. I could arrest the whole lot of the bastards and I could guarantee you two get the film."

Jane stared. "You know about the film?"

"Like I said, more holes than a tea strainer."

"Pretty critical for a guy who's looking for our help," said Jane.

"I'm not looking for help. I'm just looking for information."

Morris Black stood up, went to the big West Bend urn and drew himself another cup of coffee. He went back to his chair and put the cup down on the edge of Shivers's desk.

"Twaddle."

"What?"

"Tonsil varnish."

"Why don't you run that by me again?" said Shivers.

"This whole conversation has been a smoke screen, Mr. Shivers, and you know it." Black took a sip of the excellent coffee. "You haven't told us anything we don't already know with the exception of the presence of some addle-headed Romanov and an equally odious yobbo who's playing dilettante Blackshirt on his wife's tick. You're trying to impress us with your intelligence-gathering abilities. So what? None of it means a damn thing unless you've got the key, which, presumably, you do. What is it, other than trying to show up your opposite numbers in the navy?"

Shivers pulled open the center drawer of his desk,

took out a White Owl and stripped off the cellophane wrapper. He dug around in the drawer and came up with a bright red Ronson and lit the cigar. After taking a few puffs, he placed the cigar into a curved slot on the side of the big ashtray, looking thoughtfully through the trailing smoke at Black and Jane Todd.

"Okay, he said, "I'll tell you." He picked up the cigar again, took one last puff and began to talk. "This didn't come all at once. We've been onto this guy since '36, which is when he came out here. Before that he was in New York, and before that he was in Germany."

"Who are we talking about?" asked Jane.

"Oh, sorry. His name is Julius Rossler. From what we know, he was naval attaché in the German embassy in Tokyo during the first part of the war and he speaks fluent Japanese. He was returning to Germany and his ship was sunk under him on the way back to Kiel. He was interned in England for the rest of the war, and he learned how to speak English there."

"Convenient," Black murmured.

"He was repatriated in 1919, married a war widow named Anna, who had two children, and then had two more children with Rossler. In 1931 he joined the Nazi party, membership number 504. I'm not sure you understand the significance of that but—"

"Lower the number the earlier the membership," said Black. "And the closer you were to the high muckety-mucks, Göring and Hess and all the others."

"Right." Shivers nodded. "Anyway, he was right up there."

"Where's all this going?" asked Jane impatiently.

"He joined the Nazis in 1931 and then came to New York in 1935, supposedly because he didn't like Hitler's government."

"Doesn't make a lot of sense," said Black.

"It didn't make much sense to me either. It made more sense when he started making friends with a lot of high-ranking army and navy people here. We put a tail on him for a while last year, and he spent a lot of time taking long walks with his son Dieter around Pearl Harbor because Dieter liked sketching seabirds." Shivers tried to take a puff on his cigar but it had gone out. He lit it again with the Ronson and blew out a cloud of smoke. "He was also seen in the company of a man named Tadashi Morimura, who arrived in Honolulu in March, supposedly as a consular officer."

"Which means he's a spy," said Black.

"I wouldn't know," said Shivers bitterly. "I reported back to Washington, and I was told to back off and let Naval Intelligence handle it."

"Did you?"

"Not a chance." Shivers smiled. "We kept a loose tail on him, tapped his phone and went after his cable messages." The special agent in charge reached into his trouser pocket, took out a small key and opened one of the side drawers in his desk. He took out three onionskin flimsies and handed them across the desk. "We got the first one on Tuesday, the second one the day after, the third one today."

NO CHANGES OBSERVED AFTERNOON 2 DECEMBER. SO FAR THEY DO NOT SEEM TO HAVE BEEN ALERTED, SHORE LEAVE AS USUAL.

BURN YOUR CODE BOOKS EXCEPT FOR 'OITE.' WHEN DESTRUCTION IS COMPLETE WIRE US THE CODE WORD HARUNA.

THERE ARE NO BARRAGE BALLOONS UP. THERE IS A CONSIDERABLE OPPORTUNITY FOR SURPRISE ATTACK AGAINST THESE PLACES.

"Who knows about these?" said Black.

"I sent copies to Hoover, State, ONI and Justice."

"What were the replies?"

"There weren't any," said Shivers, letting out a long breath. Black handed the translated cablegrams to Jane. She read through them quickly.

"Jesus! It sounds like the Japs really are going to make a sneak attack on Hawaii."

"Specifically Pearl Harbor." Shivers nodded. "And no one seems to give a good goddamn." His face screwed up. "The sons of bitches are ignoring me."

"Where's this Morimura character now?"

"He was last seen early this morning with Rossler sitting in Rossler's car parked on Neho Street by the Punchbowl."

"Punchbowl?" asked Black.

"Old volcano crater," said Jane. "Didn't you read your brochure?"

"Our guys lost them," Shivers continued. "We found the car an hour ago, abandoned on Pacific Street in the industrial district."

"What's there?" Jane asked.

"Nothing. We talked to a longshoreman. He said he saw two men get into a powerboat at pier twenty-nine and head up the Kapalama Channel. One of the two men was Japanese, so presumably it was Rossler and Morimura."

"That's it?" asked Jane.

"Not quite. The name on the transom of the powerboat was *Southern Cross*."

Chapter 31

Ala Moana Park was completely artificial, having been created with landfill dredged from the construction of the Ala-Wai Canal ten years previously. The park was donated as a "gift" to Honolulu County by the dredging company, and no one mentioned the fact that the easy disposal of the landfill so close to the site of the canal saved the dredging company several hundred thousand dollars and a great deal of time. The company was Hawaiian Dredging, owned by the Dillingham family, which in turn had once used the building Shivers was in as their headquarters. The Dillinghams had made their gift a very plain and dusty one, and Honolulu had then had to spend an enormous amount of money landscaping it with koa trees and palms, grass, gardens, a running track, several baseball diamonds, a football field and several thousand tons of sand to create beaches where none had existed before. In all the park comprised approximately fifty acres, including a small municipal yacht basin where the *Southern Cross* was berthed.

The yacht was enormous, with extraordinarily good lines, bright white and brass to the Plimsoll line, light blue down to the water. She was three hundred and twenty feet long, gaining an extra twenty feet by way of her old-fashioned, solid mahogany bowsprit. She had two decks of superstructure, one cabin deck and a midships engine room below. She had a single funnel, a varnished mahogany deckhouse and twin masts, one forward and one aft, both mainly for decoration but also utilized as long-distance radio antennae.

On the slightly raised forecastle deck just behind the bowsprit was a pair of lowering davits and a twenty-two-foot-long wooden powerboat in a secure steel cradle. On the cabin deck there were ten staterooms in the aft section, a two-bedroom owner's suite forward that went from one side of the yacht to the other, as well as a fully equipped gymnasium and accommodations and facilities for the twenty-two-man crew. At full steam her twin turbines could make twenty-one knots, which was faster than the *Queen Mary* or any other ocean liner that plied the seven seas.

Screened by a group of koa trees and a large bed of shrubs at the western end of Ala Moana Park, Jane Todd and Morris Black—now in civilian clothes—and FBI Special Agent Richard Shivers had been watching the ship, Black and Shivers taking turns with a powerful pair of Leica 10×50 Artillery binoculars while Jane used one of Shivers's Bell and Howell cartridge auto-load film cameras to record any activity of note. It was now just past noon, and so far there hadn't been any activity at all, noteworthy or otherwise. No one had boarded the yacht or gotten off, and no one had appeared on deck except obvious crew members dressed in striped French-style matelot jerseys and bell-bottom white ducks. From what Jane could see, about half of the crew were black, probably Bahamian given the yacht's home port. So far she had seen two officers, both white and both wearing Wenner-Gren's version of a German *Kriegsmarine* uniform, black blazer and trousers, the fittings and rank insignia in silver.

"This could be a complete waste of time," said Morris Black, lowering the binoculars.

"Something will turn up eventually."

"Umm." Black lifted the binoculars again. "Perhaps when hell freezes over and we've missed our own invitation to the ball. Those two yobs on the airplane are almost certainly Wenner-Gren's if they weren't yours, and they undoubtedly know where we're staying."

"Could everyone already be on board?" Jane asked.

"Doubtful," answered Shivers. He nodded toward the

fisherman's wharf, where there were half a dozen brightly painted equipment shacks and a weather-beaten cottagelike office with a pair of rusty old-fashioned dial-front Sinclair Oil pumps out front, one for gasoline, the other for kerosene. "We put a couple of guys in the office last night. So far nothing. Your friend the countess came out for a tour around the deck along with Der Vacuum Cleaner Meister, and the powerboat had already been brought in and tied down like it is now, which means that Rossler and Morimura are already aboard, but I think that's it. "

Black adjusted the focus wheel on the binoculars. "Automobile coming."

Jane picked up the Bell and Howell, twisted the turret mount to the telescopic lens and swung the camera around to the right. A big dusty wood-sided Mercury station wagon turned off Ala Moana Boulevard. The car rattled its way down the steep, unpaved track, sending up a cloud of coral dust, then pulled onto the pier, stopping in front of the gangway that had been let down midships on the starboard side of the yacht. From their vantage point they could just see the bottom of the gangway.

"Three passengers and a driver," said Black.

"Screw the driver. Who are the passengers?"

"You tell me," said Black, handing the big black binoculars to the FBI special agent. Black turned to Jane. "You filming this?"

"Uh-huh," said Jane, keeping the eyepiece glued to the sight. The clockwork spring motor that powered the camera made a barely audible whirring sound. She adjusted the focus slightly, her fingers delicate on the camera's controls, balancing the camera itself securely in her palms.

"You were right," she murmured, still concentrating on the eyepiece. "Three passengers. The driver's taking their baggage out of the back."

Shivers spoke. "The tall guy in the black suit with the bald head is our pal Vonsiatsky, the Connecticut Blackshirt. The shorter, chubby-faced one is his old pal Feodor Romanov, son of the Grand Duchess Zenia and the late tsar's nephew." He paused. "I think that's how it goes, anyway."

"Who's number three?" Jane asked. "Sad-looking guy with a slouch hat."

Shivers put the binoculars to his eyes and followed the slight, bland-looking man as he trudged up the gangway, a heavy-looking briefcase under his arm. The FBI man lowered the glasses. "Your new piece on the board is a man named Emil Haas," said Shivers, sounding surprised. "Our dossier indicates that he works for Admiral Canaris at the Abwehr, but according to our Secret Intelligence Service he is also something of a freelancer. I had no idea he was in the U.S., let alone Hawaii."

"You think he's here to buy the film for Canaris?" Jane asked. "It makes sense if you think about it; throwing shit like that at the Windsor family, some of it would be sure to stick. A propaganda coup if nothing else."

"There's only one flaw in your analysis," said Shivers.

"Oh, what would that be?"

"Our sad-looking friend in the slouch hat doesn't buy things—he kills them. Usually with a little Mauser m1910 .25 caliber vest pocket pistol, which I assume he was carrying in that briefcase."

"Jesus," Jane muttered. "You need a goddamn scorecard to keep track of the players."

"I've had enough of this," said Black. "It's doing us no bloody good at all. You want this Julius Rossler fellow and his friend the Jappo, but I'm afraid we've got rather a different agenda. We're supposed to be on that boat, and if we're not back at our hotel fairly soon we're going to miss it."

"I'll drive you back," said Shivers. "We've got our two men in the office over there. Should be enough for now."

"Just take us to one of the trolley stops on Ala-Wai Boulevard," said Jane. "Wouldn't do to be seen in the company of the local head of the FBI."

They went back to Shivers's car, an old Dodge, and drove up the unpaved road that ran the length of the park and came up on Ala Moana Boulevard. After a few more turns they arrived at Kalakaua Avenue, Waikiki's main drag.

"The buses come every few minutes. The Silver Service trolleys are more expensive than the little yellow jitneys run by the Rosecrans Taxi people, but I suppose the difference between a nickel and a dime doesn't mean much anymore."

"As soon as we find out what's going on we'll give you a ring," said Black.

"I'll be in the office until late," Shivers replied. He put the Dodge in gear and drove off.

Jane and·Black walked up to the corner. A tin bus-stop sign had been tacked onto a telephone pole just down from the corner. They went and stood by the sign, and Jane rummaged in her bag, digging out a pair of dimes and a pair of nickels to cover all the bases. The night before, they had walked up and down the mile-long section of Kalakaua that ran through Waikiki. To Jane it was a lot like Hollywood Boulevard in Los Angeles; to Morris Black it was like nothing he'd ever seen before, an almost continuous strip of huge hotels like the luxurious Royal Hawaiian, cheek by jowl with a pair of guest cottages named Bide-A-Wee and Rest-A-While, complete with their own miniature gardens and lawns, coconut palms and gorgeous shrubbery, followed by any number of hot-dog stands, outdoor cafés, ice cream parlors, and the garish, wildly rococo marquee of the Waikiki Movie House, which featured a beautiful woman dressed in a feather cloak and helmet worn by the Kamehameha kings and chieftains, her only function to guide patrons to their appropriate aisles.

They waited at the bus stop for no more than a minute or two before a bright yellow wood-sided Rosecrans jitney appeared, a truck-sized big-wheeled Dodge station wagon with six doors, in this case all of them except the driver's side removed. Jane put out her hand and the jitney pulled over. She dropped the two nickels into a glass fare box beside the driver and they climbed on, taking the bench seat directly behind the driver. The bus pulled away, cutting off a much larger Silver Service trolley bus, and roared off down the boulevard.

"You know something about Haas that you didn't tell Shivers?" Jane asked. "He didn't look very dangerous to me. He looked like a policy man to me."

"Policy man?"

"The kind of person who goes door-to-door trying to sell funeral insurance policies on a time-payment plan."

"Good Lord," said Black, smiling. "I've never heard of such an occupation."

"Haas," Jane reminded him.

"He's an assassin," Black responded. "Also a blackmailer. Very efficient, according to his file. Before Hitler took power he was a Berlin detective."

"You don't think he's here to bid on the film?"

"I wouldn't say it's the kind of thing Canaris would send him off to do, no."

"Then why is he here?"

"That's what bothers me," answered Morris Black. "I don't have the foggiest idea."

The jitney roared in and out of traffic down the length of Kalakaua Boulevard, until Jane pulled the bell cord and the jitney pulled over, letting them off at the corner. They crossed the wide boulevard, careful not to get run over by the traffic that was roaring in either direction, and reached the safety of the other side. They headed into the cooling shade of the sidewalks along Kaiulani Avenue and headed for the quieter, northern environs of Waikiki and the streets that led away from the sea and the beaches and the blazing sun.

Black continued. "Money again, access to the Romanov bank accounts through Prince Theodore. Maybe propaganda."

"Sounds thin. What about the Russian NKVD man? Zarubin. The one who had our professor's goose cooked, not to mention his friends in Santa Barbara? Where the hell does he fit in? And why would he want the film? It doesn't put our Russian allies in a very good light, especially since your present king was cousin to Nicholas the Second just the way his father was."

"We've been over this before," said Black. "I don't really think logic has much to do with it at all. I think it's all perception. The film has been a secret all these years, and people always covet secrets, even if the secrets don't matter."

"For a secret that doesn't matter much it's managed to see a lot of people killed," said Jane. "And I still think we've been played like fish on a line ever since this started. There's been too much water under the bridge for any of this to matter anymore, just like you said, but it obviously does matter. Lockhart was an agent in St. Petersburg and blew some rescue mission, so what; it doesn't seem to have affected his career any and the only people Donovan could blackmail with the footage are his own allies. Where's the sense in that?" She shook her head. "We're missing something."

"Well, I suppose we'll find out soon enough."

"Feels a little bit like Daniel and his friends going into the lions' den," grumbled Jane as they turned right down Tusitala Street and reached the Ala Wai Hotel.

The Ala-Wai Hotel was a misnomer since it was a row of small one-room cabins, eight in all, with a small office building at the entrance to the crushed coral compound. Still, it was cheap, private and totally anonymous. When they'd checked in, the man in the office, a huge, big-gutted Polynesian type named Howard, had been a little suspicious of a couple who slept in separate cabins and had no car, but he'd taken their money anyway. The Ala Wai was out of the way and didn't get much of the hot-sheet trade from army and navy boys the way the motor courts on Kalakalua did.

They reached the entrance to the cabin court, and Jane stopped in the office since there were no telephones in the cabins. On a shelf behind Howard the radio was tuned to KGMB and playing Glenn Miller doing "High on a Windy Hill" with that dishy crooner Ray Eberle providing the vocals. He had the kind of smooth just-old-enough-to-be-legal voice that did very unladylike things to her.

"Any messages, Howard?"

The motel owner shook his head. "Nope." He went back to reading the newspaper, and after listening to Ray for another few seconds Jane turned with a sigh and went out the screen door, letting it slap shut behind her.

"No messages," she reported as she walked over to where Black was standing. Parked on the far side of the office was a Two Bit cab, the driver asleep with a copy of the *Honolulu Advertiser* over his face, snoring loudly.

Jane looked carefully and saw that both its headlights were intact. "What do you want to do now?"

"Change clothes and then get something to eat," Black answered promptly as they walked across the open space toward their cabins. "I thought I might try another one of those hamburger sandwiches at that stand by the canal."

"God, do we have to?" Jane asked. "Street meat can be dangerous in hot climates." It also didn't fit into her plans for a slightly more romantic evening.

"Street meat?" said Black.

"Forget it." She sighed.

Of the eight cabins it looked as though only one was occupied other than their own, or at least there was only one car parked, an old, slightly rusty rumble-seat Reo with a St. Louis College pennant hanging from the radio antenna. The name St. Louis probably meant it was a Catholic school and Jane grinned, musing about what kind of venal and cardinal sins had been committed in the rumble seat, let alone the cabin the old car stood beside. It didn't surprise her in the slightest that the curtains of the cabin were tightly drawn even though the sun hadn't set yet.

"Ah, youth," she said to herself as she walked up the short path to her cabin. She took out her key, wondering if losing your cherry at the Ala Wai wasn't some sort of rite of passage for the boys of St. Louis College.

After opening the door, she stopped and gaped. The room had been completely tossed, furniture thrown from one side of the room to the other, the mattress slashed and the bedside lamp thrown against a large plate-glass mirror above the bureau. Her suitcase had been hacked to pieces and a wooden chair had been smashed to splinters. She quickly checked the remains of her suitcase and saw that the Minox and the film Fleming had given her were gone. For a short minute Jane had a nauseating vision of the compartment on the Super Chief and the two corpses in it. There were no bodies here and she didn't intend to be the first.

She backed slowly out the door, took a deep breath, turned and sprinted to the door of Black's cabin next door, bursting through it without a knock. Once again she was stopped in her tracks. The room was neat and tidy, nothing out of place—except Black sitting stiffly on the edge of the bed while the two men who had traveled with them on the Clipper stood on the other side of the bed, Colt .45 Automatic pistols drawn, one pointed at the back of Black's head, the other one at the front of Jane's. Neither man moved or spoke. Their expressions were as bland and uninterested as they'd been on the airplane.

"I think this is our invitation to the ball," said Morris Black.

Chapter 32

The ill-mannered man from the Clipper took them up the broad stairs from the cabin deck to the main deck, then down a long, very narrow, windowless interior corridor to the forward section of the ship. They passed an open doorway, and Jane spotted a brightly lit galley and two male cooks preparing food. The wonderful odors wafting out through the doorway were almost enough to make her faint, and she realized that they hadn't eaten anything all day. Their jailer led them inexorably past the paradise of smells and into a narrow, wood-paneled vestibule that led into the yacht's dining area.

At first Jane thought they'd been called to dinner, but she quickly realized something much more serious was going on in the large room. Most of the space was taken up by a long, brilliantly polished table that gleamed richly in the overhead lights.

The three portholes on either side of the room were drawn. The carpets on the floor were Persian. The ceiling was coffered oak. At the far end of the room was a tall mahogany sideboard. Instead of a silver service on display there was an old-fashioned French Debrie 16mm film projector and a pile of bright yellow Kodak Safety Film boxes. Moura Budberg, a sequined cap over her dark hair, was standing beside it. A white collapsible screen had been set up at the other end of the dining room.

Most of the Russian demi-courtesan's guests were already at the table, but she made no attempt at introductions as Jane and Black were shown to their places. At the end of the table closest to Budberg sat Axel Wenner-Gren, trying to look as Aryan as possible with his close-cropped hair, his uniform-styled blue-gray suit, and a powerful build that at the same time managed to look dissipated.

Every few seconds he looked back over his shoulder and smiled at Moura Budberg. Black had no doubt at all that the Swedish vacuum cleaner inventor was just as smitten as the British agent, the Russian writer and the English journalist and historian had once been.

On Wenner-Gren's right sat Emil Haas, sitting quietly, his perfectly manicured fingers clasped together. Beside Haas sat Feodor Romanov, dressed in a very expensive double-breasted suit, leaning to his right, whispering into the large ear of the taller man beside him, Count Anastase Vonsiatsky, the fascist married to the Connecticut pork heiress.

The seat beside him was where Jane had been placed, with Black directly across from her. On Black's right were only two chairs, one for Julius Rossler, the German spy Shivers was sure worked for the Japanese, and the other for Rossler's Japanese contact, the supposed consular officer, Tadashi Morimura. Rossler had the flat peasant features and thick neck Black associated with beer halls and bullies while Morimura looked much more refined, his long rectangular face set in the placid expression of a Buddhist monk but with a hardness in his eyes that couldn't be disguised.

"We have one more guest to arrive," Moura Budberg said quietly from her end of the room. "And while we wait it might be of some interest to some of you to know a little bit about the film you are about to see. There is no doubt in my mind that it amounts to being the single most important 'document,' if you will, of the twentieth century.

"There is also no doubt in my mind that the events and people you are about to see represent a pivotal moment in the direction the entire world has taken over the last quarter century and will almost certainly affect the next quarter century with equal power. The film in question is some twenty-three years old now and has traveled the world for a great deal of that time, searching for the moment best suited for its revelations. This, indeed, is the fulcrum Archimedes was talking about when he proposed a theorem to move the world."

"Bit florid, don't you think?" asked Jane in a melodramatic whisper. "Levers, fulcrums, Archimedes."

"Oh, quite, quite," Black responded, putting on the plummy airs of an Oxford don.

"You two have less reason to mock me than anyone else at this table," said the Budberg woman.

Wenner-Gren was less polite. "You will shut your mouths and listen to what is being said," barked the man, his accent thick as cheese.

"I think I'd rather ask questions." said Jane, uncowed. "Like how did Miss Budgie down there get the film in the first place? Levitsky gave it to Trotsky, didn't he?"

"This is true." The woman nodded, smiling. "I applaud you on your knowledge, Miss Todd, and I can also assure you that your bad manners only reflect on yourself, not on me."

"I was born with bad manners," Jane answered back. "So answer the question. How did you get the film?"

"*Gospodin* Levitsky was given a sum of money for it."

"Paid for by your Swedish friend?"

"Yes."

"So he gets a cut of the proceeds."

"He knows a moment in history when he sees it," Budberg answered. "He simply rose to the occasion."

"How much choice did Levitsky have?"

"Very little." Budberg smiled. "He had little to barter with."

"He had the film," said Jane.

"And we had him, so to speak. My old comrade Iron Feliks is dead these many years, but I can assure you his specter still haunts the thousand rooms of the Lubyanka. There are those who say that Lavrenti Beria is his reincarnation, and without a doubt his legitimate heir." She paused, her smile broadening. "We knew where Levitsky was and what he was doing, which was making—how do you call them?—'stag movies.' His papers were also false. He knew he would be deported back to Russia if anyone found out. Confronted, he capitulated. His memory goes back to the Ohkrana and the Cheka before the NKVD was even created. He knows precisely how relentless they are, and that once they have found the spoor of their prey they never give up, no matter how long it takes. Without our protection he was a dead man and he knew it."

"Did he know you worked for the NKVD as well?" put in Morris Black.

"I'm many things to many people, Detective Inspector. I'm like most people, I wear many masks."

"So he didn't know."

"There was nothing for him to know," said Budberg. "Or that he needed to know."

"Is he still alive?"

"I have no idea."

"But you have the film."

"And there you have the meat of the matter." The Russian nodded. "I have the film."

A door opened at the far end of the room, and Moura Budberg's smile broadened even more. Wenner-Gren got to his feet and bowed deeply. Jane turned in her seat. The woman was tall, reed-thin and wore an ankle-length silk cheong-sam in a shimmering deep jade color. Her features were sharp and birdlike, her hair rigid with lacquer, her thin lips a slash of bloodred across her face.

"Your Royal Highness," said Wenner-Gren, using the title that had been denied to her by her brother-in-law, the present king of England. His Queen Consort, Elizabeth, hated the woman with an unrelenting passion.

The duchess of Windsor, née Wallis Simpson, American divorcée, stepped into the room and took her place at the head of the table.

She lifted one imperial, haughty hand. "You can begin now."

Wenner-Gren stood up from his place at the near end of the table and went to the light switch on the wall. Moura Budberg flipped the little toggle on the side of the Debrie projector as Wenner-Gren simultaneously doused the lights.

The film began abruptly with a shot of a small empty room. The first few seconds were blurred as the gate of the whirring, chattering projector came up to speed. The blurring eased and Jane saw that the walls were covered with broadly striped ornamental paper. The floor was planked, probably with birch, and a single bulb burned hotly, hanging on a piece of wire from the ceiling. There was a false arch across the center of the room and to the right a barred curved window. It was obviously night, the window uncurtained and dark. At the far end of the room were a pair of wide paneled doors.

A shadow crossed in front of the lens, probably Levitsky, and a moment later the aspect of the film changed entirely as a pan light came on, throwing long shadows to the right. The shadow crossed the lens again and a second light came on, canceling out the shadows thrown by the first. A slight movement on the right side of the frame indicated that the shadow—presumably Levitsky, the cinematographer—had taken his place behind the camera.

For a full minute nothing happened and the film showed nothing but the blank stretch of wallpaper, the archway and the barred window on the right. Then the wide doors beyond the archway suddenly opened and a young dark-haired man with a dark mustache and beard stepped into the room. He was wearing a thick jacket and heavy trousers, seemingly an odd choice for midsummer.

"The Jew, Yakov Yurovsky," supplied Moura Budberg. "The chief executioner."

Behind Yurovsky came the imperial family, and as they appeared, Moura Budberg identified them one by one.

"Nicholas the Second." The tsar, looking like the twin brother of his cousin, George V, King of England, was carrying his son in his arms. "Alexei, the tsarevitch and heir, his son.

"Alexandra, the empress.

"Her daughters, Olga, twenty-two, the oldest.

"Tatiana, twenty-one.

"Marie, nineteen.

"Anastasia, seventeen."

Anastasia was carrying her pet King Charles spaniel, Jemmy. Olga and Tatiana were both carrying pillows.

All were wearing simple white underdresses, and their long hair was informally down without so much as a ribbon. Following the daughters came several others.

"Dr. Eugene Botkin, the family physician. Trupp, the tsar's loyal valet, Demidova, the empress's maid and finally, Kharitonov, the cook."

At this point in the film Yurovsky and the empress seemed to be in conversation. The tsar nodded and Yurovsky left the room for a moment, apparently going through a doorway that must have been somewhere behind the camera. A few moments later he reappeared carrying two ordinary wooden chairs.

The chairs were set down close to the back wall of the room, and the tsar, who had continued to hold his son in his arms, gently put Alexei down in the nearest of the chairs while his wife, the empress Alexandra, took the second chair, which had been set down a little closer to the window. Tatiana and Olga took their pillows and placed one behind their mother's back and the other behind their brother's. Yurovsky then spent a few moments arranging the rest of the people in the room, forming up two lines against the far wall. With that done the tsar and Yurovsky had a brief conversation.

"Yurovsky is telling the tsar that the film is needed to prove to St. Petersburg that the tsar and his family are still being held safely and that they are still alive. You can see Nicholas nodding in agreement as he goes to stand beside his son."

With everyone lined up peacefully, waiting without any look of fear or panic, Yurovsky looked from the camera and back to Nicholas as he pulled a small, torn piece of paper from his pocket.

"This is Yurovsky reading the indictment from the Ural Executive Committee, ordering their execution."

The look on the tsar's face changed, his eyes widening. He turned to look at his family and then back at Yurovsky. The dark-haired man reached into his trouser pocket, pulled out a Colt revolver and fired a single shot, point-blank into the tsar's face. The tsar's head burst open, spraying blood and brains over his daughters behind him, and he crumpled to the ground. The single shot must have been a signal of some kind because Yurovsky quickly stepped off to one side, positioning himself just out of camera range as almost a dozen men surged into the room, at least one of them knocking against the camera, the picture suddenly shaking.

"Yurovsky's killers. Eleven of them. They had all been given their own specific targets."

Silently the eleven men lifted their pistols and began to fire, Yurovsky firing as well from slightly offstage. In the room the noise would have been deafening. The empress and the tsarina Olga each tried to make the sign of the cross, but they did not have time. Alexandra died instantly, several bullets striking her in the chest, midsection and head, tearing her apart. A single round took Olga in the head, her forehead disappearing beneath a veil of gore draining down over her face. Botkin, Trupp and the cook died quickly as well, the wallpaper behind them shredded down to the plaster and lath, blood spraying everywhere.

Alexei and the three younger sisters and Demidova the maid were still alive, although they'd all been hit. Any round fired at their chests seemed to ricochet off, bouncing around the room like lead hailstones. There was so much smoke in front of the lens that there was almost nothing to see except bodies crawling across the floor while others remained inert.

Moura Budberg solved the mystery. "It was discovered later that the three sisters and the maid had stuffed their collection of jewels into their corsets, acting like crude bulletproof vests."

The people in the dining room watched the small screen as Yurovsky stepped forward and stood over Alexei, who had crawled to his father and was clutching the tsar's bloody shirt. Blood was running out of the boy's mouth and there was clearly at least one wound in his belly. The boy was so close to the camera that Jane could see him shivering and his eyes blinking rapidly and spasmodically as though he was rapidly losing his sight. The bearded, dark-haired man kicked the thirteen-year-old boy in the head with the toe of his heavy boot, and the tsarevitch's temple caved in under the lethal blow. Still not satisfied, Yurovsky pulled his second gun, a short-barrel Mauser, out of his jacket and pumped two shots directly into the boy's ear. Alexei's head exploded. The boy's heels drummed against the floor for a few seconds and then he was still. Twenty-three years had passed since the pale, thin little prince had died, but Jane still felt tears welling up in her eyes.

Yurovsky, wreathed in smoke, surveyed the room. The pall had begun to lift off the floor, and the bodies and the bloodbath became visible, gleaming darkly in the harsh lights Levitsky had supplied. The blood was everywhere, on the walls, the ceiling, pooling around bodies and streaming out from under them. Methodically Yurovsky went from corpse to bloody corpse, checking pulses and occasionally firing the Mauser in a coup de grace.

He pried Jemmy the dog out from under the body of her mistress, then tossed the little spaniel aside like a rag. He put away the Mauser and the Colt, then waved the others forward. The eleven men began to lift the bodies and carry them back out through the doors and up the twenty-three steps that led from the basement room.

The film went dark and ended, the tail spinning around and around on the projector, flapping noisily. Moura Budberg switched off the projector, and Axel Wenner-Gren switched on the lights. Their guests blinked in the sudden illumination. Faintly, from somewhere outside, came the tinkling of someone plucking at a ukulele—badly.

"Nine minutes and forty-four seconds," said the Budberg woman. "That's how long it took to end a dynasty and change the world."

A sudden prattle of conversation and questioning erupted from around the table, everyone speaking at once with the exception of Jane, Morris Black and her dubious majesty, the duchess of Windsor. Wenner-Gren put a stop to the babbling with a single clap of his large, meaty hands.

"If you wish to discuss what you have just seen, you may do so in the drawing room in the aft section of the ship, or you may return to your staterooms. There is a steward outside who will guide you." He paused. "Mr. Black and Miss Todd, if you would remain where you are for a moment." Jane noted the fact that the Swede had called Morris "Mr." instead of Detective Inspector. Clearly they were to remain as anonymous as possible.

"Dinner will be served here in approximately an hour," said Moura Budberg. "You will be notified by one of the staff. Under the circumstances, dress will be informal."

Everyone stood up and began to file out of the room. The duchess remained where she was, her eyes on Wenner-Gren and the woman beside her. Jane and Morris Black might as well have not existed. Outside, the sound of the off-key ukulele had stopped.

Like a mongoose on the alert for prey, the duchess swiveled her head toward Morris Black. "Presumably you're the man from Scotland Yard. The policeman I've heard Moura talking about."

"Detective inspector, actually," said Morris, smiling thinly, "although I'd say the rank is irrelevant at the moment."

The duchess swiveled a second time and stared at Jane. "Which would make you the Hollywood photographer." The duchess smiled and Jane realized she wasn't a mongoose at all. She was a cobra, probably the kind that spit its venom.

"I suppose you could describe me that way. I prefer to think of myself as Kodak queen to the stars."

At the use of the word "queen" the duchess of Windsor's already thin lips thinned even more, the small eyes staring intently at Jane to see if any sarcasm was intended. Jane smiled back at the duchess blandly. This was the illegitimate daughter of a dirt-poor Virginian and a Baltimore banker, a woman who had clawed her way up the social ladder, rung by rung, until she'd married a man who had briefly been the king of England. Not someone to be idly slighted, even now, banished to near exile in the Bahamas for the duration of the war.

"We seem to be under some sort of house arrest," said Black, addressing Moura Budberg, intending to break up the staring match between Jane and the duchess. "We were locked in our stateroom."

"Do not think of it as house arrest," said Wenner-Gren, his elbow on the sideboard. "Think of it instead as well-disciplined hospitality on my part."

"It doesn't seem to apply to anyone else on board," said Jane.

"That is because they are all who they say they are," Budberg answered. She sat down in the chair at the end of the table. "While you are otherwise. Mr. Black is not a detective inspector, or at least not anymore. According to our information, he works for the Special Operations Executive at Beaulieu Abbey in Hampshire, seconded to the Secret Intelligence Service as he was a year and a half ago in an effort to track down an especially dangerous German spy."

"Not quite, but that will do," Black answered flatly.

"And you, Miss Todd, have recently been hired by Colonel William Donovan, your president's personal spymaster, the man known as Wild Bill."

"Beats me," Jane answered, shrugging and trying not to show her surprise at the extent of the woman's knowledge.

"There's no need to be coy, Miss Todd. I am merely explaining why we are being very careful about our handling of both you and Mr. Black. When the fox is in the henhouse, it is important for the hens to take precautions, *govorit pravdu, da?* This is the truth, yes?"

"What's truth to one can be a lie to another," said Jane.

"A philosopher among us. How refreshing," the duchess put in.

"You've kept us here for a reason," Black said. "What is it?"

"You will be given your dinner in your stateroom. You will then be returned here at ten o'clock for a special viewing of the film."

"We don't need to see it again," said Black. "You've proved your point."

"I think you should listen to the woman," Jane put in quickly. "I've been living in Hollywood, remember, the place where illusions are created and not everything is quite what it seems."

"And I suggest you listen to Miss Todd, *Gospodin* Black. She is speaking sense. I'm sure you can find your own way back to your cabin."

Jane and Morris stepped out onto the deck, surprised by the freedom Moura Budberg seemed to be giving them. A moment later they saw the beefy figure of Arthur, their jailer, standing only a few yards away. They were on the seaward side of the yacht and both Jane and Morris knew that there would be more guards on the landward side, clustered around the companionway down to the pier. The freedom they had been given was illusory. They turned in the other direction and saw Emil Haas leaning over the rail, smoking a cigarette and looking out to sea. Black gave Jane a look. She shrugged, raised her eyebrows slightly and finally nodded. They joined Haas at the rail and lit cigarettes for themselves.

"Herr Haas," said Black.

"Mister will do just fine," said the German agent. "You are Morris Black, the famous detective."

"That's a bit much."

Haas turned to Jane. "And you are Jane Todd, the woman who foiled the infamous assassin John Bone."

"You seem to know a lot," said Jane.

"Bone worked for us at one time."

"I see," Jane answered.

"Rather a lot of strange bedfellows on board, don't you think?" said Black quietly.

"Quite so. Half of them quite mad." He offered a small bleak smile. "Of course that applies to much of the world in these unhappy times."

"I'm surprised to find you here," said Black.

"And I you," said Haas briefly. "Although I think our purpose is the same."

"The film?" put in Jane.

"The film is only part of the game," said Haas. "The real game lies in who the players are."

"You're being suitably obscure for an intelligence officer," said Black.

"You pay me too high a compliment, Detective Inspector. I am just as much a pawn as you and your companion, toiling for my master on the board." He smiled again. "In your case, of course, your master truly is a king, while Miss Todd's is, what shall we call him, a knight-errant?" He took a last puff on his cigarette and shredded it over the side, field-stripping it like a hunter or a man who knew what it was to be hunted.

"You really are being obscure," said Jane.

Haas turned to her, his expression blank and infinitely dangerous. "I can be very direct as well, Miss Todd. In the game of chess, pawns are the first to be sacrificed so the more important pieces can press the attack. They are also placed on the board in an effort to confuse an otherwise obvious ploy or gambit. I would advise you and your policeman friend to make your greatest efforts to leave this vessel before it is too late." With that, the small gray man pushed himself away from the rail, turned his back on them and walked away down the open deck.

"What the hell was all that about?" Jane asked.

"We were being warned," Black responded grimly.

"About what?"

"Haas is an assassin. He kills people. That's his profession and that's why he's here." Black paused as the small man disappeared through a doorway at the far end of the yacht. "And that's what he intends to do."

Chapter 33

Saturday, December 6, 1941
Kewalo Basin

They each sat on one of the beds, with a folding table brought by the steward between them. The meal had been excellent: macadamia nut salad with papaya seed dressing, steak and crab legs with mashed Hawaiian sweet potatoes and other island vegetables, finished off with pineapple cake, Portuguese sweet roll and more of the wonderful Kona coffee.

Morris Black poured them each another cup of coffee from the thermos jug on the tray and they both lit cigarettes. Black looked at his wristwatch.

"Ten to ten," he said. "Our dear friend Arthur will be coming for us soon."

"Good," Jane replied. "Maybe we'll get to the bottom of all of this."

"By seeing that wretched piece of film again? I don't quite see the point."

"Well, for one thing, it was in black and white."

"Most films are in black and white. They certainly didn't have color film in 1918."

"They didn't have black and white either," Jane informed him. "It was called orthochromatic, which means it was only sensitive to blue or green. They made people up and lit sets to make it look like black and white, but the actual film stock was usually green. What we saw is a copy done sometime in the mid-twenties or maybe even later."

"Could it have been staged? You said something about illusions."

"Maybe, but it looked pretty real to me." Jane shook her head and took another sip of coffee. "No, I think it's the real thing, all right, but it's not the original film. And that's not the whole story."

"What do you mean?"

"We didn't see everything that this Levitsky guy shot."

"How can you tell that?"

"The way the film started with all that flutter, and so abruptly. Levitsky was used to shooting full-length movies." She shook her head again. "No, I think the countess just took a pair of scissors and cut off the head end of the film."

"You're sure?"

"I think we're going to find out in a few minutes. I think that's what this whole thing's been about right from the beginning and none of the others know about it."

"Including Mrs. Simpson?"

"Who?" said Jane. Then she grinned. "You mean the duchess?"

"Yes," said Black. "After all, she and her husband have the most to gain. Even without this mysterious 'head end,' as you call it, if he had the film he could blackmail his own brother with it. The film might not put him back on the throne, but it might get him a better job than being governor of the Bahamas."

"The countess isn't treating her the same as the others—that's for sure," said Jane. "And it fits. This yacht is registered in the Bahamas. It says so right on the back end. She probably sneaked on board and hitched a ride with Wenner-Gren. The duke couldn't just buzz off like that, but that skinny bitch he married could."

"He'd have to be in on it, though," said Black. "He's part of this whole bloody mess and we're right in the middle of it."

"You think the countess and Wenner-Gren have nasty plans for us?"

"I don't think it bloody matters a jot," said Morris Black harshly.

This time there wasn't even a knock on the door. It simply opened, and Arthur the thug appeared. He stood aside without saying a word. Jane stubbed out her cigarette in her saucer and went out the door, Morris Black close behind her.

Vassili Zarubin, Washington, D.C., and New York *Rezident* station chief for the NKVD, lay hidden in the low brush that covered the rising waste ground directly across Ala Moana Boulevard. Using his favorite British "Heath" binoculars, he could put himself on the main deck of the *Southern Cross* with ease. His people in both Los Angeles and San Francisco had tracked both the British policeman and his woman friend easily enough once they'd met with the countess and had continued to follow them. The trail eventually had led back to the countess and her Nazi friend, Axel Wenner-Gren.

Over the two days he'd stayed in his hiding place in the brush, using his binoculars, he'd seen an extraordinary assortment of people both on and getting aboard the *Southern Cross*. In addition to Black and his companion, who seemed to have been brought on board with some element of force involved, he'd seen Vonsiatsky, the *kruglyj durak* driveling idiot who'd married a pig heiress and played at being Stalin and Hitler on his Connecticut farm. At one point, focusing on the rectangular windows of the main cabin forward, he was almost sure he'd seen none other than the duchess of Windsor, which had seemed like utter madness until he'd thought about it for a while.

It was common knowledge that the American would do virtually anything to become queen of England, and if the film was all it was purported to be, it might take her a few steps closer to her dream, regardless of the fact that the England in question was under virtual siege by the most powerful army ever known on the planet, its leader a babbling, comically mustached idiot. He smiled at that, suddenly realizing almost exactly the same thing could be said about his own country.

Beside him, hidden in the scruffy grass and in its own custom-built case, was a Beretta Model 31 semiautomatic rifle with a nine-shot clip fitted with a British Parker Hale silencer and an Enfield telescopic sight. Between the Beretta and the Tokarev TT-33 pistol slung under his jacket he knew he could wipe out the entire crew and guest list of the *Southern Cross* in a matter of seconds.

The Russian picked up a pinch of dirt from the ground and let it dribble from his fingers. Not so different from the soil of the *Rodina,* his homeland. Dirt had no patriotism or pride, and ideology was something you hid behind; no, the only thing separating the nations of the earth was their fear and their hate and their secrets.

This secret had remained just that, a secret, for almost twenty-five years, and Zarubin wasn't about to have it revealed now. Everyone who could have been a problem had been eradicated, all but one. He took a deep breath of the perfumed night air. It was a shame, really. He'd enjoyed his short time here and would be sorry to see it come to an end, not to mention the fact that he abhorred Washington winters. Zarubin lifted his wrist and checked the luminous dial of his watch. Only another few hours to wait and the end could begin.

As before Morris Black and Jane Todd were taken forward to the dining room. The table had been cleared of any food, but a silver tray was set up on the sideboard beside the motion picture projector. On the tray were two bottles of vintage port, one Graham's, the other Smith-Woodhouse. Both were 1935 vintage, which Black knew would make them very expensive indeed.

As before the duchess was sitting on the starboard side of the table, while Moura Budberg was seated at the far end, the imposing figure of Axel Wenner-Gren standing behind her, ready at the projector. An ashtray, a large, ornate gold table lighter in the shape of a swan and a gold cigarette case on the table were centered in front of the duchess, who was already smoking.

Sitting down across from her, both Jane and Morris Black took cigarettes from the case. Morris lit both of them with the swan lighter. Jane sat back in her chair and so did Black, both of them putting on an air of nonchalance that neither of them felt. The arms of their chairs were almost touching, and Jane stretched out her baby finger slightly, just managing to touch the side of Black's right hand for an instant. He looked startled for an instant, then regained his composure, turning a little toward her and smiling.

"Do we get to drink the booze after the show or before?" Jane asked, keeping her eyes on the duchess.

"It can hardly be called booze, my dear. It comes from His Royal Majesty's private cellar."

"The duke, that would be?" said Jane brightly.

"Do you make a habit of being obnoxious?"

"Depends entirely on the company."

"It's getting late," Moura Budberg interjected. "Her Royal Highness has already seen the film, but she said she was interested in finding out what your impressions would be."

"I don't mind if she stays," said Jane.

"Be a dear and switch on the projector, would you, Axel?" said Moura. He did as he was told, then reached back and flipped off the lights. The room dropped into total darkness except for the brilliant white square of light at the other end of the cabin. Right away, Black saw, the beginning of the film was nothing like the one they'd seen earlier in the evening.

It began with a standard countdown strip of leader and opened with a long shot down a wide, dirt-packed boulevard with large Russian-style wood-frame buildings to the left and right. A few very old-fashioned automobiles were parked on either side of the road, but mostly it was lined with small horse-drawn carriages drawn up to hitching rails. Several wooden goods wagons moved back and forth. The film had a pale green overtone, but from the brightness of the scene and the length of the shadows trailing behind people it was perhaps a little past noon.

"Yekaterinburg, Western Siberia, this is Ascension Avenue, looking to the east."

The shot went dark in a way that told Jane someone had turned a multiple-lens turret.

"This is the British consulate. The man coming out the door is Sir Charles Eliot, British high commissioner and consul-general for Siberia." Eliot was on the short side, his dark hair in an upright brush. His face was broad and square with a large nose and a drooping mustache covering thick, almost feminine lips. "The man with him is Major Homer Slaughter of American Military Intelligence, nominally attached to the Czech forces as liaison officer. On July 17, 1918, Major Slaughter had no business being in Yekaterinburg, and certainly not speaking to the British consul-general."

"Why was he there?" asked Jane.

"In a moment," cautioned Moura Budberg.

The shot changed several times, once showing a palatial building that Budberg identified as the local railroad station, another rather pretty shot of a large tree-lined lake with a biplane flying boat resting close to shore, and a long continuous pan across a very old-looking cemetery with railroad tracks in the background and what appeared to be a freight yard behind it. Finally they were back in Yekaterinburg, this time facing an odd-looking house. It was large, several stories tall with a Spanish-style tile roof, two turrets, and a multitude of chimneys. What was truly odd, though, was the wooden palisade that had been built around it, completely obscuring the main and second floors as well as the entrances. The main gate was open and Jane could see a second, shorter palisade within. Six people were standing in front of the outer gates of the palisade closest to the street, one of them in uniform. As the film continued to play, an old woman dressed completely in black tottered through the shot as she crossed the street and disappeared from view. It was a strange, human detail that suddenly made the rest of the proceedings all the more real.

"This is the Ipatiev House, also known as the House of Special Purpose," said Moura Budberg, her voice flat and unemotional. "We can identify the date of this as being sometime shortly after the fifteenth of July, since that is the date the outer palisade was completed. Watch now."

The turret flipped and suddenly the people standing at the gate came into sharp focus. The tallest was Major Slaughter; the man beside him was tall and dressed in an odd-looking uniform with boots and jodhpurs as well as a plain battle jacket without any rank insignia or unit designation. The two men were talking easily together and smoking cigarettes.

"The man with the uniform is Alexander Beloborodov. At the time he was the chairman of the Ural Regional Soviet. He was also a friend of and a spy for Trotsky. In the end it was Beloborodov who managed to spirit him away to Mexico. Very little is known about him other than that."

"The next man?" said Black.

"Yakov Yurovsky. The chief assassin and leader of the firing squad that murdered the tsar and his family. He was also responsible for disposing of the bodies." The second man was slight and dark with a round face and a heavy mustache and a long, thick goatee-style beard that covered most of the bottom of his face.

"And the next?" asked Black, no longer able to delay the inevitable.

Moura Budberg smiled in the gloomy, brightly punctuated darkness. "As you are well aware, the third man is Robert Bruce Lockhart, acting on special orders from George the Fifth."

"To rescue the Romanovs?" said Jane, thinking about the flying boat she'd seen.

"Nothing so high-minded," put in the duchess of Windsor. "David told me all about this some time ago. Lockhart was there to negotiate trade agreements with the Reds, through Yakolev, the head of the local soviet. Supposedly to get a jump on the Germans. The question at hand had nothing to do with rescuing the poor creatures. It had to do with questions regarding how trade could go on after they'd been killed and would it have any effect. Very cold-blooded, I must say. David hated his father for that. I think he would have gone and rescued them himself if he'd been able, but of course he wasn't."

"Lenin and Trotsky were both aware that there would be a cinematographer in place, and he was given orders to get Lockhart on film, as well as the two men standing next to him, also there to negotiate trade agreements," added Budberg.

The camera panned a little more, and the two men at the far end of the group came into focus. One of them was tall, stooped and lanky with thinning dark hair. The other one was shorter, broad-shouldered and clean-shaven. His haircut was military, but he was wearing a rumpled dark suit that didn't seem to fit him very well.

"It can't be," Jane whispered, her eyes widening.

"Oh, but it is, Miss Todd. The man you see in front of you is none other than Colonel William Joseph Donovan, at that point late of the Fighting Sixty-ninth, I believe they were called. He was also a member of American Military Intelligence and a 'friend' to President Wilson. The other man is Father Patrick Duffy, Donovan's regimental chaplain and a high-ranking member of military intelligence himself. Since neither Donovan nor Duffy spoke Russian, Slaughter, who did, was brought in to translate for them." They watched for a few moments longer and then Wenner-Gren stopped the film and turned on the lights.

"It's impossible," said Jane. "Donovan was a war hero. He was on the Western Front. He got the Congressional Medal of Honor."

"He was also slightly wounded. In the end he was given two Purple Hearts, I believe," said Budberg. "He was taken off the front lines and evacuated back to a field hospital in a place called Château Poicens. From there he was flown to Marseille, where he caught an Imperial Airways flight to Trebizond in Turkey and then a Stetinin M9 *Devjatka* flying boat. The whole trip, start to finish, took a little less than twenty-four hours. Neither Duffy nor Donovan was even missed. Ironically, Donovan came back a year later with the American Expeditionary Force to talk to General Kolchak of the Whites to see if he could arrange the same trade deals as he had with the Reds. Hedging his bets, so to speak."

"This doesn't prove anything," said Black. "Only that Donovan and Lockhart were present in Yekaterinburg."

"It certainly proves that Lockhart wasn't planning any rescue. In fact, it obviates any further discussion about it. It also categorically proves that both Donovan and Lockhart lied about their whereabouts since neither one ever mentioned their presence publicly, either at the time or since. Combined with the film of the assassination itself the whole thing is very damning." She shook her head. "An American war hero and a member of the British Foreign Office talking in broad daylight with the man who was responsible for the mass murder of eleven people. Governments have toppled for less than this."

"Who's to say the film was shot all at the same time?" asked Jane.

"Because there are no edits of any kind. The film all comes from the same reel of negative stock."

"Why don't we get to the point of all this?" said Black. "I've seen enough."

"Not quite," Moura Budberg replied. She made a small gesture with her hand, and Wenner-Gren darkened the lights and switched on the projector a second time. Once more they sat through Levitsky's preparations for filming and then the horrible footage of the killing itself, ending with the scene as Yurovsky stepped forward and stood over Alexei. Again they saw the bearded, dark-haired man as he kicked the thirteen-year-old boy in the head with the toe of his heavy boot and the tsarevitch's temple caving in under the lethal blow. They watched again as Yurovsky pulled his second gun and pumped two shots directly into the boy's ear. Alexei's head exploded. The boy's heels drummed against the floor for a few seconds and then he was still.

On the film once again Yurovsky, wreathed in smoke, stood up and looked around the room, and once again he went from corpse to bloody corpse, checking pulses and occasionally firing the Mauser in a coup de grace.

He pried Jemmy the dog out from under the body of her mistress, then tossed the little spaniel aside like a rag. He put away the Mauser and the Colt, then waved the others forward. The eleven men began to lift the bodies up, carrying them back out through the doors and up the twenty-three steps.

But this time instead of ending, the film continued. The shot held steady on Yurovsky, standing in the thinning smoke, and then two figures passed between Yurovsky and the camera, their profiles briefly seen but forever captured on the whirring strip of celluloid. Even in the smoke and the semidarkness there was no mistaking who they were: William Joseph Donovan and Robert Bruce Lockhart. The film ran on for a few seconds as the smoke continued to swirl and then it faded out to nothing. Wenner-Gren switched off the projector again and turned on the lights.

Jane stared, "They were *there*? In the *room*!"

"It would appear so."

"But why?"

"I'm not entirely sure, but it may simply have been so that they could bear witness. Various banks and financial institutions, both of your governments, in fact, have access to enormous amounts of Romanov wealth. With the Romanovs undeniably gone the Morgans and Barings of the world could breathe just a little bit easier. Had there been any survivors it could well have led to awkward questions."

"They would have reported back to their superiors: Lockhart to Balfour, the foreign secretary, and Donovan to President Wilson," put in the duchess. "A sigh of relief heard round the world, or at least in Europe and the States," she added sourly.

"What is the price for all of this?" Morris Black asked bluntly.

Moura Budberg smiled. "For our friends down in their staterooms their version of the film is expensive. For you and your friend, think of this version of the film as a gift." She turned and glanced at the duchess of Windsor. "For Her Royal Highness it is a bulwark. Something to keep the royal dogs at bay in case they intend to visit any further indignities on her or her husband." Budberg paused. "And you, Detective Inspector Black, will deliver the bad news that she has it in her possession."

"And my copy?" Jane asked.

"Make it public and it would almost certainly destroy any credibility Colonel Donovan might have, now or in the future. It might even be enough to bring down Mr. Roosevelt."

"What if we just destroy the copies and have done with it?" said Jane.

"Then we'd make it public for you. As you must be aware, we have access to the originals."

"One question," said Black. "Why didn't you just do that in the first place? Why did you need us to run about tracking it all down? You could have released the film yourself."

"It probably wouldn't have been believed. What do my friends on Dzerzhinskiy Square call it, *Dizinformation*? This way is much more effective, much more believable."

"And what do you and your friend here get out of it all?"

"Doors will open," she said, glancing at the former Wallis Simpson. "Doors will open in many places, I think."

"When do we get the film?"

"Tomorrow, shortly after nine p.m. along with everyone else." She smiled. "I wouldn't want it to appear that I was playing favorites. Until then they will be kept locked in this sideboard, which I should caution you is quite well guarded." She paused again. "And now, if you will excuse us, Her Majesty and I have a number of things to discuss before we return to Nassau." It was a dismissal. Arthur, stationed outside the dining room door, escorted them back to their stateroom.

"Now what?" asked Jane as they were locked into their stateroom on the *Southern Cross* again. The dinner things and the folding table had been removed. "How about we climb out through the porthole? Take good old Emil's advice before he starts shooting." Black shook his head, puffing on a cigarette and thinking hard. Jane hopped over to his bunk, pushed back the curtains and tried her hand at the brass porthole bolts securing the small round windows. They were dogged down tight, and anyway it would have been impossible to clamber through an opening that small. She cupped her hands and looked out over the water of the basin. On the fisherman's wharf by the administration building all the lights were out. Below the wharf, riding out a low tide, was a long fishing boat with twin booms, an open cockpit, and a small forward cabin that was probably used in foul weather. She could even read the name on the transom, *Crunch and Des*, after the Philip Wylie stories in the *Saturday Evening Post*.

"What the hell was the name of their boat?" she asked under her breath, trying not to think about the situation they were in.

"Whose boat?"

"Crunch and Des."

"The *Poseidon,*" answered Black promptly.

"How did you know that?"

"I read the stories in the *Saturday Evening Post,*" Black answered. "My mother had an air-mail subscription. When I grew up, I was either going to be Crunch Adams having adventures in the Florida Keys or one of the Mounties bringing law and order to the Canadian West."

"I always wanted to be Gertrude Lange."

"Who?"

"One of the first famous woman photographers," Jane answered. "Like Margaret Bourke-White."

They sat in silence for a moment, side by side on the bunk. "Are we going to get out of this?" Jane asked.

"I think so. We're the ones bringing the bad news, remember."

"Yeah, and you know what happens to the bearers of bad tidings." After a pause she said, "You think they're not going to let us go, Donovan and your people?"

"They can't," Black said darkly. "We're too much of a security risk as it is. This simply makes it a thousand times worse." He let out a long, sighing breath. "The chances are, we'll be sent out on some sort of mission from which we won't be coming back. Nice and tidy and out of the way. Telegrams home to the family . . . We regret to inform you . . ."

"Except we don't have any families, which makes it even easier." She made a fist and pounded it down on the bed. "Christ, we should have seen this coming."

"I think we did," said Black. "You and I share a terrible flaw, I'm afraid."

"What's that?"

"We're too bloody curious for our own good."

"Well, curious or not I'm not going to give up without trying."

"You seem to forget we're on an island, Jane. There's not too many ways of getting off, and you know as well as I do that Shivers's people are no more than a hundred yards away in that gas station watching everything that happens."

"Quit being a pessimist. Something will show up."

"Such as?"

Without thinking very much about it Jane leaned over and kissed Morris Black full on the lips. He returned the kiss for a long moment, then broke away. "Is this part of some escape plan?" he asked, smiling. His lips and mouth were tingling hotly from the touch of her. Jane kissed him again and this time it lasted even longer. Black felt his right hand come up and gently touch her breast. She moaned softly and the kiss deepened, then broke a second time.

"A while ago I fell in love with another Limey and wound up not kissing him or making love to him or showing him how I felt in any way. I'm not going to let that happen again."

"Don't I have anything to say about this?"

"Not a word," Jane said and kissed him again.

According to his watch it was slightly after five thirty in the morning when Morris Black sat bolt upright in the narrow bunk. Jane Todd mumbled sleepily under the covers beside him.

"Bloody hell," he whispered, speaking into the gloom. At the Yard, Morris Black had been considered to possess the Sight, the slightly metaphysical sixth sense that was sometimes a little spooky to those who did not possess it. Black himself knew that there was nothing at all metaphysical about it. Most coppers thought in an entirely linear fashion, putting one fact atop another like a child playing with alphabet blocks until the tower was finished and the letters aligned in the right order. Black, on the other hand, was one of those rare policemen who could let the facts at hand simmer in the back of his mind until he was ready to make the single, simple intuitive leap that took him directly to the solution of the problem. To Black it was the subtle difference between craft and art.

"What?" murmured Jane, pushing herself up against the pillows and yawning. Still half asleep, she groped around on the table between the beds and found a lighter and a packet of cigarettes.

"Levitsky!" said Black. He took the lit cigarette away from Jane and began puffing away on it himself.

"I hand over my virtue. Twice, if you recall, and you steal my cigarette." She lit another. "And what's this about Levitsky? He's the cameraman, right?"

"Who came to America, stole a camera from a news-reel company and started making stag movies."

"You've gone crazy now, haven't you?"

"It explains it." Black grinned. "It absolutely explains it."

"Explains what?"

"Why they came here. To Hawaii. Honolulu."

Suddenly Jane saw the reason too. "It wasn't because Wenner-Gren couldn't dock his boat in the States. It's because Levitsky's here. The original film is here."

"There's tens of thousands of sailors here. A ready-made market."

"So how do we find him?"

"How many film-processing laboratories do you think there are in Honolulu?"

"Not a whole lot," Jane answered. "It's pretty specialized." She shrugged. "And he may not be doing it commercially. He may just be doing it for his own stuff."

"First we have to get the other copies."

"From the dining room? A bit risky, don't you think?"

"A lot risky, but I don't think we have any choice."

"I get the feeling the royal whippet has already got her copy safely hidden away."

"There's nothing we can do about that now."

"Then I guess we'd better get dressed."

"Sad but true," said Morris Black, climbing out of bed.

Chapter 34

Sunday, December 7, 1941
Kewalo Basin

That Sunday, sunrise in Honolulu was officially at seven twenty-seven a.m. Sunrises are as slow to appear in Hawaii as sunsets are long to fade, but by seven thirty-five Vassili Zarubin had enough light to begin his work. Over the previous two days he'd noticed that at least two and sometimes as many as four armed guards dressed in Wenner-Gren's idiotic matelot sailor uniforms patrolled the main deck of the boat. Unlike the rest of the crew, none of the armed guards were Bahamian, which probably had something to do with the Swedish Nazi's fear of putting weapons into a black man's hands. Not unreasonable since he paid his workers in Nassau next to nothing and there had already been one or two signs of unrest in the island paradise.

This morning he had noted three guards, one standing by the upper end of the companionway leading from the wharf to the main deck, one at the stern, and a third at the bow. All three men appeared to be carrying M1 Garand rifles as well as holstered sidearms. The man at the companionway never moved, but his two companions made regular slow tours, meeting in the middle, where they would stop briefly at the companionway and spend a few moments talking to their friend. With all three of them together and a range of less than three hundred yards Zarubin knew they presented no real difficulty.

The Russian opened up the case containing the rifle,

screwed the Enfield sight firmly into place and tucked himself into a knees-up downhill firing position in the grass. He lifted the rifle, eased the stock comfortably against his cheek, sighting on the chest of the guard standing by the companionway stairs. He could probably have taken him with a head shot, but he resisted the temptation. This wasn't about marksmanship. He wanted an assured kill, three of them, in fact, with no more than half a second between the three men's deaths.

Thirty seconds later, just as the sun began to clear Diamond Head, the other two guards joined their friend at the companionway. Zarubin took in a breath, then let it out, squeezing the trigger as he exhaled, once, twice, three times. The sound was like three short hand claps, followed by silence. Keeping his eye to the telescopic sight, Zarubin watched the men as they slithered down onto the deck. The way was clear.

Without haste Zarubin began to pack away the rifle, carefully wiping it off with a piece of cleaning cloth, then unscrewing the silencer. He put everything back in its place, then picked up the case. He looped the binocular strap around his neck and began to make his way down the hill.

The sun was now barely glinting off the glass of the pilothouse, and all the curtains were drawn over the porthole windows. The *Southern Cross* was still sound asleep, perhaps with the exception of the cooking staff. A sound came to him distantly, disturbing the peace of the moment. He took a moment to place it: aircraft. Probably an early-morning practice flight at Hickam Field. Zarubin ignored it and continued on down the hill. He reached Ala Moana Boulevard, crossed it and hooked slightly to the right, moving down the steep sand-and-gravel single-lane track that made up the beginning of Ward Street. At the foot of the street, parked off to one side, was the wood-sided Chevrolet Special DeLuxe station wagon he'd seen parked there for the past two days. He tried the handle, found it unlocked and tossed in the case containing the Beretta and then the binoculars, since he wouldn't be needing either anymore.

His load somewhat lightened, he headed down to the wharf and silently climbed the companionway until he was standing on the main deck of the *Southern Cross*. He looked to the west again, frowning. The sound of the aircraft was much louder, mixed now with irregular explosions. In the distance he could see dense smoke rising blackly over Pearl Harbor. It looked as though everyone in Honolulu's worst fear had been realized— the tank farm of fuel for the ships and planes had somehow ignited. That wasn't his concern, though.

Keeping the Tokarev in its sling for the moment, he spent some time dragging the three dead guards to the companionway and then down, easing them into the oily water between the ship and the wharf. All three disappeared without a trace. With that done he went forward and climbed the ladder up to the foot of the cabin deck with the pilothouse above. He cared little about being seen. Reconnaissance with the binoculars had shown him that the forward upper decks were on three levels, the bridge, the dining cabin, and below that the gymnasium, where Wenner-Gren usually did exercises in mid-morning. He turned around the corner of the deckhouse and slipped in through a doorway.

Black was already dressed except for his jacket when Jane came out of the adjoining bathroom. She found her crumpled skirt on the floor, pulled it on without bothering to slip on her stockings and shrugged on her blouse, buttoning it rapidly. Black was sitting on the edge of the bed they'd so recently occupied together, carefully pulling at the stitching behind his lapel.

"What are you doing?"

"I wasn't sent into the wilderness entirely naked." He smiled.

"You were entirely naked last night," she said. "I thought you looked pretty good that way actually."

Black flushed bright red and bent over his work.

"You really are a shy one, aren't you?"

"I'm not greatly experienced with women. I find the whole thing a little disconcerting when you get right down to it." He hesitated. "Lots of fun, mind you, but a little disconcerting all the same."

"You may find it disconcerting but you seem pretty passionate about it."

"The passion comes from my Russian side, the shyness from being a Brit."

Black managed to pull open the seam behind the left lapel and pulled out a small leather container only a few millimeters thick.

"What the hell is that?" asked Jane.

Black unzipped the little case and displayed the lockpick set inside, two or three rakes and an assortment of tension wrenches.

"You're a cop and you know how to pick locks?"

"Know thy enemy," said Black. He went to the door leading out to the passageway outside and began working on the lock. "Wait for me here," he said as he worked. "I'll see if I can get into that sideboard and fetch away the film. That should put a crimp in their plans." In the distance, miles away, Black could hear the muffled crack and roar of an approaching storm.

"Wait for you here?" Jane's tone was indignant. "Not on your life, brother."

"It'll be safer, trust me."

"Every time a man says trust me, I get suspicious. And I don't like the Prince Charming act."

"I beg your pardon?"

"Just because we slept together last night doesn't make me into a porcelain doll, Morris. I can take care of myself."

"All right." Black crooked a finger. "If that's the case, then come over here and hold this tension wrench." Jane did as she was told, kneeling and holding the slim, unfamiliar tool, while Black continued to poke at the lock.

"What do we do after we get the film—if we get the film?"

"Find a weapon and get off this wretched boat."

"Then what? Hitchhike into Honolulu?"

"There's an estate wagon parked just up the road. I think they must use it for purchasing supplies. We take that."

"If they left the keys in it."

Black looked astounded. "You can't start an automobile without the key?"

"You think just because I come from Brooklyn I know

how to hot-wire a car?" she said with mock offense. "I'm appalled."

"Do you?"

"As a matter of fact I do, but I don't like the assumption."

"Well, there you go then," said Black.

"And then what?" Jane asked. "Hand the film over to someone like Agent Shivers at the FBI?"

"I haven't thought that far yet." There was a sharp click and Jane felt the lock release. She pulled out the tension wrench and handed it to Black, who fitted it and the rake he'd been using back into his case.

"Come on," he whispered. "I'm dying for a cup of tea, and I don't think I'm going to get one until all of this is over." He eased open the door and they slipped out into the silent corridor.

At seven forty-one, Zero pilot Second Lieutenant Masaji Suganami reached Wheeler Field, his primary target. He went into a low-level strafing run with the rest of his group of nine aircraft from the Third and Fourth Fighter Combat Units. He had reached landfall at Waimea Bay exactly on time and had met no resistance whatsoever as he thundered over the hilly, heavily forested inner island, marveling at the beautiful landscape and the perfect blinding orb of the rising sun, blossoming on his left and filling his cockpit with a golden, almost supernatural light.

Suganami had already been a full-fledged fighter pilot for the past four years and a lieutenant for two. He was proud of his family, his country and even prouder of the *Hachimaki* scarf tied around his forehead, marked with the bloodred spot of his nation's flag and the inscription that meant "Certain Victory."

Coming in over the field, Suganami noted with pleasure that the Sixteenth Attack Group consisting of twenty-five Aichi dive-bombers had already completed their task, destroying the barracks and hangars as well as a number of aircraft assembled on the hardstand. Arming his twin 20mm cannon and his two 7.7mm machine guns, Suganami brought his fighter in at less than a hundred feet, blazing away, raking his fire across the remaining aircraft on the ground and the crews desperately trying to save them. He went into a low wing turn and spotted a trio of American P-36 fighters taxiing onto the longest of Wheeler Field's three runways. All three of the fighters were moving but not airborne. While Suganami knew his aircraft was much more maneuverable, the P-36 group was capable of doing considerable damage. He turned again, bringing himself on a collision heading and opened fire. The first of the enemy aircraft exploded almost instantly, and the other two, unable to stop, raced through the wreckage, igniting their own aircraft.

Suganami gave an involuntary shiver. The Zero was without a doubt superior to anything the Americans had in the air, but to gain such superiority sacrifices had to be made. The aluminum skin of the aircraft was dangerously thin in an attempt to save weight, and there was no armor plating for the pilot. Worst of all, the fuel tanks were not self-sealing, and in a dogfight a sudden fire was the realization of a Japanese pilot's most terrible nightmare: to be burned alive in an aircraft where everything was flammable.

Blotting the thought from his mind, the Japanese pilot pulled his aircraft into a steep climb, did a perfect wingover and headed for his next target.

Morris Black and Jane made their way carefully up the stairs from the cabin deck and then out into the main corridor. Jane paused and unclipped a fire ax from its bracket on the wall.

"What the bloody hell are you going to do with that?" Black whispered.

"Cut the duchess into little pieces if I run into her," Jane answered. "Keep going."

They continued toward the forward end of the *Southern Cross*, listening for the slightest sound that anyone was coming. Watching the boat with Shivers, they'd never seen fewer than three guards on deck, and neither one of them had any idea how many guards there were patrolling the interior of the yacht. As they moved down the corridor, they came up on the companionway that led down to the chief steward's quarters, and suddenly Arthur the thug appeared, coming up onto the top step, buttoning his shirt, his jacket over one arm. Jane had three thoughts in rapid succession: he's a fruit of all things, having a fling with one of the crew; he's dropping his jacket and reaching for his gun; if I don't do something fast, we're dead.

Without bothering to think anymore she swung the fire ax sideways with all her strength, hitting Arthur in the exact center of his chest with the pick end, rupturing his heart. Arthur's eyes opened very wide. Blood spurted out around the remaining inch or so of the pick end not buried in his chest. When Jane pulled on the ax handle, it brought him forward, blocking the corridor. She stood there, staring at the blood dripping from the end of the pick.

"Jesus," she whispered. "What have I done?"

"Killed him, I think," said Black. "Well done." He reached out and squeezed her shoulder lightly. Bending down past her, he rolled the dead man over and retrieved the automatic from its sling.

Jane kept on staring at the blood on the pick end of the ax and the blood pooling under Arthur's corpse.

"Thanks," she said dully. She wanted to throw up, but she couldn't take her eyes off the blood or the body. "I think I'm going to be sick."

"We don't have time for that. We have to hurry," he said, his eyes turning hard. "And bring the ax."

Vassili Zarubin knew that the most likely place for the film to be hidden was either somewhere in the dining room or the owner's stateroom directly below it. With the duchess of Windsor on board, Wenner-Gren would almost certainly have given over the suite to her and moved forward with Moura Budberg to two of the officers' cabins, probably demoting the chief engineer and the chief steward to occupy crew quarters even farther forward. As with most ships of this size the captain of the vessel would have separate quarters behind the wheelhouse and bridge one deck above.

Stepping directly from the deck into the enclosed dining room lobby, Zarubin took out the silenced Tokarev

and eased back the slide, pushing one of the nine
7.62mm shells into the chamber. He paused, listening,
and heard the faint rattling of pots and pans somewhere
nearby. The galley staff getting ready to cook breakfast.

He decided to leave them alone; if one of them came
into the dining room for any reason he would deal with
the problem, but for the moment there would be no
unnecessary noise or killing. He would much prefer to
make his entrance and exit with as little fuss as possible.
Zarubin knew perfectly well that if he was discovered,
arrested or charged, his identity would be revealed,
which would be a disaster in more ways than one. Silently he pushed open the swing door to the dining room
and stepped inside. The long, narrow room was empty,
the curtains over the portholes pulled back to let in the
weak early-morning sun.

The dining room table was set for eight. Zarubin did
a quick count in his head and came up two short, which
probably meant Black and the woman were being kept
under lock and key. Already several covered serving
platters were arranged on the sideboard as well as a
large samovar-style coffee urn. If any one of Moura's
guests was an early riser, Zarubin knew he was going to
have a problem. Speed was now definitely of the essence.

He went to the sideboard, skirting the table, then
crouched, laying the Tokarev down beside him on the
carpet. He took a set of lock picks out of his jacket
pocket and began working on the old-fashioned locks on
the sideboard doors. He judged he'd have them open in
less than a minute, and he'd be off the *Southern Cross*
in three. One more task after that and he'd be aboard
the MV *Stary Bolshevik*, a four-thousand-ton Russian-
built freighter out of Vladivostok, already docked in Honolulu and bound for San Francisco within twenty-four
hours. He smiled as he worked, enjoying the irony of
his escape.

Zarubin heard a faint squeaking sound behind him.
Instantly he realized he was no longer alone in the room.
Forgetting about the lock on the sideboard door, he
swept up the Tokarev in his right hand, dropped out of
his crouch in a tuck and roll, coming upright with the

silenced pistol already aimed at the same entrance he'd come through less than a minute before.

The Russian was too late. Morris Black had beat him to the punch. Arthur's Colt Automatic was aimed at his chest. "*Tovaristch* Zarubin, I presume?"

"And you would be Detective Inspector Black," said Zarubin. "Which would make the lady with the bloody ax in her hands Miss Jane Todd." He smiled. "The photographs we took of you don't do your beauty justice."

"Gee, thanks," said Jane. She looked nervously back out the door, but no one was coming.

"How did you know who I was?" Zarubin asked.

"You were the only interested party not represented at the table yesterday." Considering the size of the weapon in the man's hand, Black didn't want to mention anything about Fleming having mentioned the "Squirrel Cheeks" nickname, but seeing the man in person it was easy to see how it suited him.

"You look familiar," said Jane, frowning at the man with the huge silenced weapon.

"I don't think we've ever met," said Zarubin.

"I take pictures all the time," said Jane. "I never forget a face."

"Under the circumstances I don't think it matters. They had a name for situations like this in your Wild West, I believe."

"A Mexican standoff," said Morris Black. "Still, neither you nor we can afford to waste any time here.

"Dear God," Jane whispered, staring over Zarubin's shoulder. "What the hell is that?"

Vassili Zarubin smiled. "Don't be silly, Miss Todd. That one's as old as the hills."

Second Lieutenant Masaji Suganami's attack on the Marine Air Corps station at Ewa had been a complete disaster. The secondary target, which was a rear-echelon support base for the bases at Midway and Wake Islands, comprised mostly transport aircraft and amphibious PBY patrol aircraft. As far as the Japanese plan was concerned, it was a gathering point for members of the First, Second, Third and Fourth Attack Groups and a target to expend their remaining ammunition on after completing their primary mission. As planned, Suganami and several other aircraft already there did several strafing runs, low and slow over the runways. Yet the first shell in the packed sixty-round belt of the left-wing cannon jammed in the receiver, effectively taking Lieutenant Suganami's aircraft out of combat, since the jamming of one cannon made it impossible to fire the right-wing weapon as well.

Suganami desperately squeezed on the bicycle-brake firing lever on the left side of the cockpit and even ducked down between his now empty twin machine guns to toggle the cannon master switch on and off, but nothing seemed to work. Furious and ashamed, he peeled away from the rest of his comrades and headed southeast, reaching Ewa Beach, then gained a little altitude as he streamed away toward Diamond Head, the final landmark he would use to guide himself back to the pitching deck of the aircraft carrier *Soryu*.

Hurtling along the coastline at roughly three hundred miles per hour, Suganami was barely aware of the roiling pall of smoke over Pearl Harbor off his left wing and even less aware of the city of Honolulu in the middle distance. Suddenly the air around him was full of antiaircraft flak, and he pulled up on his control column in an effort to avoid it.

Peering down as he jinked the Mitsubishi fighter plane back and forth, he was astonished to see what appeared to be a relatively new-looking cargo liner with a stark white superstructure firing at him from an antiaircraft gun platform mounted on the afterdeck. He couldn't be sure, but he thought it might be flying the Dutch flag. Then it was gone and so was Honolulu.

Pushing the stick forward, he dropped down until he was almost skimming the incoming breakers as he raced for home. He gritted his teeth with anger and shame, tears forming in his eyes behind the goggles. To return to the ship with his assignment incomplete was an almost unbearable humiliation, even though the fault was not his but the machine's. He squeezed his eyes shut for an instant, knowing that such a thought was only an excuse. He was the leader of his group, and most of all he was *responsible* for everything that happened. The word "fault" had no meaning.

Second Lieutenant Masaji Suganami believed in *Bushido*, the Way of the Warrior, and a true Warrior would have become *Kamikaze*, the Divine Wind, and turned his aircraft into a blazing weapon, crashing down into the enemy ranks, even at the cost of his own life.

Just ahead of him he was suddenly aware of a mad vision—a yacht of monumental proportions was tied up to what had to be a fisherman's wharf, its prow with a long, ornate bowsprit pointing directly at him. Without thinking he reached out with his left hand, somehow knowing, almost as though someone was whispering the solution into his ear, that the reason his cannon had jammed was because the barrels had been overheated. He squeezed the bicycle brake firing lever and the cannons began to roar.

Although the cannon had a slow rate of fire and a reduced muzzle velocity, the huge 20mm caliber and the fact that it used explosive shells more than made up for those deficiencies. Each of the 120 shells in the wing magazines weighed slightly more than a quarter pound and had the destructive force of a hand grenade. By the time Second Lieutenant Suganami began to fire on the *Southern Cross* he had a total of thirty-four shells left.

Jane had spotted Suganami's Zero a split second before the lieutenant began to fire and managed to grab the sleeve of Morris Black's jacket and drag him down to the carpeted floor. Vassili Zarubin wasn't quite as quick. Spinning on his heel, he turned and stared out one of the forward portholes in the dining room cabin as the world began to explode around him.

During weapons training Masaji Suganami was deemed to be one of the most accurate and intuitive pilots in his entire squadron. Almost without thinking he knew that he was flying too fast and too low to get a reasonable shot below the yacht's waterline, and the target offered by the narrow prow was far too small anyway. Instead he concentrated on the superstructure, emptying his wing magazines into the main deck, upper deck and wheelhouse, followed by a string of hits that included the pantry, galley, captain's cabin, chief engineer's cabin and rear drawing room on the afterdeck. Of the thirty-four shells expended, eighteen of them struck home, including three in the dining cabin. The entire attack took slightly less than eight seconds, and then Second Lieutenant Masaji Suganami and his fighter, all ammunition now expended, climbed toward Diamond Head, on his way home, honor served and shame averted.

The first shell to strike the dining room hammered through the outer skin of the cabin with barely any loss of velocity, then impacted the thick oak panels at the back of the sideboard. The sideboard exploded into a hundred whirling pieces, most of them smoking or on fire, totaling immolating the copies of the Romanov film and incidentally saving Vassili Zarubin's life.

An instant later the second shell struck two feet above the first, ripping out half the ceiling, which plummeted onto the table, collapsing it. The shell exploded against the far wall, blasting it in pieces into the stairwell leading down to the owner's suite and the gymnasium. The third shell followed an instant later, roaring through the remains of the aft wall of the dining room and exploding into the galley and pantry, killing the entire cooking staff. The concussion of the third explosion, which included the secondary detonation of three pressurized containers of bottled gas, blew up through the floor of the captain's cabin, killing him in his bunk.

Jane Todd's ears were still ringing from the explosions as she began pulling the wreckage of the dining room table off herself and helped a battered Morris Black to his feet. Almost unbelievably he still had Arthur's .45 automatic in his hand. He had a few cuts here and there and his clothes were scorched, but he didn't seem to have any major injuries. Jane had a short, deep gash on her temple and her teeth felt half rattled out of her head from the multiple explosions, but that was it.

The cabin was on fire. The curtains had caught and small blazes burst up in several other corners of the room, which was now filling with smoke.

"Where's Zarubin?" Black asked.

"Here," came a small voice. With a cough the Russian staggered up out of the ruins of the sideboard. The whole front of his shirt appeared to be soaked in blood and one pant leg had been torn open, showing a five- or six-inch piece of wood and iron protruding from his thigh—one of the sideboard's old-fashioned hinges. His face was covered with dirt and blood, and his hair was singed. There was no sign of the Tokarev. He pushed himself fully upright, using the bulkhead beside him for support. "You must help me."

Jane reached down and retrieved the ax. She took a pair of staggering steps toward the Soviet spy and raised the ax a few inches. "Mexican standoff's over, pal. I think we've got more important things to deal with now. Like figuring out why we were being shot at by a Japanese fighter and getting the hell off this boat. You, buddy, are on your own.

"No, you must help me! *Poszhalujsta!*"

"What does that mean?"

"Please," said Black.

"You must!" Zarubin moaned. "I know where Levitsky is. I know where he is hiding the original of the film!"

Chapter 35

Getting off the *Southern Cross* was as easy as pushing open the door to the main corridor, stepping out onto the deck and then going down the companionway to the wharf. There was a brief moment of tension in the corridor as the duchess of Windsor appeared in a fur-ruffed robe and matching mules, demanding to know what was going on, but the moment ended quickly when Jane raised the bloody fire ax. The duchess's jaw clamped down and she rushed back down the stairs.

"Snotty bitch."

Once out on the wharf, they helped Zarubin toward an old green Chevy, but it had obviously ceased to be useful after sustaining two hits from Suganami's Zero, both of which had struck the engine, destroying both the block and the radiator.

"So much for that idea," said Jane. "You think the buses are still running?"

"Shut your pie hole," Black answered in an excellent Eastender accent. He looked down the fisherman's wharf running at right angles to theirs. If any of Shivers's men had been in the administration building, they were dead. One or more of the Zero's cannon shells had turned the small shack into a blazing pile of kindling that was on the verge of setting the two old pumps alight. Still moored in front of the burning shack was the shallow-draft net boat with the curved bow. Jane could read the name on the bow, neatly done in simple block letters in black: *Oriana B.* Behind it the fire from the shack was creeping out onto the wooden planks of the wharf and was now no more than a few yards from the two old Sinclair pumps.

"You're kidding," said Jane.

"You have any other suggestions?"

"Please decide so I do not bleed to death," muttered Zarubin. The more blood he lost, the less grip he had on the English language.

"Come on." Black took Zarubin under one arm and Jane supported him on the other side. The Russian hobbled between them as they headed for the fishing boat. Jane looked to the west. Fires burning in Honolulu were sending up plumes of smoke, but they did not compare to the sight a few miles farther on. The cloud over Pearl Harbor was black as night, a gigantic thunderhead, shot here and there with monstrous licking flames. It was now beginning to sink in that the fighter plane that had strafed *Southern Cross* was no aberration but part of a massive, concerted attack on the Pacific Fleet.

Zarubin followed her gaze. "It would appear that America and the Japanese are now at war, Miss Todd, whether America likes it or not." He was smiling widely.

"What are you so happy about?"

"I am happy because Hitler will be forced to declare war on America as well under his Axis agreements. He is already fighting a war on two fronts. Now it will be three. I am glad we are now allies, Miss Todd."

"I think we might move along a little faster," said Black nervously. "Those flames are getting quite close to the pumps, and we aren't the only ones trying to get away from here." He looked back over his shoulder, and both Jane and Zarubin saw what he meant. People from the *Southern Cross* had come out on deck, both passengers and crew. Smoke was pouring out everywhere on the upper decks, and even from halfway along the fisherman's wharf Jane could see that the pilothouse and the bridge had been completely demolished.

For a moment she saw Wenner-Gren, dressed in a long silk robe, and she was sure the imposing Swede was looking in their direction. She picked up the pace, and a few moments later they reached the *Oriana B.* Together Jane and Black eased Zarubin into the boat, sitting him down on the scarred plank top of the big fishbox amidships. Black jumped back up on the wharf, cast off the bow and stern lines, then jumped back down into the boat again. A hundred yards away people were beginning to stumble off the *Southern Cross*. Under Wenner-Gren's direction, half a dozen of his striped-jersey crew were heading in the direction of the little fishing vessel.

"You know anything at all about boats?"

"Yes, as a matter of fact, I do," Black answered. "I used to spend all my summer hols on a place in the Thames Estuary called Canvy Island. All I did was go about with the fishermen there in boats quite like this one." He paused, looking back over his shoulder at the approaching crew members. "I suggest you tend to Comrade Zarubin's wounds while I get us out of here."

Jane nodded and headed back to the hatch-covered fishbox. Black thumbed the starter button beside the wheel, and somewhere underneath him he felt the rumble of the engine turning over. A few yards away the flames from the office shack were beginning to lick at the base of the pumps. There was very little time left. He pressed the button again, felt the starter rumble and then catch. Instantly his hand shifted to the throttle mechanism bolted to the gunwale.

He eased back on the lever slightly until he was sure the engine was running smoothly, then spun the wheel and hooked the fingers of his other hand around the lever and pushed it forward, hard. They roared away from the wharf in a broad curve, the almost flat bottom slapping against the water. At Zarubin's side, Jane lurched as she began tearing the remains of his left pant leg into strips she could use for a bandage. Even before they reached the entrance to the basin, she felt a concussive explosion that felt like someone had pushed a fist into her back as the pumps finally exploded. Then they roared out into the main channel.

Ignoring the marker buoys, Black swung the *Oriana B* hard to port, taking them into the shallower water just offshore. Like the boats he'd fished from off Canvy Island in the Thames, the *Oriana B* was built for shoal fishing with a slightly more than flat bottom so she wouldn't limpet on the mud banks at low tide. The water toward shore was a pale green-blue, indicating shallow water. Cutting across the flats off Fort Armstrong would save a great deal of time.

Dead ahead, no more than a mile away, he could see Sand Island and the entrance to Honolulu Harbor. Dark columns of smoke were rising over the city, but nothing like the monstrous cloud that still raged over Pearl Harbor. Black instinctively looked out to sea, scanning the horizon for any sign of an invasion force, but saw nothing. Clearly the intention of the air strike had been to destroy the American Pacific Fleet. It was shameful, but he felt a surge of savage joy, knowing that a blow like this was exactly what was needed to push the Americans into the war. England would no longer stand alone.

Jane came forward, supporting Zarubin as he hobbled along with her. "Is there anywhere he can lie down? He should be off his feet."

Morris Black pointed to a low door with a thumb latch just to the right of the wheel. "There's probably a berth through there. Biffy as well."

"Biffy?"

"W.C. Toilet. Shitter."

"No," Zarubin croaked. "No lying down. I wouldn't get up." Grimacing, he eased himself down onto a small padded seat to the right of the doorway, keeping his wounded leg stretched, the knee locked. Jane looked out over the roof of the low cabin in front of the wheel. The ominous cloud was still rising over Pearl Harbor, accompanied by the distant rumble and roar of multiple explosions, loud enough to be heard from five miles away over the clatter of the engine on the *Oriana B*.

The sun had risen into a cloudless sky, high enough now to warm their backs. Swinging back and forth in the small invisible eddies of wind were dozens of Laysan albatross and Bulwer's petrel, waiting for a fishy treat from the boat. In this small patch of wind and sun and water there was only beauty and peace. Jane looked up and saw more birds, high above them, darting back and forth, swooping and careening.

"I can't believe that this is happening," she said, staring out at the black climbing horror above Pearl Harbor, knowing that hundreds, maybe thousands of men were dying over there. "It's such a beautiful day."

"There's a famous poem about that," said Black, keeping his hands on the wheel and his eyes forward. "It was Thomas Barry's favorite. Written by a Canadian, I think." He began to recite. " 'In Flanders fields the poppies blow, between the crosses row on row, that mark our place and in the sky, the larks still bravely singing fly.' Thomas said he'd be down in the trenches among the mud and the rats and the bodies, and sometimes there were clouds of birds overhead, flying about as though millions of men weren't dying down below."

"The first few minutes of a war beginning and you're reciting poetry about the last one."

"What better time?" he asked wryly.

"You truly are a strange man, Morris Black." She leaned over and kissed him gently on the cheek, gripping his shoulder with one hand.

Suddenly, almost as though the poem had been a signal, the air was filled with the insect drone of engines. Zarubin, already sitting facing the stern, saw them first.

"They're coming back!" he said. "Get us off the water!"

Black looked over his shoulder and Jane turned fearfully as well. Behind them, no more than five hundred feet above them, scores of aircraft were approaching. Fighters like the one that had attacked the *Southern Cross* were taking up protective positions around flight after flight of larger bombers.

"A second wave!" said Zarubin. "Turn! Turn away."

"They probably can't even see us," said Black, turning back to the wheel, but changing course to port just the same. "And we don't make much of a target."

"Don't be so sure," said Jane. She watched as one of the fighters peeled away from the rest of the group and lost altitude, veering in their direction. He was no more than a mile or two behind them now, and at his speed it was only a matter of seconds before he would be on top of them.

"Get Zarubin into the cabin!"

"There is no time for that!" the Russian screamed. "Turn to shore!"

Shore was a quarter of a mile away and he hadn't a prayer of getting that far. "Onto the deck!" Black ordered. This time Jane grabbed Zarubin and tumbled him off his perch on the padded bench. He screamed in pain as he hit the deck, then tried to drag himself into the small cover offered by the fishbox.

Morris knew that any fire from the incoming fighter craft would chew up the fishbox, the deck and anything on it like paper, but they'd all be dead anyway unless his idiot plan worked.

Looking over his shoulder again, he saw that the aircraft was now frighteningly close, sunlight glinting off the squared glass of the front of the cockpit. He could only hope that the pilot would conserve his cannon fire for a bigger target and merely use his machine guns on the *Oriana B*. The aircraft was skimming the water now, and Black knew he had only an instant of time before the pilot opened fire. He waited for one more breath, then grabbed the throttle lever, pulled it back until the engine whistled and died, and at the same time spun the wheel to starboard.

The *Oriana B* stopped almost dead in the water. Suddenly the air around them was filled with the buzzing of a hundred wasps as the pilot opened fire. Black dropped to the deck, curled into a ball and wrapped his hands over his head. A ratcheting sound like an enormous zipper being jerked down was followed by the thudding of a hundred six-inch spikes being hammered into the deck and the wheelhouse cabin. Splinters and pieces of metal flew in the air like a small tornado. A few seconds later there was the crackling sound of flames and, at last, the receding thunder of the fighter as it passed over them and rose back up into the sky to join its formation.

Black waited until he was sure the fighter was gone, then rose up off the deck and surveyed the damage. Machine-gun holes had raked the deck, the gunwales and the fishbox, with more across the top of the cabin. The glass had been blown out of the little forward steering station nest that poked up out of the cabin forward, and smoke was pouring out of it. He listened hard, but the engine sounded all right, which meant it was probably the bottled gas for the stove that was on fire.

Jane helped Zarubin up and sat him back down on the little bench, the padding now ripped by several bullet holes. The Russian looked up, keeping a wary eye on the passing hordes of aircraft overhead. Jane looked forward, knowing where the planes were headed.

"Pity the poor bastards over there," she whispered.

"Pity us if we do not reach land before we are all burned to death," said Zarubin.

"A few more minutes," said Black. "We should make it in time."

Jane picked up the fire ax she had carried with her from the *Southern Cross*. "Maybe we should start talking about where this guy Levitsky is."

Zarubin winced and shifted his leg. "When the time comes you will be told."

"This is the fucking time, you Red bastard!" She swung the ax and it crashed down into the deckhouse a few inches from the surprised Russian's head, three inches of blade digging deeply into the wood. "I don't have time for any shit! Not now! Not today!"

Zarubin held up his hands, palms out. "We are allies, remember!" He stared up at her, wide-eyed. "I am a wounded man!"

"Ask me if I give a shit!" roared Jane. She pulled the ax out of the cabin roof and held it over her head again. "All I know is you've been following us around and people have been dying. The professor, the Harte kid, some woman from the bank in Ventura, and easy money says you were behind our little Mexican driver getting killed."

"I am no different from you," the Russian answered weakly. "I have a job to do."

"Blowing the heart out of a fourteen-year-old boy?" said Jane. "That's part of your job?"

"I did not do that."

"No, but you almost certainly hired the person who did," put in Black. "I sincerely suggest you tell her where we can find Levitsky." The Scotland Yard detective nodded toward the ax in her hands. "She'll have no hesitation in burying that thing in the top of your head and spilling your brains out all over the deck and into the scuppers."

"You would not," said Zarubin.

"Spread your legs a little," Jane answered. "Maybe we'll start a little lower."

Zarubin stared up at her and she stared back.

"Make up your mind, sap. This ax is getting heavy."

"She really would," Black said quietly. He looked around. "And it's not as though we have many witnesses."

"All right. I'll tell you," Zarubin grumbled. "Just get us to shore."

Emil Haas had been moving slowly along the midships corridor on his way to the drawing room when he first heard the droning roar of the fighter plane. He had spent time in Spain during the civil war as an observer, and the sound had the same familiar, terrifying throb as the dive-bombing Stukas Göring's Luftwaffe had tested in the skies over Madrid. He managed to use a bulkhead door to get himself out on deck just as the first shells struck the *Southern Cross*, and for a split second he was covered by the capelike shadow as the Japanese fighter passed directly over his head, no more than thirty feet above him, almost close enough for him to count the rivets in the Mitsubishi's aluminum belly. Then the shells exploded deep within the superstructure of the yacht.

The concussion threw Haas over the rail. He slammed into the fouled and oily water beside the *Southern Cross*, his head narrowly missing a large floating piece of debris that might have been part of the bridge housing. He sank beneath the water, barely conscious, the visibility in the enclosed space around the pier almost down to nothing. Feeling his lungs half filled with water, Haas managed to summon up enough of himself to push hard toward the surface, eventually reaching it, his ears still ringing from the concussion of the explosions, his eyes stinging from the oil and the brine as he watched the panic-stricken crew desperately trying to put out half a dozen fires with the small soda extinguishers that had been strategically placed around the boat. He caught a brief glimpse of the duchess, her hair singed and one almost boyish breast revealed by a rip in her nightdress. Then she disappeared into the smoke. No one was paying the slightest attention to him.

Looking blearily around him, the German agent saw the broken remains of a life ring, hooked his arm around it and paddled toward the pier, but away from the boat. Scores of other planes roared overhead, too high for him to see their markings, but there had been no doubt of the bright red circle on each wing of the one that attacked the *Southern Cross*; the continuing thunder of explosions in the distance confirmed it. Germany's Japanese allies had just made a decisive and violent declaration of war on the United States.

Haas reached the pier and clambered up a metal ladder bolted to one of the pilings. Climbing, he knew that the Japanese attack on Pearl Harbor meant that Hitler would be forced to declare war, and with the Americans in the war, for all intents and purposes that would be the end of the Third Reich. He reached the top of the ladder and climbed out onto dry land, his clothes dripping. He paused for a few seconds, bent slightly, hands on knees, catching his breath. Third Reich. It was strange but no one simply called it Germany anymore.

He looked briefly back at the *Southern Cross*. There were still a few fires burning here and there but there seemed to be more smoke than anything else, members of the crew and passengers appearing and disappearing in the fog.

Haas spotted the station wagon parked at the foot of the steep track leading down to the pier and trotted across to it. There was a rifle case and a pair of binoculars in the backseat. The keys were dangling from the ignition. He climbed in behind the wheel, switched on the engine and wheeled the car around. One last errand to run and then he'd see about getting out of Hawaii and down to Mexico. From there, if he was lucky, he'd find a way to get back home. To his beloved Germany.

Chapter 36

Sunday, December 7, 1941
Honolulu

The front cabin of the *Oriana B* was smoking heavily by the time they reached Honolulu Harbor. There were several freighters and a Dutch cargo liner named the *Jagersfontein* in port, but nothing else; it was, after all, a Sunday. There seemed to be some activity aboard the Dutch liner but other than that the port seemed strangely empty, almost abandoned.

Black found a mooring at Pier Eight, just to the right of a tower with huge clocks and the single word "Aloha" on all four sides. The only other vessel, on the other side of the dock, was a small, scruffy-looking Soviet freighter with an unintelligible Cyrillic name on the bow and a yellow hammer and sickle on its single red-and-black funnel. The mooring for the *Oriana B* was at the base of a set of metal steps that climbed at a steep angle up to the wharf, and it took some time for Zarubin to make his way to the top.

According to the Russian their destination was next to a Chinese restaurant on Hotel Street, not far from the Chinatown Canal. They reached the wharf and saw that it was deserted—not a stevedore or mechanic or seaman anywhere. They reached the end of the long, low warehouse building that stood beside the pier and came out on the corner of Bishop Street and Ala Moana. There was no traffic at all, although a number of cars were parked at the curb. Spotting a small corner restaurant, Black crossed the road to ask the owner or the patrons a few questions, but halfway across the street he saw that the place was closed, dark and empty. A sign in the window, already cracked and broken, read MORI-MURA ALL DAY BREAKFAST—AMERICAN FOOD. By now a place like that would have been opened for at least a couple of hours to catch the shift change, but not today. Mr. Morimura had other problems to deal with.

The three of them kept on going up Bishop Street under the palm trees, but the bandages around Zarubin's leg were soaked in blood and he was slowing with every step. Every now and again they could hear explosions from not too far away, and clearly there had been damage inside the city. They passed another restaurant that looked as though it had taken direct impact from a bomb. Shards of glass and brick and stone were strewn all over the streets.

A Ford stood in the middle of the street, torn to shreds, its tires flat, the body of the car ripped with odd-shaped holes. Four people were slumped inside the car, all of them killed by shrapnel from exploding antiaircraft shells from Pearl Harbor. The radio in the car was still playing, set to KGMB. The song it was playing was number one on the charts and called "Three Little Fishies":

Down in the meadow in the iddy biddy poo
thwam thwee little fishies and a mamma fishie too.

"Jesus," said Jane as she regarded the two dead men in the front and two dead women in the back. Off to work and never got there.

Jane found a Rexall drugstore at Bishop and Queen Street, which was also closed. Black put the elbow of his jacket through the glass of the door and let Jane and Zarubin inside. She found a pair of shears, cut the leg off Zarubin's trousers entirely and changed the dressing, this time covering the wound with penicillin powder. She convinced the Russian to lie down on the soda fountain counter and proceeded to stitch the wound closed with a needle and some Coates and Clark waxed thread from a sewing kit she found.

"You have medical training?" asked Zarubin, gritting his teeth.

"I have sock-darning training. Same thing," she answered, continuing to stitch. "It should hold you until we can get you to a hospital."

"You mean an interrogation room with that skinny fellow I saw with you yesterday."

"You saw us?" said Black, surprised.

"Of course I saw you. Elephants in a china shop."

"Bulls in a china shop, actually."

"Who fucking cares?" grunted Zarubin. At that moment, Jane tugged particularly hard as she tied off the last piece of thread. She wrapped the wound site in yards of gauze, stuck on a pair of temporary splints and then wrapped it all up in three or four Ace bandages. "That should hold you," she said. "Fix you a milkshake?"

"*Shtoi!*" Zarubin climbed down off the counter, and Jane went to the fountain and pulled herself a glass of Coke with lots of ice. She drained it, then had another. She hadn't eaten anything since the night before, but her thirst was even stronger than her hunger. She finished the second glass, pushed open the counter flap and did a little shopping of her own. By the time she joined Black, who was waiting by the door, she was carrying a drawstring canvas beach bag and had sunglasses perched on her forehead. Zarubin was foraging through the pharmacy, looking for a display of work clothes he'd seen.

"What's in the bag?" asked Black.

"Sandwiches for later, in case we get hungry."

"Good idea."

"How are we going to do this?" Jane asked, keeping her voice low.

"Zarubin, you mean?"

"Yes."

"We could let him find Levitsky and the film, then turn them both over to the police."

"I think the cops have got other things to worry about right now," said Jane. "And I still think I've seen Zarubin before. It's starting to bother me a lot."

"If Levitsky had the film, it's the only copy left," said Black. "The others were destroyed on the *Southern Cross*." He paused. "We have to stick with Zarubin, at least for the time being."

"And if we get the film, what then?"

"I haven't thought that far," Black admitted.

Zarubin came out of the back of the Rexall, struggling to button up a pair of whipcord work pants that were at least a size too large for him. When he had the fly buttoned, he cinched his own belt through the loops, grimacing with pain from the wound in his thigh.

"Shall we go?" he said.

"How do you want to approach this, Vassili?" Black asked.

"Simple. We go to the address, you give me your gun and I go in and kill him, destroy the film."

"Destroy it?" Jane asked.

"Of course destroy it," said the Russian. He limped behind the front counter and chose a package of Camels as well as a Ronson lighter from the display case under the counter. He spent a few moments putting the flint and fluid in the lighter, then lit a cigarette for himself. He offered the pack to Jane and Morris Black, who took one each. "Destroying the film is best for us all. To have it around makes us all look bad: your government, my government, the lady's government. Destroy it forever and we can all forget about the damn Romanovs, yes?"

"And about giving back their money."

"That too. In time of wars like this governments need all the money they can get."

"True."

"So Levitsky dies. The film is gone." He grinned broadly. "I even rid you of a traitor in Donovan's organization. A happy ending, like a fairy tale." He paused again. "I think we should be on our way, though. Comrade Levitsky will not wait forever, and my leg is hurting quite badly despite the kind lady's ministrations."

Morris Black and Jane Todd stepped out through the open doorway. Parked directly in front of the Rexall was a brand-new fawn-colored two-door Lincoln Continental Cabriolet with the top down, complete with wheel covers in the rear, whitewalls all around and the spare in its own casing tucked into a little niche behind the rear bumper.

The top down made Jane's job all the easier. She hopped in behind the steering wheel, pulled out the ignition and the starter wires, then stripped an inch or two of each with a nail file she took from her newly acquired beach bag. The car started instantly. She and Black shared a smile as she opened the passenger-side door and pushed back the seat, letting Zarubin climb into the back.

"Where to?" asked Jane.

"Up the hill," Zarubin instructed. "Three blocks. Take first left past King Street."

Jane did as she was told, driving the big car slowly, weaving around debris that littered the roadway. Windows had been blasted out everywhere, and once or twice she saw that large chunks of masonry had been blown off buildings.

Reaching the corner of Bishop Street and Hotel Street, she saw that she was in the middle of the worst of the bombing. A trolley had gone off the rails and several fires were burning. The people in the streets were looking west toward Pearl Harbor, but there wasn't much to see except the giant cloud of oily smoke.

Several men in their undershirts were wandering around with rifles from the last war, but no one was trying to play either hero or self-appointed commander in chief. The look on most people's faces was a combination of fear and confusion. Jane noticed that there didn't seem to be a single Asian face in the crowd. It occurred to her that to be Japanese today was to be a target, and at the very least, an enemy.

She remembered the newsreels she'd seen from Germany about what they'd called *Kristallnacht,* the Night of Broken Glass, and hoped Americans would ever really turn on their own like that. In her heart she knew that they could, and probably would in the coming days and weeks.

She turned the big Lincoln left, heading down toward the old Iwilei red-light district and Chinatown. On both sides of Hotel Street it was wall-to-wall Wiki-Wiki clubs, barnlike Taxi Dance halls where you paid a dime for five minutes of dancing with a Filipino girl who usually couldn't speak any English. There were fifty bars to a block and twenty brothels large and small to go with them. Everything was closed, the doors and windows of the upper floors tightly shuttered. Twice along the way they passed smoking, gutted holes where buildings had once been. More cars, all of them empty that Jane could see, had been hit by the shrapnel from the antiaircraft fire as well, but there was no sign that any of the dive-bombers or high-altitude aircraft had wasted anything on the city.

The view as they drove was dominated by the big Dole Pineapple water tower sticking up over everything. The air was heavy with the sweet-sick stink of the pine-apple canneries.

"Where is it?" said Black, turning in his seat.

"There," said Zarubin, pointing. The building in question was located beside a low, faceless warehouse that sagged in the middle and was covered with dark green clapboard siding. The building Zarubin was pointing at was also wood, three stories high and at one time painted red. Now it was the color of dust and dirt. On the main floor was a Chinese restaurant named the White Orchid. The curtains were drawn over the front window, and the only sign of life was a gigantic marma-lade cat curled up in one corner by a tall, fat Chinese vase half filled with orchids. A rickety staircase on the side of the restaurant building led to the upper floors. At the foot of the stairs was a row of garbage cans in the alley that separated the White Orchid from the warehouse.

"He owns both buildings except the restaurant. He lives on the second floor and does his filming in the warehouse next door."

Jane had noticed a sign in Chinese over the narrow street door into the warehouse. "What does the sign say?"

"Passport to Paradise," Zarubin explained. "It is sup-posed to be for the taking of photographs for passports and for men to send back to China to their picture wives. Most of his market is for Orientals. They like to see one of their own schtupping a white woman."

"*Schtupping*?" laughed Black.

"Screwing," said Jane.

"*Schtupping* I already know." Black smiled.

"Yes, yes!" Zarubin nodded "*Ebala, eb Tvoyu Mat!*"

"I think we understand now, Vassili," said Jane.

The Russian shrugged. "*Khazdy drochit kak on khochet.*"

Black flushed bright red.

"What did he say?"

"Roughly translated, it means everyone has his own way of masturbating. In this case I think he is referring to Comrade Levitsky's films. Let's go and see if we can catch Levitsky in his bed," said Black.

"If I was him, I'd be long gone. If he's been living here, I think his incognito status just came to an end."

"We'll check anyway."

"And what am I supposed to do, knit?"

"As you said, he's probably already fled. We're just checking."

"Sure. I'll just sit in the stolen getaway car and wait for a cop to come by and start asking me quest—"

Suddenly her words were ripped away by an earsplitting roar as an antiaircraft shell hit the empty street half a block away, blowing a six-foot hole in the asphalt. It was enough to burst a water pipe, and a fountain erupted in the middle of the street. Jane realized that the closer you got to Pearl Harbor, the more likely you were to be hit by friendly fire. The AA shells would be firing almost straight up, and when they missed, their trajectories would be pretty short.

"We won't be long," said Black, grinning. "Maybe you should put the top up."

"Funny fellow."

Black stepped out of the car, the automatic in his hand, and pulled the seat forward. Zarubin got awkwardly out of the car, throwing his leg straight and hanging on to the body of the car as he hauled himself onto the street. They went across in front of the car, crossed the street and headed down the alley. It took a full five minutes for the two men to climb the outside stairs to the second floor and slip through the door leading off into the apartments.

Chapter 37

No sooner had they gone than Jane was out of the car and heading for the warehouse. Reaching the door, she reached into the beach bag and pulled out the Smith & Wesson .32 caliber Police Special she'd discovered behind the pharmacist's counter when she'd gone looking for Zarubin's penicillin powder. She bumped her hip into the door and turned the knob. The door opened, and when it did she slipped inside. The immediate impression was sex, even before she'd seen anything. It was in the air, a thick, dark smell that burned into your nostrils. It seemed quite a fall, the man who'd filmed the murder of the Romanovs now filming men and women rutting like dogs or, God knows, even *with* dogs.

Directly in front of her was a door with a frosted glass insert that read OFFICE. She pushed through it and found just that, a small outer office with a coffee table, a small couch, and a dwarf palm drooping in one corner. The coffee table had half a dozen magazines and newspapers on it, all of them in Chinese and Japanese and Tagalog. There was also, obscurely, a Gideon Bible that someone must have stolen from a hotel somewhere.

Right in the middle of all the magazines was the most recent copy of *Life,* Douglas MacArthur all over the cover, oddly missing his sunglasses and his corncob pipe. There were ashtrays at both ends of the couch and one in the middle of the coffee table. Jane did a quick check;

most of them had filters and lipstick stains. More women than men here.

Two doors led out of the office other than the one she'd come in through, one behind the receptionist's desk and another one beside the dwarf palm. Jane went behind the desk and tried the door there. It opened into an inner office, empty except for another desk, a leather chair behind it and a very old-looking leather couch on one wall. There were three battered filing cabinets against the other wall. Above them were framed movie posters: *Big Girls on the Beach, Sluts for Dinner* and *Honolulu Moon.* All the posters featured big, oversized Oriental men overpowering much smaller white women.

Trying to ignore the posters, Jane went for the filing cabinets, going through the drawers quickly and carefully. They all carried eight-by-tens of naked and seminaked women, all striking what they assumed were provocative poses. All the pictures had been taken with the same three different backgrounds. A studio palm tree, a backdrop of Waikiki Beach and a backdrop of the Aloha Tower. On the back of every picture was stamped COPYRIGHT MICHAEL LEVITT. Like most people on the run he wasn't wandering too far from his real identity.

Jane abandoned the rear office and went back to the front reception area. She went over to the door on her right, turned the knob and stepped through. She found herself in a maze of fiberboard cubicles, all of them connected, creating half a dozen corridors. The cubicles were eight feet high, leaving lots of space between them and the high old tin ceiling. She wandered up and down the aisles, checking out the three-sided rooms. Each of them was a permanent, roughed-in set. Four-poster romantic bed with a mosquito netting canopy and a fake window that looked out onto an alpine meadow made out of a travel poster; a stall in a barn complete with a saddle; a dungeon with whips and chains; even an ordinary kitchen. It wasn't hard to imagine what went on in each of the rooms; this was the stuff of nickel peep shows and five-dollar reels you bought for your home movie projector.

So far she'd counted twenty of the little rooms; Levitsky or Levitt or whatever he was calling himself was putting out a lot of product and making a lot of money. He probably paid the girls nothing, bribed the cops to stay out of his hair and had connections all over the islands for distributing what he made. Maybe if she'd looked harder she might have found a few reels of Levitsky's hidden in the Rexall she'd gone into.

She jumped as she heard another crash from outside, and then she heard something else, the familiar whirring squeal of someone rewinding a reel of film. She moved through the corridors bending her ear toward the sound, getting closer every few seconds, her nostrils filled with the acrid smell of developing baths. Levitsky was running his own lab and processing his own film. Before long, she found what she was looking for, a long room in the center of the warehouse floor, the only one with a door and a ceiling. She kept the gun in her hand, turned the knob and stepped into the film lab.

Levitsky was a man in his middle forties, stocky, with a dark shock of hair only just going gray at the temples. As Jane had assumed, he was hand-cranking a rewind, transposing film from a metal "core" onto a full reel. He looked up when Jane stepped into the room, scowling, his heavy brows coming together angrily.

"We're closed, you stupid bitch. There's a war on out there, or can't you tell?" There was barely any trace of an accent in his voice.

"You're Alexander Mikhailovitch Levitsky?" Jane asked blandly, pointing the gun at the filmmaker. Levitsky let go of the rewind crank and the film continued to spin on for a few seconds, then stopped. Behind Levitsky was a wall of shelves with hundreds of silver cans lined up behind a simple wooden dowel restraint. There was a cutting table with more shelves above it, these filled with new stock, and the third wall was taken up by a pair of large developing tanks. Hanging in front of the editing table were dozens of strips of films, each with an ordinary bulldog clip attached to it, the squeezes on the clips looped over nails. Not the most attractive setup in the world, but it looked reasonably efficient for a man who made stag films for a living.

At the sound of his real name Levitsky took a step

back, bumping into the chair that stood in front of the editing table. "Who are you?"

"Moura Budberg isn't going to let you get away alive," said Jane. Somewhere in some part of her brain that Albert Einstein or Sigmund Freud had forgotten about or never discovered, she'd been putting it all together and now she was pretty sure she had it. "In fact, she's hired a top-notch assassin to kill you."

"You're insane. I'm worth a fortune to her!"

"No, the film is, and when she's got what she wants, you don't have any value at all, but your silence does. His name is Emil Haas, and he's probably on his way over here right now. Haas gets a copy of the film for his superiors, and this is how he pays for it."

"Who are you?" Levitsky demanded.

"Probably more of a friend than you deserve right now. I'm an American and I work for one of the men in that film."

"Donovan."

"Apparently."

"I want political asylum!"

"You won't get it. Not today, pal."

"But I have committed no crime!"

"I know. I've been thinking a lot about that." Jane nodded. "You shot the film you were ordered to shoot, and then, being a smart guy, you saw what would happen to you once you delivered, so you went on the lam, ran away. Kept the film for insurance, right?"

"Yes." Levitsky visibly sagged. "If I brought it to Lenin, he would have killed me. So would Beloborodov or any of them. The only one I could trust was Trotsky, and even that turned out to be a mistake."

"You sure led everyone on a merry chase, though. Half a dozen people or more have been killed because of that little piece of film." She paused. "Since I'm pointing a gun at you, why don't you tell me where the original is, the negative? Then we can get this whole thing over with." She saw the frightened man's eyes flicker to the small reel of film on the rewind.

"You will shoot me."

"I'm not the shooting kind, comrade. I'm just tired and I want to go home. Like you said, you committed no crime except stealing a piece of film from Lenin. If you haven't heard, he's dead. Give me the negative and you can do whatever the hell you want."

"They will hound me to the ends of the earth." Levitsky moaned.

"Not if you don't have the film," said Jane. "Nobody's going to care once they know it's gone. It all becomes meaningless, a myth, like discovering Atlantis or Napoleon having three balls, or Hitler just one."

"*I'll* hound you, Alexander Mikhailovitch," said a quiet voice from behind them. Levitsky stared, and Jane turned and looked over her shoulder. It was Zarubin, and he was carrying Morris Black's automatic.

"Where's Morris?" She cocked the Smith & Wesson, swinging it away from Levitsky.

"Calm yourself," said Zarubin, smiling. "He's resting. A slight error in judgment on his part. He's in the automobile. You'll see him in a moment."

"He's lying. For him lying is like breathing—it always has been. He's going to kill you." Levitsky shook his head. "You don't know this man."

Jane stared at Zarubin, then the truth came to her in a rush as the last pieces fell together. She remembered the file Morris had given her to read and knew that it was the only explanation that fit.

"Jesus, I know who you are. You're Yurovsky."

"Of course he's Yurovsky!" screamed Levitsky. "Who did you think he was!"

"All this time," said Jane. "You disappeared and changed everything about yourself. Used what you knew to find a job in the NKVD and settled in to your new identity. Until Moura Budberg came along. Release the film and if even one person recognizes you it's all over. You're Yakov Yurovsky again and one big embarrassment to Uncle Joe. His little torturer Beria would have you dead and buried before you could take another breath. How many people have you killed to keep your secret, Vassili?"

"As many as was necessary," Yurovsky answered. "Almost all."

"And poor old Levitsky here was going to be the last,

thanks to Morris and me." She shook her head. "All you had to do was follow our trail."

"There has been too much talk," said Yurovsky. "Alexander Mikhailovitch I will kill here in his sordid little premises. You and Mr. Black will come to the docks with me as hostages." He smiled. "We have a boat to catch. Her name is the *Stary Bolshevik* and she's en route to San Francisco."

"Not that we'll ever get there."

"I'm afraid not, no."

Emil Haas came through the doorway, the high-powered Beretta rifle cradled in his hands. "Neither will you, Comrade Zarubin, or Yurovsky, whichever you prefer." The rifle was aimed directly at Yurovsky's chest. Jane realized that one shot at this range would rip his heart out and blow it into the next room. "Or perhaps Squirrel Cheeks," said Haas, continuing to bait Yurovsky. "Isn't that what your colleagues at the embassy call you behind your back? The cheeks you used to hide behind that beard and ridiculous mustache you sported twenty-three years ago."

I still don't see what the Abwehr's interest is in all of this," Yurovsky said with a calm smile. "I am assuming that you still work for the admiral."

"The Abwehr's interest should be obvious," said Haas, shifting the heavy rifle in his arms. "We've been hearing rumors about your real identity for some time. The film is proof of it. To have the man who murdered the Romanovs living in Washington, supposedly an ally, simply wouldn't do. The film has the added bonus of undoubtedly causing some perturbation and consternation among the royal family. A benefit to Germany, and of course to the duke and duchess."

"I only commanded a firing squad," sneered Yurovsky. "When you kill it is in cold blood."

"All blood spilled is the same temperature."

"Shoot him! Shoot him! Before he kills us all!" Levitsky screamed frantically.

Jane tried to ignore him but the man was adding a hysterical edge to everything, not what you wanted when there were three weapons cocked and ready to fire.

Eventually someone's trigger finger would get too itchy to bear and the shooting would begin. Bad enough under any circumstances, but in this room it would be like committing suicide.

"I'd advise you to shut up for the moment, Mr. Levitsky," Jane said. "And if we all keep our heads, no one's going to shoot anyone."

Several miles away, berthed for general repairs to its engines, the United States heavy cruiser *New Orleans* was caught completely unprepared both for the first- and the second-wave attacks by the Japanese forces. The antiaircraft directors were not aboard the ship. More than forty percent of the crew had no gunnery experience at all, and what experience they did have came from their most recent practice session, which had taken place in June. By the time more experienced gunners from the nearby heavy cruiser *San Francisco,* the minelayers *Tracey, Preble, Sicard,* and *Pruitt,* and men from the *West Virginia* motor launch rallied to the *New Orleans,* the first attack was over.

As the second wave began, Corporal James Atkins Sloane of the *Pruitt* was manning one of the stern AA guns on the *New Orleans,* screaming obscenities at the top of his lungs, lining himself up on an Aichi D3A1 torpedo bomber that had swung into view. At eighteen Sloane was more enthusiastic than he was accurate and he emptied a whole box of unfused 40mm shells at the retreating torpedo bomber. At least ten of the shells were duds, a further dozen went off course and landed harmlessly in the entrance to Honolulu Harbor, half a dozen more impacted on the outskirts of the city in the cannery district, but the remaining shells, each twice the size of the ones used by Second Lieutenant Masaji Suganami, fell between Hotel Street and Kekaulike Road. Real fire and brimstone had come to Honolulu's red-light district at last.

The shells rained down over a three-block area, two of them completely demolishing the building containing the White Orchid Restaurant. The sleeping marmalade cat, whose real name was Charlie, was blown out of the window and across the street. Amazingly the creature survived, minus half its tail, which had been scorched off as cleanly as if it had been cauterized. Exactly 12.3 seconds after being fired by Corporal Sloane, the last of the 40mm shells exploded three feet in front of the main doors of Passport to Paradise.

The doors were blown off, and every window on the front wall was blown inward by the concussion from the explosion. The entire building was shaken down to its minimal foundations, swaying back and forth like a tree in a high wind. In the lab it was enough to throw everyone to the ground and pour hundreds of film cans down from the shelves. In addition, the explosion sent almost a hundred years of dust into the air along with the mixed, stale odor of spermaceti oil, which the warehouse had once been used to store.

Jane scrambled to her feet first, coughing and blinking in the thick air, and found that somehow she had been blown over the cutting room counter. She'd managed to hang on to the Smith & Wesson she'd taken from the pharmacy. In front of her, on the other side of the counter, Yurovsky stood up, wobbling, the automatic held loosely in his hand. There was no sign of either Levitsky or Emil Haas except for the splintered stock and ruined action of the hunting rifle he had been carrying. Most of the spool of film Levitsky was winding was gone along with him. The only thing left was a few feet of negative stock still on the original core. "Better hit me with the first shot," she said to Yurovsky, not feeling anything like as confident as she sounded. "Half the film in here is old. Nitrate stock. You hit the wrong can and one of two things is going to happen. Either this place is going to get lit up like a Christmas tree or we're all going to be blown to Kingdom Come." It was true enough; she'd seen half a dozen of the old pale green boxes that marked nitrate emulsion film. Despite its popularity, however, nitrate film had always been chemically unstable. Not only did it decompose easily under adverse conditions, but it was also highly flammable and potentially explosive, as one of its component parts became nitroglycerine.

"You are lying," said Yurovsky. "Throw down your gun."

"Would I lie to you?" Without pausing she turned a

little to her left and emptied the Smith & Wesson into a row of green boxes to the left of where Yurovsky was standing, then hit the floor, praying that the heavy table between her and the film would protect her. A split second later the lab of *Passport to Paradise* turned into a Roman candle.

It took three hours for the Honolulu Fire Department to dig Jane out of the remains of the building, and the only reason they looked at all was because Morris Black insisted. At one point, when they were about to give up looking, Black called in Richard Shivers from the FBI to add his weight to things, and by four o'clock in the afternoon they finally reached her, angry, hungry, thirsty, covered in soot and stinking of hundred-fifty-year-old whale sperm. According to the firemen who finally reached her, the only thing that saved her life was the heavy table between her and the exploding film, as well as the fact that the force of the explosion blew her down through the rotting floor and into the basement.

When they finally had a hole in the rubble big enough to talk through, Black went down. Beside him a fireman crawled down into the hole to see if her legs were pinned or if she had any broken bones.

"You think Napoleon really had three balls?" she murmured, her ears still ringing.

"You'd have to ask Josephine," said Black, wondering not for the first time at the strange intricacies of the American female mind.

Jane spent a day in the hospital even though she insisted there was nothing wrong with her. According to the newspapers and radio, everyone was in shock at the sudden attack by the Japanese and horrified by how successful they had been. She actually heard Roosevelt's "Day of Infamy" speech over the radio and knew that the die was cast. It was a world war now, not just a European one. The United States could no longer hide behind its isolating oceans; yesterday had proved that.

On Tuesday morning Jane was released, and she and Black went immediately to the docks and boarded the Dutch liner *Jagersfontein,* inbound to San Francisco from Java and the South China Sea, where it had barely escaped without being captured or sunk by Japanese forces. It was now being used as a civilian evacuation transport and as a hospital ship for seriously injured soldiers and sailors.

Standing by the port rail as the tugs took the *Jagersfontein* out into the channel, Jane could still see smoke pouring up from Pearl Harbor. "So I guess we're more than just kissing cousins now, Morris. Full-fledged allies."

"Hitler's declaring war on the United States today. I think he'd rather not have done it, but the Japanese forced his hand."

"He'll regret it," said Jane.

Black nodded. "Yes, I think he will."

"Whatever happened to the *Southern Cross* and all those people?"

"She's gone now, of course. Probably limping down to Panama to see to her repairs. Presumably the duchess is still on board. Wenner-Gren and Budberg as well."

"The others?"

"The German's been arrested as a spy by Shivers. The Japanese fellow managed to make it back to the consulate. They'll probably just deport him. Romanov and Vonsiatsky are being held for questioning, but I don't think anything will come of it."

"And Haas? The one who looked like a bookkeeper?"

"They found a body in the warehouse. It was about Haas's size, but there's no way to identify it. Might be Levitsky's, for all we know."

"Yurovsky was going to be on board that Russian freighter. What about him?"

"The *Stary Bolshevik*? She'd already sailed before the Coast Guard could stop her. Immigration people said they'll look for him at the San Francisco end, but they don't make any promises." He sighed. "The whole world's turned upside down."

"He'll kill us if he thinks we'll divulge his dirty little secret."

"No, he won't," said Black. "He knows as much about that film as we do. He'll keep our little secrets and we'll keep his and he knows it."

"What a mess," said Jane. They were out in the main channel now, and if not for the men stringing barbed wire up and down the Waikiki beaches it would have looked like any Hawaiian Aloha.

"What about us?" Jane asked quietly.

"We saw the film. We know what's on it. That's enough, I think. Give a letter to a lawyer and threaten to have it sent to the *New York Times* if anything happens to you. Maybe that will be enough. Other than that I'm sure I'll be sent off to someplace obscure to sit out the war."

"I don't think I meant that."

Black gave her a quick glance, then carefully turned his face back to the sea. "Oh. You mean the other," he said, blushing as he always did when the subject of sex came up.

"I don't do it with everyone, you know. I didn't just pull your name out of a hat."

"I know that, but I don't see what we can do about it. Right now we're ships passing in the night."

"If Donovan keeps his promise, I'll be in London as a war correspondent before you know it."

"And before you know it Stephenson will have me packed off to somewhere in Outer Uzbekistan for the duration. Counting enemy yaks or something."

"Well," said Jane, "at least we have a few days before we get to San Francisco."

"That we do." Black smiled.

There was a long pause. "Who said, 'War is hell'?" Jane asked.

"One of yours, actually," Black answered. "General William Tecumseh Sherman."

"Well, it still is."

"And always will be," said Black, reaching out to put an arm around her against the chilly breeze blowing in from the east.

Epilogue

Jane Todd stood with her hands in her pockets, ignoring the heavy flakes of snow that were collecting on the shoulders of her coat and in her hair. It was cold and windy, and the snow was blowing around noisily with that familiar distant howling sound it made as though this wasn't New York City at all but somewhere out on the arctic tundra where the only other creatures around were wolves just outside your line of vision waiting to gnaw on your bloody bones.

She stared down into the small square hole at her feet waiting for Marco, the man who took care of the cemetery, to reappear. Today Marco had been dressed in a boiler suit, heavy boots and a hat, exactly as he'd been six weeks ago when she'd buried Annie's ashes here. Dear God, was it only five weeks? She felt as though she'd lived an entire lifetime since that day in the rain.

Jane was already late for her appointment with Donovan but she knew that this had to be done first. She also knew that Black was gone, flown away into some unknown without a trace or a word the moment they arrived back in Washington, just as he had predicted.

Fleming pled ignorance and wouldn't say anything except to tell her quietly that whatever her fears, Morris was safe, and in his own way protected from friendly fire. Now it was her turn. Coming to New York, she'd had one of Donovan's people visit her hotel with exactly what she'd requested: two suitcases full of top-notch photographic gear, a correspondent's uniform and all the paperwork necessary to prove that she was legally allowed to wear it. She reached her right hand more deeply into her coat pocket and touched the cold metal of the two keys that had been Morris Black's last gift to her—his flat in Shepherd's Bush for as long as she liked since he'd have no use for it where he was going, if the German's didn't blow it to hell in the meantime.

He'd given her the keys and kissed her, quite a nice kiss as a matter of fact, and then he'd gone away. She squeezed the keys hard in her pocket and tried not to think about any of it and tried very hard not to cry.

Marco appeared again, climbing out of the hole, this time empty-handed. He smiled at Jane and tipped his hat and then got about the business of putting the capstone back down over the shaft.

"Did you put it somewhere safe, Marco?"

"Yes, yes, very safe." The man smiled. "With your Annie, where no one else will look or find."

Marco and Jane stood together silently for a moment, watching the snow cover up the capstone cover and what lay beneath it. Jane found herself wondering if it would have been any different if Levitsky had been rewinding the negative from head to tail rather than the other way around that day they met in the run-down building on Hotel Street. She decided that it probably didn't matter a bit. A secret after all was only a secret because someone perceived it to be one. It was really just six feet of film from a long, long time ago.

She shook Marco's hand and he tipped his hat to her again and then she said a silent, final good-bye to Annie. When that was done she turned around and walked back down the path through the newly fallen snow, knowing that before very long those footprints would vanish, never to be seen again.

Author's Note

Most of the facts, details and characters described in *The House of Special Purpose* are real. Alexander Mikhailovitch Levitsky was a real cinematographer and was the cameraman for several major feature-length movies made in Russia during the First World War. He was a friend of Alexander Beloborodov, the chairman of the Ural Regional Soviet, and Beloborodov was in turn a very close friend of Vladimir Ilyich Ulyanov Lenin as well as Lev, or Leon, Trotsky.

It was Beloborodov who warned Trotsky that he had fallen out of favor and who helped him flee the Soviet Union. In all likelihood it was Beloborodov who got the assignment at the House of Special Purpose for Levitsky, under orders from Lenin. There have always been rumors that a group photograph of the tsar and his family was taken immediately prior to their assassination, and given that film cameras and still cameras looked very much alike at the time it would have been easy to confuse the two.

As far as Levitsky's escape is concerned, he *was* last seen boarding the American tramp steamer SS *Ida*, which, ironically, was covertly taking a large consignment of tsarist gold to the National Bank in San Francisco. It is not known whether Levitsky disembarked in Hawaii or the continental United States, but it is known that a Russian cameraman calling himself Mischa Levitt was employed by both Movietone News and Bellevue Pathe during the years 1922 to 1929. A company named

Passport to Paradise existed in Honolulu between 1932 and 1941, manufacturing pornographic films and photographs for the local, mostly military market.

The movements during the summer of 1918 of Sir Robert Bruce Lockhart, author of *British Agent* and a number of other books during his tenure as a member of both the British Secret Service and the Foreign Office, are extremely vague and no access is allowed to his correspondence between London and St. Petersburg from June, July and August of that year. Equally vague are any references he makes to his relationship with Moura Budberg, even then a known NKVD agent.

As to Colonel William Donovan, his own movements during that period, which supposedly place him on the Western Front with his men of the Fighting 69th, are as foggy as Lockhart's. What is known is that Donovan, slightly wounded in the leg, was taken off the line and disappeared for almost two weeks with the 69th's field chaplain, Father Patrick Duffy. It is also known that Duffy was a member of the State Department's private secret service, and both Duffy and Donovan were "special friends" of the president. It is also a matter of historical fact that Donovan reappeared in Yekaterinburg the following year on a supposed fact-finding mission.

During the first year of the Co-ordinator of Information Office more than eight-seven known members of the American Communist Party were employed by Donovan. Also employed by Donovan in Washington were more than a dozen Soviet agents-in-place, all of them run by the local NKVD *Rezident,* Vassili Zarubin.

Although Zarubin was never found on the *Stary Bolshevik* when it docked in San Francisco, he did reappear in Washington the day before New Year's in time to attend the well-known New Year's Eve party given at the White House.

Zarubin maintained his position throughout the war and returned to Moscow in 1945. He worked for the KGB until his retirement in 1972 and died peacefully while on a Black Sea holiday in 1983. Between 1945 and 1972 he traveled to the United States on a number of occasions and even visited Disneyland. There is no record that anyone ever discovered his true identity.

Moura Budberg, whose birth name was Maria Ignatie-vena Zakrevskaia, was a real spy working for the NKVD both before, during and after the war. She was also lover to Sir Robert Bruce Lockhart, Maxim Gorky and H. G. Wells, sometimes simultaneously. She was also a close friend of the duke and duchess of Windsor as well as Axel Wenner-Gren, the well-known Nazi operative. Wenner-Gren later set up a trust that is still in existence, and still deals in the "anthropological" aspects of race purity.

Miss Budberg spent much of her later years in San Francisco and Los Angeles, working peripherally in the motion-picture industry and sometimes as a translator, although her spoken and written knowledge of the Russian language left something to be desired. This might have something to do with the fact that she was actually born in Estonia. She died in Tuscany at the age of eighty-one on October 31, 1974.

There is no account of the whereabouts of the duchess of Windsor between November 26 and December 19, 1941. According to the official record at Government House in Nassau, New Providence, the duchess was on a tour of the outer islands on those dates, while her husband the duke stayed home and dealt with official business, some of which involved a submarine kidnap plot against his person.

The duchess had been forbidden by both Winston Churchill and the king himself from setting foot on Wenner-Gren's yacht the *Southern Cross,* so officially, at least, she did not travel to Hawaii. The yacht itself was registered as having arrived there on December 4, 1941, and on December 15 it is noted in the harbormaster's log that the *Southern Cross* put in to Panama City for "repairs to her superstructure caused by fire." Presumably the duchess returned to Nassau incognito, probably out of Mexico or Panama.

Immediately following the war the duke and duchess of Windsor returned to Paris, establishing residence in a large mansion on the Bois de Boulogne. On a number of occasions various dignitaries, including Lord Louis Mountbatten, the Queen Mother, the queen herself as well as Prince Philip and Charles, the young prince of

Wales, visited with the duke, pleading with him to either hand over or destroy what came to be called the Cousin's Film. Their pleas were rejected, as well as their pleas for scores of letters that did nothing to discourage the idea that both the duke and the duchess were deeply involved in Nazi politics. It was even embarrassing to the royal family that both the duke and duchess maintained a friendship with Sir Oswald Mosley, the infamous British blackshirt, until his death. On May 28, 1972, the duke died, followed in 1986 by the duchess herself.

Within thirty minutes of the duchess of Windsor's body being removed from her house in the Bois de Boulogne for transshipment to the chapel at Windsor Castle, where her husband already lay, a team of eight "cleaners" from MI6 entered the now-empty house searching for anything resembling a reel of film. It took them less than fifteen minutes to find it in a small lead box hidden under one of the floorboards in the duchess's bedroom. The lead box was removed, the floorboards replaced and the film taken to the chief archivist at Windsor Castle. It was duly logged into the archives and put away. Unfortunately, or perhaps otherwise if you are a member of the royal family, the film and a number of other unsavory documents literally went up in smoke during the catastrophic fire at Windsor Castle on the night of November 20, 1992.

In Hawaii there was a special agent in charge of the FBI unit in Honolulu named John Shivers and he sent repeated reports both to J. Edgar Hoover and the State Department regarding the possibility of a Japanese sneak attack.

There really was a German spy in Honolulu named Rossler. He was caught on December 8, 1941, tried by a military tribunal and sentenced to death by firing squad. His death sentence was eventually commuted to life imprisonment in Oahu State Prison, where his only view was the giant pineapple-shaped Dole water tower.

One of the most often played songs interspersed between bombing alerts on radio station KGMB really was "Three Little Fishies (Itty Bitty Pool)."

There really was a Dutch cargo liner called the *Jagers-*

fontein that put into Honolulu on December 7, 1941, and it was her single antiaircraft battery that first fired on the Japanese aircraft coming into Pearl Harbor. The Soviet four-thousand-ton freighter *Stary Bolshevik* was also in port on December 7, but left on that evening's tide.

Of all the people who died in the Pearl Harbor attack, forty-eight were civilians, including the youngest, Yaeko Lillian Oda, six. Lieutenant Masaji Suganami, whose cannon shell fragment was responsible for the little girl's death, was himself killed at 11:02 A.M. on August 9, 1945, while on leave in the city of Nagasaki. At the time of his death he was having breakfast with his wife, Yumiko, and his two children, Yoshio and Jitsuo, aged seven and nine.

It is estimated that a total of $750 million in Romanov bullion, cash, stocks, treasury bills and jewels still rests in British, American and Swiss banks.

As General William Tecumseh Sherman once said, "War is hell."

Acknowledgments

Many thanks are due to Wes and Lucia and their minions at Contact Editions, for all their help in finding some of the more obscure material necessary to make this book work. Thanks also to Noah's friend Eugene at Bruno's Deli, for supplying the dirty words in Russian; to several Romanovs who would rather remain anonymous; to the man who invented the KGB, STILL WATCHING YOU T-shirts available on most street corners in downtown Moscow; to the kind staff at the Trotsky Museum in Mexico City, for supplying photographs of the rabbit hutches (and Trotsky's favorite recipes for the little beasts); to Elaine and Patrice, who put us up in Paris; and once again with humble gratitude to my editor, Doug Grad, who relentlessly whips me onward toward perfection. And of course, most of all, to Mariea, who puts up with all the vicissitudes of a writer's life.

ONYX

CHRISTOPHER HYDE

Wisdom of the Bones
A Novel

Master of suspense Christopher Hyde takes us to
Dallas in November of 1963, where Homicide
Detective Ray Duval is about to collide with history.
His girlfriend's mother used to talk about the wisdom
of the bones: "When you're close to dying, you can
see the truth." Now, with six months left to live,
Duval is putting that wisdom to the test. He's trying
to save one last life before he loses his own to a
terminal heart condition. But the President's
assassination has sent shockwaves of panic
throughout the city. The killer has kidnapped another
girl. And—unless Duval can break the pattern—she'll
be dead in forty-eight hours.

0-451-41065-3

Available wherever books are sold, or
to order call: 1-800-788-6262

ONYX

CHRISTOPHER HYDE

The first conspiracy of World War II begins with

THE SECOND ASSASSIN
A Novel

The year: 1939—and the world readies itself for a war
that is sure to come.
The conspirators: A group of powerful men who want to keep
America out of the approaching conflict—at all costs.
The plan: Assassinate the King and Queen of England on
American soil, destroying any hope of an alliance between
Great Britain and the United States—and ensuring victory for
the Nazis in World War II.

0-451-41030-0

Available wherever books are sold, or
to order call: 1-800-788-6262

S630

Penguin Group (USA) Inc. Online

What will you be reading tomorrow?

Tom Clancy, Patricia Cornwell, W.E.B. Griffin,
Nora Roberts, William Gibson, Robin Cook,
Brian Jacques, Catherine Coulter, Stephen King,
Dean Koontz, Ken Follett, Clive Cussler,
Eric Jerome Dickey, John Sandford,
Terry McMillan…

You'll find them all at
http://www.penguin.com.

Read excerpts and newsletters, find tour
schedules, enter contests…

Subscribe to Penguin Group (USA) Inc. Newsletters
and get an exclusive inside look
at exciting new titles and the authors you love
long before everyone else does.

PENGUIN GROUP (USA) INC. NEWS
http://www.penguin.com/news